"In *Elusive Dawn*, author (
elusive. Her skillfully craft
will pull readers into the ː
Writer's Digest Magazine

"*The Summer Before the Storm* by Gabriele Wills is a beautifully written story that shows humanity from all walks of life – from the very wealthy to the poorest." – *Writer's Digest Magazine*

"*The Summer Before the Storm* is a richly detailed, complex novel – one that will stay with you long after you've turned the last page." – *The Book Chick – Jonita Fex*

"If you are a fan of Downton Abbey, you will love [the Muskoka Novels] series!" – *Teddy Rose, So Many Precious Books, So Little Time*

"I did not want it to end. I am giving *Lighting the Stars* a very well deserved five plus stars." – *Locks, Hooks and Books*

"Highly compelling and absolutely captivating... Wish that I could give [*Lighting the Stars*] even more than 5 stars!" – *Betty Bee on Toot's Book Reviews*

"The [*Summer Before the Storm*] is sweeping and epic in scale and feel with a marvelous grandeur of times past." – *BookNAround*

"There was never a moment in reading *Elusive Dawn* that I wasn't completely captivated with the story. I absolutely adore Gabriele Wills!" – *Peaceful Wishing*

"Ms. Wills is one of the most talented writers I have read in a long time... She has written more than a story. She has written a world to get lost in." – *A Book Lover's Library*

"*Lighting the Stars* has compelling characters, beautiful prose and that extra something that makes a novel truly touching. I couldn't put this book down!" – *Linda Lu - Guest Review on All Things Jill-Elizabeth*

"*Lighting the Stars* [is] beautifully researched and marvellously written. Of all of the great historical fiction novels that I have read over the past year, this was definitely one of the best." – 5 Stars - *Bookgirl86*

"When I came up for air, I was actually surprised to find myself in 2012 instead of 1914." – *Popcorn Reads*

"Wills writes her characters in such a way that you literally feel like you're on this journey with them. The second book in this series [*Elusive Dawn*] is fantastic." – *To Read, or Not to Read*

"[*Lighting the Stars*] is a treasure and one that is not to be missed! Five out of five stars!" – *CelticLady's Reviews*

"Following this latest chapter [*Lighting the Stars*] in the Muskoka chronicles is as enchanting as it was in the previous books. It is a joy to be completely immersed in this bold family saga once again." – *BookNAround*

"Ms. Wills... truly brings history alive through her descriptions and her characters. I didn't want the story to end." – *Broken Teepee*

"A stunning blend of emotionality and research, *Lighting the Stars*... is both unmissable and unforgettable." – *Sal - Guest Review on Bound 4 Escape*

"Gabriele Wills has once again combined impeccable research, actual events, and real people with a finely embroidered story, poignant and vividly detailed." – *The Eclectic Reader*

"An exceptionally well-told story.... *A Place to Call Home* offers a delightful glimpse into Canada's past, told through characters who come to life and jump off the page." – *Writer's Digest Magazine*

Once Upon a Summer

Gabriele Wills

MIND
SHADOWS

Copyright © 2024 Gabriele Wills

All rights reserved. No part of this book may be reproduced or used in any form or by any means, including graphic, electronic, mechanical, recording, or information storage or retrieval systems without prior written permission from the publisher, excepting brief passages used in reviews. For information contact Mindshadows via email: info@mindshadows.com.

This is a work of fiction, which sprang from the author's imagination. AIs were not allowed to participate.

Cover photo by Melanie Wills
Cover design by Amitav Dash of dubs & dash (www.D2-Group.com)

ISBN: 978-1-7750354-3-5 (print)
ISBN: 978-1-7750354-4-2 (e-book)

Thank you for supporting the author by purchasing this book!
Comments are always appreciated at info@mindshadows.com

First Edition
Published by Mindshadows
Mindshadows.com
Printed and bound in Canada

Welcome to Westwind Inn

But be careful what you wish for. . .

Dedicated to my husband, John, and daughter, Melanie,
who share my love of "cottage country".

Prologue

Paige clung to the overturned canoe, but the wood was slimy, giving her little purchase. Wind-lashed waves crashed against her, trying to tear her away. The air was liquid with driving rain. Hard to breathe.

Blinding lightning ripped apart the inky sky. Thunder rumbled up from the depths of the lake with volcanic wrath.

She tried to shout Rebecca's name, but the black, churning water swept over her.

And then she heard the hollow scrabbling of bony fingers digging at the canoe. Her mind screamed for Rebecca. She must be there, clinging to the other end or in the air bubble under the capsized boat. She couldn't have drowned. Those skeletal fingers that reached from the angry waves were not hers.

She tried to scream again, but this time in terror as the flailing claws crept ever closer. Seaweed snaked around her legs, tugging tenaciously as she struggled against the insubstantial water. Down she drifted, ever farther from the surface, now calm and blue with reflected summer sky.

The girl with dead eyes standing among the swaying weeds reached for her.

1997

Chapter 1

"Now I feel like we're heading through a portal into the past," Brett jested as they bumped over a private road through towering woods along the last stretch to the resort. The sign at the entrance read *Westwind Inn: Making holiday wishes come true since 1882.* "I won't be surprised if I see women in Victorian gowns."

"You just might," Paige said happily. "When we used to stay here, they had a weekly masquerade dance, if people wanted to dress up. And lots did! My parents kept some of the vintage clothes from the old cottage, so we always brought something to wear. I loved dressing like a flapper when I was a teen."

She never thought she'd return to the lake or the inn, much as she had once loved it and still dreamt of it, usually with poignant pleasure. But the nightmare had returned.

And then she had read in the newspaper – just a small ad which she'd almost missed – that this was the last season for the renowned Westwind Inn.

It was time to come to terms with the past.

Although Paige had booked in for three weeks, Brett was only staying for one, and then rejoining her for long weekends. Unless something cropped up at work, which it often did.

"They actually seem to have a decent golf course," he said, spying the close-cropped green turf through the thinning trees.

Paige clenched her hands tightly, almost afraid to catch her first glimpse of the place that had been the epitome of summer. But seeing its white clapboard siding and red roofs sent a thrill of pleasure through her.

The three-storey inn rambled lazily along a rise overlooking the lake. It had sprouted from a farmhouse with several additions, giving it a haphazard but welcoming look.

Manicured grounds and colourful gardens flowed around it. A dance pavilion perched on stilts over the lake at right angles to a long wharf and extensive boathouse complete with an enticing rooftop bar.

It was so unchanged that Paige almost burst with happiness. She now knew what people meant by that overwhelming emotion, that pounding of blood through the veins, the feeling of breathlessness, as if one's heart actually ballooned with joy.

They walked in through the double-door entrance to the reception area, which had changed little since it was originally hand-crafted from local oak and pine. The scent of old wood with a whiff of lemony polish instantly took her back a decade and more.

Although she rarely acknowledged it, Paige had a "sensitivity" to atmosphere, perhaps even to people's thoughts. She had vague premonitions, and strong feelings about certain places. There were old buildings that she could barely enter without feeling suffocating emotions - sadness, terror, revulsion.

But Westwind had always felt like being embraced by a warm hug.

The middle-aged woman at the front desk greeted them with a large and friendly smile. "Paige Latimer! How wonderful to see you again!"

"It's good to be back, Louise. How's the family?"

"Very well, thank you. We'll have to catch up when you have a few minutes."

"Absolutely! Louise, this is my husband, Brett Turner."

"Welcome, Mr. Turner. We hope you enjoy your time here." She had the reservation quickly to hand. "You have a one-bedroom cabin with two double beds . . ."

"Do you have any with a king bed?" Brett interrupted.

"Only in the Water's Edge Suites, which have been fully booked for months, sir. For our cabins, we provide as many beds as possible for families. Yours can sleep six."

Brett scowled.

"Paige is familiar with the drill, but I'll run through it anyway. All your meals are included except Sunday lunch, which is our turnover day, when most of our guests depart. You can get burgers, sandwiches, salads, and such at our rooftop bar."

She circled a little house on the grounds map, saying, "Yours is the very last at the north end of the property, on a narrow stretch of the beach where few venture, so it's quite private. Do you need help with your luggage?"

"Thanks, but we can manage," Paige responded before Brett could. "I can't believe that this is Westwind's last summer." She could see that it needed a facelift, but nothing major that she could discern. "What's going to happen to it?"

"It's been sold to a developer from the city. He's keeping this part - the original inn - but will completely renovate and winterize it. Everything else will be bulldozed to make way for townhouse condos and a recreation complex."

"Now that *does* interest me," Brett said.

"There's a model of the development in one of our meeting rooms behind the lounge. And here's a brochure, Mr. Turner."

"Westwind Beach Club," Brett read, taking a glossy promo booklet. It exuded money, class, exclusivity.

He was already reading as they walked out. "'Luxury villas starting at $325,000. New, world-class golf course.' This definitely interests me! It would be a terrific investment. You could spend all summer here, babe. When you don't want to use it, the management company rents the place and splits the profits with you. They'll offer cross-country skiing on the golf course and skating on the lake in winter. You do wonder how these places have survived so long, only being open four or five months a year. Things are certainly looking up," he added cheerfully.

She put her arm through his and said, "Great! Why don't you drive over to our cabin, and I'll walk?"

"Sure. We can check out the development later," he agreed, looking at the property map as he walked off.

Paige was glad to be alone for a moment. She breathed deeply of the fresh, pine-scented air, and felt her soul nourished by the sight of the sparkling blue water, the rugged islands, and the busy waterfront activities. How could she have stayed away so long? She had expected to feel again the anguish and sorrow that had shrouded her departure. There was nothing but a sigh of sadness wafting across a thousand happy memories. Not enough to obliterate or negate them.

With childish glee, she strolled along the familiar, broad veranda that flowed around bays and wings with inviting bandshell corners and bump-outs furnished with wicker sofas and chairs set around small tables.

At the far end of the building, a flagstone path led her past shuffleboard players and the Lodge - a two-storey building added in the 1920s - past the free-form pool and hot tub, between the dozen tennis courts and the beach, where cheerful yellow-and-white sun shelters provided shade, and along the double-string of cabins that squatted near the water's edge.

Brett was pulling into a small parking lot behind, and she went over to help him unload.

"We could have used a bellhop," he muttered, looking askance at the pile of luggage they had to haul to the cabin.

"They're needed in the main buildings, which don't have elevators. And for the elderly and infirm," Paige ribbed, grabbing his golf bag, and setting off for cabin #19 at the farthest end of the waterfront row. The cabins were well spaced and staggered so that each had a view of the lake. They were afforded privacy with screening shrubbery, interspersed with trees that offered shade in a cozy woodland nook.

She spotted it at the last moment, just as she shifted her heavy load and looked up at the three steps to the deck. It sat there belligerently.

Paige froze in terror, dropping the bag, but unable to move. She could almost feel it crawling over her, its legs probing and assaulting her skin, and shivered in revulsion. It was the size of a hand, its eight strong legs narrowing like talons, gripping the deck where it now hunched menacingly.

Just as Brett came up behind her, the creature leapt down the steps and scuttled across the grass toward the shore. Paige yelped and jumped back.

"Holy shit! What the hell was that?!" Brett asked, dropping the suitcases and hugging her. He was well acquainted with her arachnophobia and had always been considerate and gentle with her. At first, she could barely stand to be touched, as if she felt a thousand spiders swarming over her. But then her heart stopped thundering and her breathing calmed, and she managed to say, "A dock spider."

"What? That thing the size of a plate? That's got to be somebody's pet tarantula that escaped."

She shuddered and shook her head. "I saw one before," she stammered. "It bit me!"

It had happened that last summer.

"It was like a bee sting. One of the staff was studying biology and told me that I'd put my hand into a dock spider nursery web. Where the hatchlings mature. The mother is very protective of them, which is why she bit me. They don't otherwise. I hated spiders before that, but I've had a dread of them ever since."

"Jeez, I'm not surprised! I'll go and scout out the premises," Brett offered. "And when we've unloaded the car, I'll take you for a stiff drink."

The cabin was clean, with not a cobweb evident in any corner. "This isn't bad," Brett conceded when he led Paige inside. A large picture window overlooked the deck and the tranquil lake beyond. The living room was tastefully, if rustically, furnished with a sofa-bed, a couple of easy chairs, a small TV, and a table ready for a game of cards or a laptop computer in Paige's case. The honey-coloured pine walls and floor cast a cheerful warmth. Above the mini fridge was a counter with a bar sink and shelves of beverage glasses. The separate bedroom was decorated with colourful quilts, and Brett quipped, "I suppose we can fit into a double bed, for a while anyway."

"Until I want some sleep," she shot back with a grin.

"That's pretty unromantic, actually wanting to *sleep* in a bed," he teased.

Paige's gaze was caught by the painting on the wall. A single Muskoka chair on a dock beckoned against a misty sunrise over the lake. It was surreal and totally enchanting. And the style was so familiar that it felt like home. Of course, Simon was the artist.

"I've done the spider search, and everything is A-OK, ma'am," Brett declared, coming out of the bathroom.

"Dock spiders are supposedly skittish, disappearing as soon as they hear a noise or sense movement. That's why people don't often see them. Anyway, they prefer to be by the water."

"Glad to hear it! I can't even imagine the size of their webs."

"They don't build them, other than to protect their offspring. They can walk on water and dive down to get their prey, like small fish."

"Jeez! Now I need a drink as well."

She laughed.

Holding hands, they ambled to the wharf, past the line-up at the ice cream kiosk, and climbed the steps to the sundeck bar above the long, open-sided boathouse. Yellow and white striped umbrellas shaded some of the tables, but they chose one that basked in the late-afternoon sunshine. Boxes of red geraniums, white petunias, and trailing ivy lined the railings, and the sparkling blue lake surrounded them.

"I *can* see the charm of this place," Brett conceded after they had ordered drinks. "Like an adult version of summer camp. A bit shabby, but the make-over under new management should take care of that."

Paige, fiercely loyal, was stung by the criticism, as if she had some stake in this place. And perhaps she did. For years – from the time she was ten until that last fateful summer, when she was nineteen - it had been her paradise. She said, "This has been one of the top summer resorts for over a century."

"I don't doubt it. But it hasn't kept up with the times."

"I love the quaintness of this place, the connection with people who enjoyed it before we were even born. I wish I could see into the past, experience the days when people were more carefree and didn't lug their computers and cell phones along on holidays."

"Idle hedonists, the lot of them," Brett joked. "We modern people have to earn our way."

His grin evaporated as a man came up to the table.

"Welcome back, Paige."

Her heart cartwheeled. Trying to subdue the rush of colour to her cheeks, she turned to smile at him. "Simon! Nice to see you again."

Their eyes locked for a moment, each probing the other to see what still remained of the affection they had shared all those years ago. Her pulse quickened when she found vestiges of the familiar tenderness in his startling blue eyes. But the easygoing manner of the boy she had known and loved seemed shrouded. And his abrupt severing of their relationship was still a raw wound, so she looked away.

Almost as an afterthought she said hastily, "This is my husband, Brett Turner. Brett, this is Simon Davenport. His family built Westwind."

They shook hands, assessing each other warily.

Brett said casually, "I didn't think much of your welcoming committee."

"Oh? Is there a problem with one of our staff?" Simon asked, looking puzzled.

"A spider the size of a Frisbee greeted us on our deck."

"A dock spider," Simon remarked with relief, although he glanced at Paige regretfully. He was obviously recalling her last encounter with one. She wondered if he also remembered the feel of her sun-warmed skin against his when he'd comforted her. Did he ever think about how that moment had finally unleashed their suppressed passion for each other?

"As compensation for your traumatic introduction, your drinks are on the house," he said. "And I trust you won't see any more. We have guests who've visited us for decades and have never seen one. I'll make sure there aren't any nursery webs near your cabin." He looked at her meaningfully.

"Thanks.... I was surprised to hear that you've sold this place, Simon," Paige said, glad to change the subject.

"Mom died a couple of years ago and Dad passed away last year."

"I'm so sorry to hear that!"

He nodded in acknowledgment. "The resort needs a major overhaul. Younger guests want big suites with Jacuzzi tubs and fireplaces. And exercise facilities – as if there's not enough to do outdoors. We added a few waterfront suites, but it would have taken a lot of money and dedication to completely modernize the resort. I never wanted to be an innkeeper. So, I bought my freedom. But I've kept the house."

"I noticed that you're still painting. The picture in our cabin is wonderfully evocative."

"I've decorated the entire place with them and my photographs. They're for sale if people want a souvenir."

She and Simon used to sketch together, those summers long ago. When she was twelve, and he, fourteen, they discovered their mutual love of art, and took sketchbooks and cameras with them whenever they went out in a canoe or sat at the end of the dock. They talked about going to Paris to study, to wear berets and paint on the streets of Montmartre.

Brett was obviously getting bored, but Simon was quick to pick up on it. He said, "I'm sure Paige has told you some pretty crazy stories about life as a waterski instructor. She helped teach the more advanced tricks and starred in our weekly shows."

Brett, struck silent for a moment, looked at her challengingly. "I haven't actually heard much about that."

"It was a long time ago," she replied.

She recalled how she and Simon would ski side-by-side. She'd drop her outside ski, step onto his bent knee, and drop the other ski as she hoisted herself onto his shoulders. Once they had perfected that, she would hook one foot under his arm, lie back and raise her other leg gracefully into the air, so that her head dangled just above the spray from his skis. But being held in his arms when she dismounted had been even more sensual.

"Well, I should get back to work," Simon declared. "Enjoy your stay and let us know if there's anything you need. Good to meet you, Brett." He gave Paige a rueful smile and left.

Brett cocked an eyebrow and drawled, "Old boyfriend?"

"Old friend. I've known Simon since I was ten."

"Why did you never mention you did stunt skiing?"

"I told you that I taught here." But since he didn't waterski, he hadn't shown any interest.

"But not that you're an expert skier. That surprised me."

She *had* been a different person here. More carefree and daring. In high school, where both her parents were teachers, she'd blended into the background, painting the sets for the drama club and sometimes directing a play, but never on stage. She helped create the décor for the elaborate, themed formal dances she never attended. She did run the library club, which never had many members. After all, her mother was the school librarian. But it was during the summers here that she'd felt really confident.

"Well, I couldn't do it now. It's not exactly a useful skill. Come on, let's explore."

From the sundeck, they went through French doors into the bar.

"When my mother worked here in the summer of '60, this was an ice cream parlour also serving pastries, burgers, fries - that sort of thing. The Latimer cottage is only two miles away by boat, so my father dropped in one day with friends, and the rest is history."

"You mean it was love at first sight?"

"Dad came by for a sundae every day for two weeks until Mum finally agreed to go to a dance with him."

Brett chuckled. "That's some sacrifice, having to consume all that ice cream."

"That was the bonus, he claims."

At the far end of the room, a short flight of stairs led down to the large dancehall. The floor was somewhat warped - not surprisingly since it had perched over water for more than seventy years - and attempts to hide battered woodwork with fresh paint just added to the sadness of its general decline.

But it was still an active venue, as a poster of daily events listed dances with a live band, a musical revue, and a play by a professional summer theatre troupe.

"Cottagers from around the lake come to these," Paige told him. "There were talent shows as well as the weekly costume ball."

"So, what did you do?"

"There were always aspiring rock stars among the staff, who played guitar." Including Simon. "And some of us girls were happy to sing with them. Upbeat, summery songs like 'It's a Beautiful Morning' and 'Dancing in the Street'."

"At least I knew you could sing before we came here."

"Wouldn't it be too boring if you knew everything about me after only three years of marriage?" she asked coyly.

"Almost four," he amended with a grin.

Perpendicular to the long wharf were shorter sections for visitors to park their boats. Off-duty student staff were sunning themselves on those quieter docks where they wouldn't interfere with the resort guests.

At the end, where the water was deep, was a wide stretch where the large steamships had disembarked passengers in the days when that had been the only way to get to hotels and summer homes on these popular lakes. This arm was dominated by a long, open-sided gazebo, its red roof topped with a small, faux tower, reflecting the hotel's design. Guests and their luggage had sheltered here while awaiting transport. Some benches remained where people could seek refuge from sun and rain, and enjoy the wide-open vista. A poster invited them to sign up for boat cruises.

"We should definitely do that," Paige suggested, "since you don't know this lake. And I can already see that it's changed." Distant islands that had still been mostly wild had sprouted massive cottages and boathouses.

"Sure thing!"

Looking back at the resort that spread out before them, Paige was happier than a child at Disneyworld. The historic inn perched majestically on the rise, seeming cheerfully complacent. Lush, terraced gardens edged by granite walls rippled down to the waterfront flagstone terrace atop a rock retaining wall that stretched from the dock to a distant octagonal gazebo. Three dozen Muskoka chairs in bright, stoplight colours alternated along its length. Beyond them were the Water's Edge Suites that had arisen since she'd been here. But she hadn't wanted one of these modern, luxury units that had no connection to her past.

And beyond them, the substantial Victorian house was Simon's family home.

As they walked back along the wharf, Paige noticed two elderly women sitting in the Muskoka chairs along the shore. "Just a minute, Brett. I know those ladies."

She went over to them and said, "Miss Emmeline and Miss Abigail! How wonderful to see you again!"

"Good gracious! Look, Abby, Paige has come back!" They beamed with delight.

She introduced Brett.

"You've done well for yourself, young man, finding a treasure like our Paige," Abigail said.

"I'm constantly discovering that."

"The ladies have been coming here for years," Paige explained to Brett.

"Seventy-seven to. be precise," Abigail stated. "1920 was our first year. I was ten and Em was eight. And we haven't missed a summer, even if we could only manage a week. Now that we're retired, we stay for much of the season. Simon is such a dear and gives us an excellent rate. We're quite pampered."

"Do join us for a chat," Emmeline suggested.

Brett said quickly, "Yes, why don't you, babe, while I go and check out the golf course. See you back at the cabin. Ladies, delighted to have met you."

"He's a handsome devil, your husband. Plenty of self-confidence," Abigail said with a hint of criticism. Her blue eyes were still sharp as they scrutinized Paige's face.

Paige admired the sisters' candour and keen intellects. Neither had ever married, but Abigail made no secret of her suitors, some of whom were quite illustrious.

Although in their late eighties, the Pembrook sisters were slim and attractive, and looked at least a dozen years younger. Always smartly dressed, they exuded a classic sense of style and poise without being dated or stuffy.

Paige chatted with them for half an hour, catching up on ten years of news. She learned that they still lived in their stone bungalow in Ottawa's Rockcliffe Park and spent the coldest months of winter in Florida. When they had first retired, they traveled extensively each spring and autumn, but now that they were less mobile, they were content just spending their summers at Westwind.

"Even after everything I've seen, I still think that this is the most beautiful spot on earth," Abigail declared.

Emmeline agreed and added, "Sometimes I do wish I could go back to those days when we were young and danced the night away. There wasn't a more fun or welcoming place on the lake."

"I wish I could, too," Paige said. "You've told me so many wonderful stories over the years, that I wish I could spy on the past."

"You would have loved it, dear. Would have fit right in. But it's lost its heart," Abigail bemoaned. "We've decided it's the people who come here now. They're too self-absorbed."

"Simon's wife maintains that the inn is no longer attracting the 'right' crowd, and they were already sinking so much money into renovations," Emmeline said, eyeing Paige carefully. "She was eager enough to run this place at the outset. You probably remember her. She was on staff here for a couple of summers.... Veronica."

Paige missed the knowing glance between the sisters.

"I certainly do. She was new the last summer I was here." And had insinuated herself into Simon's small group of friends. Outgoing, helpful, with a friendly word for all, she was popular with the guests. And Paige soon realized that Veronica had her sights on Simon.

The yearly Westwind brochures that had initially kept coming to the Latimer home included a newsletter about the changes and improvements returning guests would find that summer. One year it mentioned that Veronica had been taken on staff full-time as Social Director and Assistant Manager. Two years later they announced that Simon and Veronica had married.

Until she read that, Paige had been considering coming for a week that summer of 1992 when she'd finished university, to see if there was any spark left between her and Simon. Not long after that, she met Brett.

Emmeline looked wistful. "It *is* sad that all this is going to end."

"So, you won't be buying a condo here?" Paige asked.

"Heavens, no!" Abigail cackled. "It would spoil everything to see this turned into some pretentious Yuppie haven."

"We're staying until the bitter end this year," Emmeline said. "We have lots and lots of memories to sustain us."

"You'd best run along now, dear," Abigail advised. "Some men don't like to come second."

"Abby!" Emmeline chided.

"Paige knows I speak from experience and won't take offence at good advice."

"We'll see lots of you, I'm sure," Emmeline said, grasping Paige's hand in a wrinkled but firm grip. Her embrace seemed to communicate something more than friendship – reassurance, support. "My, but it's good to have you back again." *I've been waiting for you.*

Paige did hasten to the cabin but slowed down before reaching it. Carefully she looked around to see if the dock spider had returned but saw no signs of it. Brett was putting his flip phone away when she walked in.

"You actually got a signal?" she asked.

"Barely."

"Business?"

"Can't get away from it," he replied, shrugging.

"You could turn it off. Tell them there's no signal here."

"You know I can't do that."

"Why not? You're supposed to be on holidays."

"One of my assistants is tackling a new account. There are a few last-minute glitches that need to be resolved before the weekend."

Paige noted how carefully he avoided identifying gender. "Then she should have asked another colleague, and not disturb you."

"Do I detect a note of jealousy?"

"Is there any reason for me to be jealous?" she countered.

"Says the woman who blushed bright red when she met her old boyfriend again," he needled.

She didn't correct him this time, but just stared back, waiting for a proper answer. When they were alone together, he usually seemed completely enthralled with her, which is how he had won her over. But she'd soon realized that he was like that with everyone, at least initially, which was why he was so attractive. When he disliked someone or found them a bore, he could just as easily disengage and move on. But when he wasn't with her, did he even think much about her?

"Of course not, babe. Surely you have more faith in yourself. And in me. Anyway, you took your time with the old biddies, so my little bit of work didn't interfere."

"Don't be rude, Brett! They're like cherished great-aunts. They were formidable women in their day. Abigail worked for CBC radio in its infancy, the National Film Board during the war, and then as a producer for CBC in the early days of television, when most women were still chained to their Betty Crocker kitchens. Emmeline is an art historian as well as an artist, and became a curator at the National Gallery. She taught me *plein air* painting when I was a kid. We'll be lucky to be as sharp as they are when we're that age."

"You're absolutely right. So, what's next on our agenda? A swim?"

"Yes... Alright."

The lake was refreshing, though pleasantly warm in the shallows. Through the crystal-clear water, they could see the rippled, golden sand underfoot as they waded out. Because the beach area was recessed in a bay, they were nearly level with the sundeck bar by the time the water was deep enough for swimming.

Paige loved being enveloped by the silky, calm water, feeling the long, hot rays of the late afternoon sunshine penetrating the coolness of the lake to caress her skin. So unlike the last time she'd been in this lake. Those memories were never far below the surface, so she was grateful that Brett was beside her.

Being immersed in the immense body of water, she felt like a part of its vastness. The gentle push and pull of the water were like the pulse of the lake, so that it seemed life-sustaining.

And she allowed herself to remember the treachery of the lake. Cold, black, frenzied, the water had lashed her as she clung desperately to the overturned canoe.

Brett swam farther out while Paige lingered in the shallows, never going deeper than where she could easily stand, absorbing the landscape of water and rocky islands as if re-infusing her lifeblood. This gentle, nurturing warmth was a long-awaited antidote to that horrible day when the lake had fought to claim her.

She concentrated on the softness of the water as she stroked her way gently through it. Its sensuous touch was benign. And she allowed herself to feel pleasure, to dispel the fear, to relax. And with the melting of the oppressive burden came a burst of joy that caused her to gasp, and nearly inhale water. She flipped onto her back and gazed thankfully at the boundless blue sky.

It was the most wondrous start to dispelling the stranglehold of the past.

As they dressed for dinner, Paige pointed out the tradition of more formal attire. "Women wore evening gowns and jewels in the old days, the Pembrook sisters told me. Even in our day, my mother wore cocktail dresses and high heels. Now they just expect 'dressy casual', but I like to think of it as a special night out."

"Which is why you packed my sports jacket."

"No tie necessary. Open-necked shirt is fine. In fact, it's more you," she added with a grin. "Casually dapper."

"Now there's an old-fashioned term I haven't heard in ages. You're reveling in this historical ambience, aren't you?"

"Did you ever doubt that?" she asked as she fastened her grandmother's pearls around her neck.

He guffawed. "I should know better."

The spacious lounge in the inn had a floor to ceiling granite fireplace and plenty of deeply comfortable chairs and sofas. It opened into the extensive dining room, the beautiful wood and craftsmanship from the last century well preserved throughout. Walls of windows maximized the lake view beyond the enveloping verandas. Tables were laid with crisp white linens and gleaming silverware, and decorated with crystal vases of fresh flowers. Formal wear seemed almost imperative in this elegant setting.

Brett requested a table by the window.

"Could I have your name please, sir?" the Hostess asked.

"Turner. Cabin 19. In my wife's name, however - Latimer."

"Yes, Mr. Turner. We have table 37 reserved for you. It will be yours throughout your stay. If you'll follow me."

"Is it a window table?" Brett asked, not moving.

"I'm afraid not. But you still have a view," she said cheerfully.

"That's fine," Paige said, but Brett ignored her.

"The one in that bay seems to be available," he suggested with an encouraging smile.

"I'm sorry, sir, but those tables are reserved for our regular patrons, the ones who return every year. They're a bonus for loyal guests."

"My wife came regularly years ago, and has booked in for three weeks. Surely she deserves the same consideration."

Embarrassed, Paige murmured, "Leave it, Brett. That's part of the tradition."

"It's antiquated. I just expect to be treated fairly." Turning to the flustered girl, he said smoothly, "I should speak to Simon. I know you're just doing your job and have no authority to change the rules." He flashed her an understanding smile.

Paige cringed inside. She hated when he became supercilious.

She hadn't noticed the Pembrook sisters come up behind them. Abigail said, "That won't be necessary, Mr. Turner. Em and I are here until Thanksgiving, so you're welcome to use our table during your stay."

"No, we couldn't..." Paige began, but Brett interrupted her.

"Thank you, ladies. That is most considerate and generous of you."

The Hostess looked gratefully at the Pembrook sisters and said, "This way, Mr. Turner."

When they were seated, Paige challenged, "Was that really necessary?" The Pembrook sisters, presumably sitting at the table assigned to her and Brett, were only a few feet away.

"You have to stand up for your rights. Outdated conventions should be challenged. No wonder the place is going under."

"I enjoy and appreciate traditions."

"I know, babe," he said, placatingly patting her hand. "I'm sure they were acceptable in their day, but not as we move into the 21st century." His well-worn smile signified an end to the discussion, as he perused the menu.

Her anger abated when he instructed the waitress to offer the Pembrook sisters whatever drinks they wanted for the duration of Paige's stay, to be added to his account. She was glad to see that the ladies didn't hesitate to order something extravagant. They raised their glasses of excellent Châteauneuf-du-Pape in acknowledgement of Brett's largesse.

Behind her smile, Abigail whispered to Emmeline, "Charming, but ruthless. I fell for men like that, too. But I'd never have married one. Poor Paige."

Emmeline silently agreed.

"I'm pleasantly surprised not to see any little kids here," Brett said, tucking into his wild mushroom bisque.

"There's a separate dining room for families with children under ten. They eat earlier."

"That's very civilized. And this soup is excellent!"

She had to admit that much as he often found fault, he also acknowledged and applauded things well done.

Most of the staff were students earning money to attend college or university, so Brett engaged their pretty waitress in conversation as she delivered their various courses, asking about her studies and goals.

"Psychology, eh? Have you ever thought of going into advertising? We need bright young people with innovative ideas. You might have seen my latest TV commercial," he said.

His ad highlighted something special in each Canadian province and territory, all tied together by happy people toasting with a particular brand of beer. Although the beer seemed almost incidental to showcasing Canada, sales had skyrocketed. Paige had contributed suggestions when he'd run the idea past her, and he'd incorporated them. Although he'd conveniently forgotten that.

"That one's brilliant! I don't normally like ads, but it makes us feel proud of our beautiful country."

"Here's my card. If you want to go that route, just remind me where we met. I'll pay special attention," he added with a wink.

"Is it fair to tantalize her just to ensure good service?" Paige asked. And to make sure everyone on staff knew that he was an important person, not to be trifled with.

"I meant every word. We're always looking for new talent."

And new conquests, Paige thought. She often had to rein in her suspicion that Brett was cheating on her. When she'd finally confronted him last year, ready to walk away, he'd assured her that he loved only her, despite his penchant for "harmless" flirtations. "Just a bit of spice," he'd said dismissively.

While they were having dessert, a woman came to their table. "Paige Latimer! I could hardly believe it was really you when I saw the guest list!"

"Hi, Veronica. I hear that you're Mrs. Davenport now."

She chuckled. "Lady of the manor, which is about to be torn down. But you've done well for yourself, Paige! I've enjoyed your articles." She assessed Brett, who responded in kind, as he always did with attractive women.

Paige introduced him, and Veronica said, "I've already heard that we have a celebrity here. Your clever commercial touched a nation, Mr. Turner. Kudos to you!"

"Call me Brett."

They smiled at each other.

Overhearing, Abigail murmured to Emmeline, "Now those two would go well together."

Emmeline pondered how she could set things right. She wished – fervently, with all her heart – that dear Simon and Paige would find each other again.

Summer wishes. They had worked before. But sometimes with unexpected consequences.

Chapter 2

It was the music that drew her – jazzy tunes from the 1920s. They echoed over the moon-glazed water. As in other dreams, Paige felt awkward walking outside in her flimsy satin nightgown, but she couldn't turn back.

The ground was chilly beneath her bare feet, although the night was still warm. Mist swirled around her like a witch's cauldron in the moonlight. She drifted along the path towards the dancehall, whose lights spilled into the calm night. When she looked behind her, the cabins were gone, and only the looming shadows of ancient trees appeared through the fog. Where the pool should have been stood a gazebo large enough to house a brass band.

The doors of the pavilion were open to the night, and Paige could see the gyrating bodies through the haze. The Charleston. She had seen it in old movies. But the dancers looked insubstantial. Like phantoms.

An antique mahogany launch pulled up at the end of the dock and a giggling flapper scrambled out. Her debonair escort tied up the boat, and the pair ran hand in hand along the wharf to the pavilion, not even glancing at scantily clad Paige who felt almost naked. Their passing was like a cool breeze.

It was the roughness of the wood beneath her feet that suddenly roused her. She hadn't sleepwalked in years.

She looked in awe at the revelers, those shimmering ghosts of a bygone era. She was so shocked she couldn't even scream, although she felt the prickle of fear. Mist still swirled around her like a live thing, twisting and mutating.

A thin hand gripped her shoulder and Paige shrieked.

"Hush, dear. It's Emmeline."

Paige glanced about in alarm. The old lady had an encompassing silk shawl draped over her cotton nightdress, but she was real, her hand warm and reassuring.

"Yes, I see it, too. You're not dreaming or crazy. You *did* want to see the past, my dear. One must be careful what one wishes for here."

Emmeline took Paige's trembling, cold hands in her strong embrace.

"I don't understand," Paige stammered.

"Some of us are more sensitive to the larger spectrum of existence. We can see things that others can't. A gift or a curse – I don't know. Abby quite envies me the ability to see the past. She, of course, is much too sensible and ever rooted in the present."

Paige glanced uneasily at the spectres that still quivered to the strains of long-ago music.

"They won't hurt you," Emmeline assured her. "We're just witnessing a moment in time."

Paige realized that they didn't know she was there, as another couple breezed by without acknowledging her. It was like watching a play through a scrim.

And yet her skin crawled. She was tempted to pinch herself to see if this was indeed real.

Emmeline seemed to read her thoughts, for she said, "Notice there's no sundeck bar, just a boathouse. Look up at the inn."

In the bright moonlight, Paige could see the differences. The dining room wing was shorter; the bandshell veranda corner didn't exist at the north end; the trees were smaller.

"That's how it looked in the '20s when we first came. See how new the Lodge is, and the Water's Edge Suites aren't there."

"The pool wasn't there, or the cabins!" Paige exclaimed. "I didn't see them when I looked back."

Emmeline nodded.

"But how will I get back?" Paige cried, trying to keep panic at bay.

Emmeline remembered how surprised and frightened she had been when she first had the visions. And she'd had no one to guide and reassure her. "Just think yourself back to the present. But you must be calm, my dear, and not allow the past to threaten or unnerve you."

Paige shivered. "If this isn't some freaky dream, then I know I'll be sorry if I don't appreciate this moment. But I'm scared."

Emmeline took off her shawl and draped it around Paige's shoulders despite her protest. "No, I insist! I am quite warm, and you're in shock."

The heavy, embroidered silk was comforting. When her shaking had subsided, Paige said, "Does this happen often?"

"I catch glimpses every now and again. This is the strongest manifestation I've ever experienced. Probably because you're helping to make it happen. Your desire is powerful. I can even recognize people I knew long ago. It's eerie." It was like witnessing the blazing glory of a thunderstorm, where she had seen only distant, silent flashes previously. Paige herself was enveloped in a bright aura of power.

But she hadn't seen Edward. No matter how strong her desire, Emmeline had never been able to conjure him up.

"Were you there?" Paige asked cryptically.

But Emmeline understood, and chuckled, "I haven't seen myself, but I remember this night. I was seventeen, and my parents never believed in restricting our enjoyment or enlightenment." Edward had danced with her that evening, but he had still seen her as a gangly teenager, while she had already been smitten by his dry wit, his charm, his easygoing nonchalance. Sometimes she wondered if her aged heart could stand these remembered bursts of ecstasy.

"I recall this summer particularly, because we had the stock market crash that fall of '29 and summers changed after that. So many never came back." She sighed. "It was like a war. People ruined, disappearing forever from our lives."

Paige could hardly believe she was witnessing an evening that actually took place almost seventy years ago.

"Don't fight this power you have, Paige. This *is* real. It seems as if you have to re-examine your entire relationship with reality, but don't deny this."

And Paige suddenly saw something she recognized all too well. "Oh my God! That dress! I've worn it! It belonged to my grandmother. And the pearls!" Which Paige had worn to dinner. "Oh dear God, that must be her!"

She peered searchingly at the glamorous young woman whose blonde bob was decorated with a beaded, fringed headdress that Paige had also worn. And the suave man at her side was her grandfather! She recognized them from old photographs. But seeing them so young and vivacious brought tears to her eyes.

"They're so beautiful," she whispered.

"I remember you looking equally dazzling in that outfit."

Her favourite, Paige had worn it several times at the costume balls, including that last summer.

"Do they get to dance here forever? Will we?"

Emmeline smiled and said, "Oh, I do hope so!"

"Wait, you said this was 1929. Nan was 29, exactly my age! This is so weird!" Was she somehow connecting with her grandmother? Why?

Paige was suddenly sapped, as if this manifestation was feeding off her, draining her. And the images grew fainter. Emmeline patted her shoulder and said, "You should go back now, dear. You're exhausted."

She returned the shawl but was reluctant to leave Emmeline's side, to venture alone along that dark path. But suddenly the dimmed landscape lighting was on again, and the dancehall, slumbering.

Paige gazed into Emmeline's ancient, knowing eyes and said, "Will you remind me tomorrow that this was real?"

"Oh, you'll know. But yes, we'll chat." Her smile was warm and reassuring.

Embarrassed that someone, like the night watchman, might see her in her thin nightgown, Paige hurried along the lit path to her cabin.

"Where the hell have you been?" The angry accusation startled her when she walked in, and a lamp came on. Brett, whiskey glass in hand, was sitting on the couch glowering. "And dressed like that? Couldn't even put on some clothes before you snuck off to visit the old lover, eh?"

"Don't be silly!" She tried not to lose her temper. After all, it must appear bizarre to him. And while she wanted to pour out the story, to have him soothe her fears, she knew he would think her crazy. He would have no sympathy or understanding for what she had just experienced. "I was sleepwalking."

"Oh please! Give me more credit!"

"It's true!" Paige poured herself a glass of wine to steady her nerves, and sat down next to him, tucking her icy feet beneath her. "I used to when I was a child, but I haven't in years."

"So what brought it on?"

"I think it's time you knew the story," she said, "If you're willing to listen."

He cocked a skeptical eyebrow, but she ignored it.

"It's because of something that happened a decade ago – the last summer I was here. I've been trying to forget. Mostly the nightmares had stopped, but they recently started again. That's why I had to come back this summer."

She glanced at him uneasily, but he challenged her with, "Go on."

Paige took a deep breath. "Simon had a distant cousin, Rebecca, who came to live with his family when she was thirteen. Her parents were killed in a car accident, and there was no one else to take her. She was two years younger than me, and I got to know her quite well."

Having had, as an only child, the magnanimous, unconditional love of her parents, Paige had pitied Rebecca, who had been her own worst enemy. Beneath her abrasive shell of arrogance and defiance, she had been a lonely child seeking affection and attention.

"That last summer we were canoeing and were ambushed by a sudden storm." Paige paused, recalling things that she would never tell anyone.

"I haven't been able to forgive myself for her death," Paige admitted after giving Brett an expurgated version of the story.

Especially after Simon seemed to hold her somewhat responsible.

Pulling her cool, shivering body into his arms, Brett said, "Don't be silly, babe. You can't take responsibility for her drowning. How could you have saved her? Jeez, it sounds like you hardly managed to save yourself!"

Others had told her that, but it was nice that Brett was sensitive to her grief and remorse.

"I just don't understand why you've never told me this before."

"I can't talk about it. You can't imagine how many times I've wished that things had been different! Nothing stupid, like wishing it had been me instead of her. But wishing that we'd been wearing our lifejackets. That I'd insisted we wait out the storm." That they hadn't parted in anger and bitterness. That was hard to bear.

"And that's why you never sail with me," he stated. He liked taking friends and colleagues out on Lake Ontario on his family's 30-foot cruising sailboat, but she always declined. So, what better place for him to have liaisons with other women?

"Yes. I need to be close to shorelines. Will you go canoeing with me tomorrow? I mean later this morning?" she amended. "I need to revisit that place." She shuddered. "But only if it's a calm day!"

"Of course I will. Now come to bed."

As twilight crept into the cabin, Paige allowed herself to be led into the bedroom, where she fell into a deep and dreamless sleep.

* * * * * * * * * *

August 18, 1987

Paige and Rebecca pulled their canoe up to the sandy shore of a tiny, rocky island with a couple of jack pines and a splendid beach, great for a dip after a vigorous paddle. It was amongst an enclave of larger islands, but since the water between them was generally too shallow for motorboats, it was delightfully secluded.

Paige and Simon often came here on their drawing excursions and had named it Silver Sands. This summer it was the perfect place to get away from the resort in the early mornings for their trysts.

She was surprised that Rebecca had come here. "So, what did you want to show me?" Paige asked.

"You shouldn't think that Simon's in love with you just because he screws you here," she sneered. "I followed you to see what you were *really* up to."

Hiding between the larger islands, Rebecca could have been spying on them. Although how much could she see from a distance? Certainly not what they did beneath the overturned canoe and the rocks.

"You don't know what you're talking about."

"Don't I? I've seen you sneaking up to the boathouse suite most evenings. You're just the fling of the moment, so do yourself a favour and stop drooling over him. Girls are always throwing themselves at him. Look at that scheming bitch, Veronica. She's been sucking up to me so that she can get closer to *him*, offering to come over to the house to paint my nails or some other BS. It's pathetic!"

"That's different. Simon and I have been friends for years."

"So? His university girlfriend, Trish, was here the week before you arrived. She had the boathouse suite, and Simon spent all his free time there. But I scared the crap out of her.

"She hates spiders – like you - so I drew one on her bathroom mirror with greasy fingers. You don't see anything until the mirror steams up from the shower, but the marks stay bare. That must have given her a rude shock! I'd already warned her about dock spiders, and how they crawl up from the boathouse and get under the sheets."

"They don't!"

She shrugged dismissively. "But then she made Simon check out her suite every night before bed. Or so they claimed." Rebecca snorted. "Just an excuse for sex, of course.

"So, when that backfired, Edward Davenport's ghost came and scratched on the outside walls." She grinned maliciously. "With a whisk broom. I mentioned at breakfast the next morning that I thought I'd seen him wandering about the place again. Which meant that something awful was going to happen to someone.

"Simon had to admit that some people have seen what looks like a ghost, but he never had. I told *Trish-Trash* afterwards that she'd better watch out in case old Edward didn't like her. One of the maids claimed that someone had tried to shove her down the stairs, but there was no one there. You should have seen how pale she got. Like a ghost!" Rebecca giggled.

"That's mean."

"Just protecting my territory."

"Simon is not yours."

"He's going to marry me when I'm old enough! I'm a Hawksley! The only one left! Hawksley Bay is named after me, and the marina, which my great-grandfather started. Simon told me it was only right that I have a stake in the inn!"

"He said you might work there one day, but nothing about marrying you."

Paige recalled the surly fourteen-year-old Rebecca whining about having to do menial chores at the resort – like gathering used towels by the pool, helping with dishwashing in the inn's kitchen, sweeping the paths. "Why can't I just have fun, like all the other girls?"

"Because they're our guests, and we have to look after them," Simon had explained patiently.

"It's child slavery! I don't even get paid!"

"That's part of being in the family. You get room and board, a generous allowance, and a useful education. Think of it as an apprenticeship. I did my stints in the kitchen, housekeeping, landscaping, maintenance, and a dozen other things before I was allowed to take over the skiing lessons and boat tours."

"You mean I'll be running the inn? With you?"

"We'll see if you end up with a job here once you're old enough. But you sure won't if you don't learn the ropes and show some initiative. Oh, and be kind, helpful, and friendly to staff and guests. Being crabby is not attractive."

She'd stuck her tongue out at him and laughed helplessly.

By the following summer, Rebecca was eager to help at the waterfront, where she outfitted skiers and canoeists, rented sailboats, took reservations for lessons and cruises, and helped visitors tie up their boats. She was also near Simon and Paige there.

Now she screamed, "How do *you* know what he promised? He's too much of a gentleman to touch me now, which is why he needs you *whores* to satisfy him in the meantime!" Her freckles seemed to glow and her unruly red hair to catch fire in the sunshine, as if her entire being were ablaze.

This rabid anger was a side of her that Paige had rarely seen.

The summer that Rebecca had come to Westwind clutching her well-loved bunny, Simon and Paige had felt sorry for her, and tried hard to make her feel welcome in her new home. She'd exploded when they'd called her 'Becky'.

"I'm NOT Becky ANYMORE! That's what my parents called me! And they were stupid and hateful! Always fighting. At the funeral I heard someone say that they argued at the party and got drunk and that's why they lost control of the car and crashed into a tree. They didn't care about ME!"

"That's not true. Adults have their own lives, and if they had problems, that was with each other, not you," Simon had reassured her.

"Then they should have divorced. Not killed each other!"

"Maybe they would have. But no one knows the circumstances of people's private lives. Or of the accident. Maybe they swerved to avoid a deer. And you shouldn't trust gossip. You have us now, Rebecca," he'd replied compassionately. "So, what would you like us to call you?"

"Rebel!"

"Hmm... That's more of a declaration of war than a name." She'd stifled a grin.

"How about Bex? That's short and punchy. And you'd be the only Bex I know."

"Rhymes with sex."

"And vex, and hex, and Tyrannosaurus Rex."

She'd giggled. Simon was good at drawing her out of her cantankerous moods, but he was away at the private boys boarding school at the top end of the lake, along with his Rowan cousins, for most of each year, and later, at university, so his parents didn't have an easy time with her. He often had to do his big-brother chats over the phone to appease her.

While Paige and Rebecca argued at Silver Sands, neither noticed the sinister clouds moving in. It wasn't until they heard the distant rumble of thunder that they realized the danger.

Thunderheads were massing quickly, and Paige suggested, "We should wait out the storm. Take shelter under the canoe."

"We can make a run for it. Or are you too chicken?" Rebecca smirked.

"It's not safe! We'll be a target for the lightning!"

"Bwak, Bwak! You're spineless! You've been so pampered, *Perfect-Paige*," she mocked. "You don't know what it's like to have to rely on yourself. You're just a spoilt brat!"

"You're the brat!" Paige countered.

"Stay if you like!" Rebecca snapped as she started pushing out the canoe.

Paige didn't want to be stranded without shelter, so she clambered in. "You'd better paddle like hell!"

Rebecca was now the more experienced canoeist, so she took the stern seat where she had the most control.

The festering sky and water turned a malevolent black. Lightning forked ever closer; thunder blasted obscenities from the heavens. A ferocious wind whipped up the waves as rain pelted down. The storm felt like an embodiment of Rebecca's rage.

"Pull up to that dock!" Paige shouted as the waves began washing over the bow.

But Rebecca steered against Paige's efforts to redirect them.

"Bex, don't be stupid!" Paige shouted into the fierce wind. "And put your lifejacket on!"

They had been kneeling on them out of habit. As Paige reached for hers, the boat suddenly veered sharply and was struck broadside by a powerful whitecap. They capsized into the cold darkness churned up from the vast depths of the lake.

Few could appreciate how the lake, benign on a hot, tranquil summer day, reflecting the relaxed blue of the sky, could turn into a roiling black cauldron of horror. It pushed her down, pulled her under. Water invaded her: clogging her ears, snatching her breath, blinding her eyes. Suffocating her.

Paige thrashed about as she fought to regain the surface, coughing and sputtering as she emerged into the driving rain. She grabbed onto the bow of the overturned canoe.

"Bex?" she panted, struggling against the pummeling waves and frigid, lashing rain to maintain her precarious hold on the canoe. She daren't let go to look for Rebecca.

"Bex!"

But there was only the cacophony of the storm, finally splintered by the sound of a motorboat approaching.

"Grab the rope!" a young man yelled as he tossed it to Paige.

She flailed for it with one hand but couldn't snatch it. Shivering and growing weak, she lost her grip with the other, sinking beneath the punishing waves. It took all her remaining strength and willpower to stroke for the chaotic surface.

Suddenly, a strong arm clamped around her and dragged her up. The guy hauled her to the swim platform on the back of the boat, which was heaving wildly. Another one pulled her into the boat where she lay gasping like a landed fish. He buckled her into a lifejacket and covered her with his own rain jacket.

"My friend," she managed to wheeze.

"Oh shit!" one of the young men exclaimed.

Her rescuer grabbed a length of tethered rope, and jumped back in, searching under the canoe in case Bex was in the sheltered air bubble beneath. But he came up alone.

Paige's blood ran cold. Surely Bex couldn't have drowned!

He dove down several times, but to no avail. The lake seemed impenetrable and gave up nothing.

"It's no use, Zack! Get back in the boat!" the driver shouted as lightning crackled between the embattled clouds above them.

Once they had him safely aboard, he said to Paige, "I'm sorry, but it's getting too dangerous to stay out here."

She nodded as tears mingled with the rain.

At the rescuers' nearby cottage, the boys' parents, having witnessed the capsizing, had already called the police, and now put a call through to Westwind. The mother pressed a cup of sugary tea into Paige's icy hands and enveloped her in a thick towel and blanket. The storm raged southward and ten minutes later the lake settled into placid contentment.

Everything became a blur after she arrived at Westwind. At one point, Simon gave her a brief hug and said, "Thank God you're alright! We thought you would have sheltered somewhere, so we didn't come looking for you. We had some novice canoers who were in trouble near Blackthorn Island. They didn't realize that they could pull into any dock and get help. But at least they were wearing lifejackets."

The police reinforced that sense of carelessness when they asked questions to establish what had happened and why. Their divers recovered Rebecca's body standing in the weeds at the bottom of the lake, not far from the overturned canoe.

No one needed to state that her death could have been prevented. Although Paige had tried, she felt that her actions hadn't been forceful enough, and the crushing weight of guilt descended upon her.

She couldn't even look into Simon's eyes before her shaken parents took her home.

Chapter 3

They slept late, so Paige just had yogurt and coffee, although the buffet table tempted with anything one could wish for breakfast. A sous-chef even created made-to-order omelettes. Brett had porridge and fruit before choosing Eggs Benedict, but she was too nervous to eat.

She tried to hide her impatience. Now that she had decided to go out in the canoe, she was anxious to get started. So far it was still calm, but she knew that on such a clear and sunny day, there was usually a wind by mid-morning, and the lake could become choppy. She didn't want to lose her nerve now.

"I have to admit that the food is pretty good," Brett declared, finally finishing his third cup of coffee. It was high praise indeed, for he was not gastronomically easy to please. Paige was an accomplished cook, which made that aspect of their relationship easy. He even liked to help her in the kitchen when he had time, thinking himself something of a cordon bleu chef in training. It amused him to boast of his culinary skills when they entertained, and he would make something extravagant as proof.

"Ready to tackle the canoe? I have to warn you that I was an excellent canoeist at my summer camp when I was ten. My partner and I won the race."

"So, I can just sit back and enjoy the ride?"

"Hardly! I expect energetic paddling, madam!" he replied playfully.

But the lightheartedness quickly faded as they arranged to take out a canoe. Her mouth dry, throat constricted, heart pounding, Paige forced herself to step into it, taking her usual position in front. This time she put her lifejacket on over her swimsuit, despite the heat.

"Alright, babe?" Brett asked solicitously.

"Yes," she croaked.

She panicked for a moment, clutching the sides, white-knuckled at the wild rocking of the canoe as Brett stepped in. But he quickly had it steadied.

Of course it all came back to her - the rhythmic paddling. Like breathing. It was hypnotic. She had always loved the nearness of the water, feeling herself immersed in it, yet separate.

And the elation of physical exertion, of reaching out to propel them through the vast fluidity of the lake, dispelled her fossilized fear. So, another crusty layer of the past was sloughed off like a scab.

"I forgot how much I love this!" Paige said, her words powerless to convey the euphoria that had been released from years of bondage.

"Ready for a break? I haven't done this in too many years."

"There's a perfect spot just around the next island."

It was as she remembered - a beautiful little oasis with champagne-coloured sand beneath the pristine, shallow water. Under the benevolent warmth of the sun, it harboured no terror. Silver Sands.

As soon as the canoe was beached, Paige jumped out and tore off her lifejacket. "I can't stand the heat anymore!" She plunged into the water to cool down, instantly thrust back into the days when she and Simon used to swim here. They had been exultant as only privileged children can be, she thought, the subsequent years of sorrows, disappointments, and responsibilities weighing heavily on the adult soul.

"This is refreshing," Brett said, joining her. They sat on the hard, sandy bottom, lying back to let the silky water lap gently around their shoulders. "Our own little deserted island. We should have brought a picnic."

"What, and forego a gourmet lunch?' Paige said, staving off an amorous embrace. The memory of making love here with Simon was too intense and precious to be clouded by casual sex with Brett.

She tried not to dwell on that last time here with Rebecca.

She just needed an uncomplicated moment to wash away the past. And suddenly her face was wet with tears. A knot of emotion that had long lodged between her heart and stomach was unravelling, leaving her free to breathe.

"What's up, babe?"

"Poor, desperate Rebecca!" Looking back with adult eyes, she could see how bitter Bex had been. Paige forgave her the spite and jealously that had marred their last few minutes together. "How I wish that she were here now so that I could tell her how sad and sorry I am about what happened."

Brett put his arm comfortingly around her shoulder.

She wiped away the tears.

Brett's cell phone rang. "Sorry, babe," he said, giving her a reassuring pat before going over to the canoe to fish the phone out of a waterproof bag.

She cursed under her breath. His apology was merely politeness, and not regret. He had that familiar gleam in his eyes at the possibility of something new and challenging to occupy him.

Surprised that he actually had a viable connection, she listened only half-heartedly to Brett's side of the conversation, catching enough words to know that work was calling him back.

"Well, babe," he said with a self-satisfied grin. "More accolades for your brilliant husband! We've just landed a new account with a huge telecommunications company, thanks to my inspired beer commercial. Hal golfed with the CEO at the country club yesterday, and they want to meet with me on Monday afternoon."

"That's wonderful! Congratulations! So, when do you actually get a holiday?"

"I expect I'll be back in a couple of days to finish out my week here. You know how crucial this is to my career," he said, stroking her cheek.

"Of course I do. If your client intends to promote cell phones, then you already have personal experience you could draw on. Sitting on this deserted island in the wilderness but still connected to the office," she said with a hint of sarcasm.

"Hmmm. . . . Not a bad idea! Well, the bonus from this one will help buy you that condo at Westwind. In fact, let's go back and you can pick one. That whole concept really appeals to me. It'll be like living at a country club but having the added advantage of also being on a prestigious Muskoka lake. You've really hit on something there."

As they paddled away, Brett was using her as a sounding board for ideas for his new project, actually expanding on her suggestion. He didn't expect more than the occasional grunt from her, just to show that she appreciated his genius. She was interested, of course, but would have preferred to enjoy the silence of the lake just now.

But it wasn't silent. Jet skis zoomed past; deafening, supercharged speedboats roared by; boats towing skiers or inflatable tubes weaved in and out amongst others. Float planes roared overhead seeking open water to land. A few graceful sailboats skimmed across the water, but not as many as when she was young. Now everyone was constantly in a hurry, even on holidays. The lake had more of a crazed atmosphere.

Paige stopped paddling when they came to the scene of the accident, off the point of her rescuers' island.

It was beautifully calm, showing no signs of its violent past. But her image of Rebecca standing amid the seaweed forest at the bottom of the lake haunted her. Bex, with floating arms outstretched as if pleading for rescue, her undulating hair tangling with the slimy weeds. Her dead eyes, accusing.

Brett must have sensed Paige's tension because he stopped talking.

Suddenly the canoe lurched violently. Paige shrieked and gripped the sides frantically as she tried to regain her balance. She glanced around, demanding, "What the hell are you playing at?!" just as Brett said, "Steady on! What are you doing?"

They both said, "It wasn't me!"

"Must have been a wave," Brett conjectured.

"I didn't see any." It was an oddly tranquil spot amid all the hectic activity on the lake. Only gentle ripples reached them; certainly nothing large enough to have almost tipped them over.

Surely Brett wouldn't deliberately scare her like that? She shivered as she sensed something evil. Cautiously she turned around to look at Brett again, almost expecting him to have been transformed into a leering monster, but he just seemed bewildered.

"Could have been a fish, I suppose," he offered.

"Not that big! Let's get away from here. This place gives me the creeps!"

He seemed to understand, and silently resumed paddling.

Although they were in the fresh open air in blistering sunshine, Paige felt as if she were under the gaze of a malevolent presence. She turned often to look at Brett, but he just smiled at her.

"Still here," he said, amused.

You and who else, she wanted to ask. Brett was not someone she could read, or with whom she was in tune in any sort of extra-sensory way.

It wasn't until they were within sight of Westwind that she no longer felt spooked. Surely it had been just a reaction to revisiting the scene of the tragedy that had haunted her these many years. Maybe it had been a catharsis.

She tried not to dwell on it as she and Brett went for another swim before changing for lunch.

"Business before pleasure," he said, as he ushered Paige into the conference room behind the lounge.

"Oh Brett, really!"

"I wasn't kidding. We're going to buy one of these places."

"Glad to hear it," a young woman in a business suit said, greeting them with a chuckle. "I'm Amanda, the agent looking after sales. Have you seen our brochure?"

While Brett asked her to clarify some points, Paige wandered over to a large table that housed a model of the new development. There was the old inn and an expanded pool, but nothing else was the same. Replacing the Lodge, the cabins, all but four tennis courts, and even the new Water's Edge Suites were attractive blocks of three and four attached two-storey townhouses. Behind them sprawled a redesigned golf course.

Paige wondered if, like the Pembrook sisters, she could bear to come back here when the place was so completely altered.

Yet now that she had returned, she realized how much she loved it here, how she had missed it, craved it, how her very soul seemed entwined with it. Even staying in this proposed condo resort was better than losing the chance to ever be here again. The lake, the vistas, the air would be the same. And she would own the right to enjoy it whenever she chose. That had immense appeal.

Amanda was saying, "Here we have computer renditions of the floor plans. Do sit down and take your time browsing through. We have a pretty good interface, but if you have any problems or questions, just let me know."

It didn't take Brett long to decide. He wanted the waterfront, four-bedroom corner unit, which had the advantage of a wraparound veranda, part of which was a screened, three-season "Muskoka room". At 2,700 square feet, it was $425,000 before any upgrades, although granite counters and hardwood floors were already included.

"I'll have my lawyer contact you. In the meantime, I'll give you $5,000 now to guarantee this unit. And I'll see you in a couple of days, Amanda," Brett said as he handed her a cheque. It amused him to impress or astonish people. He'd clearly done both to the poor girl.

"Well, you obviously know what you want, Mr. Turner. I spend longer than that shopping for shoes!" Amanda responded.

"So do I, "Paige chimed in. She drew Brett into the lounge saying, "Aren't you being a bit hasty?"

"The money isn't an issue. I like the fact that we'll have nothing to maintain, but have access to all the amenities, including a couple of restaurants on site. You obviously like it here, and I think it's a great investment. A no-brainer. The only thing to think about is choosing the finishings, which I will leave in your artistic hands."

Brett's family had always holidayed at luxury resorts, which gave them the freedom of being somewhere different every summer, including Europe. But his eldest brother, Mark, had recently built a cottage on Lake Muskoka, which was connected to this one by the lock in Port Carling, and Brett had been pondering buying into this prestigious area as well. Many of his friends and colleagues had cottages in Muskoka, some on Millionaires' Row.

So, it had only been a matter of time before he settled on something. Why not here? She wrapped her arm gaily around his.

As they walked through the deserted lounge, he noticed an ornate grandfather clock. "For a moment I thought we were late, but it doesn't seem to be working."

"That's because it's haunted."

"Some excuse!"

"No, really." Paige stopped in front of it. It had always given her chills, as if it were somehow alive. And watching. "Edward Davenport was an Englishman who fell in love with Muskoka and the daughter of the house and married her. He brought this clock with him from England - it had already been in his family for generations. Apparently, when he died, it stopped working. They had clockmakers in to repair it, and they declared that there was nothing wrong with it. But it kept stopping, and so eventually, they didn't bother with it anymore. Just kept it as an ornament.

"So, you can imagine how spooked everyone was when it suddenly started chiming one day. It rang just three times. And it does every time something bad is about to happen to someone in the family or close to the family."

"Bullshit!"

Paige shrugged, not caring if he believed the story or not.

"Surely you don't buy that." He cocked an eyebrow at her as if to say that anyone who did was of questionable intellect.

Paige wondered what he would say if she told him about last night's experience, which she really hadn't allowed herself to think about yet. He'd probably have her committed to a mental institution. She was saved from answering by the Pembrook sisters, who were just arriving.

"You've heard Edward's clock chime, haven't you?" Paige asked them.

"Indeed, we have," Abigail answered. "The first time was before Florence's death - she was Edward's wife."

"I heard it on the day of your canoeing accident, Paige," Emmeline added.

Abigail placed a wrinkled but strong hand on Brett's arm as she said astutely, "Skepticism is healthy, but not to the extent of closing your mind to possibilities."

During lunch, Paige became aware that Emmeline kept glancing at her, looking somewhat perplexed. She was surprised that Brett picked up on that, however.

"Your ancient friend is trying hard not to stare at us," he muttered.

"She's probably wondering if I'm OK. She found me sleepwalking last night." Paige couldn't think of any reason not to reveal that much, at least.

"Will you be alright while I'm gone?"

"Yes, of course. You usually sleep like a log, so you wouldn't be much help anyway," she teased.

"Gee, thanks! And here I was trying to be chivalrous." He grinned fulsomely. "I won't head back to the city until early Monday morning. The traffic should be fine then." They were well aware of the heavy cottage-country traffic that flowed out of Toronto on Fridays and crawled back on Sundays. "So that gives us another full day together tomorrow. But now I'm going to get in a round of golf before I challenge you to tennis. Alright?"

"Perfectly," she replied truthfully.

"What are your plans?"

"To do whatever strikes my fancy, which is the beauty of holidays."

"I thought you did that every day," he teased.

"I'll remember that when you expect to have your shirts ironed and a feast on the table after I finish *my* work."

"Touché! I'll catch up with you around 4:00."

She didn't accompany him back to their cabin because she decided to join the Pembrook sisters on the veranda. The other guests had gone off to pursue afternoon activities. The playful shrieking of children was far off at the beach or in the even more distant "Adventure Day Camp". Paige settled into the comfortable solitude. "Is this a good time to talk?" she asked Emmeline.

"Yes. I've told Abby."

"What a trial for you, my dear," Abigail pronounced. "It seems that you have an even worse case than Em."

"Oh dear! You make it sound like a disease," Paige said.

"Perhaps more of a burden."

"But I've never experienced anything like that before. Why now? And here?"

"Because you wished so fervently for it," Emmeline explained. "Not once, but twice. I've found in my travels that there are certain places where the veil between our world and the other is thin, and concentrated thought manages to draw it aside momentarily."

Paige wondered what else she had wished for, which would suddenly surprise her. "Have bad things ever happened to you because of that?"

"I've certainly been frightened, felt threatened in places where one suspects evil intent or deeds that occurred in the past. But never here." In fact, she wished for these glimpses into the past, longing to see Edward again.

"Miss Emmeline, you keep looking oddly at me," Paige said. "Is there a problem?"

Emmeline was momentarily flustered. How could she tell Paige that out of the corner of her eye she detected a faint shadow quivering behind her. But whenever she looked directly at Paige, there was nothing there. "I do apologize, my dear. Your aura is a bit off today."

"I confronted the past this morning. Perhaps that's why."

"How did you do that, dear?"

When Paige had explained, Abigail said, "Good! And now hopefully you can leave that behind you."

But Emmeline wondered with growing unease whether Paige had made any dangerous wishes.

Chapter 4

Sunday was turnover day, so the resort was busy as people dragged unhappy children away from the tempting beach and pool, and trundled baggage to their cars.

"This is the perfect day to introduce you to the old Latimer cottage," Paige told Brett. "Marshall's not coming until later this week, but I have a key. It's only two miles south by boat, but twelve by road because we'd have to go through Port Carling and back up another peninsula."

"I'm game."

They bought sandwiches and the "world's best butter tarts" from the rooftop bar and added a bottle of chilled Sauvignon Blanc to their cooler.

Taking a canoe, they hugged the shoreline south and crossed a half-mile stretch of open water towards Old Baldy – a humpbacked, cliff-faced island - and from there they had an easy paddle past the tranquil shorelines of a string of islands leading to the mainland.

Paige was overjoyed when she glimpsed the white-trimmed green cottage perched above the rocky shoreline of a point that slid into the water in one direction and crumbled into a sandy beach in the other. Substantial but not ostentatious, it settled comfortably into the landscape, blending into the many trees that disguised its size. "Arcadia" was painted on the matching boathouse.

Paige grew up here in the summers with her parents and grandmother, Delia Latimer, with cousins from Great-Aunt Esther's brood – including Marshall - living next door.

Delia and Esther had met as young teens at Brightwell Girls' Academy in Toronto, and Delia first visited here in 1913. After the war, she married Esther's brother Raymond, who was ten years older.

Because Esther loved the place so much, Raymond severed off a few acres of the large property when he inherited, so that Esther's family could build their own, albeit more modest cottage called Esther's Nest.

"You've got to be kidding!" Brett exclaimed. "Look at the size of the boathouse!"

"The second floor was used as a ballroom in the early days, but my grandparents rebuilt it in the late '20s so that there was a large 'cocktail' deck and sitting room with a bar, after Prohibition ended. It was Nan's sanctuary when we lived here. She loved being so close to the water." As well as a bedroom and bath, Delia had a chaise lounge and a desk for letter writing, and comfy sofas and chairs for invited guests. "Wait until you see the cottage."

In 1895, Paige's great-grandfather, an industrialist specializing in precision instruments, had erected a summer mansion like so many of his wealthy peers – a showpiece large enough to house an extended family, invited guests, and sufficient staff to cater to the lot.

Her father had inherited it from his father, Raymond, in 1960, with the proviso that Delia was to have use of it until her death. Her parents found it too large and expensive to maintain, so they reluctantly decided to sell after Delia died in '76. Just the money saved from the upkeep easily paid for their annual jaunts to historically significant places and several weeks at the Westwind Inn.

"My grandfather stipulated in his will that his sister Esther's family should be given first refusal if we ever wanted to sell. So, Dad sold it to his cousin – Marshall's father - who restored and modernized it. My parents could never have afforded to do that."

Her second-cousin, Marshall Warrick, who was in his mid-forties, recently took over Arcadia from his aged parents. He knew how important it was for Paige to return to the lake, so he'd given her an open invitation to use the place.

It was through Marshall that Paige had met Brett. She sometimes wished she hadn't attended that party.

* * * * * * * * * *

November 1992

Just west of trendy Yorkville, the epicenter of the annual Toronto International Film Festival, north of the sprawling university, and beneath the brooding majesty of Casa Loma basks The Annex. Marshall had bought one of the late Victorian houses on a quiet, tree-lined street when the area was still relatively affordable.

It and the attached neighbour stood out because they weren't mirror images and flowed together to look like an imposing single home - whimsical, gabled, turreted, with tucked-in balconies and ornate trim. Paige had already written a well-received article about the unique Toronto "Annex" architectural style that defined the area.

The attached neighbours had become Marshall's close friends. Chef Duncan and sommelier Gavin owned the renowned "Maison d'Étoiles" only blocks away in Yorkville. So called because pinpricks of light in its black ceiling simulated mystical starry heavens. The fact that Hollywood stars attending TIFF frequented their establishment further justified the name, and had turned Duncan and Gavin into minor celebrities as well.

Paige and her best friend from university, Michelle, rented a delightful attic flat in another Victorian gem in the next block. Michelle had landed a job with CBC television, and was working that evening, so Paige attended Marshall's party reluctantly.

"You need to make connections, Kiddo," Marshall had said when she demurred. "Hard enough to get freelance writing jobs, but almost impossible if you don't mingle. Just be yourself and they'll fall under your spell."

She knew that he was right. Unlike her, Marshall was a master at engaging people in conversation and making them feel welcome and important. She had a lot to learn from him.

So now she was politely fending off advances from a drunk Englishman who looked like a dissipated '60s rock star. He claimed he was a music promoter based in London, and just happened to be visiting a friend in Toronto who had been invited.

"It's destiny that I'm here. Meeting you. I have an utterly romantic houseboat on the Thames. You really *must* come live with me there, darling girl. Even sex is better on the boat. I promise you won't be disappointed," he murmured as he pulled her close.

"No, thanks. I get seasick," she retorted, pushing him away as she dodged a kiss.

"You wouldn't on my boat."

Brett intervened, saying, "Hey, Paige, long time no see!" To the Brit he said, "Do excuse us while I catch up with an old friend."

As Brett took her arm and steered her away, she asked, "How do you know my name?"

"I asked our host who that ravishing young lady is who wants to escape."

Paige laughed. "Thank you for rescuing me, kind sir. . . . I think." She raised a suspicious eyebrow.

It was his turn to laugh. "Brett Turner at your service. I promise I won't be a bore or a pest. Just say the word whenever you've had enough of my company, and I'll depart like a gentleman."

"Fair enough," she admitted with a smile. "So how do you know Marshall?"

"He's going to be filming one of my ads. He's rather brilliant."

"That's terrific!" His "bread and butter", Marshall called the TV commercials he created. Which had also won him several awards.

"And your connection?"

"He's my favourite cousin."

"Ah, so we already have something in common – our esteem for Marshall."

"Notice how deftly he's ushering out the tipsy Brit and presumably, the friend who brought him."

"All done most hospitably, I expect."

Marshall caught her watching as he closed the door behind the pair and gave her a wink. Was that a sign of approval for Brett?

He monopolized her that evening, insisted on walking her around the corner to her flat – with not even an attempt at a goodnight kiss - and invited her to dine at Maison d'Étoiles the following evening.

She was surprised that he'd managed to get a last-minute reservation on a Saturday, and even more that they were seated in an intimate alcove away from the main restaurant, usually reserved for close friends or celebrities who didn't want to be seen.

"What's your secret?" she asked as he toasted her with a glass of exquisite wine.

"Family members frequent the place. And I had a word with Gavin at the party after you left last night to see if he could accommodate us. 'Anything for Paige', he said. And then warned me there would be dire consequences if I trifled with you."

She chuckled. "He and Duncan have kind of adopted me as a niece, which is really sweet."

"I can understand why they're protective of you," Brett said, gazing at her with admiration. "You seem so unpretentious. And innocent."

"Naïve, you mean. I'm just a small-town girl. Not used to the sins and temptations of city life," she said with a twinkle in her eye.

He chuckled. "OK, I'll stop being patronizing."

"Thank you."

"But you're still different from the girls I know."

"I'm old fashioned. And not interested in playing games."

"How about tennis?"

"In November?"

"At the Granite Club. Just blocks from my family's home."

"I'd love that!"

* * * * * * * * * *

"There was a servants' wing with a dozen rooms that stretched back from the kitchen, but it was deteriorating, so Marshall's father demolished it," Paige explained when she'd finished giving Brett a tour of the rambling, eight-bedroom cottage.

"This place is amazing!"

"Especially when you consider that the only way to get here in those days was by train and then steamship."

"I had no idea your family came from such wealth."

"Well, there wasn't much left of it, other than this place and our house in Launston Mills that Nan inherited," Paige explained.

"How did that happen?"

"My grandfather, Raymond, was never interested in the family business. He was shell-shocked from the first war and had some damage to his lungs from chlorine gas, so he frequently struggled with bronchitis. My dad wasn't born until '38, so at age 47, Raymond thought he'd have no heirs. When he had an offer for the company, he sold, and paid out his sisters' shares, although it was a bad time to sell during the Depression. Anyway, since my grandmother, Delia, had inherited her family home in Launston Mills, they moved from Toronto because they thought the clean country air was healthier for him. And she preferred the small-town ambiance.

"He fancied himself an inventor and had a keen interest in telecommunications. He built a facility and hired a couple of engineers to help him bring his various ideas to fruition, like making radios smaller and more portable. But others beat him to it with the transistor radio, despite all the time and money he poured into his research. He did have a couple of patents, but they were never used.

"He never scaled back his extravagant lifestyle either. So, by the time he died there was enough money left to keep Nan comfortable, but not much for her to pass on. Not enough to help us keep this place going. We were still lucky to have had it, though."

Paige knew how important money and its status were to Brett's family. His parents owned an intimidating estate in the Bridle Path, the most affluent neighbourhood in Toronto. His father was a stockbroker, his older brothers, Mark, also a broker, and Chad, in high-end real estate. They had married private-school girls from among the family's elite social circle, and so Paige felt out of place among them.

Marshall's reputation and their shared ancestry from an old Toronto dynasty gave her at least some credentials, even if her parents were *"just* teachers". More importantly, Marshall's Warrick grandfather had founded a prestigious Bay Street law firm, which Marshall's father and now older brother had taken over.

She should have backed away then, but being romanced by Brett was the first time she'd felt good about herself as a woman since the summer she'd lost Simon.

They dined frequently at Maison d'Étoiles and other popular bistros, attended concerts and theatre performances, and played tennis regularly at the Granite Club.

She eventually accepted his invitation to a meal at his Harbourfront condo – with takeout from a nearby French restaurant. But the place hadn't appealed to her, with its walls of windows overlooking the vast, threatening expanse of Lake Ontario from the twenty-fifth floor. On clear days you could see the far distant mist over Niagara Falls. On stormy days, the water raged across the endless lake while belligerent clouds brushed too close and lightning seemed within reach.

She declined his offer to go sailing on Lake Ontario once weather permitted, so they'd just dined at the Royal Canadian Yacht Club on Toronto Island, with its unrivalled view of the city across the harbour. His family were members of the exclusive club, and brother Chad was a champion sailboat racer, having won medals in North American and international competitions.

The more she'd resisted Brett's attempts at seduction, the more ardent and determined he'd become.

He was at his most charming when she'd introduced him to her parents. He admired the stately century home that her paternal great-grandfather – a successful lumber baron – had constructed using the finest woods.

They lunched at a nearby lakeside inn that had at its heart an historic log house carved out of the primeval wilderness, now surrounded by a golf course, which, of course, he was eager to play. Her father approved of Brett after the men golfed together, and her mother conceded that he seemed to be a good person, if a bit too suave at times.

The following weekend they spent in Niagara-on-the-Lake to tour wineries and attend a clever play at the Shaw Festival, staying at a luxurious Victorian inn - two rooms booked - where she had finally succumbed.

She'd been a challenging conquest, which was probably why he asked her to marry him after she refused his invitation to move in with him.

"I'm flattered. But not convinced that I'm the right person for you," she'd prevaricated. She didn't feel the intense love for him that she still had for Simon. Perhaps that wouldn't have lasted, but she was reluctant to commit herself to Brett.

"How could you not be right for me?" he'd asked taking her seductively into his arms. "You bewitch me. Enthrall me." He trailed kisses down her neck.

"I can't become Paige Turner."

"Hmm. ... OK, Paige Latimer Turner."

"A big mouthful."

"Keep your maiden name then. We'll be a modern couple."

"I can't live in the condo," she'd floundered. "I don't like heights and don't care to access home from an elevator."

"Ah yes. Used to getting from one end of town to the other in five minutes," he'd teased as he'd released her.

"And living on tree-lined streets where homes relax into expansive gardens," she'd added.

So, he found a house in Wychwood Park, a private enclave that resembled an English village within a woodland. With only one entrance from a minor street and a narrow looping road, it didn't invite outside traffic, so the community was a tiny sanctuary just west of Casa Loma and the Annex.

She adored the early century Arts and Crafts English Cottage style house with its leaded and stained-glass windows that overlooked beautifully landscaped grounds. She delighted in the name, which harkened back to medieval England. And she loved the fact that it had been founded as an artist's colony in the late 19th century when the area was on the pastoral edge of the city. It seemed as if that had been encapsulated and would forever be its own bucolic, tranquil nook in the heart of the otherwise frenetic city.

"It will be yours, milady, if you marry me."

She discovered later that Brett's father had bought a house for each of his sons as a wedding present. It wouldn't do to have any of them carrying a mortgage.

At the time, she'd thought that Brett must truly love her to be so considerate, but also worried about fitting into his fast-paced, sometimes snobbish world. She sensed that his father didn't approve of her, and although his mother was friendly and welcoming, the others were rather dismissive, the women, also subtly disdainful. She took some satisfaction that she easily beat the women in tennis and managed to hold her own against the men.

And she wondered how happy she would actually be, living in the city when she craved the slower pace and friendliness of a small town.

"Why don't you live together for a few years?" Marshall suggested when she'd solicited his advice. "No need for a ring to have sex these days."

"Don't let my parents hear you say that! Do you wish you'd never married Liz?"

He and his ex-wife were good friends. But with her career as an actress and his also taking him away for long periods of time, they'd realized that they were better off not tied to each other. Their son lived with whichever parent was home, or with grandparents.

"Although she's still my best pal, it was better for us to divorce than to feel tied to a shotgun marriage. It was the right thing to do at that time, to save Liz's reputation and Craig from being considered a bastard. Fortunately, that crap doesn't matter anymore. But we don't need a contract to bind us as friends. I can see us happily growing old together. Isn't that the important thing? To share your life's journey with your soulmate?"

But her soulmate had married someone else. The sentiment had obviously not been mutual.

"Monique and I have no intention of getting hitched," Marshall said of his current girlfriend, who was a set designer. "We value our time together, but also our private space, which we need to indulge our creativity. So, we won't even move in together, although we're there for each other when needed. That freedom to be apart has kept us together for seven years. I'm probably impossible to live with anyway," he added with a smirk.

But Paige did want someone to share every day, every joy, every adventure.

With Marshall, Duncan, and Gavin coaching her, Paige worked hard at being the perfect hostess for Brett's friends, colleagues, and clients, knowing how important it was to his career. Her new culinary skills – under Duncan's tutelage - and their exceptional wine cellar – thanks to Gavin - won many a devotee.

Their condo at Westwind would be a hit as well, although she felt possessive of her Muskoka sanctuary, and not willing to share it with that crowd. And she *could* see herself spending all summer as well as autumn and winter weeks at the lake, since she could write anywhere once she'd done her research.

While Brett went to use the facilities, she stepped out onto the commodious wrap-around veranda where her family had lived during those long summer days, the inside only used in the evenings or on cool days. She was happy to see some of the old wicker furniture among the modern.

She stood beside Delia's favourite rocker and whispered, "Oh Nan, I miss you. How I wish I could talk to you again!"

A breeze blew a forgotten autumn leaf along the veranda, subsiding as it reached Paige. The chair suddenly moved. At first alarmed, she felt a calming presence beside her. "Oh my God! Nan!"

Chapter 5

Dressed in her cozy Roots track suit against the early morning chill, Paige wrapped her hands around a steaming cup of coffee while she waited for the sunrise from the Muskoka chair on her deck. She'd looked carefully for spiders before sitting down.

Brett had told her not to bother getting up to see him off, but she loved dawn on the lake, and had already taken photos of the rosy horizon reflected in the mirror-still water.

He joined her with his coffee, which they'd brewed in their cabin.

"I wish I didn't have to go back to the city already," he confessed. "I am enjoying this place with you."

"So, the magic is beginning to work," she quipped.

"You certainly seem happier."

"Very much so. Hopefully, I've laid a ghost to rest."

"About time!"

Although it was only 5:30, a young man in a crisp chef's uniform arrived in a golf-type cart bearing a tray of food, which he offered to Brett. "Ms. Latimer told us that you had to leave early, Mr. Turner."

"Very thoughtful!" Brett said in surprise. Breakfast wasn't served until 7:30, although coffee and pastries were available in the lounge at 6:00 to tide over early risers.

There was a generous egg salad sandwich made with freshly baked bread, a blueberry muffin still hot from the oven, an apple, and a small bottle of orange juice.

"What a treat! Thanks, babe," Brett added when the young man had left.

"They've always prepared hampers for fishermen who want to be out early. That's one of the ways they make us feel at home."

"Good strategy to keep people coming back. Want some?"

"I'll grab a muffin with my next coffee."

"Are you sure you'll be alright here without your car? You could come home with me and drive back later today."

They'd brought her Volvo because Brett was supposed to be getting a lift back to the city on Sunday in his brother Mark's floatplane, from his Muskoka Lake cottage. Then Brett would drive back and forth on weekends in his Jag.

"I don't need to go anywhere by car. Marshall will pick me up when we want to get together, or I can canoe over."

"Be careful when you're out on the lake." He looked at her seriously as he got up to leave.

"I expect I'll just be lazing around here, planning my next article."

But as soon as he left, she set off with her Canon camera to capture the sun rising behind distant rocky and pine-bearded islands.

Although the pastry chefs had been busy well before dawn, the rest of the resort was slowly coming to life. The grounds staff were brushing away spider webs from the corners of every veranda post and roofline, raking the beach, watering the flower gardens, restoring the stop-light Muskoka chairs to their precise chorus line locations.

It was there that she took the coffee and muffin she picked up in the lounge, confident that the staff had removed all the spiders when they'd wiped off the dew.

Being the only one at the waterfront now, she savoured the serenity. A canoe slid through the water around a headland and a distant fishing boat perched between sky and water, perfectly reflected. It might have been like this a century ago. Tranquil. No boat noises.

Not even from that steamship heading towards the dock.

It must be the *R.M.S. Segwun*, the last of the many large steamers that had plied these lakes for almost a century. After two idle decades, she'd been restored and relaunched in the early '80s, and had often visited Westwind. Paige had been thrilled to cruise aboard the enchanting, historic ship that had turned 100 that summer of 1987.

But the passengers aboard this *Segwun* peered out from the 1930s.

Paige hadn't expected this to happen in daylight. It didn't scare her this time. Just fascinated her.

"It is exciting, isn't it?" Emmeline asked as she settled down next to Paige.

"Yes. But a bit disconcerting that it just happens out of the blue."

"You were thinking about days gone by."

"I suppose I was, but . . ."

"I was on our balcony, up behind you, and could feel a tingle of anticipation. When I saw you sitting down here, I knew that you were channeling this."

"Now you're scaring me!"

"Don't be, dear. I can't thank you enough for this opportunity to revisit my youth. Somehow, I recognize this particular day. June 25th, 1933. Mother had died of pneumonia that winter. She never fully recovered from the influenza that almost took her in 1918, during the pandemic, which is one of the reasons we spent the entire summer here every year. Heartbroken, Father died just three months later. Abby had been helping him the past two years and was now running the family business, because it wasn't easy to sell it during the Depression. But she had a good manager and needed time to pursue her own career, and I had just finished university. So, we had a glorious summer of freedom and healing ahead." It had seemed that her life was only whole here, and the rest of the year was consumed with anticipation of seeing Edward again. It was the summer that changed her life.

The old *Segwun* didn't fully materialize as it neared the dock. But a young gentleman stood up from a bench in the gazebo to welcome the ship.

"Edward!" Emmeline gasped. Astounded that she could finally see him. That it really was a moment relived. He'd always greeted the guests, who arrived aboard the steamers in those days. His face had lit with a warm smile whenever he spotted her.

Shakily she rose and hastened to the dock. Paige jumped up to accompany her, taking her by the arm.

Edward Davenport suddenly turned towards them as the *Segwun* dissolved into the lake. Dressed in light trousers and dark jacket, a silk ascot about his neck, he looked every bit the dashing hero of some period film. His face softened, and he extended his arms in greeting. Emmeline quivered with emotion.

As they drew nearer, he dispersed like smoke from a bonfire.

"No! Edward! Don't leave!" Emmeline cried softly.

Paige embraced her as she began to crumple, suspecting that Emmeline had been in love with Edward Davenport. Suddenly, strong arms relieved her of the burden. Simon scooped Emmeline up and headed for the inn.

"Do put me down, dear boy," she said as they arrived at the veranda. "I'm quite alright. Just surprised." She looked at him astutely. "You saw it, too, didn't you?"

He put her on her feet but kept a firm hold. "Let's talk in your room."

Emmeline took Paige's arm as well, and they escorted her to the third floor.

The sisters' spacious suite was one of only four in the original building that had balconies – two on each floor. They were in what had once been an L-shaped wing over the dining room beneath, but with further extensions of the dining area and additional rooms, it jutted out prominently from the centre of the building. At the turn of the century, a tower had been added just to this section, proclaiming the resort's grandeur. The door to it was right across the hall from their room.

"Goodness, what's happened?" Abigail asked with concern. "I'm afraid I've had my nose in a book."

"We saw the *Segwun*. That day we arrived in '33," Emmeline said.

"All of you?" Abigail asked, looking at Simon in astonishment.

"I couldn't believe what I was seeing," he admitted. "I was walking over from the house when a phantom ship suddenly appeared by Blackthorn Island, heading towards us. I thought it must be a trick of the light, some mist perhaps making the *Segwun* look so odd, although she's never up here this early. By the time I arrived at the dock, she just disappeared! Along with a shadowy figure. What the hell is going on?"

"We like to think it's heaven rather than hell," Abigail began as she enlightened Simon. "And Paige seems to be the power source that has amplified this gift for Em. I can't see a damn thing!"

Simon eyed Paige strangely. "Why now?"

She shrugged. "I've never experienced this before."

"Your motto is not just an idle boast," Abigail snorted. "Making wishes come true, indeed!"

"Paige has been focusing on the past," Emmeline said. "Probably like us, being nostalgic about losing this place that has meant so much to us."

Simon looked distraught.

"Em is fine," Abigail assured him. "As happy as a kid in a candy shop, I'd say. So why don't you two run along and catch up?"

"Brett's in the city for a few days, so will you ladies please join me for meals? At your old table?"

Abigail cackled. "That we will, dear!"

Paige and Simon walked downstairs silently. Awkwardly. Out on the empty veranda, he said, "I have to get to work, I'm afraid."

"We don't really have anything to discuss, do we?" She hoped yet feared that he would say something about regretting what had happened between them. But what good would it do now that they were both married?

He looked at her searchingly. "No. . . . I suppose not."

She turned away abruptly and hurried down to the waterfront to fetch her camera. She couldn't give in to the silly tears that threatened.

Watching from the balcony, Emmeline said to her sister, "Oh dear. They're not making up. If only they realized that one day it might be too late." She would have to wish harder.

• • •

Paige had made no plans because she just wanted to be inspired by her surroundings. But after a morning swim, she realized that she needed to capture every corner and nuance of Westwind with her camera before it *was* too late.

If there wasn't a definitive history of the inn, then perhaps she could write it. And use excerpts for articles. 'Lake Life' magazine would undoubtedly be interested in seeing the transition from the old to the new, and she had written for them before.

She went into the gift shop between the reception area and the senior staff quarters, which turned away from the lake at a right angle. As well as postcards and chocolate bars, the shop carried everything anyone needed, from toothpaste to swimsuits. There were original watercolours by Simon as well as his art photographs for sale. He really was talented.

She scanned the bookshelves and was happy to find nothing about Westwind.

"No, we don't, although lots of people have asked for an illustrated history," the sales lady responded to Paige's question. "Especially now. Many of our guests have been coming for years, and there's such a sense of melancholy this summer. But we've done very well with our souvenir clothing. Top quality and Canadian made." The subtle logo was stunning, with windswept pines lapped by "Westwind Inn" written to look like waves in a lake.

"I love this logo!" Paige said. "It was different when I was last here in the '80s."

"Yes, it's a big hit. Simon Davenport designed it a few years ago."

Which is why it looked more like art than advertising.

Paige bought an entire wardrobe of those branded clothes for herself – including tennis outfit, sweater, flattering skinny T-shirts, beach cover, terrycloth bathrobe - and a golf shirt for Brett. She picked up a few more rolls of film and noticed the sign that mentioned processing available.

"We take the films into the camera shop in town every day," the lady explained. "Town" being Bracebridge, a forty-minute drive by car, so not accessible to Paige at the moment. "They do a quick turnaround for us. People who are staying more than a week are especially anxious to start seeing their photos."

"I will definitely take advantage of that."

Paige was delighted with her purchases and thrilled at the thought of writing about the inn and illustrating it with historic photos as well as her own. It could be as much visual as textual, since photos conveyed so much.

She needed to talk to Simon about it, but in the meantime, she set to work collecting memories for herself.

The waterski school was still popular, although Simon no longer taught, of course. There was still a tennis pro, but with fewer students. Cottagers still pulled up to the dock to enjoy humongous ice cream cones. She even caught the Pembrook sisters, immaculately dressed and coifed after their daily swim, toasting with their afternoon cocktails in the Muskoka chairs by the lake.

And she wanted to snap loyal Louise at the front desk. Fortunately, no one required her attention, so Paige said, "Do you have time for a quick chat?"

"Of course! I'm glad to see you looking so well...."

Paige saw her struggling for words. "I'm sorry it's taken me so long to return. I've missed all this. It feels like a second home, especially with the Pembrook sisters and you and Barry, who stopped to chat with me, still here and virtually unchanged."

Louise chuckled with relief. "Hardly unchanged. See the silver streaks?"

"Very becoming!"

Paige realized that Louise, the office manager, and her husband, Barry, who was the maintenance manager, would be able to give her valuable first-hand accounts for the book about the past thirty-five years at Westwind, having worked for three generations of Davenports. Both had grown up in the village and worked summers here from the age of sixteen. Eager and dedicated, they became full-time employees and had their own small house on site.

"What are Adam and Laura doing now?" Paige asked after their children. They were several years younger, so she hadn't interacted much with them, although they were always helping around the resort, earning "allowances" from the Davenports before they were old enough to be properly employed.

"Adam became an architect, but after a year of working in the city, decided he was a Muskoka boy after all. So, he came home and began renovating old cottages and building new ones. Laura starts teaching grade 6 in town this fall. She got lots of experience working at the kids' Day Camp here over the years, and that's her favourite age group."

"Good for them! You must be proud, and happy to have them nearby."

"I count my blessings every day. Including how lucky we've been to work here. But Simon was right to sell. Barry says it's becoming increasingly difficult to maintain all these old, seasonal buildings. I just hope the new owner does justice to Westwind's legacy."

"I noticed on the model of the development that the pavilion and sundeck bar aren't there, although there's going to be a waterside pub and a residents' clubhouse beside a big array of docks."

"Exactly my point! Why not rebuild those to look like the originals? That's part of the lakeside appeal of Westwind, as the cottagers tell us. There are some folks that are mighty upset. There've been too many changes on the lake recently."

"I have a feeling you won't be working at the new resort."

"You're right! With our savings and a generous bonus and mortgage from Simon, we've bought a small, four-season cottage resort on Lake Muskoka not far from Port Carling. Adam is renovating the main house and the six self-catering cottages, and we're allowed to build four more, so he's having fun designing those. Our house is almost finished, and he's already living there. It's a beautiful, seven-acre property tucked into a calm bay, with a sandy beach and spectacular sunsets, so we're really excited."

"It sounds wonderful!"

A guest came to ask Louise something, so Paige excused herself.

She didn't mention her book plan to Brett when he phoned her a short time later. He was effusive about his own new project. "This will be a gamechanger. Possibly a partnership for me."

"That's terrific, Brett! And well deserved."

"I'm off to dine at the club with Hal and the others now, so I won't call again tonight. Miss you, babe! Enjoy the place, but not too much," he jested.

She told the ladies of her idea over dinner.

"Brilliant!" Abigail declared. "We've been following your career, and you're just the person to do this."

Although much of her income still relied on copywriting and editing, Paige also wrote occasional scripts for Marshall's documentaries as well as magazine articles that often focused on historical places and architecture. Most also included her photos.

"I hope that Simon thinks so."

"He'd be a fool not to."

"You could include a few of his paintings in the book," Emmeline suggested.

"Yes, of course!"

"And we can certainly provide context for you about the last seventy-seven years," Abigail offered. "There's plenty of social history in the changing culture, not only of the times, but of how people vacation."

"You're so right. This *will* be fun!"

"Simon is off duty by six, so you should talk to him after dinner. Veronica works evenings, since she looks after the entertainment. Would you like to join us for the play afterwards?"

"Thank you, but I'm eager to take more photos. The clouds are so interesting right now, so there could be an amazing sunset."

The best place to shoot that would be from a canoe, if she had the courage to go out alone, but the end of the wharf would suffice.

Paige brushed her long pale hair back from her right shoulder, although it wasn't in the way. There was just a sense of something there. A bug perhaps.

Emmeline was disturbed when she spotted the dark shadow behind Paige again, which disappeared when she looked directly at it. If it were Edward, she would surely have felt him, and have no need to worry.

But she was overwhelmed with dread.

■   ■   ■

Paige pondered the suggestion of visiting Simon but decided that it was inappropriate to disturb him when he was off duty. She'd make an appointment with him in the morning. She changed into slim capri pants and one of her new Westwind T-shirts before heading out with her camera.

With the everchanging sky and water and so many different angles to shoot from, she easily went through several rolls of film. She also realized how large the resort really was, and how difficult it must be to maintain and update it. No wonder Simon wanted out.

She saw him swimming from his private dock, but looked away quickly so that she didn't have to acknowledge him. Or make him feel spied upon.

So, she was surprised when he joined her a little while later as she was snapping photos of the now empty Muskoka chairs along the shore, people having migrated to the play or to the rooftop bar.

"The Pembrook sisters mentioned that you had something important to discuss with me. They seemed keen."

"Well... yes."

"Will you join me for a drink on my veranda?"

"If I'm not intruding."

"There's nothing I'd rather do." His smile was tentative.

His house was mostly screened from the resort by a copse of mature trees and shrubs parading from the shoreline up to a high stone wall which enclosed the back garden over to a granite cliff-dubbed the "Ridge Dragon" - that sheltered the property from the northwest winds.

A path snaked up the south slope of that massive rock, with a lofty outlook over the lake, which she and Simon had painted in different moods, sometimes under Emmeline's tutelage.

A "Private Property" sign was prominently attached to one side of the entrance through the stone wall because – as legend had it - an elderly guest in the '50s had wandered into the house while everyone was busy working at the inn. He'd chosen a book from the library and a scotch from the liquor trolley, and made himself at home on the veranda, thinking it was yet another part of the resort but with finer amenities. When Edward had found him there, he'd offered the old gent another drink and engaged him in conversation. The widower had admitted that he was often confused as to where he was, but grateful that his daughter had included him in the family vacation, which he was enjoying immensely. Edward invited him to join in several cocktail hours in the tower for the rest of his stay. A letter from the daughter that autumn had thanked Edward for his kindness to her ailing father, who had spoken often of that special holiday before he passed away.

Inside the enclosure, an ornate, century-old carriage house sheltered the vehicles. Flagstone paths meandered past sparkling, rocky outcroppings artistically revealed by departing ice-age glaciers, and through pockets of fragrant gardens.

To distinguish the house from the resort and make it recede into the landscape, it and the outbuildings were painted a cloudy grey with forest-green roofs.

Paige had once spent plenty of time here. The capacious, partly screened veranda had been a favourite place to paint on rainy days and practice their acts for the talent shows.

She drank deeply of the delectable Sauvignon Blanc Simon poured them before telling him about her idea.

"Who would want a history now that the resort's going to disappear?" Simon asked.

"The people who've loved it. The new owners who are cashing in on its reputation. Anyone interested in Muskoka history."

"A few, sure. Is it worth your time? And who would actually publish it? Won't be a bestseller."

"With lots of photos and some of your paintings to illustrate it, it could be a coffee-table book. Anyway, I'd do it just for me and you and the Pembrook sisters. And I'd find a way to print it if we couldn't find a small press to publish. I'm not expecting to make much money from this. I just want to ensure that Westwind isn't forgotten, that people can access the remarkable history of this place."

"That's one of your specialties. The sisters keep me well supplied with your magazine articles."

"I'm sure this is the longest running family resort in Muskoka, if not Canada. But it's also pretty well the last of the old ones on these lakes. Where will people go now to enjoy all this?"

"They build or rent cottages. Someone bought Rowanwood Lodge for the site of a luxury four-season hotel with a spa. They've already torn everything down." He snorted. "Remember how we used to have a friendly rivalry with Rowanwood? When they had better bands, our guests and staff would go over there. Kept us on our toes."

She and Simon, with Rebecca sometimes tagging along, had gone there for dances as well, since the lodge had focused on the younger clientele, unlike the family atmosphere of Westwind.

"But we usually won more regatta races," she said with a grin.

"And had *their* guests sign up for our ski school."

"So, what happened to them?"

"Doug's a civil engineer and lives, as he puts it, 'between the mountains and the sea' in British Columbia. He hardly ever comes back. And Greg became a vet."

She knew the Rowan boys, since they were Simon's second cousins and best pals.

"Greg lives in Collingwood between the 'hills and the lake', which he says is good enough for him, and comes here for a week every summer with his young family. Unfortunately, you've just missed him."

"Too bad!"

"Since the guys had no intention of running the place, their parents sold to a hotel chain in '89. But the new owners changed things so much that regulars stopped coming – many stayed with us, in fact. And it just kept spiraling downward until they bailed out last year. One of the former guests told us that it became too impersonal once the family no longer ran it. Just a hotel getting rundown and no one caring."

"I didn't want that to happen here. To keep going to the bitter end. I want people to remember it fondly."

"They already do, and it will help if we give them a legacy to hold in their hands. To reminisce with."

She held her breath as he looked at her intently. "Alright, let's do it. But I have the final say on everything."

"Agreed! The Pembrook sisters are eager to help, but could you ask your other long-time guests if I could interview them?"

"No one comes close to the ladies' record, but we do have people who've been coming fairly regularly for decades. I'll introduce you to those you don't already know."

"What about former staff?"

"Quite a few have booked in this summer. Tony and Angela are coming next week. They'll be happy to see you."

They already became friends with Paige and Simon in 1985 – their first summer working as ski instructors and boat drivers.

"Cool! What are they doing now?"

"They have a house on Lake of Bays, but still come for a week each year. Tony got his Ph.D. and is doing research on lake health and ecology, and Angie's a pharmacist."

"Good for them!"

"I was glad to see that your parents will be here for the first week of September."

"They're in Britain with my grandparents this summer. But they wanted a memorable retirement. What better way than starting September here rather than at school?"

"We'll give them special treatment. We really appreciate all those who've worked for and supported us all these years, and became friends as well."

She couldn't meet his eyes.

"I'll deliver cartons of documents to your cabin tomorrow. And maybe we can go through old photos together here in the evening. If your husband's not back. You might find some of mine useful as well, taken in all moods and seasons."

"Sure! And may I give you my backup disks to store? Here perhaps? I feel uncomfortable unless my work is duplicated from my computer and offsite as much as possible. Usually in my safe deposit box at the bank."

"Of course! I can put them in our vault here. Now, tell me more about that bizarre incident this morning. I still can't believe what I saw!"

Reluctantly, haltingly, she told him about that first night, when she was sleepwalking. "It scared the hell out of me. It was so real and yet unearthly at the same time."

He shook his head in disbelief. "I remember that '20s dress you wore. So, you actually recognized your grandparents?"

"Yes. And now I've seen your grandfather as well. But I don't know what all this means." She looked at him beseechingly. "How did I suddenly become a conduit to the past?"

"My father once warned me that a few people have seen strange things here, including a ghostly figure. He tried to brush it off by saying they'd probably imbibed too much or been dreaming. But Miss Emmeline told me after dinner this evening not to dismiss what we'd seen. It seems that the two of you together are making this ... time warp happen."

He ran his fingers agitatedly through his dark hair. "Are you OK?"

"If this is as scary it gets, then yes. I love these glimpses into the past. I wished for them, after all."

"I'm here if you need me." He had the same affectionate look that had always seemed to be reserved for her.

But she couldn't allow herself to be seduced by that again. She was a married woman now, not a love-struck teen.

"Thanks. And for the wine and this exciting project, but I should go since I want to catch the sunset."

"That's best done from a boat, as you know. I'll take you out if you like. And bring my camera as well."

"If you're sure."

He grinned. "We'll see if my Nikon can outdo your Canon."

"You're on!" she laughed.

They went down to Simon's private three-slip boathouse where a gleaming mahogany launch held pride of place. Returning from the Great War, shattered after leaving his beloved elder brother behind in a French cemetery, Simon's great-uncle, Fred Hawksley, had tried to rebuild his humanity and his life by painstakingly building boats. This was one of the twenty-five that he crafted to perfection in his lifetime, one each winter.

It was all too familiar to Paige. She and Simon had daringly made love in it under the stars. She tried to ignore those exquisitely nostalgic memories as they pulled away from the dock.

And realized that she had sealed those off along with the horror of that fateful day.

Rebecca's revelations had made Paige doubt her own thoughts and feelings about Simon after the accident. Had he been in love with a girl he'd met at university? With whom he might already have had a lengthy affair? Was theirs just a convenient summer fling?

With her crushing guilt augmented by the sense that Simon held her somewhat accountable for Rebecca's death, she hadn't even been able to read the letter he wrote to her until months later.

They stopped close to Blackthorn Island, which gave them a long vista towards the inn and Hawksley Bay.

Fiery clouds radiated from a vortex behind Westwind like swirling flames and charcoal smoke that drifted overhead into the encroaching darkness behind them. The horizon glowed amber below the ascending blues from aquamarine to indigo. It was all reflected in the calm water.

"This is spectacular!" Paige exclaimed.

"One of the best I've seen in a long time," Simon agreed.

"I did wish for some good photo ops."

"Those kinds of wishes we can usually accommodate here."

While the saffron afterglow lingered, Simon drove over to the site of the former Rowanwood Lodge, around the headland from Hawksley Bay. Although the resorts were half a mile apart across the water, Rowanwood had been tucked into a secluded cove, so they'd only been visible to each other from the very tips of their long docks.

All that was left of it now was a concrete wharf along the shore.

"This is terribly sad," Paige said. "We had fun times here as well."

"Doug had a crush on you."

"Did he? He was always keen to dance with me."

"Paige . . . ," Simon began, but she sensed that he was veering toward their relationship and wasn't ready for that. The last thing she wanted right now was to know why she hadn't been good enough for him.

"I need to get back, Simon. Brett's going to call, and he might be worried if I don't answer," she lied.

"Of course."

They were silent while Simon docked the boat in its slip, and they made their way back to the veranda.

"I wondered where you'd gone. I've finished the wine," Veronica drawled, raising her glass to them. "My *coffee* break."

"Photographing the sunset," Simon said dismissively.

"It set ages ago."

"But the most colourful skies are afterwards, as you know. Paige is going to write a history of Westwind, so she's taking plenty of pictures."

Surprised, Veronica said, "Whose idea was that?"

"Mine," Paige admitted. "And the Pembrook sisters are happy to help. I want to interview you when you have time, since you've experienced this place as summer help and now as an owner."

"Oh, I'll have plenty to tell you!" Veronica assured her.

"Great! I'll be off now. Thanks, Simon. I think these photos will be epic. Westwind going out in a blaze of glory."

"I'll walk partway with you, since I need to get back to work," Veronica offered.

Once they were out of Simon's hearing, she said, "You have to be careful what you wish for. I thought it would be fun to run the inn with Simon. But the work is relentless. Summer is consumed by long days, different shifts, so we rarely have time together or days off, and winters are deadly isolated here. And even then, the work doesn't stop. We have to do maintenance and renovations, prepare for the next season, hire and train staff, take reservations."

"I expect that Louise and Barry provide invaluable help with all that."

"Of course. And when Simon's parents were in charge, it *was* less hectic, and we could all take regular days off during the summer. They'd go to Europe or Britain after Thanksgiving, and we'd look after the fall clean-up and renos until they returned before Christmas. Then we had a couple of months in the winter to travel somewhere for a real holiday. The Caribbean, California, Hawaii. But once his mother was ill and his father was failing, Simon couldn't leave for more than a few days. I'll be glad when this season is finally over."

They stopped on the path below the inn and above the row of Muskoka chairs.

"Just a word of warning. Don't believe everything the Pembrook sisters tell you," Veronica said. "I sense that they blame me for us selling the place. Anyway, I think they're witches."

"If so, then they're good ones."

Veronica harrumphed. "So, they've put a spell on you as well. Simon actually considered keeping the place going until they died. Christ, that could be another ten or a hundred years!"

Paige chuckled. "So, what will you do after October?"

"Enjoy life and summers! Going to visit my sister in Seattle first. Her husband is a software developer at Microsoft. I spent my winter holidays with them when Simon couldn't get away. Sis and I pop down to see Dad in San Diego. That's the place to be in winter!"

Paige knew that her parents had divorced when she was young, and she'd lived with her mother and sister in the city. Her father had been an American "draft dodger" who'd made his home in Toronto during the Vietnam war, but had later returned to the States.

"I'm glad to see you've recovered so well from . . . the trauma. The Davenports were sad that your family didn't return, but I can understand. And who wouldn't rather spend the summer in Britain than here? Anyway, I can spare you some time in the late mornings. I generally go on duty after lunch. But don't spoil your holiday by just looking into the past. You've landed yourself a classy guy, so enjoy your time here together."

What little there would be of it, Paige thought as she headed to her cabin. Although she missed Brett in some ways, she was also relishing just being on her own. Being able to savour this place without his digs, to revel in treasured memories of days when she'd been truly happy. To allow herself to recall with poignancy her passionate affair with Simon, which left her moist and longing for him. She would definitely have to shut down those thoughts when Brett was back.

She knew she should feel guilty, but she wasn't convinced of Brett's loyalty, especially after what his brother Chad had implied a few weeks ago. And she had to admit that she still loved Simon. It was why she'd never allowed a man into her life, other than as a friend, until she'd met Brett.

Paige reached her cabin as the last of the muted colours reflected in the lake drained away and stars awakened in the darkening sky. She closed the curtains and moved one of the chairs, wedging it under the door handle to – hopefully - prevent herself from sleepwalking outside again.

She donned her new Westwind pajamas – a light T-shirt with capri-length bottoms – in case she wandered into the night. At least that was more substantial than the flimsy nightgown she'd worn last time.

With invigorating thoughts about her new project, she couldn't concentrate on the novel she was reading, and turned off her light.

Afraid of total darkness, she always brought flashlights in case the power failed, and nightlights to softly illuminate her environment. She'd left the door to the sitting room ajar, and there was enough dim light to see that there was nothing untoward in the bedroom.

But she suddenly felt spooked. Like she'd been in the canoe with Brett. As if there were an unearthly presence here. Watching. Waiting.

She rolled over to face the other bed, opening her eyes occasionally to check that it was still empty. She was terrified of seeing flashes from the past again. Or Edward Davenport staring at her.

Despite the warmth, she pulled the sheet over her shoulders against the breathy night air wafting in.

Chapter 6

The nightmare returned. Paige awakened, panicked, as the bony fingers scrabbling against the upturned canoe came ever closer.

But the noise didn't stop. Something was scratching at the cabin. It must be the branch of a shrub. A refreshing breeze was blowing in, so the wind had picked up. *Don't dramatize. Go back to sleep.*

But she was too overwrought by the dream, so she turned on her bedside light to read. The noise became fainter and more intermittent.

When she woke again, it was 5:15 and getting light. The book was lying beside her, so she must have fallen asleep reading, although she didn't remember turning off the light, which was too far to reach when lying down. Had she sleepwalked? At least the chair was still in place, blocking the outside door.

She would have loved to start the day with a swim but wasn't brave enough to venture into the lake with no one else around. Even the main beach near the inn was deserted so early, and the pool didn't open until 8:00.

As she was pulling on her shorts after a quick shower, she happened to glance at the other bed and noticed a faint impression on the edge. As if someone had perched there momentarily.

Strange that she hadn't seen that last night. She hadn't touched Brett's bed or thrown anything on it since the housemaids had made it yesterday. She tried to shrug it off but couldn't suppress a tingle of unease.

When she went outside to photograph the sunrise from her deck, she realized the sheltering shrubs and trees around it weren't close enough to have rubbed against the cabin, even in a gale.

Had there been an animal clambering about somewhere? A mischievous raccoon perhaps? Hopefully there weren't mice in the walls. She might have to mention that to Simon.

She went down to the inviting lake, kicked off her flip-flops, and waded into the shallows, snapping photos from various angles, even crouched so low that she was almost sitting in the water. The dock and dance pavilion seemed a long way off and made for an interesting shot.

She walked in the other direction where a creek trickled into the lake, its banks busy with marshy plants, the water icy cold as it coiled lazily around her feet. She knew that there was a small bridge over it on the path that led through the pine woods to the marina.

She captured a macro of an iridescent green dragonfly perched on a striking magenta swamp milkweed. Then she turned her lens back to the lake and saw a dock spider running towards her on the surface of the water. She shrieked and had the impetus to move away this time, but realized that she had sunk into soft, sucking sand, and struggled to pull herself free. It was like a dream where she tried to escape danger but was held fast in molasses.

She shrieked again.

And then Simon was there, his waves chasing the spider into the reeds. He enfolded her in his arms, like he had ten years ago. "It's gone," he reassured her as he stroked her back.

She laid her head against his shoulder, trying to subdue her shuddering. Feeling the dangerous tenderness of his embrace.

She pulled away reluctantly. "Thank you. I don't know how I got so stuck." But she wasn't anymore. The sand was softer than at the main beach, but not like the quicksand that had imprisoned her only a minute earlier.

"The creek washes silt in, so it can feel a bit boggy here."

He held onto her firmly as they walked back to the shore. She saw a cart parked outside her cabin, loaded with the cartons that Simon had promised her this morning.

"I thought you might be up early. If not, I was going to come back later."

"Good timing then! But I'm glad you didn't get wet." She was a bit surprised to see him in shorts.

He chuckled "I don't look like the boss, do I? It's one of things that I *do* like about this job. I handle the behind-the-scenes work, and Veronica is the social face of the resort. I don't get into proper office attire until I have to. This morning, I have outside work. But I will borrow a towel to dry my feet."

When he'd slipped back into his boating shoes, he hauled in the boxes, saying, "These are the early years and up to the second war. There's probably lots of boring stuff to plow through to find the nuggets. I've never read any of this."

"I'm practiced at skimming historical documents. . . . Tell me about Edward Davenport, now that I've sort-of met him."

"That's just too strange," Simon said, shaking his head. "Granddad was twenty-one when he came to Canada in 1922 – a graduation and birthday present to explore the 'colony'. His father was a solicitor and Edward was the youngest of six kids. His two eldest brothers had been killed in the war, but he'd been too young to join. Anyway, he came here for a month and ended up staying for the season because he fell in love with the landscape and my grandmother, Florence.

"Her eldest brother died in the war as well. And shell-shocked brother Fred wasn't interested in anything but boats. Younger sister, Maggie, married into Rowanwood, so Florence was to take over the inn and needed to find a suitable partner."

"Because women couldn't possibly manage on their own," Paige scoffed.

Simon chuckled. "From all the stories I've heard about other farms-turned-into-resorts up here it was often the women who made them successful. But she was also supposed to produce an heir to carry on. Anyway, Grandma was five years older than Granddad, and by all accounts, lucky to land him. Handsome and charming, which made him popular with the guests, he also brought money into the marriage, which he used to build the dance pavilion and the Lodge, with large rooms and ensuite bathrooms - quite luxurious in those days."

"And he brought a haunted clock."

"Yes." Simon became suddenly serious. "I heard it chime the day of your accident. You have no idea how terrified we were because you and Bex hadn't returned."

He looked at her with such compassion that she almost asked why he'd deserted her when she'd desperately needed his love and reassurance.

They jumped as Simon's painting of the Muskoka chairs crashed to the floor.

"The nail popped out of the wall," he said in puzzlement when he went to examine the damage. The frame was unbroken.

"I heard something in the night. Scraping noises. Could there be mice in the walls?"

"I wouldn't have thought so. We take precautions and constantly monitor pest activity. But I'll have it checked out."

The moment for intimate revelations had passed – fortunately, Paige thought – as Simon went to fetch a hammer from his toolbox in the cart. After he'd put the painting back up, he said, "I should go. But I'll give you my home and cell phone numbers in case you have any further encounters with unwanted guests. And if they don't work, I can always be paged through the main desk. Call me anytime, day or night if Brett's not here."

"Thanks. I do appreciate that," she added with a smile.

He turned back at the top of the steps, saying, "By the way, I'm not going to charge you for your stay here, since you'll be working on the book. Do you think another two-and-a-half weeks will be enough, or do you want to extend your stay? We're pretty well booked right now, but there are usually a few cancellations. . . . And there's always our boathouse suite."

She wasn't sure Brett would approve of her staying longer, since he wasn't going to take any more time off to join her. But this was *her* work, and she would definitely need more time here. She could always stay at Marshall's cottage. The boathouse suite would only remind her of Simon and what she had lost.

"I think that would be a good idea. But you really don't have to waive the cost."

"Brett can't complain if you get free room and board," he said with a wink.

Don't be so sure.

Paige finally made herself some coffee and began tackling the oldest box. By the time she went for breakfast at 7:30, she already had a good sense of the Hawksley family from England, who had claimed a free government land grant in the Muskoka wilderness in 1869. Their hundred acres was doubled because they had a child, and Howard Hawksley had cleared the requisite fifteen acres in five years. Their first abode was a rudimentary cabin constructed of the pine logs he had felled. Two years later, the second, but not final home, with two storeys, four bedrooms, and a veranda, was also hewn from the primeval forest, but sawn into lumber at a nearby mill.

"It's all quite fascinating," Paige told the Pembrook sisters over breakfast. "And the hardships those people had to endure! Howard's wife gave birth to six children here, with only a neighbour to help. Three of them died as infants and were buried on the property. So tragic!"

"Only the hardy survived in the backwoods," Abigail said. "We did a documentary about pioneer life in Ontario when I was with the National Film Board. The European settlers were lucky to have had advice from the indigenous people who had been living in harmony with the land for millennia. Although this beautiful, rocky landscape that we so admire didn't provide much fertile farmland, it did entice outdoorsmen and tourists."

"It seems that the Hawksleys got into innkeeping accidentally," Paige said. "A couple of British gentlemen had come to hunt and fish in the fall of 1879 but had been blindsided by a fierce blizzard. They stumbled upon the Hawksley farm and sought shelter from the storm. It lasted three days, and they ended up staying until the spring thaw!"

The sisters chuckled. "The days when it took months to get mail from abroad and people didn't worry if you didn't check in with them for a year," Abigail quipped.

"Exactly! The toffs enjoyed the hospitality and the cuisine. Helped Howard hunt their venison dinners, learned how to ice-fish and cut timber, paid the family handsomely, and suggested they rent rooms to adventurers like them. So, the Hawksleys rented their original log cabin that summer, and Howard, realizing they could make more money from tourists than their farm, began building the inn."

"It makes it even more sad that so much of this history will be lost," Emmeline lamented. "Photos in the lounge show the rugged farmhouse next to the inn when it opened, and how it looks today under a new façade and connected through the gift shop. You can be sure that old section will be torn down."

After breakfast, Paige went to look at the two dozen vintage photos from different eras displayed in the lounge. She had seen most of them before, but never with the keen interest she had now. She looked first for Edward and Florence.

With his tidy moustache, his sense of style and poise, Simon's grandfather was rather a heartthrob in his day. Paige saw some of him in Simon – the sparkling eyes, dark wavy hair, and engaging smile.

Florence, although not unattractive, looked stern, like she tolerated no nonsense. She was surely the driving force behind the inn, while Edward was the suave and personable host.

Paige couldn't help wondering if Edward had been an opportunist who bought his way into the business through marriage and a modicum of monetary investment. And recalling Emmeline's reaction to him, she wondered if Edward had been a ladies' man, breaking hearts. Having affairs.

Was that why Emmeline had never married? It wasn't something Paige could ask, but she wished she knew more about that relationship. She sensed the sisters had long-held secrets.

She dropped off several rolls of film at the gift shop for processing.

Back at her cabin, she tried valiantly to skim through the papers, but kept getting caught up in intriguing details.

From Florence's mother's journal:

Sept. 30, 1913 – So strange to have both girls off at boarding school in Toronto, Bill at the university, and Fred still working and living in Gravenhurst. Florence is happy to be back at Brightwell Girls' Academy with her best friend Lucinda, but sad that it's her last year. Maggie would rather be home, but there's no schooling beyond primary here. I do wonder if the children will be content to take over from us when the time comes.

Paige was surprised that the Hawksley girls attended that prestigious private school, and around the same time as her grandmother, Delia. Surely they had known each other!

She made copious notes - much of which would never be used. But they still gave a sense of the times, which was critical for setting the context.

At lunch she said to the Pembrook sisters, "You must have known Florence quite well. I'm eager to know more about her."

"She was a rather private person, working behind the scenes, not interacting much with the guests. That was Edward's purview," Abigail elucidated. "She ran the kitchen, as chef when necessary, and supervised all the staff. We know that she loved this place and was completely invested in it."

"And Edward was the perfect match because he made sure guests were happy and would keep coming back," Paige ventured.

"Exactly! By '39, he and Florence were in charge. So, after the war he convinced her that they should make the rooms in the inn larger, with private bathrooms, because that's what people wanted by then. The Lodge had always been more popular and was where our family stayed after it was built. But it doesn't have balconies, as you know. So, when fifty rooms were renovated into thirty, Em and I moved back in here and grabbed the best one of the four with balconies. The view is splendid. We like it so much that we've had the same room now for forty-nine years."

"That's amazing!"

"We always booked for the next summer before we left. Of course, they gave the place a facelift every decade or so, but that doesn't seem to suffice anymore."

"Now people want holiday suites or condos out of the pages of Better Homes and Gardens," Paige said, and described their new "cottage".

"Would you ladies come to stay for a few days every summer once it's built? I'd love for you to be here with me. When Brett isn't."

"That's very sweet and considerate of you, dear. Simon's invited us to stay at his house as well, so we'll be sure to meet up here, one way or another," Emmeline said.

"That's kind of him. And wonderful! You won't have to entirely lose your summers here." She left them with a dazzling smile.

"She's genuinely happy," Emmeline observed after Paige had left. "Much more so than when she arrived."

"It's the magic of the lake. And this book project with Simon is undoubtedly helping."

"Yes. And allowing them to get reacquainted."

The sisters looked at each other.

"Are you going to tell her?" Abigail asked.

"If . . . When the time is right."

■ ■ ■

Trying to regain her confidence on the water, Paige took out a sit-on-top kayak, wearing a lifejacket. She felt more stable in the kayak than a canoe, and was really enjoying her paddle, staying close to shore, but avoiding Hawksley Bay. It was busy with boat traffic, since the marina not only rented dock space to island cottagers, but also had a small general store with everything from bread to batteries to live bait, saving locals a trip to the village.

So, when she got back, she decided to buy herself a lifejacket rather than use the damp ones shared by all the guests. And she decided she would purchase a kayak when they had their condo cottage.

Beyond the parking lot for the cabins, a gravel path led near the shoreline to the Hawksley Bay Marina, founded by Fred Hawksley but no longer in the family. An arched stone bridge spanned the creek into a pine woodland, the discarded russet needles forming a thick mat on the forest floor which glowed in shafts of sunlight. A short section of boardwalk skirted a small wetland with blooming lily pads and other aquatic flowers. Frogs perched on the floating leaves, a family of ducks rested on a rotting log, and a majestic blue heron stood at attention in the shallows. Paige was glad she'd brought her camera.

At the end of the boardwalk was a sign announcing, "You are leaving Westwind Inn", the reverse side warning, "Westwind Inn. Private Property."

One of the things Paige loved about resorts, marinas, and cottage country communities was the infectious cheerfulness of the holidaymakers. Excited kids were coming out of the store with inflatable boats that looked like swans or pirate ships, plastic buckets and shovels for sandcastles, Frisbees, beach balls, and pool noodles.

In fact, she thought one of those unsinkable foam noodles would be helpful for just floating in the lake, as well as making her feel safer.

The marina carried high-quality lifejackets, and she didn't mind paying the price when she found one that was a good fit for her and comfortable for kayaking.

After a swim with her new, turquoise noodle at the supervised main beach rather than her own waterfront – where she feared the mysteriously shifting sand – she got back to the boxes.

Marshall called her mid-afternoon. "Hey, Kiddo, I'm finally at the cottage. Man, it's good to be here! I need some downtime to regenerate. How are *you* doing?"

She knew what he meant and explained, adding, "I feel mostly at peace now. I even told Brett about it."

"Good! Can you join me for lunch tomorrow? I have a project that might interest you."

"You're only having a half-day off?"

"Working from here's not really working, is it?" he jested.

"I'd love to! But Brett had to return to the city, so I don't have a car. I can kayak over."

"Not a chance! I'll pick you up at the dock at noon."

Brett called her just before 6:00. "I'm afraid I won't make it back tomorrow as I'd hoped," he said. "Sorry, babe. But I *will* be there by mid-afternoon on Friday. Are you bored yet?"

"I'm never bored here. In fact, I'm working on a new project." She told him about the book with exuberance, since she suspected that it wasn't necessarily work keeping him in the city.

"You seem excited."

"Very. In fact, I'll have to stay longer to do my research. So, you can at least join me on the weekends if you can't take more time off. Simon's not going to charge me for my stay."

"That's generous! And your book sounds interesting. Coffee-table chic as well as informative. That should sell well with the new condo owners."

She was surprised that he approved so readily. And suspected that her continued absence suited his own plans. *Damn him!*

"I have a dinner engagement with my parents, so I'd better get going."

"Is everything alright?"

"Of course. Just a bit of business Dad wants to discuss."
Good excuse.

Paige brightened up over dinner with her elderly friends. "Marshall always offers me plum scripts to write. Usually historically oriented. He was the one who encouraged me to study film as well as journalism at Carlton."

"If we'd known you were at the university, we would have invited you to visit," Abigail said.

"I left this part of my life behind after . . . the accident." Paige admitted. "But next time I'm in Ottawa visiting my grandparents, we should get together. I'd love for you to meet them. They live by the canal near Dow's Lake."

"Sounds delightful!" Emmeline said. "Did you know that Simon studied film at Ryerson Polytech? It's a university now, of course."

"No!" Paige said in surprise. "Last I knew he was at U of T."

It was where they had been eager to meet up that fall of '87, Simon in his third year at the Toronto university and she, in her first. He'd rented a private room in a Victorian house, part of a student-run co-op in The Annex. She was to have moved into a university residence, but his place would have been their love nest.

But she'd been so traumatized that she didn't go.

"He dropped out in the fall of '87 to travel," Abigail said. "And returned just after his father's accident in the spring. Richard was lucky to survive the crash with a drunk driver. The ER doctor speculated that he wouldn't have if he hadn't been in a Volvo. And that's thanks to your family, who had one that Richard admired, so he bought one."

"Wow! We all still drive them."

"So does Simon. Anyway, when he returned, he was enthusiastic to know all about my career with the NFB and the CBC, because he said he wanted to study something he was passionate about."

"Is he planning a career in film now?"

"You'll have to ask him," Emmeline suggested.

But Paige didn't want to discuss anything that would refer to that summer of '87.

This new knowledge made her a bit nervous when she went to his place after dinner. Hearing a Moody Blues CD playing when she arrived was almost her undoing.

"Your Wildest Dreams", their big hit from their "Other Side of Life" album, came out in the summer of '86 and became an instant hit with Paige and Simon. She had already been a fan and knew their earlier records through Marshall, who had been listening to them since before she was born. Some of the summer staff, like Tony and Angela, also listened incessantly to that album, so a small group of them created the Westwind Moody Blues Fan Club, which met frequently on Simon's veranda to binge their earlier LPs, which Simon ended up buying that summer.

"Marshall took me to see the Moodies in Toronto in '93. They were fabulous!" she enthused, trying to regain her equilibrium.

"Lucky you! I didn't manage to get tickets."

Throughout his years studying filmmaking at Ryerson, Marshall was a waterski instructor at Westwind during the summers. He'd taught Simon as well as her to ski.

"I do see Marshall occasionally. He drops in for a burger and fries on the sundeck and stocks up on butter tarts at least once a summer."

She laughed. "He says that he got hooked on those when he worked here."

"Lots of people do. Which is why we don't divulge our secret recipe," Simon added with a grin.

He already had photos spread out on the long refectory dining table, and she was quickly caught up in the fascinating historical ones that they looked through.

"Juxtaposing some of these with modern views would really tell a tale," Paige said. "Like this one showing the vegetable gardens and the cattle and sheep grazing on what are now the tennis courts and golf course."

"They produced most of their own food for the resort in the early days." Riffling through a stack of photos, Simon showed her one from almost exactly the same angle. "I'd already thought of that when I took this shot. And you can see the old barn was replaced by the first tennis court."

"What a difference!"

He showed her more then-and-now photos – the waterfront with and without the dance pavilion and rooftop bar, the beach narrow and hemmed in by trees where there were now chaise lounges and a beach volleyball net, and beyond that, a former copse where the cabins now squatted.

"These are wonderful!"

"I'm trying to capture everything before it changes yet again. And it illustrates the evolution of resort life. I might make a little film after the next version of Westwind is built."

"That's a terrific idea." She hesitated and then plunged in. "The sisters told me that you studied film."

"Like you did, I heard. I've seen a couple of the docs you worked on with Marshall. You've done really well. Seems we still have similar tastes and ambitions."

In the background, the Moody Blues sang "I Know You're Out There Somewhere" as his eyes caught hers. The poignant lyrics expressing the yearning for lost love resonated between them. Was he also haunted by the promises they'd made each other?

Looking away, he said, "I dropped out of U of T. Couldn't see the point of getting a general arts degree anymore since I was destined to run this place, so I bummed around Europe for a while and ended up in Australia for the winter. I landed a job with a film crew, as a Production Assistant. Bottom rung of the ladder, as you know, but it allowed me to see what goes on behind the scenes in filmmaking, and I decided that I wanted to pursue that. Some day."

"Why not start with your Westwind documentary? Now."

"Sure, why not? It's still hard to fathom that I won't have to worry about next season once Thanksgiving is over." He smiled. "What do you think of these photos?"

There were spectacular autumn shorelines reflected in glassy water, loons sailing through morning mists, a pumpkin moon floating over the lake, flaming Northern Lights, tumultuous clouds, and brooding skies.

"They're stunning! So artistic! You could have a book of just your photos, Simon."

"That occurred to me as well. I have hundreds more."

There was an odd squeaking noise and a whoosh overhead. Paige ducked instinctively.

"How did *you* get in?" Simon remarked as the bat swooped back over them. "Open the door to the veranda, Paige. You can wait outside and watch for it to fly out. It's a bit frantic right now."

Simon closed the French doors to the library wing and turned off most of the lights as the bat flapped erratically around the rooms.

"Ok, little guy, let's get a draft going so you can find your way home," he said softly as he opened the back door beside the kitchen.

A few minutes later he called, "It's out!"

Paige closed the screen door but stayed out for a moment to watch the encroaching night, thinking of the photos and that the constant here was the lake. Aside from some new cottages on the islands, the view would have been the same when this home was built at the turn of the century.

Shadows suddenly moved amongst young trees between the inn and the house, and Paige noticed two indistinct people in a passionate embrace. They held hands as they walked towards Simon's private boathouse.

"Simon! Come quickly!"

"What's up?" he asked as joined her.

"Do you see them? Going to the boathouse?"

Paige couldn't make out any features, but suspected that one was Edward Davenport. Was Emmeline the woman?

Simon paused. "Yes. But sometimes we just need to leave the past behind. Let's get back to the book."

The phantoms disappeared, and the screening trees once again reached their mature height.

"We're not exactly doing that by creating this book, are we?" she observed wryly when they were back inside.

"This is different."

"Because we only see what people have chosen to leave us?"

"Exactly! We all have secrets. . . . Don't we?" He gazed at her intently.

They had often met in the boathouse suite.

For a moment it seemed that they were back in '87, and she just wanted to throw herself into his arms. The touch of his lips on hers and trailing down to her breast was seared into her memory. As was the urgency and intensity of their lovemaking in those stolen moments. If he touched her now, she didn't know if she could resist.

Desperately needing a diversion, she said, "Would you consider working with Marshall to produce your documentary? I'm meeting with him tomorrow."

"Of course! I admire his work and would feel privileged to learn the craft from him."

Envisioning two of her favourite people creating together made her suddenly ecstatic. "Perfect! I'll arrange a time when we can get together."

The phone rang and Simon answered. His brow knit as he listened. "I'll be right there!"

"Sorry, Paige. One of the staff thinks she saw a ghost."

They looked at each other.

"May I come along?"

"Sure."

When they entered Simon's office, Veronica was trying to calm the hysterical girl, who was rocking back and forth in a chair.

"I can't stay, Mrs. Davenport! I want to go home!"

Simon squatted down in front of her and took her clenched hands reassuringly in his. "I hear you've had a nasty shock, Tammy. Can you tell me about it?" he urged gently. "Take your time. Breathe slowly."

Haltingly she began. "I delivered the extra pillow 313 requested, and was just walking past the entrance to the tower . . . when I felt a cool breeze around me." She began shaking. "I realized the door was slightly open, which surprised me. So I opened it a bit more and saw . . . part of the darkness separate . . . and look like a person!"

Her eyes were huge. "He was coming towards me, so I ran!" She began sobbing.

"That sounds frightening, Tammy. But I'm sure there's a rational explanation. Sometimes people play tricks. Maybe he was trying to surprise someone else. Or sweethearts found a private place for a kiss. But we're not likely to find out who they are." He let go of her hands and said, "But we don't ever want you to be uncomfortable here. Do you feel safe in the girls' dorm?"

"Yes, sir."

"Good. How would you feel about working in the kitchen? You'd be around other people all the time and never have to deal with the guests or their rooms."

She seemed to gather strength and finally said, "I could do that."

"Excellent! Take a few days off. Go home if you like. And know that we value your contribution here. But we understand if you feel you can't return."

"Thank you, Mr. Davenport.... I'll be OK now."

"Good!" he said with a warm smile. "Now I'm going to make sure the tower is properly locked to discourage mischief and romance."

Tammy smiled tentatively.

When she'd left, Veronica turned to Paige and snapped, "Why are you here?"

"Seeing what's involved in running this place."

"This isn't the sort of thing we want advertised. Ghosts, for God's sake!"

"What difference does it make now?" Simon asked.

Veronica was speechless for a moment. "I have to get back to the pavilion. It's coming up to intermission."

When she had swept out of the office, Simon took a key and flashlight out of a desk drawer. "The only keys to the tower are this one and one on Barry's keyring. And he's off today. So, someone must have taken this and replaced it. Let's see what we find."

Aside from the creaking of the warped wooden floor, the third-storey corridor was eerily quiet. People with children needed the larger rooms in the Lodge or the cabins. The Pembrook sisters were at the musical revue in the pavilion along with many other guests.

The door to the tower was closed. And locked.

"That's odd."

"Can it be locked from inside?"

"Yes."

Simon strained to open the door. "Hardly any of the door frames in this old building are square anymore," he complained. "And then the wood swells from the humidity."

He finally pushed it open. Faint moonlight struggled down the stairwell that turned 180 degrees from a landing halfway up, but did little to dispel the darkness. Paige realized she was holding her breath in anticipation of seeing Edward Davenport standing there.

Simon flicked the light switch, but the bulb flared and went out. "We never bothered to replace the ancient wiring in the tower. So much of the infrastructure needs upgrading that the new owners will probably find it cheaper to raze the whole place and begin anew. We've always worried about fires from faulty wiring or the dry old wood being set ablaze by a careless smoker.

"You should have seen how quickly Windermere House burned last year when it caught fire. We could see the flames from here." It was another century-old resort, six miles across the lake. "Sad and terrifying. But fortunately, it was winter, with no guests."

He turned on the flashlight and shone it around, revealing only cobwebs in the corners and a layer of dust on the stairs.

They both froze as they heard faint footsteps above.

"Who's there? Simon called.

Paige gripped his arm when there was no answer.

"Stay here. I'm going up. But don't close the door."

"I'm coming with you."

Although the tower had been built before Edward Davenport arrived at Westwind, he had claimed it as his sanctuary. The spacious room at the top was furnished with a few rattan chairs, a sofa, and a drinks trolley – already devoid of glasses and bottles when Paige had been here on a sunny day over a decade ago. The windows had afforded Edward a 360-degree view of his beloved realm. Florence had wanted his favourite hideaway left intact after his death.

Rebecca had tried to claim it that last summer, when she was seventeen. Already thinking that Westwind would be her future, she snuck into the tower whenever she could to "keep an eye on my domain", as she'd explained to Simon when he hauled her out and admonished her for stealing the keys from the office yet again.

A cool wave brushed past Paige.

"Did you feel that?" she whispered, spooked.

"Maybe a window's broken."

But there was no window damaged or open, or anyone there when they reached the top. A breeze would have been welcome in the stifling, musty, trapped heat.

"Can you smell tobacco smoke?" Paige asked in alarm.

"A whiff maybe. Granddad used to smoke a pipe. The scent must have permeated the wood."

Paige doubted it would it still linger after twenty-five years.

"There's no obvious sign of anyone having been here. I wonder if there are squirrels or racoons in the walls," Simon said. "We've found them nesting in the attics before."

"Didn't sound like an animal."

Paige startled as the door slammed shut.

"Damn! One of the staff must have noticed it was open," Simon said.

They arrived at the bottom of the stairs to discover the door was jammed. Simon passed Paige the flashlight as he banged the corners and edges and then put all his weight behind pulling the handle, but it didn't budge.

"I'll have to call for help." His cell phone didn't turn on. "I must have forgotten to charge it."

"This is really creeping me out," Paige admitted. She suddenly had an image of fire erupting in the tower and being imprisoned here. She focused on calming her fear, but the reek of burning tobacco grew stronger.

Simon pulled a penknife from his pocket and dug the blade in by the latch to pry it open.

The flashlight died.

"Damnation! Now what?" Simon took the torch and fiddled with it. "Batteries must be dead. OK, so when our eyes adjust to the dark, we'll see light seeping in from the hallway around the door, and I'll be able to locate the gaps better."

Paige jumped at a feather-light touch on her shoulder. She brushed frantically at it.

"What's wrong?"

"Something touched me!"

"A bug probably."

"No! It felt like a static shock!"

The atmosphere surrounding her became oppressive, choking. As if she were only inhaling darkness and doom.

Gasping, panicked, she grabbed the door handle and pulled. And fell hard against Simon as it opened easily.

"What the hell?" he exclaimed as he steadied her.

She was able to breathe again once they were in the hall.

The door closed easily. Simon opened and closed it a couple of times. Effortlessly.

"We need a stiff drink. Come on," he said after he locked it.

Back in his office, he tried the flashlight before putting it away. It came on brightly. "Must have a loose connection."

"Try your phone."

It worked. "Probably interference from somewhere."

"But it didn't even turn on."

"Let's look for logical explanations," Simon suggested when they sipped cognac on the screened veranda at his house a few minutes later. "Tammy saw something in the shadows and over-reacted."

"And that sticky door that was supposedly locked, opened on its own?"

"Maybe Barry had to go in for some reason and forgot to close it properly."

"A door you had trouble opening both ways. And then it just miraculously worked. We were trapped, Simon, with no light or way to get help, unless you battered the door down. That scared the hell out of me."

He ran his fingers through his hair. "I refuse to believe it was a ghost orchestrating that! My grandfather, you're thinking."

"Maybe he's unhappy that it's all going to change. Think of what you said. About Westwind being torn down."

"Oh hell! . . . And I've failed to live up to the legacy he helped to create."

"You should never feel guilty for wanting to live your own life! Your ancestors chose their path, and shouldn't burden you with sustaining *their* dreams."

"Dad told me, 'It's not just a job, it's your life. So you have to want that. Otherwise, find what inspires and delights you.' He said that he'd already been talking to a potential buyer, and thought we should just go ahead, unless I was determined to keep the inn going. I think he knew when I went to study film that my heart wasn't here."

"So, you had his blessing."

"But not Granddad's. You think he's haunting the place? Me?"

"Maybe he never left because it's where he was happy. And now he's upset."

"Do you believe in ghosts?"

"I don't want to. But I've sensed something. Seen inexplicable things. . . . My grandmother, Delia, was a driving force behind saving the Launston Mills Opera House and running the Little Theatre group there. She loved acting and producing plays, so she spent a lot of time at the old theatre, which has a ghost - Mary. She'd been a caretaker there, along with her husband, at the turn of the century, but died from a fall down the stairs.

"So, she's never left the place. Nan often took me to rehearsals, as I love that gracious old theatre, too. And I saw some of Mary's antics. She particularly liked to steal costumes and jewellery, which would either be found in the Green Room – which had once been her apartment – or back exactly where they'd been left, even though everyone had done a thorough search in the dressing rooms, including me.

"One day, I was sitting alone in the middle of the theatre, watching a rehearsal of 'Blythe Spirit'. All the rest of the seats in the auditorium were up, as usual when the cleaners had finished. The chairs three rows in front of me suddenly fell one after the other, as if someone were walking along flipping them down.

"I shrieked and the director, who was in the front row, jumped up, startled. Nan was on stage playing the medium, who inadvertently summons up a ghost during a seance. She rose and said firmly, 'Mary, that's enough now! You're scaring the child.'

"Suddenly it seemed peaceful in there, and I didn't feel afraid anymore. I was nine. Nan said to me afterwards, 'Isn't it delightful to think that we can still have fun when we pass into the next realm! Mary just wants to play.' Nan died a few months later, but I've always felt comforted by her words."

"Have you seen her?"

Paige hesitated. "I sense her reassuring presence when I need it."

* * * * * * * * * *

August 21, 1987

Paige loved living with Nan in the house that Delia's father had built in Launston Mills. Grandfather Raymond had died just before her parents, Tom and Jane, married, so Delia invited the newlyweds to take over the bulk of the grandiose Victorian house while she kept a suite of rooms upstairs and the glorious sunroom as her private domain.

Paige felt privileged to be invited into those spaces, to chat with Nan in her boudoir as she dressed for dining out or prepared for her role in a play. As well as that room in the corner tower of the house, Delia had a bedroom next to it, a closet-dressing room leading into an ensuite bathroom that opened into another dressing room and then Raymond's bedroom, which Delia had turned into her parlour.

Paige once asked, "Nan, why did Grandfather have his own bedroom? Mum and Dad share theirs."

"He was shell-shocked from the war, sweetie. He had terrible nightmares and didn't want to disturb my sleep. So thoughtful of him." But Nan had looked sad. Was it because she'd been lonely after his death or even more so, before?

Paige's favourite place to spend time with Nan had been in the cheerful sunroom. Exotic flowering plants and palms thrived within the six-sided walls of glass that stretched twelve feet high and overlooked the flagstone terrace and park-like property with its riot of perennial gardens.

A swath of trees flowed between the backyard neighbours from the next street, with vines clambering over low, forgotten, drystone walls that no one claimed. They became castle ramparts in what the few neighbourhood kids had deemed their enchanted forest. It was a magical place to grow up.

Her mother found her in the sunroom in a pool of moonlight only a few days after the canoe accident.

"Paige, are you alright?"

Paige looked at her blankly and then gave her head a bit of a shake. "Mum? Where did Nan go? I was just talking to her. She said that a friend of hers drowned in the lake years ago. Before the war. She said it was so tragic, and she knows how I feel."

Jane stroked her hair. "Paige, you're sleepwalking. Wake up, sweetie."

"I am awake." Paige looked around and suddenly remembered that her grandmother had died a decade ago. "MUM! I saw her! She was so gentle and understanding. What's happening?" Paige frantically gripped her mother's arms.

"It was a dream. They can be very real, especially when you're sleepwalking. Come, let's get you back to bed."

"She sat right there, in her favourite chair.... It's still rocking."

They both looked at it with a shiver.

"I must have disturbed it when I came in," Jane said without conviction as she hastened Paige from the room.

Paige looked exhausted at breakfast, as she had barely slept. Her father put down the paper and said, "How did you know someone had drowned in the lake in the '30s?"

"Nan told me. Or did I just dream that? But it was SO real, Dad!"

"Perhaps she mentioned it to you years ago, and it surfaced now that..." he faltered.

"Not that I can recall.... Then it *is* true, isn't it?"

He hesitated. "I found a newspaper clipping amongst her personal papers when I was clearing them out. A British guest at the Westwind Inn was out in a canoe one evening when a thunderstorm hit."

"Perhaps one of Aunt Millicent's friends," Jane suggested. Raymond's eldest sister had married a minor aristocrat with a sizable country estate in the Cotswolds before the first war.

"She did say that Millicent intrigued the Brits with tales of luxurious cottage life, so he wouldn't have been the first to come with expectations of being wined and dined in the wilderness."

"With better amenities than they had in England," Jane chimed in with a grin. "I remember all too well how cold and uncomfortable my early childhood was."

"Had?" Tom teased. "They've hardly entered the 20th century in some places, even now as we're nearing the 21st."

Paige giggled. She remembered the ancient pubs and inns they had stayed in during their visits, with their wonky plumbing and little acquaintance with showers or central heating.

"Mom did tell me about a fellow who came expecting to see bears, moose, and lumberjacks everywhere. But he brought his tuxedo. Just in case," Tom said.

They laughed.

But Paige wondered how she had known about the drowned visitor. Much as she loved Nan, it unsettled her to think that her spirit dwelt here.

But recalling what Delia had said about Mary, Paige whispered into the silence of the sunroom later that day, "I hope you're dancing and laughing... wherever you are, Nan."

Chapter 7

Paige woke late. And was surprised to see her light on. Had she sleepwalked?

She hadn't been able to relax enough to easily get to sleep. Much as she tried to stop it, her vivid imagination conjured up Edward perching on the edge of Brett's bed, watching her.

Before turning out her light, she'd implored, "Edward Davenport, please don't scare me. Your grandson and I are good friends. In fact, I'm in love with him, and always have been."

It felt liberating to say that out loud. Even if she had to keep it to herself, and not act on it.

Having been reminded of her ghostly conversation with her grandmother ten years ago, she was eager to question the Pembrook sisters at breakfast.

"Yes, I recall that incident quite well," Abigail said. "Cliff Basildon. So tragic! He was a friend of Edward's from England, here to escape for the summer after his wife left him. Quite a stigma attached to divorce in those days. Anyway, he took to resort life, and especially enjoyed canoeing, often going out in the evenings to watch the sunset and the stars. A violent storm blew through one night, and they found his canoe washed up on Old Baldy the next morning."

"It sounds like you knew him well!" Paige said in surprise.

"Oh yes. Cliff was a fine figure of a man. I could have fallen for him, given time. He was an avid tennis player, so Em and I often played doubles with him and whoever else we could muster."

"I wonder why my grandmother Delia kept a clipping of that incident."

Emmeline gave Abigail a quick look and chose her words carefully. "*Cordelia* Latimer?"

"Yes!"

"Goodness me! She knew him as well," Emmeline disclosed. "She sometimes came to the dances with friends. And she occasionally played tennis with us."

"Gosh! I didn't realize that you knew my grandparents."

"Not your grandfather, but we did get to know Cordelia a bit that summer."

"You've never mentioned that."

"It was so long ago, and Cordelia was a dozen years older than me. But I do remember that she was great fun, always ready for adventures and finding something to be cheerful about. She laughed easily and enjoyed talking to people."

"She certainly did. Wow, it's strange to have that extra connection with you."

The sisters smiled.

"I discovered that Florence and her sister were at the same school in Toronto that Delia attended. She only overlapped with Florence for a year, but did either of them ever mention that?"

"Not to us," Abigail said.

"And you didn't see her other summers?"

"We saw her at the occasional dance. But she usually played tennis at the SRA Country Club with her sister, I believe, who was abroad that year."

The Latimers and their crowd had belonged to the Summer Resident's Association since its inception in the 1890s.

"That was my grandfather's sister, Esther Warrick. They were best friends, so Delia must have felt at loose ends. What year was that?"

"Goodness, that's hard to recall exactly. Mid '30s."

"Did Cliff stay in the Davenports' boathouse suite?"

"I believe so," Emmeline replied warily. "Their long-term guests usually did. Why do you ask?"

Paige shrugged. "I saw, well . . . you know. A bit of *history* yesterday evening when Simon and I were sorting through photos. A man and woman going into the boathouse."

Emmeline caught her gasp before anyone could hear. "So, it's still happening?"

"Yes." Paige decided to say nothing of the events in the tower last night. She needed to think that through.

But with her thoughts constantly circling back to that, she had difficulty concentrating on the old documents. Until she found a postcard of an earlier incarnation of the famous Breakers Hotel in Palm Beach Florida.

Dear family. Marvellous place! Endless summer, with flowers & palm trees. We swim at the bathing pavilion & in the ocean. Long walks on beach & Lucinda is teaching me golf. Imagine running this hotel, with 425 rooms. Only open 4 months as well. Love, F

Paige sometimes struggled with the old-fashioned handwriting, but this was an example of exquisite penmanship. And she suspected that "F" was Florence. The postmark was January 5, 1914. During Florence's last year at the Brightwell Girls' Academy. Lucinda must have been a wealthy school friend who invited her along on a family holiday.

Paige was intrigued. And amused that Florence had devoted so much precious space on the card to the hotel. It seems she was already an avid innkeeper.

Although probably not essential to her research about the inn, Paige undid the ribbon that held a collection of letters to Florence's mother.

November 27, 1918,

Dear Mrs. Hawksley,

Thank you for your kind condolences regarding Stanley. It is indeed tragically ironic that it was the Spanish influenza that took him from me after he had survived 3 years of unspeakable hardship in the trenches. Too many of our friends never returned. My heart was broken for all of you as well when I heard about your Bill. We cannot even mourn at the gravesites of our brave and beloved men.

Had Stanley and I known that war would separate us so quickly and forever, we wouldn't have waited to be wed. Our honeymoon month in Florida will have to last me a lifetime.

I truly appreciate your generous offer to stay at your beautiful lakeside home whenever I can manage. I so enjoyed my time with you all that last, wonderful, unforgettable, precious summer of 1914 when Florence helped me plan my December wedding. Before our world went mad and our lives were shattered.

Warmest regards to you and your family, Lucinda Edgerton.

The Breakers,
Jan. 19, 1920
Dearest Momma,

We've just put Maggie and Glenn on the homebound train. They enjoyed their 2-week honeymoon, but Maggie's eager to get back and move into the little house that the Rowans have built for them. So thoughtful of them.

It is glorious to be here and to think that Lucinda and I still have a month to bask in this magical place....

Now that Pappa has bought up another two hundred acres, I do think that we should consider adding a small golf course to Westwind. We know how popular the new course at Windermere House is. Lucinda has decided to take up golf seriously, since she is not only crazy about the game, but also quite expert. There are several prestigious women's tournaments she can enter, here and abroad. So, along with our new tennis courts, we could offer another enticement to keep us competitive. I have to admit that I also enjoy the sport.

Much as I miss you all, I am savouring every moment here. It helps me to rejuvenate and prepare myself for the endless work in the summertime. This is definitely _my_ "summer" place.

Love to all, Florence

Already feeling a connection with them, Paige was eager to read the documents from Florence and Edward's reign.

And she was interested in discovering more about the disarming Cliff Basildon.

She skipped ahead and sought letters, since they revealed so much more about the people than the journals did.

But those addressed to Edward were daunting in number. His English family wrote regularly with domestic details that were irrelevant, so Paige leafed quickly through some.

There were also a surprising number of letters from Florence every winter, sent from Florida, with intriguing tidbits.

The Breakers, Jan. 16, 1925
Dearest Edward,
... It's so relaxing, but also inspiring for me to be on the receiving end of another resort's hospitality. It's also healing after the sadness of another miscarriage.

... With the success of the dance pavilion and your personal investment in financing the Lodge as well, it's only right that Pappa has agreed to make us full partners in the business. I am thrilled. Thank you a million times!

Love, Florence

The Breakers, Jan. 27, 1932
... This Depression is not impacting The Breakers or much of Palm Beach, it seems. I'm so blessed that Lucinda pays the lion's share of our $25/ day room and board here, and feels it is equal compensation for staying in our boathouse suite for several weeks every summer and autumn. That has cost us nothing, as she didn't even occupy a room we could rent.

I'm amazed that we are doing so well, when some of the other resorts, including The Royal Muskoka, aren't. But you've created loyal patrons of the professionals who still have money for holidays. And you have so many innovative ideas to augment our income. Adding the bakery and sundeck snack bar to our ice cream parlour has been so popular with guests and cottagers, even in these dire times.

Expanding the golf course and opening it to the public is also a brilliant idea. That makes it accessible to guests from other resorts.

Lucinda is thrilled to become Westwind's golf pro, and to have her own small house between us and the resort. She believes she might be only the second woman in Canada to have achieved that milestone.

I can't thank you enough for your devotion to Westwind, Edward.
Love, Florence

Paige was eager to read more, but it was time to meet Marshall, so she left the letters in several piles on the table.

She was dressed in a floral, jersey split skirt that was pretty but also functioned as shorts, so it was easy to clamber in and out of boats or go for a hike. She had an entire wardrobe of these practical culotte-skirts ranging from mid-thigh to knee length, some with matching tops. Loose and flowing, often dressy, they were also cool in the summer heat. She would ask Brett to bring up more of those, now that she'd be staying longer.

She stuffed her swimsuit and beach cover into her bag and grabbed a large hat.

Marshall had arrived early to fill his cooler with butter tarts, and there was already a crowd of curious people admiring his polished mahogany Greavette Streamliner, with its voluptuous curves and elaborate chrome detailing.

"Custom built in 1949. Still has the original 6-cylinder Chrysler engine," Marshall was replying to a curious onlooker.

"A work of art. How does she drive?" someone asked.

"She glides through the water so smoothly you don't even realize you're going 45 miles an hour," Marshall replied.

"Incredible!"

"Sexy!"

"*Diva* is well named," Paige said with a grin when they pulled away from the dock.

"She's an enchantress. Had me hooked since I was a kid. Someone offered me $50,000 for her recently, but I turned him down. Told him she and I would grow old together. Anyway, Dad would disown me if I sold his pride and joy."

Paige chuckled.

"Well, Kiddo, you look radiant."

"I didn't realize how much I've missed this place. It feels like part of my soul."

"I get it! Because we grew up here. Only summers matter when you're a kid, don't they?" he jested. "You know you can always use Arcadia when I don't have a houseful of guests. Monique is arriving Friday for a long weekend. Mum and Dad are coming for the last two weeks of August and all of September, but it sits empty too much. Liz and Craig were here in June, but now she's filming a TV series in B.C., and he's in Europe with friends for the summer before heading off to law school," he said of his ex-wife and son.

She told him about the Westwind condo Brett was planning to buy.

"I'm glad the new owners are at least preserving the main building. Do you realize how many of the hotels and resorts have disappeared here?" Marshall asked.

"Plenty, since there used to be over a hundred at the turn of the century, Dad told me."

"With only a handful left. Which is what we're going to discuss."

"I feel a frisson of excitement already! But we're not going to Arcadia?" she asked, realizing they were heading in the opposite direction.

"Not yet."

He didn't enlighten her as they raced across an open stretch of water. But as they rounded the top of the largest of the many islands, she knew they were headed for Windermere House. Or at least, where that popular resort had been before it burned to the ground last year.

She gasped when she saw it on the eastern shore in all its historic glory.

Marshall grinned at her astonishment. "Rebuilt to look exactly like the original, but up to code. With all the mod cons, including an elevator."

"How amazing. And wonderful!"

Long, white, red-roofed and anchored by twin turrets, crowning a manicured green hill, it was one of the iconic landmarks on the lake. Her family had never stayed there, but they had strolled about the grounds.

The flagstone patio spilling out from the rock-hewn lower-level pub was packed with diners.

"The stone foundations, fireplaces, and veranda pillars were all that survived the fire," Marshall informed her as they walked up the steps to the deep veranda that ran the length of the façade and around both ends. People were lunching here or relaxing with drinks in white Muskoka chairs.

"I reserved a table in the solarium. I thought it would be less busy inside on a day like this."

The enclosed corner of the veranda wrapped around the south side of the building, above the pub, and opened through sets of French doors into the lounge. Arched windows filled in between the low granite walls and columns, the middle casement panes open and screened to allow lake breezes to waft in.

"You'll be happy to know that all this granite is original," Marshall said once they were comfortably seated by a window overlooking the lake.

Paige ran her hand along the rough red and black stone beside her. "Considering it's billions of years old, I'm not surprised. But I *am* happy."

"You probably heard how the fire started."

"I read in the paper that a film crew was shooting a Hollywood movie. They had a hot light set up in a bedroom window for a night scene on the lake."

"It was never determined whether it was the lamp or a problem with the antique wiring. In any case, the wooden walls were hollow inside, like a chimney. So, once the fire got hold, it rampaged through the building and nothing could be done to save it."

"Thank God it happened in the off-season."

"Exactly! It hasn't always. Eleven women died when the WaWa Hotel caught fire on an August night in the '20s. One foolish girl ran back inside to rescue her jewellery and never reappeared."

"How tragic!"

"The Beaumaris Hotel was deliberately set ablaze by a young employee in the summer of '45. Fortunately, all the guests and staff managed to evacuate."

"You've been doing some research," Paige accused, cocking an eyebrow.

"Which I hope you'll take over. I'm planning a documentary about a vanishing lifestyle. Before all these seasonal resorts are gone."

"I'd love to be part of that!"

"Terrific!" He clinked his wine glass to hers.

They eagerly discussed the project over a leisurely lunch. When she told him about Simon's idea of producing a documentary about Westwind, Marshall said, "Perhaps he'd like to be part of this one. What you said about this being Westwind's last summer as well as Windermere burning inspired me."

"He already told me that he'd love to work with you. You've been his hero since you taught him to waterski when he was four."

"Ha! You're making me feel ancient."

"Never! We're just catching up to you." She grinned. "Can you join me for dinner today or tomorrow? Brett won't be back until Friday."

Marshall looked at her quizzically. "Everything OK with you two?"

She didn't meet his eyes. "He's busy. As usual."

"Tomorrow then."

"I'll ask Simon if he can join us. And we can chat with the Pembrook sisters, so come early for a drink. They like to have their cocktails by the lake or on the veranda."

"I remember them sitting in the Muskoka chairs on the terrace watching us waterskiing. Let's film an interview as soon as possible."

"They're still mentally sharp. And physically fit," she added with a grin.

"And they'll provide a wealth of facts and anecdotes that will inform our – your – research."

"True enough. . . . Speaking of admirers, a woman in the lounge keeps looking at you. Here she comes!"

"Oh Jeez, not again!"

"Please do excuse my intrusion, sir. Miss. I couldn't contain my excitement. I understand that there are celebrities who vacation on the lake. And I just want to say how much I admire your talent.

Pride and Prejudice was . . ." the middle-aged lady took a deep breath, "absolutely magnificent!"

Paige was surprised and then had to restrain a giggle when she understood.

"Madam, I hate to disappoint you, but I'm not Colin Firth – unfortunately for both you and me. But I'm immensely flattered that you mistook me for him." Marshall smiled kindly at the flustered, blushing woman.

"Dear me, I am SO terribly sorry! I'm afraid I've made rather a fool of myself."

"Not at all. There are Hollywood stars who cottage on the lake and sometimes dine here. Perhaps you'll have better luck another time."

When the lady had hurried off and closed the lounge door behind her, Paige teased, "You *do* look a bit like Mr. Darcy."

"Ever since that damned series came out, I've had women swooning over me because I have dark curly hair and a brooding visage. I'm considering shaving my head."

"Please don't make me laugh out loud," Paige begged from behind her napkin.

"In that case, we'd better get down to work."

They began by boating over to Tobin Island across from Windermere. Beside a rocky promontory where the land sloped down to the lake, Marshall said, "That path up from the lake is all that remains to show where the Wigwassan Lodge was. It was the liveliest resort on the lakes because it catered to the young crowd. Larry often came over with his friends to meet girls at the dances, but it closed when I was fifteen, so I never really experienced it. I just drove past sometimes with my pals – very slowly - and ogled the sexy girls in their bikinis, on the docks and the sundeck. There was always cool music playing – the Beach Boys, the Beatles.

"Most of the buildings were demolished, and it's been private, but unused property ever since. The interesting thing is that the lodge had two previous incarnations, the second being the Epworth Inn, which was the home of the Muskoka Chautauqua during the '20s and early '30s. *The* place to nourish mind, body, and soul."

"Of course! Dad told me about that. Canada's Literary Summer Capital."

"Exactly! And there are descendants of the founders still cottaging here, so we'll have to set up interviews."

He took her for a tour along the mainland shoreline, pointing out where other resorts had been, some replaced by just one mansion and matching boathouse, others by several cottages not shouting wealth so loudly.

"That's the peninsula the luxurious Royal Muskoka Hotel presided over for a mere fifty years. It was the largest and most splendid summer resort in Canada when it was built. Our grandparents often dined and danced there in their finest gowns and jewels. It burned in a mysterious fire just before the summer season in '52. Patronage had been declining since the war. Those who could afford to stay at the Royal spent their time and money travelling abroad or investing in their own cottages."

"Arson?"

Marshall shrugged. "They never established the cause."

Dozens of cottages from 1950s modest to modern monstrosity now lined the shore.

When they arrived at the gravesite of Rowanwood, Paige said, "Simon told me that there's going be a hotel built here."

"A nod to but bigger than the old Royal, from what I've heard. It will give the public a place to enjoy the lake, since there are so few resorts now. But it's also upset some cottagers."

"Why?"

"Concern about what it might do to the environment. More traffic and noise on the lake. Transient tourists don't have the same connection to the lakes or incentive to keep them healthy and preserve the ethos. But the middle-class who were able to buy and build here post-war generally can't afford to anymore. Even those who inherited are being pushed out, as you know.

"Arcadia was assessed before my parents transferred ownership to me last year. I'll owe Larry half of that when they've passed away. So, if we inherit any money, I'll be able to pay him from that. But I doubt it will come close to the $600,000 I owe him."

"Holy cow!" At $1.2 million, Arcadia was now over three times what her father had sold it for twenty years ago. But Marshall's father had obviously spared no expense to turn the century-old cottage into a modern showpiece. "I don't suppose Larry would share the place with you."

"Never! He built his luxury, all-season cottage to Judith's specs. And *she* actually hired her own property assessor to ensure that my parents and I weren't cheating Larry out of his fair share of Arcadia. So, I avoid her as much as possible. She sees the world strictly through her narrow lens and is intolerant of people and ideas that challenge her opinions. Jeez, I'm not even allowed to call my brother 'Larry' anymore! It's not *dignified* enough now that he's head of the firm. So, 'Lawrence' it is. And I get a scathing look whenever I call her 'Judy'."

"Oh dear. She *is* rather intimidating."

"Shit, she's terrifying!"

"I suppose she had to be tough to climb the corporate ladder."

"Ever notice how high her stiletto heels are? Look for the bloodstains next time."

Paige burst into laughter.

"So how will you manage?"

"I asked some cousins, but they're happy sharing Granny's smaller cottage next door. Duncan and Gavin like it here and are coming for a few days next week. They're renting it for the first week of October, once the Film Festival brouhaha is over, and are happy to take it at other times."

"That's cool!"

"I'm glad Dad winterized it when he finally retired a few years ago. I enjoy spending downtime here in the silence of winter. Getting snowed-in by a blizzard is quite satisfying. Now that I'm getting into my dotage." He gave her a mischievous glance.

Page snorted. "The opportunity of being here in all seasons really appeals to me as well. And I'm just a kiddo, right?" she quipped.

He guffawed appreciatively. "Right on!"

She was trying to imagine owning here as they passed Westwind. But what popped into her mind were the potential neighbours. Privileged, pretentious people like the Turners and their friends. It suddenly didn't seem private or enticing enough.

Farther south, Marshall stopped in front of a new development of discreet, identical cottages scattered among tall pines and landscaped grounds flowing down to a long, shallow beach.

"Sandy Bay Resort. Replaced with these fractional ownership cottages. Also four-season. Tucked into the landscape rather than overwhelming it. Tastefully done. But there's no hint of its Victorian past or access for the public to one of the best beaches on the lake."

Paige recalled the elegant old inn with its three white towers and gingerbread trimmed veranda.

"Wow, what happened to Hidden Cove?" she asked as they drove close to the ragged remains of a dock farther down the lake.

"I don't know. Yet. But it's been left to rot for almost a decade."

"That's crazy! It's prime lakefront. Surely someone owns it."

"Undoubtedly. So, it'll be interesting to discover what the plans are. Cottage? Condos? Castle? In the meantime, we need to start getting footage before a bulldozer levels it."

Even from their distance and through the wilderness of rampant vegetation that had taken over the grounds, they could see the shattered windows, the saplings growing tall through the decaying sundecks, birds flying in and out of exposed roof rafters.

"This is strangely beautiful. Nature reclaiming her own," Paige said. "But sad at the same time. I can almost hear the echoes of long-ago laughter and see ladies in lacy white gowns twirling parasols as they stroll across to the croquet lawn."

"I expect you can. Which is why you'll write a brilliant script."

As they pulled away, Paige had a sudden inspiration. "'Once Upon a Summer'.... Working title?"

"Brilliant! Like I said, Kiddo." He grinned at her as they sped towards Arcadia.

After a swim, Marshall brewed coffee, which they took out to the veranda dining table, along with a couple of Westwind butter tarts and his laptop.

"OK, let's get some thoughts down and a rough outline. I want a crew up here ASAP to film."

The preliminary research they had both done already fueled their ideas about the potential storyline, what shots to take, what historic photos to include or seek, and who to interview on camera. But surprising facts always emerged from the raw footage and could take the film in unpredictable and exciting directions.

They spent the rest of the afternoon in intense and enjoyable collaboration.

"That's a great start! Time for wine and relaxation before I take you back."

"Can we use plastic cups so that we can go down to the point?"

"For sure!"

Paige loved sitting on the rugged slope with her legs in the water. "I feel like I have a primal connection to these rocks," she said, stroking the sun-warmed granite. "It's part of what defines Muskoka for me, along with the fragrant pines, which is why I'm looking forward to having an escape up here. . . . If we end up buying the condo. Brett made an impulsive decision, so I know he'll now ponder it and come up with some plausible excuse if he's changed his mind." Or had it changed for him. His father always needed to weigh in on big decisions, and his brothers would mock him if they could find any fault.

"So, I won't pin my hopes on it." She'd been disappointed often enough even with simple things, like Brett saying they'd go somewhere for a weekend getaway, and then cancelling at the last minute.

Once, when he'd claimed that the drive to Ottawa was too far after all, she'd gone by herself and stayed with her grandparents for a week. That was one city she did like and knew well from her five years there.

It was where she had begun to climb out of the black hole of despair that had engulfed her after the accident.

Her maternal grandfather worked at the Department of National Defence and, having been a fighter pilot and eventually Wing Commander during the Second World War, he knew all too well about Post-Traumatic Stress.

Paige had unrelenting, terrifying nightmares, mental fog, breath-snatching panic attacks, sudden flashbacks that plunged her into the grasping waves. She withdrew into herself, not wanting to see or talk to anyone except Delia's ghost, who visited her constantly. That's when her mother took her to Ottawa to meet with her grandfather's psychotherapist friend. Early counselling intervention had helped.

But she'd stayed on because another of Grampa's friends, a retired Major-General and colleague during the war, was writing a book about WW2 RCAF heroes – including Grampa, who earned his first Distinguished Flying Cross in the Battle of Britain - and wanted help with research. Paige suspected that Grampa had engineered that to distract her, but it had opened a career path for her. And the Major-General had been thrilled with her work and generously rewarded her.

She discovered that she loved history, researching, writing. And after hearing wartime memories from Gramma as well, she realized how lucky she was to have never had to experience war. Those stories of living in Britain under bombardment and rationing, of war brides travelling to a vast, unfamiliar land, had also given her material for a few articles that she'd eventually managed to sell.

Because she had been such an emotional mess, her father didn't mention for months that Simon called shortly after she'd gone to Ottawa. He had inquired if she was going to attend the university in Toronto, as planned, and had asked Tom to pass along his family's best wishes, and suggested that Paige could call him anytime, if it would help.

Her father didn't give her the letter from Simon until she came home at Christmas.

She had been furious at first. But when she had it in her hands, she was afraid to open it. She couldn't face rejection or any reminders of the accident. And her own crippling sense of negligence.

"So, I really appreciate your offer to use the cottage," Paige said to Marshall as she trickled cool water down her arms. "Arcadia is special." Even when they were at Westwind, she and her parents had spent plenty of time visiting and always staying at Arcadia for a few extra days at the lake. "Do you ever feel ancestors lingering here?"

"Do you?" he challenged.

"I sensed . . . something when we were here on Sunday. It felt like Nan was looking after me. I know that sounds crazy, but . . ."

"I feel welcome here, in a strange way. As if I were attending a gathering and people were happy that I'd shown up. If that makes any sense."

"It does! I'm so glad you're trying to keep it."

"For as long as possible, Kiddo."

Some of Esther's brood, including Marshall, had spent as much time at Arcadia as at her cottage next door. It had always been the epicentre for parties, games, cocktails, special dinners, and provided bedrooms for overflow visitors, which was why Marshall's father had been only too willing to buy it.

"Preserving our heritage is a huge responsibility. Fortunately, Craig is invested in this place. He spent a lot of summers here with my parents while Liz and I were too busy working to enjoy it."

"Now that my parents are retired, they would probably love to rent Arcadia from you, especially in the off-season, which they've never had time to enjoy anywhere. Help you keep it going."

"There's an idea! What plans do they have now that they're foot-loose and fancy free?"

"You know them. They belong to various clubs and sit on multiple Boards. Dad's planning to write a definitive history of Launston Mills as a retirement project. But helping to preserve

Arcadia would surely be top of his list. Although he probably can't buy in."

"I'll talk to him about it."

As they walked back up to the cottage, Marshall stopped to pick up a rock by the path at the bottom of the veranda.

"I've seen you pet stones twice today, so here's a piece of Arcadian granite to take along as a good luck talisman," he said, handing her a palm-size, pink-and-grey chunk.

"It's gorgeous! Look at the all the sparkly quartz bits! I didn't notice this before."

"Oddly enough, neither did I. Although I've been along here numerous times since I arrived."

They looked at each other with cautious disbelief.

"I will treasure this," Paige said, clutching it tightly. *Thank you, Nan.*

■   ■   ■

"Marshall suggested that Westwind be the focus of the doc as an example of the many owner-run resorts that were here, because he can easily film the daily operations and interview guests and staff," Paige told Simon when they were going through more photos after dinner. "We'll have to find vintage pics and home movies for the other places we mention, but you have a treasure trove right here."

"Miss Abigail always took holiday movies. Every year for Christmas, she'd send us a short compilation of that summer's visit."

"That's perfect!"

"Lots of footage of me, which I wouldn't want included. And there are some of us waterskiing."

"I'd love to see them! Will you show us at least a few tomorrow?"

"If you want."

Impulsively she said, "Would you be interested in co-authoring the script with me? Suggest questions and help with research and interviews?"

He was startled. "Are you sure?"

"You're the expert and I'll bring the perspective of the inquisitive outsider. I'm happy to share the workload and the rewards."

He looked at her gratefully. "That's a generous offer."

She had to pull her gaze away as she said, "Teamwork."

The lyrics from the Moody Blues' romantic songs playing in the background were often a strangely appropriate soundtrack. She hoped that she and Simon *would* always be there for each other.

Distracted, she almost missed the photo. She was astonished.

"This is my grandmother!" Yet that wasn't her grandfather Delia was smiling at, but a handsome younger man. Paige turned the photo over. The faded ink read "Cliff with guests 1937". *Cliff Basildon, surely!*

"Are those the Pembrook sisters in the background?" Paige asked. They were cradling tennis racquets. Had Delia and Cliff just played a match against them?

"I think so. They would have been in their mid-twenties."

"Gosh, they're beautiful!"

"So's your grandmother."

"May I take this and ask them?"

"Sure."

Paige eagerly searched for more photos. There was one of Cliff laughing with Edward, and a few of Cliff on his own – preparing to dive off the end of the dock, beaming while he's driving the Hawksley launch, and looking introspective as he's sitting in a canoe.

There was something familiar about him in that last picture. Did one of Cliff's children or grandchildren become a famous actor, rock star, Olympian?

"Do you know much about Cliff Basildon? This is surely him." She told him what little she knew.

"He and Granddad met at a boys' school in Oxford, and then attended the same college at university. They were best friends, so Granddad was devastated when Cliff drowned."

"How old was he?"

"The same age as Granddad, so he would have been thirty-six."

Another surprise was seeing Delia at the wheel of the Ditchburn runabout custom-built for Paige's grandparents in the '20s. Cliff was in the seat beside, and the same young women were sitting behind them. The reverse side read, "Cliff and friends off to Lookout Rock."

Paige scanned a shot of a small group at the masquerade dance. There was Delia, stunning in the beaded flapper dress and headband that Paige had also worn for the costume dances. And the lumberjack beside her looked like Cliff. Edward sported a deer stalker hat and pipe, à la Sherlock Holmes, and probably the Pembrook sisters were dressed as an Edwardian lady and a fortune teller. "Cliff enjoying being Canadian" was the caption.

"May I take these as well?"

"Wow, you resemble your grandmother in that dress you used to wear."

They heard the distinctive slap of the old-fashioned screen door. Veronica rushed in. "I need a big glass of brandy!"

"What's wrong?" Simon asked with concern.

"Someone tried to push me down the stairs!"

She was pale and shaking, so Simon took her into his arms. "Hey, you're OK. Tell me what happened." To Paige he said, "Cognac's on the drinks trolley in the living room. Would you mind?"

As Paige went into the adjacent room, she heard Veronica stammer, "I was walking down the stone steps from the veranda when I suddenly felt a push on my back. I managed to grab the railing as I fell. I wrenched my shoulder and scraped my leg."

Paige returned as Veronica added, "But when I looked back to see who had done that, there was no one there! No one anywhere on the veranda. No doors closing to the lounge. No footsteps. It was like the person had disappeared into thin air."

Simon and Paige exchanged glances.

"Are you sure it wasn't a gust of wind? Sounds like we're in for a storm," he said, releasing her.

"It was a deliberate push!"

Seeing the blood dripping down Veronica's calf, Paige said, "Where do I find the first aid kit?"

"I'll fetch it," Simon stated. To Veronica he said, "I'll get you fixed up and then investigate. You're off duty now."

Paige felt a sharp pang of jealousy, and realized that she had been allowing the music and the intimate times with Simon to distort their relationship. This was not a romance, but business with an old friend. Perhaps she should never have started any of it.

"Unless I can be of help, I'll be off," she declared.

"Thanks, but I don't need anything." *From you*, was the implication in Veronica's dismissive tone.

Bruised clouds were gathering in the charcoal sky, and the lights along the paths and dock were already on.

From the flagstone walkway that bisected the rise and gardens between the inn and the waterfront, she looked carefully up the stone stairway to the wooden veranda and the double front doors that opened into the lounge and reception area. No one could have pushed Veronica on these exposed stairs and silently disappeared.

Paige noticed that the Pembrook sisters' balcony overlooked those stairs. It was too high to see if someone was sitting there, but she'd ask them at breakfast if they'd witnessed Veronica's fall, or anything unusual.

A blast of wind suddenly unbalanced her as thunder growled in the distance. The atavistic fear that now always gripped her during storms triggered a panic attack. Heart pounding, she hurried past the pavilion, where strains of laughter drifted out from the audience watching the weekly movie.

In the open stretch between the pool and beach – both empty – she could see continual lightning splitting the ponderous clouds, unleashing a wall of water that raced across the lake towards her, obscuring everything behind it as if it had washed away the islands and shorelines.

She reached her cabin as it swept onto her deck. Once inside, she leaned against the door for a moment, but then hurried to close the windows against the driving rain. Only then did she notice what a mess lay before her. The letters she had been reading earlier were scattered on the floor. Only her Arcadia rock sat defiantly on the table.

If wind had managed to penetrate that far into the room to blow the papers down, why weren't they all on one side, instead of in a haphazard circle?

She picked up her rock and clutched it tightly, it's rough, cool weight reassuring. *Nan, please protect me from whatever mischief or evil lurks here.*

A simultaneous explosion of lightning and thunder shook the cabin and snatched her breath. The lights she had left on for her return went out. There was only blackness outside her streaming windows.

Trembling, she gripped the rock so hard that it hurt. She needed something to anchor herself to sanity.

You're safe. Calm down. Breathe.

A brilliant flash lit the room, and Paige thought she saw a figure in the corner. The thunder contained a maniacal laugh.

"Stop!" she yelled as much to herself as to whatever was there with her.

The psychotherapist had told her that the shadow shapes, strange noises, and disembodied words she sometimes saw and heard were pareidolia – "perception imposing meaning to amorphous stimuli". She found that difficult to believe. Especially now.

Trying not to scream, she groped her way to the counter by the bar fridge with one hand, the other still clenching the rock. Ready to lash out should anything touch her. She was almost surprised to find the hurricane lantern where she had last seen it. In its welcome light, she could suddenly breathe again. And noticed no one in the room and nothing else untoward.

Playing it safe, she went to fetch her own flashlight from the bedside table. Both beds were unruffled.

Paige poured herself a drink and sat on the sofa trying to figure out what could logically have made this mess.

Had she done it herself? She sometimes had brief memory lapses during panic attacks. Had the papers been on the floor when she arrived, or had she knocked them down in her haste to close the windows?

Had someone with a key come in and deliberately created havoc? Who and why?

Veronica trying to scare her away? Was she afraid that Paige and Simon were getting too close?

Had Veronica been pushed, or did she slip on the steps and decide to use that as another scare tactic?

Was Edward Davenport trying to chase Paige away? Or send her a message.

She took a photograph of the mess before going over to examine the papers.

Paige was startled when her cell phone rang.

"Hey, Kiddo. Just checking to make sure you're OK. The hotel phone line's down, so I figured you've lost power as well. Helluva storm. I expect you're not fond of them these days."

"Thank you, Marshall. It's a bit terrifying. But I'm safely inside and have a couple of flashlights."

"Anything I can do to help?"

"Not at the moment. But there are some . . . weird things. I'll tell you tomorrow."

"Jeez, Paige! Want to stay here tonight? I can be there in twenty minutes if there are no trees down en route."

The storm was still raging outside and felt like it wouldn't soon relent. She was actually grateful for the lightning, more distanced now, because it offered some dimension to the outside. There were no cottage or resort lights spilling onto the black lake.

"Thanks, but I think I can cope. I have to confront my fears."

"You don't have to be so brave, Kiddo. Especially if this is about more than the storm."

"I have the talisman stone in my hand right now. It will keep me safe."

"If you're sure. Call anytime if I can help. Or if you just want to escape."

"I will. Thanks, Marshall."

She started to tidy up the papers. Luckily, they hadn't become too disorganized by date. There was an interesting one from Florence that ended up on top.

Palm Beach.

February 27, 1934,

Dearest Momma,

I'm well and fit and sun-kissed, as Edward says, so you mustn't worry about me. Edward and Lucinda are looking after me splendidly, and we're savouring every moment of this extended, relaxing vacation. I love that our villa overlooks the vast ocean and is steps from the beach, as I find bobbing about in the saltwater makes me feel light and buoyant and carefree. We can also walk for miles in the warm, white sand if we choose, although I don't go too far these days. Yes, I assure you I've given up golfing for now. Lucinda is practicing for a tournament in April.

Edward has found us a small flat in Toronto, close to Women's College Hospital, where we plan to arrive by the end of March. Much safer to give birth there at my age. It will also give us and the baby a bit of time together before we head back to busy Westwind. Please be assured that there's no need for you to come to Toronto to be with me. Of course, we will inform you if there are any problems.

We so appreciate that you've taken all the work off our shoulders for the time being. So now, prepare yourselves for being grandparents.

Love to all, Florence

Paige jumped when the hotel phone rang. The power was still out. Was the phone working again or would there be no one on the other end? Or something worse. She was almost afraid to touch it.

She held it gingerly to her ear.

"Paige, it's Simon. I just wanted to make sure you got back alright. The storm came in fast."

"I made it inside just as it hit. Marshall called on my cell. He said the phone lines were out here."

"Now that the generators are going, we have power to the phone system again. But we only have enough for critical things, like the kitchen fridges and freezers. We have emergency lights in the buildings, but the cabins have to rely on the lanterns. Yours is working?"

"Yes." *For now.*

"Good!"

She wouldn't tell him about the papers just yet.

"Don't hesitate to call anytime if you need help. Or if anything strange is going on."

"I appreciate that."

There was a pause as if he wanted to say more. "Goodnight then."

"Thanks for checking on me."

Paige went eagerly back to the letters, not only to distract herself from the storm, but also because she was certain there must have been correspondence between Edward and Cliff.

Basildon Books,
St. Ives, Cornwall,
May 7, 1937
Dear Edward,

I am indeed grateful for the generous offer of hospitality at your resort. I've been keen to visit your wilderness domain since you moved to Canada, and this is the perfect opportunity to disappear from here for a while. As you know, I have a reliable second-in-command who is delighted to mind the bookstore for a few months.

As you can see, I'm living above the shop again, as the house has sold. Fenella could hardly wait to return to her ancestral estate, less than an hour's train ride from "exciting" London. She could no longer abide living at the "edge of the world" and needed to return to "civilization".

This place is heaven to me, as you know. I'm inspired by the temperamental sea, the wind-swept cliffs, the hidden coves, the sandy beaches, and the artists' colony.

But you are right that a change of scene might allow me to finally complete my novel. And give me a new perspective on life. Your boathouse suite sounds delightful.

I don't know what Fenella and I ever saw in each other, besides the attractive outer shell, as we have such different interests. Love, or in this case, ephemeral passion, does indeed blind us. She doesn't have a poetic soul, reads only The Tatler, Vogue, and their ilk, and mocks my "attempts" at writing. Granted, my oeuvre so far consists merely of informative tourist guides for the area – popular ones, however – and a few slim volumes of poetry, which have garnered praise from the artistic and literary crowd, if not from my wife.

She will seek a suitably wealthy husband to provide the lifestyle she feels she deserves, and which I failed to give her, being just an "unambitious shopkeeper". Her parents will keep her in luxury in the meantime.

I have yet to find the woman I am pining for.

Poor little Isobel is caught in the middle. She doesn't understand why she and Mummy are moving away without me. I've assured her that she can come and live with me as soon as things are sorted out, if she doesn't mind living above the shop. She replied that she would be happy to live _in_ the shop. She has spent so much time here that she's not only a great help, even though she's only eight, but loves being among books. I will ensure I obtain custody of her. I would hate for her to grow up in an intellectual vacuum like Fenella did.

Before I leave for Canada, Izzy and I will spend a few days with my parents and several more with Enid and her brood. Fortunately, Izzy and Enid's youngest are best friends, and she's happy that she'll now be close to Hazel, who has already told her she must come to stay every weekend and all summer holidays.

The scandal of Edward VIII's abdication over Wallis Simpson makes our pending divorce recede into the background, for which I'm grateful. Fenella is lying low as she slowly reintegrates into society.

I expect that she, through her London friends, will insert herself into some celebration of next week's coronation of King George VI and Queen Elizabeth as a first step.

I will soon be indulging myself in the company of another new Queen. I've booked passage on the reputedly fabulous RMS Queen Mary for June 18th. I have no desire to linger in New York, so I'll be with you before the end of June. I'll send a telegram with travel details from NY.

I shall bring a good supply of vintage Scotch, although I am impressed that you managed to get a government licence to serve wine and beer in your dining room. Prohibition must have been hell, so I understand why you were eager to return to England every autumn during those years.

Very much anticipating a memorable summer with you, dear friend! Cliff

St. Ives had been one of Paige's favourite stops on her family's tour of Britain, the summer after the accident. They had stayed at the Tregenna Castle Hotel high atop the sea, where her grandparents had spent their brief honeymoon in December of 1940. She readily agreed with Cliff that Cornwall was far more appealing than London. She wished she could read his poems.

Looking more carefully through Edward's letters, Paige found at least one a year from Cliff. Although intrigued by him, she had to keep her focus on the projects, so she put them aside for now.

It was after midnight before the lights finally came back on. Along with a crackling noise emanating from her bedroom.

Although she hadn't used it, the clock radio had come on between channels, and contained broken words, which sounded like "go . . . a . . . waaay". Quickly she dialed in a station and was relieved to hear music.

But was surprised it was the Moody Blues singing the long-ago hit, *Go Now*.

Chapter 8

"Good gracious! That *is* us!" Emmeline exclaimed, looking at the photos Paige had brought to breakfast. "And Cliff, Edward, Cordelia. How young we were." She sat back in her chair. "Sixty years ago. A lifetime." Hastily, she brushed away a tear.

"I'm sorry if this has distressed you, Miss Emmeline," Paige said.

"It's wonderful to see these photos. It's just sad to realize that they and so many other friends have left us."

Abigail snorted. "Which is why we make new friends, Em. To see us through our next decade. In any case, we still have work to do. I'm looking forward to helping with Marshall's documentary."

"So is he," Paige assured her. She had already told them of the plans at dinner yesterday.

"I came across some interesting letters from Florence to Edward in the '20s and '30s. They were sent from Florida. I was wondering why Edward wasn't there with her, except for the winter she was pregnant."

"Apparently, after a two-month honeymoon in Britain, Florence had no desire to return to the 'Old Country'. Edward didn't much like Florida, so he usually went home to England for a couple of months after Westwind closed in the fall."

"Cliff mentioned something about him escaping Prohibition." Paige told them about that letter.

The ladies chuckled.

"That doesn't surprise me," Abigail said. "He was fond of scotch and cocktails, and once Prohibition was repealed in '27, he would hold private parties up in the tower room for his friends, including us, once we were old enough. He couldn't sell spirits here in those days, but he did as soon as the government allowed it. Several of the resorts were teetotal, Windermere House until '71, if you can imagine! So Westwind never lacked for business. Of course, people brought their own booze and imbibed in their rooms."

"As we still do. So, then he and Florence took their vacations separately?"

"She liked her golfing and sunshine holiday in the Palm Beach season. He'd be back here by Christmas, and worked on renovations and such for the rest of the winter."

"Which reinforces what I thought about that not being a love match," Paige opined.

"Perhaps. But they seemed happy with their arrangement," Emmeline responded. "That's the important thing, isn't it?"

"You're absolutely right, and I shouldn't be judgmental. I will probably spend the summers and lots of other time here even if Brett can only get away for a couple of weeks and weekends."

The sisters smiled.

"I was also intrigued that Florence's friend, Lucinda, became the golf pro here."

"Oh yes, she was very talented," Abigail said. "Won several women's tournaments. She was popular with the guests, and encouraged quite a few young women to take up the sport. Including us." She grinned.

"I understand she had her own house on the property."

"Do you remember the old place where the Water's Edge Suites now stand? It was used by a few senior staff in your day."

"Tucked away in a stand of trees? Yes, I do, although I never took much notice."

"Lucinda lived there when she wasn't travelling to tournaments or in Florida for several months every winter."

"She never married again?" Paige mentioned Lucinda's letter about her husband of a few weeks going off to war and never returning.

"There was a scarcity of men after the war," Emmeline explained. "Plenty of women took up rewarding careers. But Lucinda had the support of a wealthy family and didn't need to work. She just loved golf."

"So, she was part of the resort. More like family," Paige surmised.

"Yes, indeed."

"Oh! I almost forgot to ask if you were on your balcony before the storm hit last night and noticed anything unusual. Veronica said that someone pushed her when she was walking down the stairs from the veranda."

"I sensed the storm coming, so I was sitting out to watch it," Emmeline said. "I did notice her, but then looked out to the lake as the wind was picking up. I heard her cry out and saw her grab the railing. But I didn't see anyone else."

Had there been any suspicious *shadows* lurking, Emmeline wondered. She was mightily relieved to have NOT seen one near Paige recently. But she had to be vigilant.

■ ■ ■

Paige had returned too late yesterday to pick up her photos from the gift shop, so she went eagerly after breakfast.

Back at the cabin, she leafed through them quickly, thrilled with many of them, especially the sunset ones from the boat. They went right into the "exceptional" pile. Then she examined them all more carefully, thinking how to re-shoot some from different angles or in other light conditions.

There was one of the inn that she had caught at a dramatic moment, shooting up from the waterfront as the evening light glowed through the many windows of the tower room. But there appeared to be a silhouette of a person standing there. She needed a magnifying glass to check. The front desk could probably provide her with one.

Simon happened to be there when she arrived.

"I got some fabulous photos the other day," she told him.

"Great! I should send mine in for processing."

"I have an interesting one that I need to examine with a magnifying glass."

He understood her look. "Come into my office."

After he'd closed the door, she handed him the photo and said, "I won't tell you what to look for. Maybe it's just my overactive imagination."

"It's a great capture, getting that lighting effect. . . . Hell! Someone's in the tower room!"

"That's how it looks. I don't think there's a shadow effect from anything up there. Nor a bug flying in front of the lens."

He examined it under a magnifying glass and then gave it to her as he said, "I can't tell who it is, but it certainly looks like a person."

"Shape."

"I'll think trespasser before ghost."

"Why weren't there footprints in the dust the other night?"

"It was difficult to see properly by flashlight."

"I expect you're right." She decided not to tell him about the mess in her cabin. "How's Veronica?"

"A bit rattled, but her leg wasn't as bad as it looked. She's taking the afternoon off, but we have a comedian on stage tonight, so she wants to be there when he arrives."

"That's good. Well, I should let you get back to work."

"I'll see you and Marshall at 6:30."

Paige couldn't face going back to the letters yet, so she changed into her swimsuit and took out a kayak. The lake was invitingly placid under the storm-rinsed azure sky.

She stayed close to the shoreline that she and Marshall had followed yesterday until she reached the derelict Hidden Cove Resort. Not exactly hidden and with long vistas of the lake, the cove was nonetheless sheltered and peaceful, since there were no cottages here.

She was tempted to beach the kayak on the shore between the evergreens and birches that were trying to reclaim the waterfront. But having noticed a few warning signs posted, she didn't want to be caught trespassing. Marshall probably needed only to ask at the SRA Country Club to discover who owned the property, and they could go from there.

So, she just drifted in the shallow water and looked out at grizzled Old Baldy, which was the nearest island. Cliff Basildon must have been ambushed by a ferocious storm, like the one last night, in the half-mile stretch of open water to this shoreline.

How well she knew this part of the lake – every island, every shoal, every old cottage. It had been her playground since she was born. Except for the last ten years.

How had she and Simon lost each other?

* * * * * * * * * *

June 24, 1987

Paige was thrilled to be a waterski instructor, which meant she had the entire summer to look forward to at Westwind. It not only gave her some funds for university, but she'd be close to Simon for two months now instead of the usual few weeks.

Her parents would spend a couple of weeks here in mid-August, so she had unprecedented freedom for most of the summer.

It was fun to share a room with Angela and two other waterfront staff, tiny as it was. She enjoyed the camaraderie and hijinks amongst the large contingent of students – most at university, who had already been here since May, while she had just arrived on the weekend. There was no curfew or supervision of the staff quarters, and often a party somewhere.

One of the waterskiers – a hot pre-med student - asked Paige out to a local bar the previous evening, but she had no intention of dating anyone. Other than Simon.

They were sitting on the end of one of the short docks, below the sundeck, having just finished practicing their waterski tricks.

From a cute boy, Simon had matured into a dreamboat. She had a huge crush on him, but tried to hide it because he hadn't given her any indication that he wanted more than just their long-standing friendship. Although there seemed to be a magnetic force that drew them together, something almost tangible when they touched.

She had fantasized about him all winter, imagining the different ways he might fall in love with her. In her favourite daydream, they would be swimming at Silver Sands and then lie on the beach, partly immersed in the water as they often had. But this time he would prop himself up on an elbow and gaze at her in wonderment as he began stroking her cheek. Then he'd kiss her as his hand slid down to remove her bikini, and tell her he was madly in love with her.

So, sitting on his shoulders for their stunt and being held in his strong arms when she dismounted made her long to feel his sensuous lips on hers and his hands liberating her from her suit and stroking her bare skin. Igniting a flame deep within her.

She gripped the edge of the dock to shut down her arousing thoughts, and felt her fingers sink into a horrifically sticky mess. She pulled her hand away and saw it crawling with dozens of tiny spiders. She started screaming as she tried to shake them off. Suddenly, hundreds more were streaming over the edge of the dock, as well as a huge spider, which lunged at her, sinking its fangs into her thigh. The others on the dock jumped up in a panic.

Simon pulled her into the chest-deep water where he washed off the spiderlings and drew her into a tender embrace, all the while whispering calming, soothing words, and stroking her head until her shuddering subsided.

From the compassionate look that he gave her when he finally released her, she realized that their relationship had changed into something much deeper.

At the dance that evening, they hung out as usual with Tony and Angela and some of the other waterski staff, but they danced together more than usual, and he held her seductively close. Embraced by his comforting strength, breathing in the intoxicating summer scent of him as she laid her head on his shoulder made her crave more.

"Meet me at my boathouse in ten minutes," he whispered while they swayed to Bryan Adams' "Heaven".

He left first and she snuck out a couple of minutes later. He was waiting for her at the entrance to the upper suite and drew her inside. The lake reflected the last of the burnished clouds, casting soft light through the many windows.

His passionate kiss stoked the fire within her. She strained against him, his swelling desire fueling her own.

"I've been dreaming of this for two years," he murmured, trailing kisses down her neck.

"Didn't you know I was crazy about you?" she asked breathlessly.

He caressed her cheek and said, "I thought so. But Dad warned me early on not to trifle with guests and staff, and that I had to avoid summer romances. It was damn hard to keep our relationship platonic, especially when I saw that other guys were interested in you. So I thought that once you were at U of T, we could start dating officially and tell our families. But I don't want to wait any longer. Can we keep this a secret for the summer?"

"Of course! I can't wait until fall either." She hesitated. "But I've never . . . done it."

He smiled reassuringly as he pressed her harder against him. "Just do what feels good. We'll stop if it doesn't."

Paige felt weak thinking about having him fill that yearning void inside her.

She looked into his eyes in the growing twilight, seeing her own love and adoration reflected. "I never thought I could be so happy. This will be the most wonderful summer ever!"

"Let's savour every moment. Slowly," he said, removing her blouse.

* * * * * * * * * *

Paige had finally read his letter four months after he'd sent it.
September 17, 1987
Dear Paige,
I've started this letter so many times but can't find words that don't seem trite or trivialize what happened. It would be so much

easier if I could just hold you in my arms and tell you that I love you and worry about you.

I tried to call you a few weeks ago, but your dad said that you were away and didn't give me any contact information. He thought it best if you weren't reminded of the accident. Said you needed time to heal, and weren't coming to the university this year. I wish I could help.

I can't forgive myself for not going to look for you and Bex. I was so sure that you would have sought shelter as soon as the storm hit. I should have sent Tony out to pick up the floundering guests and come looking for you myself. I'm not blaming you, of course, but I wish I knew what happened. You were always sensible, so I expect Bex was being stubborn and foolish.

How I wish you were here now, as we'd planned. Call me anytime if it would help to talk. My number here, at the residence, is...

Love, Simon

It was what she'd been hoping, not dreading, to hear. She wrote back immediately.

January 7, 1988
Dear Simon,

I'm so sorry for my delay in replying! I've been in Ottawa with my grandparents and didn't see your letter until Christmas. My parents have been very protective, because, quite honestly, I've been a mess. PTSD, Grampa's therapist friend said.

Although I'm improving, I couldn't open your letter right away. Just thinking about last summer triggers flashbacks that paralyze me. I wish I could remember the wonderful things more easily.

I wish I were in your arms again as well.

Thank you for not blaming me, although I still can't forgive myself. I'm older. I should have stood my ground, but when I tried to, Bex threatened to leave me behind on Silver Sands. She was so angry with me. She found out about us and said some terrible things. She also claimed that you belonged to her and were going to marry her when she was old enough.

I've come to doubt myself. Was I angry with her? Jealous of her? Did I do enough to try to save her?

When I concentrate on what happened, I know I didn't have a chance. I barely saved myself.

We won't be coming to Westwind this summer. We and my grandparents are going to England to visit family. They all think that I need a complete change of scene.

In truth, I don't think I can face being at the lake right now, much as I love you and miss you. Perhaps when I get back, we could meet somewhere else. Would you come to Launston Mills?

Thank you for reaching out to me, for caring. For still loving me.
All my love, always. Paige

P.S. - Please send letters to my grandparents' place at this address until June.

Her letter had been returned to sender from the student residence in Toronto. When she called the phone number he'd given her, she was told that Simon had left in the fall. No one knew where he'd gone.

She called Westwind, disguising her voice with a British accent, like Gramma's, so that whoever answered wouldn't recognize her. She couldn't face any mention of the accident or a cold reception from Simon's parents if they held her responsible for Rebecca's death.

"Simon's abroad at the moment, but we expect him back in May," his mother had said. "Can I give him a message? Tell him who called?"

"That's OK. I'll connect with him later. Thank you."

She hung up quickly, already shaking and gasping for breath.

His mother called hers in early March, asking about Paige and whether she wanted to work as a ski instructor again. She said that they'd kept the Latimers' usual cabin available for them, and wondered if they were coming that summer. She was saddened to hear that they weren't.

Paige re-sent the letter to Simon at Westwind in late May, with a note to explain the delay.

But she didn't hear from him. She made sure her parents weren't holding her mail back. She was tempted to call him but began to panic every time she lifted the receiver. And jumped every time the phone rang. Perhaps he hadn't returned home yet.

They went to Britain. She sent him a postcard from St Ives. No letter awaited her on their return. She'd cried herself to sleep for weeks, thinking that he must have gone back to his girlfriend Trish, or found a new one. She wrote and tore up several letters, deciding she shouldn't prolong the agony. If he loved her, he would surely contact her.

If he'd moved on to someone else so quickly and completely that he didn't even acknowledge her letters, then their relationship couldn't have meant much to him. Maybe Bex had been right all along – that Paige was just a convenient summer fling. But it seemed so unlike him, especially after that heartfelt missive he'd sent in the fall.

Bewildered, heartbroken, doubting herself, she wondered if something in her letter had changed his mind about her culpability in Rebecca's death, or revealed some undesirable personality trait.

She enrolled at Carlton University, moved in with her grandparents, whose house was a short walk away, and devoted herself to her studies.

And decided never to return to Westwind.

■ ■ ■

Marshall arrived half an hour before they planned to meet up with the Pembrook sisters. Paige showed him the old photos with them and Delia, as well as a few of the new ones.

"This one of the masquerade dance conveys a lot about resort life. And it will be a perfect counterpoint to the sisters now. So, tell me what's going on."

"Have a close look at the tower in this photo."

"Great capture with that figure in the window."

"Yes. But no one could have been there."

She told him about what had happened when Tammy saw a ghost. "I know it sounds crazy, but Simon and I both sensed, heard, smelled a presence."

"And you think it's Edward Davenport?"

"Perhaps." She wasn't ready to tell him about the glimpses into the past. "You don't seem unduly shocked."

"When we were doing renovations at Arcadia, one of the carpenters complained that someone kept hiding his tools. Four screwdrivers went missing in one day, and the next morning, all were lined up in a row on the kitchen counter – although he had been the last to leave and first to arrive. His assistant refused to work there because he felt a hand on his shoulder when there was no one else in the room. Those strange things stopped after the workmen left. Dad figured that perhaps his grandfather was agitated with strangers messing about with his cottage."

"Wow! But you don't feel uneasy there?"

"Nope. Sleep like a baby. My ancestors seem to approve of me." He grinned. "Try not to worry, Paige. Edward has no reason to blame you for any changes about to happen here."

Unless he felt that she was a threat to Simon's marriage.

"There was something else unsettling last night." She told him about the radio.

"Well, that was probably skywave. That's when radio waves are reflected back to the earth from the ionosphere. Sometimes not very clearly. Amateur radio operators take advantage of that skip for long distance communications."

"Thanks for that rational explanation. Sometimes I've questioned my sanity since the accident."

"Nothing wrong with you, Kiddo. Imaginative, empathic people experience the world differently. C'mon, let's go meet the ladies. I'm certainly ready for a drink!"

They met up in a bandshell bump-out of the veranda. The chairs were arranged in an arc with a circular coffee table in the centre, making it easy for conversation while offering a lake view from each chair.

Greetings had barely been made before a waiter appeared with a tray of glasses and a bottle of champagne in an ice bucket.

"I took the liberty of ordering this for us, but you're welcome to request something else if you'd prefer," Marshall informed them.

"What a treat!" Emmeline said.

"I'd like to make a toast to two very accomplished ladies, who must also be the most devoted patrons of a resort in Canada, if not the world," Marshall said, raising his glass to them.

"Will that put us into the Guinness Book of World Records?" Abigail quipped.

"Perhaps. But it will definitely make you the stars of our documentary."

"Heavens!"

"Sandy and Rosemary Wyndham send you their warmest regards, Miss Abigail. They told me that you were their shining star when you worked with Wyndcrest Films."

For once she was speechless. But not for long. "How did you know?"

"Paige told me that you'd worked for the National Film Board during the war, so you must have known each other there. I began my career with Wyndcrest. The Wyndhams have cottaged on an island not far from here for over a century, so our families have known each other for generations. It's how I wrangled a job with them."

"Astonishing! I left the NFB with them when they started Wyndcrest. What exciting days those were!" She took a satisfying draught of champagne.

"When they retired, they chose to fold Wyndcrest rather than sell it, as you probably know, but I did manage to buy some of their equipment."

"Our bungalow in Rockcliffe Park is only a few blocks from their house, so we see them around, and get together yearly for a dinner party. I suppose you know that we produced a documentary about Muskoka in the '40s."

"I do indeed! And Sandy's given me permission to use any of that, which captured the major resorts, some that have vanished without a trace."

"Excellent!"

"I've been pondering how best to approach this project. With your long history illustrating the summer lifestyle and how it's changed over the decades, I'd like you remarkable ladies to be the human-interest focus that ties the doc together, if you're willing."

"Goodness! How flattering!"

"Would you write down your thoughts, impressions, anecdotes – especially humorous ones? You know how to engage an audience, Miss Abigail. You'll both be credited and paid as story consultants. We'll do the voice-overs in the studio later, but I also want to film you on location now, telling us a few of those stories."

"Delighted, dear boy! I can provide vintage film footage. I took some every year to act as a journal. Seems like miles of it now," Abigail chortled. "In fact, I have clips of you teaching Simon to waterski," she added to Marshall.

"Wow! Does Simon have that? He's going to show us some of the ones that you sent," Paige said.

"Yes indeed. We consider the Davenports more as family than just friends. Since we have no nieces or nephews, we like to think of ourselves as great-aunts to Simon. It's brought us joy to watch him grow up here, so I wanted to ensure he had a record of his childhood."

"A professional one, no less," Marshall observed. "What a legacy! When did you start filming here?"

"I bought the Bolex H 16 when it first came out in '35. And still have it, although I opted for the Super 8 in the '60s because it's easier to take on holidays."

"Do you have it with you?"

"Always."

"Good! So will you capture special moments and anything that you consider interesting for our doc?"

"Of course!"

"Perfect! And one of these days I'd love to see that original Bolex."

"An antique. Like me," she said with a mischievous grin.

"Still in prime condition then," Marshall bantered with a wink.

Abigail broke into joyous laughter. "Oh, this is going to be fun! Just like the old days."

■   ■   ■

"I've already dined, but I wanted to meet Marshall before I go to work," Veronica said when he and Paige arrived. "I understand that Westwind is going to be immortalized in your documentary."

She had a knack for looking casually elegant without seeming overdressed for resort life. Today she wore a V-neck, elbow-length cream blouse with a slinky, leopard-print midi-skirt, which hid her bandaged calf. A striking, gold filigree tiger pendant drew the eye to her ample cleavage.

"Deservedly so," Marshall replied. "Generations of a family's vision and hard work have created this iconic landmark that defines Muskoka for many of us. That's an achievement to be celebrated."

"You're too kind!" Veronica gushed, as if it was all her doing. "I look forward to helping where possible. Now I have to run."

It was barbeque buffet night, and the kitchen had delivered a sampling of the many salads and side dishes, already laid out on the table on the screened veranda. While the inn's guests had a selection of chops, burgers, ribs, and sausages, Paige and Marshall were treated to filet mignon, cooked to perfection by Simon.

"I've already received some interest in the documentary from CBC, and PBS in the States," Marshall told them as they dined. "Lots of prominent Americans have vacationed in Muskoka, including Woodrow Wilson before he became President. He ended up buying an island."

"Formosa Island, not far from here," Simon explained. "It's part of our boat tour, although the Wilson family hasn't owned it for decades. We've had quite a few loyal American guests over the past century."

"We'll be sure to interview as many of them as we can. And we'll try to snag the Hollywood stars who have cottages here and dine at the resorts. Always good to have potential viewership outside of Canada. I'd like to sell it to European distributors, since it's a rather exotic lifestyle in a unique landscape."

"Celebrities sometimes come to our sundeck bar for lunches or afternoon drinks."

"Perhaps you could ask them if they'd be willing to participate with a brief interview, or even if they just want to pass along comments we can use."

"Sure!"

"So, what's the scuttlebutt on Hidden Cove?"

"It's changed hands again. The previous owner was trying to get planning permission for several four-story condo buildings with 2000 units and legions of docks. There was a lot of backlash from the cottagers, as you can imagine."

"Jeez, yeah! Spoils the whole reason why people come here – for nature and tranquility."

"Apparently, the new owner will build a private cottage and boathouse. There's 1000 feet of shoreline, and he wants to preserve the rest of the hundred acres as forest, so the neighbours are happy."

"I'll find out who it is and hopefully get permission to film the old relic before it disappears. OK, let's discuss what else is time sensitive, so I can have the crew here."

"The Segwun is scheduled for a luncheon cruise from here after the August long weekend. Some people on a day-cruise of the lakes come to dine with us, while some of our guests lunch on the ship during a two-hour cruise. We do that a few times over the season. It's really popular, and that one is already booked up."

"Cool! We certainly need to film that. It's such a throwback to the old days."

"We have photos of the Segwun and other ships dropping off passengers when that was the only way to get here."

"Excellent!"

"And our regatta is next weekend."

"Of course!"

"It's only us now, since the neighbouring resorts have gone. So, we opened it up to cottagers and get a decent turnout. Just canoe races, though. Miss Abigail filmed quite a few regattas over the years, which show a variety of events."

"Lucky for us!"

"I have the projector set up in the music room, if you're ready to have a look at a couple of the films she gave us," Simon offered.

The first one he showed them was Marshall teaching him to waterski in 1970 when Simon was four.

"That's awesome!" Paige said. "You're both so cute!"

Marshall snorted.

"Is that your grandfather on the dock?" Paige asked Simon. "Talking to Miss Emmeline?"

"Yes. It was his last summer."

Paige was intrigued to see him in "real" life. He had an aristocratic bearing, with a friendly gleam in his eyes and an infectious smile. A man who loved life.

Although in her late fifties, Emmeline was a sophisticated beauty, willowy and fit.

They made a lovely couple, and Paige suddenly felt incredibly sad for them. By the way they interacted and looked at each other, she was convinced they'd been star-crossed lovers.

The next reel was from '86, showing Simon and Paige practicing their waterski tricks, and then performing at the weekly show alongside Tony and Angela. She was amazed to see how professional they seemed, especially when she and Angie did the "lay-back" move on the guys' shoulders in unison. The intimacy of the stunt and being held in Simon's arms for the landing afterwards was a visceral memory.

"I didn't see enough of you two in those days to realize how good you'd become," Marshall admitted.

"Thanks to you, Cuz."

"You can't blame me for the acrobatics."

"Do you want to do some skiing while you're here?" Simon asked her.

"I'm really out of practice." Although she suddenly longed for the thrill of skimming across the water and slaloming through the wake on one ski.

"You'll get into the groove again in no time," Marshall assured her. "Dad still skis, even though he says he's too old to look after the cottage."

They laughed.

"I'll ski in tandem to get you started, if that would help," Simon offered. "I don't get out enough these days."

"OK, thanks!"

"Ski lessons begin at 9:00, and we still have lots of cottagers who sign up. So, we could go out at 8:30, if that works for you."

When she was fifteen, she started helping with lessons a few hours a day, so her skiing was free. She and the waterski staff would practice in the early mornings, late afternoons, and whenever no one was booked during the day. So it had been a natural progression for her to be hired as an instructor for the summer of '87.

"Sure! I'm not up for a long ski anyway."

"So, Paige told me that you're going to share the research and scriptwriting, for which you'll be credited and paid, of course. But what other roles do you aspire to in filmmaking?" Marshall asked Simon.

Without hesitation he answered, "Editing and directing. And I enjoy cinematography. I bought a Sony digital video camera when it came out two years ago, so I've been messing about with that."

"The VX1000?"

"Yes."

"Cool! Anything you want to show us?"

"Just done for myself. But sure."

It was a three-minute film called "Muskoka Moods" showcasing exceptional footage of the seasons. There was no voice-over, no text, no music. Just the sights and sounds of nature and humanity, so aesthetically crafted that Paige and Marshall were spellbound.

"Awesome!" Marshall decreed. "You do have an artistic eye. OK, so you can be involved with the editing as well. Paige has a knack for that, too."

"All part of storytelling," she said.

"Exactly. Goes hand-in-hand with that and directing, which is why I like to do the lion's share of the editing."

"And why you produce award-winners. You took Brett's idea of that beer commercial and turned it into a work of art."

"I work best with people who listen to my ideas and allow me creative licence. It's brought me more business as well. In fact, I might need to get another team together to handle all the work," he added, eyeing them thoughtfully.

"If I had you two on board, you could be part of a new documentary team and I'll keep most of the present crew on ad creation."

"You mean I could give up the boring stuff?" Paige asked with glee.

"That would be the goal. It won't happen instantly but gives you creative endeavours to look forward to."

"Sign me up!"

"A dream come true for me," Simon admitted.

"See if you still feel that way after we wrap up this project," Marshall advised. "I'm a hard taskmaster."

"Baloney!" Paige scoffed. "You just have high standards, which we mere mortals try to emulate," she quipped.

He guffawed.

"Thank you for a delicious dinner and delightful evening. Excellent music as well. The Moodies are still the gurus of my life," Marshall said with a grin. "But I'm going to head back. I dislike being on the lake at night now that there are so many more boats out there. And too many novice drivers. Just because they can afford a mansion on the lake doesn't mean they have boating skills. Or common sense."

Marshall had parked *Diva* at Simon's boathouse dock, so they walked down to see him off. The lake burned crimson as if the sun had melted into it.

"I can't thank you enough for including me in this project," Simon said to Paige as they headed back up to his house. "With a new career opening up as well."

"It'll be fun, even if demanding. A good start to your new life."

Glancing up at the veranda, Paige saw someone standing in the shadows watching them. "It looks like Veronica's back."

"I don't see her."

There was no one there now. But she was certain it had been a human form. *Edward again?* "A trick of the darkness descending, I guess." Or her imagination running rampant. But she shivered as they walked up the veranda steps.

"Have you had enough for today or do you want to work on interview questions?"

"Let's go through more pictures. Brett's coming tomorrow afternoon, so I won't be free again until Sunday evening."

"Sure."

"I'm particularly interested in seeing photos of Lucinda Edgerton. Being the second female golf pro in Canada is worth a mention in the documentary as well as the book."

"We have entire albums of her. She was Grandma's best friend."

The earliest photos were of them as carefree schoolgirls. Then Lucinda staying at Westwind, her wedding, yearly photos enjoying Florida, golfing, and plenty at Westwind as the pro, Godmother to Simon's dad, teaching him to golf when he was hardly taller than a club, on the veranda of what must have been her little house, having cocktails with Florence, Edward, and the Pembrook sisters. And also a few with Cliff Basildon. Although not as alluring as the sisters, Lucinda had an infectious joie de vivre.

"Wow, these are wonderful. And evocative," Paige said. "I keep wishing I could see more of that time."

"Be careful what you wish for," Simon advised with a pointed stare.

"Hmmm. . . . It just occurred to me that when Cliff Basildon came to stay in '37, he might have brought your grandfather copies of his published poems, which he mentioned in his letter." She gave him a précis of the missive. "Could we check to see?"

"It makes sense, although I've never heard of them. Granddad was a voracious reader and book collector, which is one of the reasons he added a library in the wing he built."

It was a spacious, but not overwhelming room. The bookshelves were beautifully carved oak. An antique secretary desk with a flip-down front, where Edward undoubtedly penned his letters, straddled the corner between the fireplace and a window. A couple of deep leather armchairs were invitingly perched for reading in natural light, and two more sat opposite for intimate, firelit conversations. The anachronisms were the Apple laptop on a modern computer desk and a printer on a stand beside it.

"Nothing is catalogued."

"Not the Dewey Decimal system," Paige agreed as she started examining the shelves. "But there is some vague alphabetical order. At least the authors appear to be under the first letter of their last names."

She discovered three slim black volumes stuck at the end of the "Bs". "Oh my gosh! Here they are!"

She looked at the books beside them and pulled out one with no title. Although leather-bound, it was a notebook. "And here's his handwritten novel! I wonder if he finished it." She leafed to the end. "It's hard to tell. But there are poems as well. He might have written those here! Listen to this one, entitled *Eternal Love.*"

Reflected in the mirror lake
Stars flow to the firmament,
No beginning, no end
Just the love we give and make.

We touch as two, become one
Nothing twixt my love and me,
Our souls sing in harmony

And vow to share eternity.

Adrift between the sky and earth
Caressed by soft ethereal waves
Embraced by endless joyful days
Our souls transcend to rebirth.

It wasn't his handwriting, which puzzled her, but it also didn't have any edits, like the novel did.

"He mentions lake, not sea, so I would suspect it is here," Simon said. "A lover's poem."

"I hope he did find the woman he was pining for. I wonder if it was Miss Abigail! She said that she could have fallen for him. Perhaps he had been the love of her life, for what little time they had together."

"That's sad."

"Especially since I think that Miss Emmeline was in love with your grandfather, so perhaps both were heartbroken."

"Why do you believe that?"

"You saw how she reacted when he . . . his spectre disappeared on the dock."

"She's nostalgic for the old days. It was a shock to see him."

"Yes, but I think there's more to it than that. Anyway, may I borrow these?"

"Of course."

They found two more photos of Cliff – one of him and Abigail playing tennis against Emmeline and Edward, and the other, showing the four of them enjoying cocktails in the tower room.

Simon didn't respond to Paige's quizzical look.

But now she wondered whether the couple she had seen meeting at the boathouse in the past was Abigail and Cliff.

And what about Lucinda? She obviously spent time with him as well. The poem sounded like lovers skinny dipping. How easy for them when his boathouse suite and her house were practically side by side?

Later in bed, Paige read what she considered his Muskoka poems in the notebook, for surely he was describing this landscape, which had no equal in Britain. There was such awe and reverence, such joy in his descriptions of granite and pines, islands floating on vast lakes, moon and stars and sunsets reflecting their glory in the still water, and an adored lover who embodied all this beauty of nature. Ironically, he described thunderstorms with enthusiasm and eloquence.

She was moved and saddened that such talent as well as the man had been lost too soon.

Was he another soul who still lingered at Westwind?

"Cliff Basildon, I love your poems. I hope you're enjoying eternity here."

The mournful wail of a loon echoed across the lake.

Chapter 9

"Jeez, I can't imagine doing that every weekend! I left at 1:30 for what should have been a two-hour drive, and was beginning to wonder if I was going to be late for dinner," Brett complained when he arrived at 5:00.

Paige was sitting on the deck working on her laptop. He gave her a brief kiss and added, "Make me a double scotch, babe, and then how about a swim? I'll just fetch your bag after I drop off my stuff."

"You didn't bring your clubs?"

"I couldn't see the point since I basically have one day with you. Mark flew up Thursday and wants to leave by mid-afternoon on Sunday. Miranda is expecting a friend and her three kids to arrive for the week."

So, her sister-in-law would have a good excuse not to invite them for lunch on Sunday, Paige thought. Which was a relief. There had been too many awkward gatherings in which she had been snubbed by Miranda.

While she poured drinks, he brought a suitcase with the extra clothes and items she'd requested.

"Are you planning to stay for the rest of the summer?" he asked as he hauled it up the steps.

"Who knows, but I need something other than shorts and T-shirts to do interviews."

She handed him the whiskey as she said, "You look tired."

"It's been a tough week."

"Anything I can do to help?"

He looked at her as if really seeing her for the first time. His expression softened for a moment as he replied, "Nothing . . . I'm afraid."

When he sat down beside her, he gazed out over the lake as he took a deep drink and asked, "Have you been enjoying yourself?

Working on the book, I presume, from the box of papers in the cabin."

Simon had picked up those she'd finished with, but two remained. Next week she'd tackle the batch from 1940 on.

She told Brett about the documentary as well. "So, I've been keeping happily busy."

"Sounds good. Marshall does excellent work. Nice for you to be part of that. I'm hoping he can film the new ads."

"How's your project unfolding?"

"The client likes my ideas, especially how promoting internet and cellular coverage in cottage country is seductively appealing and can change the work dynamic. People don't have to rush back and forth on Fridays and Sundays when they can work from the cottage for a while."

"I'm glad he liked my snide suggestion," she couldn't resist saying with a grin.

"You did steer me in the right direction. But it takes more than a casual thought to sell the idea to a giant corporation."

"Of course. Congratulations! Oh, I almost forgot. I have a present for you."

She gave him the Westwind golf shirt, the logo small but distinctive on the left breast.

"Cool! Thanks, babe."

She prattled on a bit about the storm and lunch at Windermere House, but couldn't think of anything else from her week that she wanted to share or thought he would be interested in.

"Sorry to be such a bore. My head's still at the office."

Or with someone else.

"We both have our creative endeavours that distract us. Let me show you some photos I took this week. You missed a spectacular sunset."

"These are amazing," he conceded when she showed him. "If you get more photos of Muskoka like this, especially throughout the seasons, you could create another coffee-table book. Ready for a swim?"

They went into the lake in front of their cabin. Paige stayed in the shallows and away from the creek area while Brett swam towards the end of the long wharf in the far distance. Feeling abandoned on the isolated beach, which was merely a narrow strip of sand between the lawn and the lake, she walked over to the broad main beach where a few people were still playing volleyball, most having decamped to dress for dinner.

Brett joined her. "I needed that! Now I'll race you back to the cabin. Winner bags the first shower!"

"Not fair!"

He was already showering when she returned.

"Mind if I don't dress for dinner? I want to feel that I'm truly on vacation. At least for a couple of days." He was in beige chinos and a black-and-tan-checked short-sleeved shirt when she joined him on the deck later. He was finishing another scotch.

"You're fine like that," she agreed with a reassuring smile.

"And you look particularly sexy in that outfit," he murmured, pulling her into a hug and kissing her.

Her simple black jersey top with off-shoulder sleeves was paired with a flowing black midi-skirt splashed with stunning fuchsia, aqua, and gold flowers. It buttoned down the front, but she left it open below the knee. A necklace of turquoise inlaid in silver, matching bracelet and earrings completed the outfit. He'd bought her that set on their second-anniversary holiday in Arizona because he said the gemstones matched her dazzling eyes.

She pushed him away playfully, saying, "Save that for later."

He was his usual charming self to the Pembrook sisters and their waitress at dinner, although he was unusually quiet while they dined. And poured himself generous glasses of wine from the bottle he'd ordered.

Paige was surprised that Veronica came by, although she knew that there was a small turnover of guests on Fridays, with some coming just for a weekend, freed up by those for whom five nights was enough. Not like the old days when people stayed for weeks or even months.

"So good to have you back, Brett! Executives need to snatch what little time they can for some relaxation. I hope that you manage to do that here."

"I've already started," he agreed, leaning back in his chair as he eyed her over his glass.

"Paige and Simon have really committed themselves to the book and the documentary, so she doesn't seem to be having much of a holiday. But it was nice to see her back on skis today."

"Was she? I guess she forgot to mention that. She'll have to give me a demonstration," Brett stated.

"I'd be delighted," Paige shot back, annoyed at being spoken of as though she weren't present. "I'd forgotten how much I love waterskiing. It's so liberating. Perhaps you'd like to try."

"I prefer windsurfing to being dragged behind a motorboat."

This was no place for a confrontation, so Paige ignored his challenging look.

"I hope you'll join us at the dance tonight," Veronica urged. "We have a cover band that caters to all eras of rock fans."

"Since you've gone to such effort to entertain your guests, we'll certainly make an appearance."

"Great!" Veronica said before she moved on to another table.

"You might want to back off on the booze," Paige said quietly as Brett poured himself another full glass.

"Don't be a bore, babe," he drawled. "I'm just unwinding in your idea of *holiday heaven*."

The Pembrook sisters exchanged rueful glances.

"What's wrong?" Paige asked Brett as they wandered back to the cabin after dinner.

"What do you mean?"

"You're not usually unkind."

"Was I?" He stopped and turned dramatically to look at her.

She knew she had to tread carefully. He could be scathingly sarcastic if he felt he was being unjustly criticized or that she was trying to control him.

"Is there a problem at work? Something you want to share?" she asked, gently placing her hand on his rigid arm.

She held her breath as he stared at her for a long moment. She could feel the tension leave him, and her own eased.

"There's always crap to deal with," he confessed. "Sorry to take it out on you, babe. Do you mind if we skip the dance? I need an early night."

"That's perfectly fine with me," she said, taking his hand. "Why don't I make coffee, and we can sit on the deck to watch the sunset?"

"As long as the mosquitoes don't carry us off."

"There are plenty of dragonflies around to protect us."

He settled into a Muskoka chair while she went inside.

In the bathroom, she put her hands over her face and massaged her forehead as she breathed deeply.

When she felt calmer, she looked into the mirror. And gasped when she caught a glimpse of someone behind her. The mocking face disappeared in an instant, too quickly to discern any features or whether it was male or female.

She scanned the tiny room, but there was no nebulous form there. Was her distressed mind playing tricks on her? But she had that hair-raising sensation again that she wasn't alone.

Are you thinking of ghosts because you're afraid to face the possibility that real people are a threat to your happiness?

Just shut up!

She had to regain her composure and stop shaking before she rejoined Brett.

"Do they rent sailboats around here?" he asked as she brought out mugs of coffee.

"Westwind used to have a few Sunfish for rent. They do have windsurfers."

"I think I'll take one or the other out tomorrow. Some quiet time on the lake will help me reset."

"I understand. I've taken to kayaking."

"Much better than a canoe when you're on your own. But always be sure to have your phone with you, just in case."

"I do."

An iridescent blue dragonfly landed on Paige's hand, which rested on the broad arm of the chair.

"He seems to like you," Brett said with amusement. "Not afraid of dragons?"

"No. They have an affinity for me. And bring me joy."

When they had watched the last of the colours bleed out of the sky, he said, "I'm ready for bed. Up early for a swim if you want to join me."

"I'd like that."

"I won't be long in the bathroom."

By the time she had prepared for bed, he seemed to be fast asleep, his face turned away from her.

She was relieved he didn't seek intimacy, since she was definitely not in the mood.

Still tense, she lay wide awake, wondering what was really going on. It seemed as if he were trying to alienate her. Or was starting to disassociate himself from her, as he did with people he was culling from his life.

Remembering all too vividly what his brother had said to her a few weeks ago, she felt lost.

* * * * * * * * * *

4 Weeks Earlier

Paige was stretched out on a chaise lounge beside her in-law's lavish pool, waiting for Brett to arrive for dinner, a straw hat over her face to shield her from the late afternoon sun.

She had just finished writing the last of a series of articles exploring the rich and forgotten history of the shape-shifting islands that guarded Toronto Harbour, so capping the day off with a swim was a treat.

But she must have drifted off because she suddenly felt a seductive hand travel up her thigh to her crotch.

"Brett!" she admonished as she removed her hat. "What the HELL?!"

Chad leered at her.

"Get your hands off me!" She attempted to push him away, but he pinned her down.

"Mom's in the kitchen getting mellow with her gin and tonic. So, there's only you and me and the cabana waiting for some action."

"Let go of me or I'll scream bloody murder!"

"You think anyone will believe your histrionics? Grow up, Paige."

"Stop acting like an adolescent bully!"

Chad snorted as he abruptly released his hold. "Ask Brett about Alexis."

"Hal's daughter?" Hal was Brett's boss.

"She and Brett were engaged, but she fell for a slick opportunist who turned out to be an asshole. She's divorcing him and wants Brett back. He's never gotten over her. He latched onto you because you're the antithesis of her. Quiet, dull, prim. So he could try to forget her. But it didn't work."

"You're cruel!"

"I'm honest. Haven't you realized that you don't fit in?"

"Then why are you hitting on me?"

"To see if there's any passion in you, or if you're just a cold fish."

"Bullshit! You're trying to prove that you can have any woman you want, even your brother's wife, and sabotage our relationship."

"I don't give a fuck about your relationship. But I think Brett's coming to his senses. He knows that if he wants to advance his career, he needs to keep his boss and Dad's best friend happy. As well as having a socially acceptable and astute wife."

Chad smirked as he sauntered to the house.

* * * * * * * * * *

Paige trod carefully up the steps, split by brawny weeds, onto the veranda. It was bristling with grasses growing between the broken boards, and shrubs that had sunk roots into the rot. A thick vine slithered along, weaving through the gap-toothed railings, new shoots snaking up the posts and reaching for her.

There were no lights in the abandoned inn, the windows gloomy in the eternal twilight. But pale faces stared out at her, expressionless. They were the dead faces from old photos. And Rebecca, not so faded, glowering at her.

Suddenly Simon was there, stepping out, offering his hand to invite her inside, away from the smothering vine creeping ever closer. But as she touched him, he turned into a decaying Edward, flesh dripping from the skeletal hand that imprisoned her wrist. She screamed soundlessly. The onlookers brayed hideously.

Paige awoke, breathless, her heart racing. It was a long time before she slept again.

■   ■   ■

"Wake up, sleepyhead," Brett said as he kissed her on the forehead. "It's almost breakfast time."

Paige was startled. "Oh my gosh!" She felt disoriented, not having slept much. "Did I miss our swim?"

"Hours ago," Brett exaggerated. "But the bathroom is all yours now, milady."

Over breakfast, he said, "Are you up to showing me some waterskiing?"

"Sure! If you really want."

"I was a bit of a jerk last night. Sorry, babe. At least I remember it." He grinned boyishly.

"I appreciate that," she responded with a smile.

"I've booked a Sunfish for the afternoon."

"Perfect! I'll take a kayak out."

With Brett watching her from the ski boat, Paige was nervous as she sat on the edge of the dock fitted out with a slalom ski. This was no time to face-plant in the water.

She and Simon had started on two skis yesterday until she felt comfortably familiar with skiing again, which hadn't taken long. They switched to single skis and did some of their old side-by-side routines. Her biggest fear had been falling into deep water, despite wearing a lifejacket, so she was grateful for his support.

It had been exhilarating! She was determined never to lose the skill, nor ever again forget how much she loved the thrill of it. She would emulate Marshall's father and ski when she was seventy-seven and beyond.

After a flawless start, she did a few ballet moves. Then she gave the signal to increase speed and began slaloming across the boat's wake, leaning hard and creating an impressive curtain of spray. She patted her head to indicate a return to the dock and did a controlled shallow-water landing in front of the Muskoka chairs, where the Pembrook sisters were watching. They applauded enthusiastically.

Brett gave her a hand out of the water, saying, "I'm blown away! You look like a pro, babe."

She laughed. "Marshall taught me to ski when I was four. It's as natural to me as riding a bicycle, but more fun. Sure you don't want to try?"

"That's a hard act to follow."

"It's not a competition. I'm happy to teach you."

"I'll think about it," he conceded. "Now I'm planning to whoop you at tennis."

"Oh yeah? We'll see about that!"

He did, but only just.

They spent the rest of the morning swimming and lounging on the beach under one of the striped shade canopies.

"I'm going ahead because I want to talk to Amanda about the condo," Brett said while Paige was dressing for lunch.

"Is there a problem?"

He didn't look at her as he replied, "My lawyer thinks we should investigate the developer to ensure that he can pull this off. The last thing we want is to be stuck with an expensive property that doesn't deliver what it promises, and becomes almost worthless. It's happened."

"That makes sense. And for that money, we could probably find a modest cottage."

"True."

When she joined him in the lounge a little later, she asked," Any issues?"

"No. Amanda handed back the cheque, saying that she'd be happy to help with any concerns we might have."

Over lunch Paige suggested, "We might consider buying into Arcadia. It would be more expensive, but look at the size of the place."

"If we buy, I want something that's exclusively ours."

"I'll keep a lookout when I'm out then, shall I?"

"Sure. Now tell me a bit about the lake. Where I should go, what I should see."

Without hesitation she replied, "The SRA Golf and Country Club. The Arcadia cottagers have belonged to it for over a century. It's only half a mile beyond Arcadia. There are lots of stretches of wide-open water nearby, which is where the annual sailboat races are held. I'll show you on the map in the lounge after lunch."

He returned from sailing, cheerful and energized. "That was great! I stopped at the Country Club to look around and talk to people. The Latimers and Warricks are well known and have their names on a few trophies in the case. Certainly sounds like the place to belong if you cottage here."

"Yes, indeed," she agreed happily.

They had a pleasant dinner, spent a little while at the dance with the same band they had missed the previous night, and went to bed early.

Brett made love to her seductively, and she fell asleep in his arms.

■   ■   ■

It was a cool morning with mist dancing off the water, but Paige and Brett braved the lake.

"Swim out to the end of the dock with me. Just a relaxed breaststroke. I'll stay right by your side, so you don't need to worry about the deep water."

Even in pools she only swam in the deep end when someone else was present.

"OK," she agreed reticently.

She was fine until they were beyond the sundeck bar and the bottom suddenly slid away. There was nothing in the darkening depths to hold her up. Just her own fluid movements.

She had a sudden nightmare vision of Bex standing below, reaching for her.

Something slimy twined around Paige's leg. She shook it off frantically, and tried not to panic, since Brett was within reach. But she felt a heaviness on her back, pushing her down. She kicked and pulled harder against the insubstantial water, her breathing ragged with fear. She couldn't see Brett anymore!

She felt faint and her muscles refused to obey. A moment later she was gazing up, the water so transparent in the morning sun, the sky beyond, a fresh blue. A dark shape slithered past her feet, startling her, and she scissored hard towards the surface.

Brett suddenly hooked an arm under hers from behind, pressing her against his chest as he backstroked towards the ladder at the end of the dock.

Simon was there and took her from Brett, helping her onto the dock. He sat her down on the bench and draped his jacket over her shoulders, having already discarded it in preparation for jumping in to rescue her.

"Did you inhale any water?" he asked.

She shook her head.

"Put your head down and lean over your knees. Breathe in slowly. Exhale slowly. Again," he instructed, rubbing her back.

Brett was beside her. "What happened, babe? You suddenly took off like you were going for gold in the Olympics and got ahead of me."

She realized that what had seemed like minutes underwater had probably been merely a few seconds.

She was still gasping and began shaking from cold. But she had enough sense not to say that she thought some... *thing* was trying to drown her. Who and how when there was no one else around?

"Got spooked... By the deep water... Sorry."

Brett put his arm around her and pulled her close.

"You don't have to apologize! I didn't realize how bad things were for you." Turning to Simon, he said, "Thanks for your help, but I can handle this now."

"Sure. I'll grab you some towels."

There were plenty stored in the waterfront booth, so he returned within minutes, draping two around Paige who was shivering uncontrollably, and handing a couple to Brett.

"I can give you a lift back in the utility cart. It's at the end of the dock."

"That would be helpful. Thanks."

Paige was still light-headed and shaking as Brett escorted her to the cart. Back at the cabin a few minutes later, Simon said, "I'll send someone over with a pot of hot tea. Let me know if there's anything else we can do."

"Much obliged."

"Your jacket," Paige said, realizing she was still wearing it.

"I have more. I'll get it back from you later." He gave her a warm smile.

"A hot shower for you," Brett ordered, ushering her inside. "Are you still dizzy?"

"No, I'm OK. Thanks."

"I'll be nearby, so shout if you need me."

But the shower calmed her down. Dressed in her warmest hoodie and track pants, sipping tea, she was finally beginning to relax. She didn't bother to change for breakfast, although it was promising to be a warm day.

"Let's blow this joint," Brett said after breakfast. "I'll take you shopping. Buy you something special as a souvenir."

"I really don't need anything."

"You don't have to *need* it. Just like it."

"We could check out real estate listings. They always have some posted in the windows," she jested.

"I was thinking of something smaller. A silver bracelet or a carved loon."

She chuckled.

"And we'll find a nice place for lunch. You'll have to drop me off at Mark's by 3:00."

"Makes for a short weekend. I hope you can actually take the holiday Monday off next week and go back early Tuesday morning."

"We'll see."

They did check the listings in the real estate office windows in the village, but there was nothing under half a million that suited Brett's tastes. Too small, too old, too ordinary, and not even close to being as posh as Mark's place or the proposed Westwind Beach Club. Arcadia would easily trump both, though.

In an artisan's gallery they found a delicate, handmade silver dragonfly necklace, which Paige adored and now wore.

"To protect you," Brett said.

"From mosquitoes?" she quipped.

"Those, too."

As usual during the summer, Port Carling was bustling with cottagers and tourists, some queuing outside restaurants. It straddled the river and falls with a lock connecting the two lakes, which the steamship Segwun was now approaching from the south.

"We'd better get back across the bridge before it goes up, or we'll be stranded here for some time," Paige explained. "It's why I parked on the south side."

On the road to Westwind was a one-lane lift bridge connecting to a third lake through narrows. Brett had remarked that waiting for a tall vessel to pass through there on a Friday afternoon would be the last straw after the long trek from the city.

"If I'm already at the cottage, I could pick you up by boat and we'd fetch the car later," she'd said. "Or in Port Carling, if the bridge is up there."

"Double jeopardy!" he'd complained.

Now she said, "We might as well go into town and try to find a restaurant there. It gets just as busy, but it's a lot bigger, with more options. It even has a Tim Horton's," she joked.

"I was thinking of a leisurely meal with wine or beer. Not coffee and donuts."

The Irish pub in Bracebridge had a table for them after a short wait, and they were only twenty minutes from Mark's cottage, so they arrived in good time.

Brett hugged her, saying, "Look after yourself and be careful on the water! Wear your dragonfly," he added with a wink. "Love you, babe."

But there was something else in his eyes. Regret?

She was barely back at Westwind when he called to say that they'd arrived safely at the civil airport just north of the city.

"This beats the hell out of driving, even if it's still half an hour to home. I'll have to consider buying a floatplane if we get a cottage." He had his pilot's licence but had rarely flown since she'd met him.

"Now I'm going for a sail. Perfect weather for it! And I'll dine at the Yacht Club, so you won't have to worry that I'm being properly fed," he jested.

"I never worry about that." *Just who he was dining with.*

Paige was happy for the diversion of work, so she pulled files out of the box and put them on the table. She picked up her camera to move it and was shocked to find the back slightly open. Damn! How did that happen and when? The film was likely ruined. But she shut the door quickly and decided to rewind and send it in for processing to see if any photos survived.

She tried to recall what she had shot so far on this roll. A couple of Brett in the Sunfish were the most recent. And the one showing the papers lying on the floor the night of the storm.

■   ■   ■

"Are you up to coming over tonight? Or do you want to take time off?" Simon asked over the phone before Paige went to dinner.

"I have nothing else I'd rather do. But I can always work on my own here if you have other plans."

"Not at all!"

Paige was happy to be dining with the Pembrook sisters again. She realized how stressed she felt in Brett's company when he was supercilious or demanding. It was obvious he felt Westwind wasn't up to his standards.

Emmeline was delighted and relieved to see her so cheerful, but troubled when she detected that shadow behind Paige again. She sensed it wasn't Edward. But was it malevolent or protective? Who and why?

"Simon and I made the most amazing discovery the other evening." Paige told them about Cliff's book and poems. "Did you know about them?"

"Oh yes," Abigail said. "He read us some of his poetry. I don't know if he finished his novel, although he said it was coming along nicely."

"Some of the poems he wrote here seemed to be inspired by a profound new love," Paige revealed, watching the sisters carefully.

"He certainly fell in love with the landscape and lifestyle," Emmeline agreed.

"And Lucinda?"

"Not that we were aware of."

Paige realized she would get no more from them about Cliff's love life.

For the rest of the meal, they discussed potential scenes that Marshall might want to incorporate from Abigail's sixty years of films.

Paige had dried Simon's jacket on the deck and remembered to take it with her. But first she slipped it on for a moment, feeling comforted by the faint scent of him, by the soft caress of the fabric that had touched his skin.

And she felt guilty for being so eager to spend time with him. Was she becoming as bad as Brett? Out of sight, out of mind? Was that nightmare on Friday her subconscious warning her not to become entangled with Simon again?

But she couldn't deny that her spirits lifted when she saw him. His long-time friendship was deep and precious to her, even if that summer of '87 hadn't been more than a diversion to him. The fact that they were working together on something that enthralled them both was intoxicating.

"Can you tell me what happened this morning?" Simon asked as he poured glasses of wine.

She hesitated. For a few insane moments after Brett had flown off today, she'd wondered if he had somehow pushed her down in the water. But she hadn't actually felt a hand on her back, just amorphous pressure. Probably her muscles spasming from panic. Why would she think that Brett was trying to drown her? Even if he was planning to leave her for Alexis. Was she losing her mind?

But what if Simon hadn't been there this morning, ready to rescue her? Allowing someone to drown wasn't the same as murder, especially if you "try" to save them with no witnesses to prove otherwise.

She told Simon about the sensation and her logical explanation for that. And the odd creature that had propelled her back to the top.

"We get some fairly large bass and pickerel around here in the early mornings. I was coming back from the tennis courts when I noticed you and Brett still a distance out from the dock. I had to check on something at the pavilion, but when I stopped the cart, I could faintly hear Edward's clock chime."

She stared at him in shock.

"I rushed down to the end of the dock and saw you sprinting ahead of Brett. You looked terrified. I could see you were hyperventilating, which is dangerous around water and probably caused you to lose consciousness for a moment. I've taken courses on drowning and rescue. It looks like Brett has as well."

"He and his family are sailors."

"That explains it. Are you alright now?"

"Yes."

"Miss Emmeline was waiting for me after I dropped you off. She'd heard the clock as well and was frantic to know what had happened and that you were safe."

"She didn't mention anything at dinner."

"I asked her not to. Don't swim on your own right now, Paige. I'm available as a buddy before 7:00 AM and after 6:00 PM."

"I can't impose on you like that!"

"It's not an imposition," he stated. "Leave a swimsuit in the boathouse suite. We can't work all the time. And you know we have a gently sloping beach here. We won't go deep."

■ ■ ■

Paige looked guardedly into her bathroom mirror as she prepared for bed, wary of seeing something that shouldn't be there. But determined not to let fear tyrannize her. If it was her mind playing tricks, then it was time to take control.

Lying in bed, she replayed what Simon had said about the danger she had been in because she was hyperventilating. With his training, Brett would have known that, too.

She tried to recall how the pressure on her back had felt. Not the heaviness of a hand, but what about the weight of waves? A hand scooping the water just above her would create that sensation – to which she had over-reacted. Perhaps Brett had been too close and created a wake. She refused to believe he had done it deliberately to frighten her. He wasn't a monster.

To distract herself from distressing thoughts, she picked up Cliff's novel, and was instantly captivated.

The first time the mysterious lady entered his bookshop in a cobbled lane of St. Ives was even more unusual than Sam Bedford had envisioned. During the past weeks, he had espied her several times on his early morning rambles, standing dangerously near the edge of cliffs, gazing out to sea. Unmoving, save for her long, ashen hair lifting and dancing on the breeze. He feared she was about to jump, but then she would turn and stride away, lost behind rocky outcroppings before he had a chance to hail her, to warn her not to stand on the unstable precipice.

"Are you seeking something in particular, Miss? Or do you prefer to browse?"

She looked at him sardonically. "I'm always seeking something. But at this moment, it's a book of local poetry, if there is such a thing."

"I can offer you my own small collection, if you'd care to have a look," he said proudly. He was a writer who, nonetheless, required the stable income which his shop provided.

"Ah, Samuel Bedford. Of the eponymous Bedford Books."

As she took the slim volume and skimmed the first poem, he was able to study her, to marvel at her flawless, pale complexion, to appreciate the slight lifting of an eyebrow and corners of her lips that paused on the edge of a smile.

"There are others in this section," he offered.

"This will do nicely. Being new to the area, I'd appreciate a tourist guide as well."

"Which I can also provide, Miss . . .?"

"Westbrook."

"I believe I've seen you on my early morning perambulations. You'll find these useful."

"Your work as well! Have you a novel to add to your accomplishments?"

"Not yet. Have you joined our community or are you visiting?"

"That is yet to be determined. I have taken a cottage overlooking the sea. Whether I stay or go is of no consequence to anyone and will depend upon what I find here."

"May I be of assistance?"

"Perhaps," she said with an enigmatic smile. Hers was a fragile beauty. He was afraid she might crack like porcelain and fall to pieces in front of him, not from age, for she was surely near his own of six-and-twenty.

Impulsively he said, "Then may I begin by offering you a cup of tea? The shop is usually quiet on a Wednesday morning."

"Yes, why not?"

"Are you here with family, Miss Westbrook?" he asked as he poured her a cup.

"Do call me Daisy. Dorothy died with the others. Daisy is a cheerful name, don't you agree, Mr. Bedford?"

"Sam. . . . Yes . . . yes, indeed," he replied in confusion.

"I have no family." She fixed him with wide, sea-blue eyes. "I live with ghosts."

Paige read far enough to realize that the story was an indictment of war, about the tragedy and trauma of loss, and the guilt and pain of the survivors.

Sam – like Cliff - had been too young, although he'd been prepared to lie about his age to enlist. His older brother, all of twenty-one, was killed at Ypres. His sister had perished in the flu epidemic just as the war ended.

Daisy – formerly Dorothy – had lost her only brother, new husband, cousins, and friends. Her widowed mother had died of a broken heart.

"Every death tore out a piece of me. I drove ambulances in France, not caring any longer if my bus was shelled. Every broken boy I transported took another slice of me. Until there was nothing left. So, you see, Sam, I'm looking for who Daisy is or can be. If she regains a heart and soul."

As dawn crept in, Paige felt the blanket pinning her down. She fought against the claustrophobia of confinement.

Brett, why are you pulling the blanket so tight. You know I hate that. Stop it!

Suddenly awake, she sat up, alarmed. Alone.

The book was lying next to her, as if she had dropped off to sleep with it, with the light on as well.

But she remembered placing it carefully on the bedside table and turning off the lamp.

Chapter 10

Looking up from her computer, Paige was overwhelmed again by the joy of working by the lake. She loved the long vistas and everchanging sky. Simon had supplied her with a patio table and umbrella this morning so she could be even closer to the water, feel the breezes, smell the nearby pines.

She knew how lucky she was not to be confined to an office in the city with only the hope of escape on the weekends. And understood why Marshall loved his peripatetic life even beyond the creativity it entailed. He was right that it didn't feel like work here, but a love pursued in an inspiring setting.

And out here in the embrace of benign nature, the unease and confusion of her awakening had dissipated. Daytime logic had conquered the nighttime mind shadows. She'd probably been sleepwalking again.

A dragonfly landed on the edge of her laptop. Its transparent, lacy wings belied its power and agility.

"Well, my little friend, have you come to offer support? Advice? Shall I shed my carapace like you did and flit to freedom?"

Paige had begun to consider what she really wanted out of life, not what she felt she had committed to irrevocably. Certainly not the heartache and constant suspicion that Brett was unfaithful. Concern that she didn't fit into his world had changed to the realization that she really didn't care to.

If she was about to be dumped for Alexis, then she was actually grateful to Chad for having alerted her. She would steel herself and make her own plans.

She'd start by telling Brett that she wanted out of the marriage.

It didn't matter that she couldn't have Simon. With their shared past and similar tastes, they would always be friends. It was finding her own path that was essential.

That suddenly felt wonderfully liberating!

And she wouldn't allow herself to feel jealous of Veronica when they met for coffee and a chat this morning.

"This is a beautiful place to call home," Paige said as they sat on the veranda of the family's house gazing out at the lake and the dockside activities. A novice water-skier clung doggedly if shakily to the towrope. A couple breezed by in a canoe. It was another perfectly sunny, calm day, the water a slightly deeper blue than the cloudless sky.

"It is at moments like this when I can relax," Veronica admitted. She was lounging in a loose, silk caftan.

"It'll be a big change for you to be able to enjoy summers."

"For sure! We agreed to stay on and run the inn for this last season because the new owners offered us generous salaries and a percentage of the profits. None of which need to be plowed back into the business, for once! They also offered us positions to help run the new resort, but Simon's not interested, and I don't want to be tied down. I want the freedom to travel anytime. Before kids come."

"Makes sense." Paige opened her steno pad and said, "OK, so what brought you to Westwind?"

"I was studying hospitality and tourism at Ryerson. So, when I discovered that I could get a summer job here, it was a no-brainer to apply. That was in '87, as you know. Simon's parents invited me back at the end of the season, so I worked the next summer, too. Which was lucky because I was able to help a lot after Richard's accident. Put my education in hotel management to good use. The Davenports were so grateful and impressed that they said if I wanted a full-time job when I graduated the following spring, they would hire me."

"It must have felt like a dream job."

"It sure did. At the time. Simon started at Ryerson during my last year and lived in a student co-op just a couple of blocks away from Mom's apartment, so we spent plenty of time together. And fell in love." She stretched out her scarlet-tipped fingers and examined the glittering diamond as if to emphasize her success.

"Of course it made sense for me to take the job. I even had my own little house the first year, just beside here, where the Water's Edge Suites are now."

Lucinda's place.

Paige couldn't suppress the hurt that Simon had so quickly fallen for Veronica after he'd confessed his love for her that summer of '87. And she'd been surprised because she thought that Veronica wasn't his type. But she'd never been able to compete with gregarious party girls like Veronica. Or Alexis.

"So, it was odd to move in here with his parents after we got married. An old tradition that no one thought awkward, except me, I guess. The only saving grace was that we had the wing that Edward built soon after he married Florence - the library and music room with his baby grand, with a back staircase up to the suite of two generous bedrooms with a bathroom between them. There's a door to the hallway, which we kept closed when his parents were in the original master bedroom at the other end of the hall. Simon had moved into his grandparent's suite after Florence died, so I just moved in with him. Not into our own house where I could do as I pleased."

"I grew up in my grandmother's house," Paige said. "It's a big place, too, so we never felt constrained by her presence."

"It wasn't all bad, of course. During the season, we're too busy to spend much time here, and we take our meals at the inn. Off-season, they were gone for two months, and then we were. So, we didn't overlap all that much, which is what made it tolerable. Also, the fact that Simon's mother liked to cook and I don't. But when she got cancer, things became difficult. Luckily, she didn't linger. . . . In pain, I mean," Veronica added hastily to soften the callous comment.

Paige remembered Simon's mother as a kind, compassionate person, genuinely concerned about her staff and guests. She had worked a couple of summers here in the '50s, which is how she met and eventually married Richard.

Paige queried Veronica on her experiences as student staff and as an owner, jotting down salient points.

"Have you noticed any major changes in resort life since you joined?" Paige asked.

"Oh yes! Even the first summer. I knew that the model which had worked for over a century was outdated. Once people could get here quickly and easily by car, there was no need to stay for weeks or months. And some don't want three set meals a day. They want to go exploring, dine out at other places, different cuisines, and not have to return at specific times. But there's never been an option to book only a room or bed and breakfast. Of course, in the old days, there wasn't anywhere else to eat around here, especially when you arrived by steamer and had no other transport. But resorts have to change with the times to survive.

"Richard didn't agree, partly because aged clients like the Pembrook sisters enjoyed the status quo. And because that was all he'd ever known. But Simon understood and didn't want to be that kind of hotelier."

"So, I presume you're responsible for the chic new dining staff uniforms?" The girls wore sky-blue V-neck blouses with a discreet Westwind logo on the left, and black, A-line skirts. The guys had matching blue, open-necked shirts, with black pants.

"Yes, it was time to dispense with demure, servant-like frocks and bowties. The staff feel more comfortable and are happy with the flattering look. People who feel good work more efficiently. I also decided to up the game for Westwind clothes, not just souvenir T-shirts with Muskoka and our name plastered on them, but high-quality clothes with a subtle logo, which people are proud to wear."

"I'm enjoying mine," Paige admitted.

"Glad to hear it! That's one of the fun aspects of the job. But meeting people is the best part. There are quite a few celebrities who drop in for drinks on the sundeck, or even stay for a few days. Hollywood has discovered Muskoka! And I'm always on the lookout for important contacts," she added with a sly grin.

"But things are never what they seem or as you imagine, are they? The inn was exotic and exciting when I was here as a student. Now I'm excited that we'll be rid of the old money pit. New adventures await."

Paige thought her cavalier attitude to this family legacy despicable. Veronica had obviously never forged a bond with the place like she had. She quelled the *if-only*s that needled her.

But as she walked back to her cabin, she wondered how she would have taken to the demands of running the resort had she and Simon married. What would have happened to her talents and ambitions?

Now she was looking forward to spending an uncomplicated, relaxing afternoon at Arcadia with some of her favourite people.

"Here's our ray of sunshine!" Duncan enthused when Paige arrived.

"Even more glowing and gorgeous than usual," Gavin added, giving her a peck on the cheek.

"I come bearing gifts," she announced as she pulled Westwind beach towels from her bag. "Different colours so that you don't get them mixed up. Methinks lemon yellow for Duncan, lime green for Gavin, and royal blue for Marshall."

"Brilliant!" Duncan said. "Let me guess what colour you have. Turquoise?"

She laughed as she pulled out her aqua towel.

"I adore this logo!" Gavin said. "Ta, Luv!"

"Simon *is* talented," Marshall agreed when she told them he'd designed it.

They lunched on Duncan's "simple fare" of barbequed salmon steaks and a gourmet salad accompanied by an exceptional Pinot Grigio from Gavin's cellar. Dessert was local wild blueberries and vanilla ice cream, which Marshall insisted they eat on "Paige's Rock, as I've dubbed it".

So, the four of them sat in a row with legs knee-deep in the water that lapped the granite slab of the point.

"I'm going to lend you one of our boats," Marshall told Paige. "That way you have freedom to come and go here, and interview people or do other research on the lake. Much faster than driving around it by car."

"How wonderful!"

"You were driving the 21 ft. Ditchburn when you were ten, so I think I can trust you with her now." His eyes glinted with amusement.

"You still have *Miss Chief*!" Paige cried delightedly. Whenever they stayed at Westwind, her father had borrowed the mahogany launch that had been built for his parents.

"I know your dad is attached to her, so he'll get first dibs if we ever plan to sell. He can even keep her here if that helps."

"That's so thoughtful! And an enticing incentive for renting Arcadia."

"Good point! Anyway, I talked to Simon, and he says there's a spare slip in his boathouse where you can berth her."

"Perfect!"

"This lifestyle that you two grew up with is to die for," Gavin exclaimed. He and Duncan had been in Canada for only ten years. "Summers spent in cozy cottages or lazy mansions on endless lakes, classic boats that tiny tots learn to drive, canoeing, waterskiing, sailing. Tennis and golf at the nearby Country Club. If we ever tire of the city, we could consider opening a restaurant up here. Someplace with a large patio overlooking a lake."

"You'd have to be really close to town, since it's pretty dead here in winter. Or shut down until spring like so many other restaurants and spend your winters somewhere warm," Marshall advised.

"Now there's a thought! Wine country California, here we come," Gavin joked.

"I'm happy just to spend downtime here for now," Duncan said. "So, do you want to make up a foursome for tennis at the Country Club tomorrow, Pet? Marshall says you're an ace on the court."

"Sure!" Paige knew that he and Gavin were avid tennis and squash players, and took care to stay fit.

"Now I'm going to use my new designer towel for a swim," Duncan declared with a wink.

"I'll watch from here," Paige said as the others got up to get changed.

Marshall sat back down. "Is there a problem, Kiddo?"

"The wind's kicked up waves. It's a bit rough for me right now," she admitted, rubbing her palms nervously against the rock as if trying to ground herself. Staving off a panic attack.

"Simon told me to keep an eye on you if we were swimming. He didn't tell me why. So, what happened?"

Reluctantly, she told him.

"Jeez! Too far too fast. Brett should have known better! You're a strong swimmer, Paige. You just need to take baby steps to regain confidence. And it doesn't matter if you never swim any deeper than where you can easily stand. It should be fun, not frightening. Let's walk along the beach, not deep, so we don't even need swimsuits."

She nodded.

The beach was in a cove sheltered from the prevailing winds by the rocky point, so the water was relatively calm, and Paige relaxed again as she strolled the shallows. The other two were racing each other to the nearest island.

"So, what else is going on? I sense a tinge of melancholy."

She explained about Brett's reneging on the Westwind Beach Club.

"You can always buy into Arcadia."

"I would love to if it weren't way out of my price range. And Brett wants sole ownership of a cottage. By the way, he might have some work for you, so be sure to make it worth your while. Deep pockets there."

Marshall snorted. "Thanks for the heads-up! I'll give you a kick-back."

She giggled.

Gazing towards the back of Old Baldy, she said, "You must have known my grandfather fairly well. How old were you when he died? Nine?"

"Yup. But none of us kids knew him well. He liked his peace and privacy. He was a bit . . . temperamental, so we gave him a wide berth."

"Nan told me about his shellshock and nightmares, how they had separate bedrooms because of that. Did you ever overhear talk amongst the adults about their relationship?"

"That's a curious question. Parents and grandparents don't have sex, you know."

She burst into laughter. "That's precisely my point! Were they a happy couple?"

"Granny cautioned us to avoid Uncle Raymond when he had his *dark moods*. I rarely saw him without a cocktail or whiskey in hand, so I thought that's what she meant. I remember Aunt Delia always cheerful and fun-loving, even when she seemed wistful underneath. Where's this leading?"

"Something I discovered has been nagging at me. Do you still have the old books here in the reading lounge?"

"Now I'm really intrigued! Yes. Aside from the odd one that someone borrowed and never returned."

"May I have a look at them?"

"Of course! But only if you tell me where this is leading."

"I will."

She found Cliff's last book near the end of the poetry section. She'd been right to speculate that he brought several copies to give as gifts. Raymond probably didn't read poetry, so Delia had hidden the book in plain sight.

She flipped through it and found a loose sheet in the middle. *Eternal Love* was signed, "Forever, Cliff." And there was a photo of the two of them, he, gazing down lovingly at her as she leaned against him with a radiant smile.

"Oh Nan!"

"Wow! What's that all about?"

"I think Nan found the love of her life. And he of his. That's Cliff Basildon. He was in the old photos I showed you with Nan and the Pembrook sisters. He drowned off Old Baldy one stormy night in '37. Returning from here, no doubt. Read this poem."

"Evocative! Lovers skinny dipping."

"Exactly! But I thought it was Abigail or another woman at Westwind."

"Poor Aunt Delia! No wonder she looked like she was pining for something. Do you think she was going to leave Raymond?"

"Perhaps. But I know who can tell us."

"The sisters."

■   ■   ■

"I'm afraid I won't be coming up this weekend after all," Brett said rather too cheerfully when he rang her just before dinner. "I ran into an old friend at the Yacht Club last night. He made it big on Wall St. and has a place in The Hamptons. He invited me down for a weekend of sailing. I know you have work to do. Filming a regatta."

"I'm sure someone else can interview participants. We already have the questions prepared," Paige replied, not because she wanted to go, or even could, considering the work that needed to be done, but to see what excuses he had.

"Sailing's not your thing though. There wouldn't be anything for you to do there."

"Explore Long Island. Seek Gatsby."

He chuckled. "Dean has a neighbour who might be interested in doing business with us. So, it's not a family invitation. I'm sure you'll be happier up there anyway."

Paige could almost see his condescending, dismissive smile.

"You're right! I will be."

Ask him about Alexis.

But she didn't want to know if he was going there or somewhere else with her.

"Dean's in Toronto on business for a few days, so I'll be dining with him in the evenings. He's going to send his private plane back on Friday afternoon to pick me up."

"I'm sure you'll be in your element there."

"I have a busy week, but I'll call you when I can. Bye, babe."

It was a relief that he wasn't going to be here for the weekend. She wouldn't have to worry about unpleasant scenes.

And she would embrace her first step towards independence.

•   •   •

"I'd like you ladies to take possession of this table again, and I'll join *you* if I may," Paige said to the Pembrook sisters at dinner. "Since Brett's not here most of the time, he has no say in the matter. The drinks are still on us, though," she added with a smile.

"Thank you, dear, although not necessary," Abigail assured her.

"I'll feel better if you accept. Hardly compensation for his high-handedness anyway."

"Do look after yourself in that power dynamic."

"I certainly will!"

"Never too late to alter course," Abigail emphasized.

"Yes. Which brings me back to research. I've deduced that Delia and Cliff were lovers. I suspect they may have been planning to elope – for want of a better word," Paige concluded, skewering the sisters with a challenging look.

"Well... yes, that was the plan," Emmeline admitted, dicing her chicken into ever smaller pieces. "Sadly, Fate intervened."

"Raymond was damaged by the war and living in his own hell," Abigail continued. "Cordelia blossomed under the love and attention that Cliff lavished on her, and he likewise flourished. It was a joy to see two people so attuned and deeply devoted to one another."

"Nan must have been heartbroken when he died."

"Undoubtedly. But she took to her bed with a 'summer flu', and we didn't see her again, except very occasionally over the years," Emmeline added. "I felt so sorry for her to be locked into that hollow relationship."

Paige's thoughts were spinning. "Oh my God! My dad was born the following May. *That's* who that photo of Cliff in the canoe reminded me of! Is that possible?"

The sisters looked at each other in resignation.

"It's probably why Cordelia never came here with him. It wasn't until we saw your father courting your mother that we noticed a resemblance to Cliff," Abigail said. "We asked her about her handsome beau and when she mentioned Latimer, we realized why."

Paige sank back into her chair and took a big gulp of wine. "Bloody hell! Should I tell Dad? I *can't* tell him!"

"Perhaps we're wrong. Cliff had died over twenty years before so we may not have remembered him well."

"But I was struck by a resemblance, too."

"If Cordelia had wanted your father to know, she would have left him a letter or told him before she died," Emmeline declared. "Perhaps she did, and he doesn't care to share that information. But don't feel it's your duty, Paige. We all have secrets, and it makes no matter now."

"Except that Dad has a half-sister in England and I could have cousins!"

"Who might be appalled to discover that. I expect that Delia would not appreciate being remembered as an adulteress. Or for your father to know that he was technically illegitimate. Things would have been different if she'd been able to divorce."

Paige felt as though she'd been hit by a thunderbolt. Her beloved Nan had planned to desert her husband, and had a lovechild that she must have convinced Raymond was his. Her father never had a bloodline claim to Arcadia. And Nan had to make a viable life for herself within the prison of her untenable marriage. No wonder she had spent so much time and energy in theatre, where she could escape into another persona, for a short time at least.

And Paige's biological grandfather sounded like just the kind of person she would have loved to know. But she couldn't even share that with her parents. Obviously, her father wasn't aware, or he would have recognized Cliff's name in the news article about the drowning.

It was all surreal.

And the Pembrook sisters had prevaricated to mislead her. Although she appreciated them trying to keep Delia's secret, she wondered what else they were hiding.

Veronica detained Paige as she left the dining room. "Could I talk to you for a minute?"

"Sure."

Veronica led her to the private office. Installed behind the desk, a meaningless smile on her face, she said, "Do sit down. I know you booked into a cabin for three weeks, Paige, but since we're not *charging* you, I wondered if you'd consider giving up next week for a room in the inn, which became available. We just had a request from a family of five for a cabin."

She paused to drive home that they would have significant income from that. Charges were per person, with reduced rates for children under twelve.

"And the inn room is one of the best, with a balcony. Right next to the Pembrook sisters, in fact."

And across the hall from the tower entrance.

Paige hesitated, but she'd have to move out the following Sunday anyway.

"As it turns out, Brett just informed me that he has a business meeting in New York, so he won't be coming this weekend. So yes, that would work for me."

"Excellent! So kind of you, Paige. But unfortunate for you that Brett won't be here."

"I have work to do as well. We start shooting on Friday, so I'm going to set up interviews."

"We've alerted the staff, who are really excited. And we're putting notices out to the guests. This will be quite a special weekend! OK, so we'll store your belongings here on Sunday morning and give you priority move-in to the new room by early afternoon."

Paige mentioned the change of accommodation to Simon a little while later.

"That really wasn't necessary," he said with annoyance. "There's no space for you to work there." He paused. "So, I'll set up the boathouse suite as your office. You can even work under the covered balcony there. And you can access all the photos and other boxes in the house whenever you need to. I'll give you a key."

"That sounds delightful! And efficient."

"Even more so if you stay there."

She couldn't look into his eyes to see if he was deliberately reminding her of what that place had once meant to them, or if it didn't matter to him now. Either would hurt.

"I've never stayed in the original inn, so it will be good to have first-hand experience for the book," she stated.

In the background, the Moody Blues were singing about waking up in the protective embrace of a true love.

She and Simon had never spent a night together. Paige wouldn't start speculating about how glorious that would be.

She realized that Delia possibly never had the comfort and bliss of sleeping in a lover's arms.

Chapter 11

Paige gazed up in surprise at the summer-blue sky as she drifted feather-like to the bottom of the lake. Dragonflies zipped past her to break the liquid ceiling and zoom into the lightness of freedom. The ribbed sand, like brutal sinews, began flexing and writhing beneath her feet, trying to grab and anchor her to the bottom.

The girl with dead eyes smiled maliciously. And began walking towards her.

Paige woke gasping, thankful to fill her lungs with the invigorating morning air wafting into the bedroom.

∎   ∎   ∎

"OK, Nancy Drew, what did you find out about the great romance?" Marshall asked.

"Not Miss Marple?" Paige quipped.

"Too old."

They had won a tie-breaker tennis match against Duncan and Gavin at the SRA Country Club and were now swimming in the shallows at Arcadia, Paige feeling comfortable with her pool noodle while the other two were racing again.

"We were right."

"Wow! Anything else?" He eyed her probingly.

She looked away.

"Kiddo, you don't have a poker face. Not hard to figure out, considering your grandparents had been married for seventeen years with no offspring, and suddenly your father appeared in a timely fashion after a passionate affair."

"Dad mustn't find out!"

"Not from me, anyway. Hey, I'm happy for Aunt Delia! She was my favourite. I expect that having Cliff's child not only gave her a part of him to cherish forever, but was also the greatest joy of her life."

"You're right!" Paige could imagine feeling like that if a child were all she could ever have of Simon. And was so thankful that she was still on the pill and not about to find herself pregnant with Brett's. It was another wake-up call to realize that she didn't want any permanent ties with him.

"Oh my God! I just realized that you and I aren't related after all!"

"Not through blood. But you'll always be my little cousin."

She smiled. "And you're still my favourite cousin."

He chuckled.

"I wish I had known Cliff. I've been reading his unfinished novel and it's fascinating."

"Then you can be proud to be his granddaughter, even if no one else will ever know."

"You're right."

"Why not finish it?" Marshall raised a challenging eyebrow.

She gaped like a fish and then said gleefully, "Why not?"

"But first we have work to do!"

Marshall had discovered who owned the derelict Hidden Cove Lodge and had obtained permission to film. After a quick, delicious lunch prepared by Duncan, they all went on a tour of the lake to scout out other filming locations and determine what further research Paige needed to do immediately.

Simon had already given them contact info for the existing historic resorts on these three large, interconnected lakes, and had talked to the innkeepers he knew personally.

So, when she saw him that evening, they finished a rough draft for what scenes to shoot at Westwind, and the list of questions to ask staff and guests. Then they sat on the veranda with a nightcap to watch the last of the light clinging futilely to the darkening sky.

"Did I mention that Tony and Angela are arriving Friday? They always stay over two weekends to include the Regatta, but this year they're staying an extra week as well."

"That's great! I hope we have time to spend with them."

"You've already done an amazing amount of work, so we should be able to take a few evenings off."

"May I make a copy of Cliff's novel?" Paige asked hastily to cover the Moody Blues singing "Want to Be With You".

"Of course! Do you have plans for it?"

"I might try my hand at finishing it. It's out of copyright by now, and his name would be on it as first author, so I don't think I'd be infringing on anyone's rights."

"His family in England, perhaps. It might be considered part of his estate."

"It seems he left it to his friend, Edward. Judging by what Cliff said about his wife, she didn't even like his literary works."

"Yes... Well, if it's my property, then I say go for it! Bring it into the office tomorrow morning and one of the staff can copy it."

She beamed. "I'll give you half the profits. If I make any."

■   ■   ■

Paige awoke in the dead of night to the menacing creaking of a door.

"Who's there!" she demanded breathlessly, heart pounding.

The door responded more quietly.

Grabbing her talisman rock and flashlight, she crept out of bed and tiptoed into the sitting room. The bathroom door was almost closed, with just a sliver of nightlight showing. She had left it wide open.

It was silent now but seemed to hold back something threatening.

A cool breeze skittered around her.

She turned on the overhead light.

"Who's there!"

She went up to the door and kicked it open. The room was empty. Thankfully.

Paige swung around as she heard clicking behind her. The outside door was slightly ajar and clattered against the latch at the whim of the wind.

How had that opened? Oh God, had she been wandering again? Hopefully not outside.

She checked cautiously under the beds and in the closet to make sure that no racoon or other nocturnal critter had ventured in. When all was clear, she wedged a chair under the door handle again, which she'd stopped doing when Brett was here on the weekend.

But it took her a long time to get back to sleep.

In the morning, the cabin looked just as she had left it. Towelling off after her shower, she gasped when she looked at the mirror. Most of it was steamy, except for the shape of a huge spider. She quivered with revulsion as she wiped it away with a towel, which she hurled into the tub as if a real spider were contained within.

Where the hell had that come from?

She suddenly recalled what Rebecca had told her about trying to scare Simon's girlfriend away by drawing a spider on her mirror with greasy fingers. Who else had Bex told?

Paige knew she would *never* have done that herself, even unaware.

"You looked troubled, dear," Emmeline said at breakfast.

Paige realized she'd been inattentive. "Sorry, I just got lost in thought."

"It might help to talk."

Why not? The sisters probably wouldn't think her crazy.

"There've been some strange things happening," Paige admitted, lowering her voice so that others couldn't hear. "And I don't *think* it's me flipping out."

She mentioned the scattered papers, the face in the mirror, and other unsettling incidents that could be attributed to her stress or sleepwalking, but she ended with the tower room "ghost".

"At least Simon was with me for that, so it's not just my imagination." She looked at the sisters for reassurance.

"If Edward is here with us, he would never hurt either of you. Or deliberately distress you. Of that I'm certain!" Emmeline declared. "And what happened Sunday morning?" She gripped Paige's hand tightly. "I heard Edward's clock chime."

She blanched as Paige told them. *What was that shadow that was too often lurking behind Paige?*

"You mustn't be afraid to tell us these things, dear. We understand and are here to help," Abigail said. "I'm not sure that the cabin is the best place for you to be alone right now."

"It's the last place I would have thought would be haunted," Paige replied. "Anyway, I'm being moved into the room next to yours on Sunday."

"That's reassuring! A hearty knock on the wall would alert us. There's only a half-wall and partial screen between us on the balcony. You could easily step across if necessary."

It's not the cabin that's haunted, it's you, Paige, Emmeline thought with deep misgiving. And she had a mission to intervene. "If there are restless spirits here, perhaps we need to reassure them," she ventured.

"How?" Paige asked.

"Why don't we visit their graves? Pay homage to them. Let them know they're not forgotten, but also not required to linger."

Paige brightened. "Good idea! Where is that?"

"At the Eden Point Church. The Hawksleys were founding members, along with several other local resort owners like the Rowans. They have family plots there."

"That's not far. There are docks there so we can go by boat."

"That will be a treat!"

"I'll stay and keep working on our notes," Abigail offered.

"And I'll round up some flowers," Emmeline announced. "There are always fresh ones on the tables, so I expect they have a few left over."

Paige and Emmeline were like eager schoolgirls when they boarded her launch a little while later.

"*Miss Chief*! I've never forgotten that name," Emmeline said with delight as Paige helped her aboard. A portable set of steps with a railing, supplied by Simon, made the boat easily accessible. "Cordelia took us on excursions in this a few times that summer."

"Did she ever take you to Arcadia?"

"Well . . . yes. What a grand and beautiful place! But we didn't want to reveal that we knew more about her than necessary. Now you know why."

"I appreciate that. But now I want to know as much as possible about her in that era. And Cliff. How I wish I could get a glimpse of their past!"

"Cliff was a sensitive soul. Like you, dear."

Paige grinned.

Beyond the headland that sheltered the doomed Hidden Cove Lodge was a little bay with docks inviting worshippers to pull in. A sign read, "Eden Point Church. Summer Sunday Protestant Services at 10:00 AM. All Welcome."

The small, fog-grey board-and-batten building seemed to grow out of the rock that dominated Eden Point at the end of the bay. The pines surrounding it reached heavenward much higher than the tiny steeple. The few narrow, Gothic windows were stained glass, but the church seemed content in its relative obscurity.

Behind it was a small cemetery with tombstones dating back to the 1890s.

Emmeline went unerringly to Florence and Edward's graves. Beside them lay Simon's parents. The empty plot next to them must surely be awaiting him. The thought made Paige shiver.

She was surprised to see a stone beyond that with the Pembrook sisters' names and birthdates inscribed.

"You're going to . . . be here?" she stammered.

"Oh yes. We bought these plots twenty years ago. We want to rest amongst our friends. No matter where we've lived or travelled, Westwind has always felt like our real home. Can you imagine anywhere more beautiful to spend eternity?"

Emmeline laid down the bouquets she had gathered beneath the two Davenport headstones, but saved one blossom for Paige.

"You can put this on Cliff's grave."

He rested behind Edward, with Lucinda Edgerton next to him.

"Gosh!" Paige ran her hand across the granite headstone and traced the carving of his name with a finger. "Hi, Granddad. Here's a daisy for you. Appropriate, don't you think? Your work has touched my soul. I'm so proud and honoured to be your granddaughter. I hope you don't mind that I'm going to try to finish your novel. The world should read it." She brushed away a tear.

As did Emmeline.

When Paige looked up, she glimpsed a shadowy figure behind a gravestone at the far end, which disappeared in an instant.

Emmeline gasped. Was this the spectre that sometimes hovered around Paige?

"Bex?" Paige murmured, quivering. "Was that Rebecca?" she asked Emmeline.

"That's her grave. Next to her great-grandparents. Come. I think we need to talk to her." *Oh God, what had Paige wished for that had summoned that wicked child?*

Emmeline had never warmed to the selfish, scheming chit who'd acted as though the world owed her because she was an orphan. Resentful and rebellious, Rebecca had been a handful for Simon's family. And Emmeline had noticed often enough that Rebecca had tried to undermine Simon's friendships, especially with Paige.

She took Paige's icy hand and led her to the black granite that marked Rebecca's grave. "Maybe you can finally put the past to rest. Just don't wish anything," she cautioned.

Paige nodded but realized she had already conjured up Rebecca at Silver Sands to make amends.

"Bex, I wanted to tell you how terribly sad I am about what happened. I did value our friendship, and wis... am sorry that we parted in anger. Rest in peace, Bex. Please."

A dust devil suddenly swirled up dried leaves, hissing as it whipped across them. Paige tried to shield Emmeline from the stinging onslaught. It stopped just as abruptly, dropping debris at the other end of the churchyard.

They looked at each other uneasily. Was that Rebecca's wrath that had just slapped them?

"Maybe she can't move beyond the bounds of the cemetery," Paige speculated as she helped brush off Emmeline and pull pine needles from her usually well-coifed silver hair.

But Emmeline feared that she already had.

They were happy to see that the flowers they brought lay undisturbed.

"Edward and Florence, you mustn't be distressed at the changes coming to Westwind," Emmeline advised. "You know better than most that catering to the Zeitgeist is necessary for survival. Rather than disappearing as most of the resorts have, Westwind and your legacy will live on in a new format for a new century, still classy and appreciated. And Simon will be free to use his talents and live *his* dream."

Paige took a poignant photo of Emmeline communing with Edward. She snapped Cliff's grave and the tranquil, sun-dappled setting with the backdrop of the humble church amid towering pines, the sparkling blue lake beyond, and Old Baldy in the distance.

She stroked Cliff's stone once more, realizing it was the same pink and grey as her talisman. How had Nan managed that? She suspected that Delia had been here regularly.

"I'll visit you often, Granddad. Perhaps you could send me your thoughts on the novel so that I don't mess up what you had intended."

"That's a lovely sentiment," Emmeline said as they walked away. "But don't come here on your own just now. I feel uneasy about Rebecca."

Once they were safely in the boat, she asked, "What happened between you two that day? Why did you part in anger?"

Paige hesitated.

"It could be important, dear."

"She discovered that Simon and I . . . had fallen in love. She hated me then. Said that he was going to marry her and was just using me. She was in a rage when the storm hit and refused to take shelter."

"So, the accident was entirely her fault. It's time you relinquished that oppressive guilt."

"I've tried."

"Perhaps you need to tell Simon."

Paige looked away, unable to respond.

"It was obvious to Abby and me that you two were happily in love. We never understood what happened between you. What kept you apart."

"I don't know either."

Sensing Paige's bafflement and sorrow, Emmeline didn't prod. But she wondered if there was any way she could help set things right.

■   ■   ■

The rest of the day and the next were hectic, so Paige had little time to think about the alarming encounter with Rebecca. Except at night when she looked cautiously into the mirror and scanned the cabin for unusual shapes and shadows.

She was mightily relieved that there were no lights going on or off, no strange sounds, no disturbance of her things. Perhaps she had put Rebecca to rest at last.

She tackled her many tasks with renewed energy, and found a moment to take her latest rolls of film into the gift shop for processing.

Marshall's crew – cinematographer, Pierre, and sound recordist, Terry - arrived Thursday afternoon and were staying at Arcadia. But Simon had invited them to have their meals at Westwind and set up a small meeting room to be at their disposal. It was there that he, Paige, and the Pembrook sisters joined them and Marshall for dinner that evening.

It was mostly shop talk because they would be filming the following day, with a full schedule of interviews already arranged.

"Simon, when you have time, shadow Pierre to get tips on cinematography. I'll leave a camera with you to capture anything interesting or unexpected, like celebs showing up," Marshall said as he and his guys were ready to depart. "We'll be here at dawn, filming the morning tranquility and all the behind-the-scenes bustle that keeps the resort ticking."

When the others had gone, Simon and Paige went to his place to discuss the final preparations. They had just sat down when Veronica came storming into the living room.

"What the hell is going on here?" she demanded.

"What do you mean?" Simon asked.

"I mean, who's been tampering with my things?! I laid out my outfit for tomorrow, and my gold tiger pendant is missing! Someone stole it! Or is playing games." She glared at them.

"The house has been locked," Simon reminded her. "It doesn't look like anyone's broken in. Maybe you put it somewhere else."

"I've searched everywhere! It's not here."

"You can always wear another necklace."

"That's not the point! Anyway, it's my favourite."

"I'll have a look. It can't have gone far. Try not to worry about it."

"This is important to me! Can't you take it more seriously, for Christ's sake?!" Veronica spat as she turned and stomped out.

Simon and Paige sat in embarrassed silence.

"It could be Bex playing tricks," she finally said. To his astonishment she explained, "Miss Emmeline and I encountered her in the cemetery yesterday."

She related the events and concluded with, "Remember what I told you about Mary, the ghost at the theatre? So don't be surprised if Veronica finds her pendant where she left it."

He eyed her astutely. "So, tell me what else Bex has done to you."

She hesitated. "I don't know that it was her. I'd rather not talk about it right now."

"I won't think you're crazy, believe me. I've had strange things happening as well lately. Faint footsteps. The piano playing when there's no one else here. Veronica doesn't even know how to play. And it's not Dad or Granddad."

Paige knew they'd been highly talented pianists, as was Simon.

"Elton John's 'I'm Still Standing' – Bex's defiant anthem against her parents. She played that often, especially when she was angry. Just faintly now, but..."

"Oh God! I think I summoned her! I wished I could make peace with her."

"Christ!" He ran his fingers through his hair. "I wished she were out of my life that summer. She'd become so obsessed with me. Wouldn't leave me alone. She even climbed into bed with me one night. Naked. I chased her out and locked my door from then on. But she was relentless."

He looked at her in anguish. "Then you had the accident and almost drowned as well. I feel so damn guilty!"

"Oh, Simon! We all make wishes like that without meaning anyone harm."

They were startled as a door slammed violently shut upstairs.

"Probably a crosswind," Simon suggested without conviction. "I'll check."

Paige's senses were on high alert when he left. She scanned the room for flitting shadows. Feared a ghostly touch or menacing sounds.

But there was nothing diabolical in the atmosphere or any premonitions that made her skin crawl. Just a gentle evening breeze drifting into the welcoming room.

When Simon returned, he said, "I checked for Veronica's necklace while I was upstairs. It was lying on the floor where she couldn't have missed it. I'll tell her I found it under the dresser."

"Will she believe that?" Or would she think that Paige was causing mischief?

He shrugged.

"Tomorrow's going to be a long day. I should get back for an early start," she said.

"Will you be OK?"

"I'm trying not to let anything terrify me. And it helps to know that it's not me doing things in my sleep or imagining them. Thinking you're being terrorized by inner demons is worse than battling something external."

"I'm sorry, Paige. For everything." His soulful eyes held hers. "I wish..."

Her eyes widened in alarm.

"That I could be of more help," he finished lamely.

She breathed a sigh of relief.

Chapter 12

The crew filmed the busy, deliciously fragrant pre-dawn baking in the kitchen. A few early risers set out in canoes and kayaks on the glassy lake that glowed pink and peach, outlining the slumbering islands, as the golden swath of sunrise heralded another glorious day. Beneath the lens, the outdoor morning preparations were done with pride and precision by eager staff as the resort slowly awakened.

After a hearty breakfast in their command centre, the team filmed snippets of the daily activities of guests and staff, interspersed with interviews, which Paige and Simon conducted.

The Pembrook sisters were outstanding, mesmerizing onlookers with their captivating memories, presented with humour and elan. Paige could easily envision where in this segment they could intersperse the vintage photos that she and Simon had selected.

Abigail concluded with, "Westwind has not only given us eight decades of incomparable fun and treasured memories, but it also helped to shape the women we became. Formidable with our tennis racquets," she quipped. "My experience writing and staging skits for the talent shows propelled me into filmmaking when the opportunity arose. The scenery inspired Emmeline's art and fed her soul. And the friends we've made here have been like family... At least the kind you would choose if you could." She grinned mischievously amid chuckles.

Paige thought again how lucky she was to be part of this creative endeavour, as well as part of the sisters' circle.

At Simon's request, Tony and Angela Vanderbeck arrived before check-in for their interview.

"Paige, how wonderful to see you again!" Angela said as she hugged her warmly. "It's been such a long time. You look fabulous!"

"And you look radiant! Am I right that there will soon be an addition to the family?"

Angela laughed delightedly as she stroked her slightly round belly. "A Christmas present."

"That will keep on giving," Tony added with a grin.

"You'll have to come and stay at our house next summer," Simon offered. "The little tyke needs to be introduced to the place where his or her parents met."

"You're on, buddy!" Tony said.

Because they had been part of the waterfront staff for three summers, they were interviewed sitting on the bench at the end of the dock.

"Hardly a hero," Tony chuckled in reply to Paige's request to relate an anecdote. "When you grow up living or camping in the Ontario wilderness, you have to become bear-wise. I was escorting Angela to the girls' quarters to fetch a sweater. It was getting dark, and we noticed a large, hulking shape at the screen door. Angela shrieked when she realized it was a bear. It turned around, got up on its hind legs and huffed. I maneuvered Angie behind me as we backed away, raised my arms to make us look bigger, and said as calmly as possible, 'Hey Teddy! Off you go! There's a good bear.' He was snorting as we retreated far enough to give him plenty of room to leave. Then he got back down on all fours, gave us one last look, and bounded towards the woods."

"It was an amazing encounter, after I got over my initial shock," Angela remarked. "Some of the girls had heard the screen door rattling, and went into the hallway that ran down the middle of the building to see what the problem was. When they noticed the bear, they bolted back into their rooms and barricaded their doors. The only phone in the building was in the hall, so they couldn't even call for help. No cell phones in those days, of course. Tony was certainly a hero to us. And luckily, none of the guests encountered the bear."

Tony concluded the interview by saying, "When the movie *Dirty Dancing* came out in 1987, our last summer, it really struck a chord with us. We sure had the 'time of our lives' working here."

"Which is why we were married here the following autumn and have been coming back every summer for holidays," Angela added.

Paige was sad that she had shut them out of her life, along with Simon and Westwind, for all these years. But even close friends can lose contact for a while. Hopefully, they could pick up the threads that had bound them together.

Starting that evening, when the four of them got together on Simon's screened veranda.

"It must feel strange that this is all going to change," Angela mused as she sipped her Perrier while the others had wine. "It does to me, and I've only known it for thirteen years."

"It's certainly weird that I no longer own Westwind. But I'm glad we were given the chance to run it for one more season so we could say goodbye to our loyal guests.

"At least the new owners are preserving as much of the old inn as feasible. Everything has to be brought up to code, and we know that there are no fire stops between the walls or in the ceilings. It was scary how quickly Windermere was consumed. Fire was always my dad's worst fear and constant worry.

"I remember one time we were walking along the veranda and noticed a cigarette butt smouldering between the boards. We couldn't get it out without possibly pushing it down onto the tinder-dry debris beneath, so I ran into the dining room and grabbed a pitcher of water ready for the lunch service while Dad stood guard. The wood was beginning to ignite when we doused it.

"He was already negotiating with the developer before he died and urged me to close the deal."

"He knew you're going to be an awesome filmmaker," Tony said. "So let's celebrate your freedom and future!"

"You were both impressive in the interviews," Angela said. "We arrived in time to watch the Pembrook sisters. Not that they needed much encouragement. Miss Abigail is a consummate professional."

"And still filming. Oh, Simon, can we show Angie and Tony the footage of us waterskiing?"

"This is so cool!" Angela said as they watched their acrobatics on screen. "I couldn't do that lay-back now even if I weren't pregnant."

"We made it look so easy," Tony added.

"But we girls took all the risks. Trusting you guys not to drop us."

"Never deliberately," Tony said, stroking Angela's arm affectionately, for they'd had their spills in practice.

Simon showed them clips from other movies that Abigail had compiled, which Paige had never seen.

"Oh my gosh! 'Dancing in the Street' was such a fun song to do for the talent show," she said. "I'd forgotten how much it resonated with the audience." Who were not only singing along, but dancing as chairs in the pavilion were abandoned.

"We made that song last for what, six or seven minutes?" Tony asked. "What a hoot that was! And we sound pretty good!"

They had cleverly added to the lyrics, naming Canadian cities in the song, as well as places in Muskoka, ending with Westwind, where "dancing on the beach" had the audience applauding and cheering.

"And look at the costume ball! I loved dressing as a hippie," Angela said.

Wearing that sequined '20s dress, Paige was surprised to see how much she resembled Delia.

"We're so lucky to have experienced this time in history. Still enjoying elegant remnants of the 19th century, but with all the mod cons. We do like our Water's Edge Suite, Simon. Figured you constructed those 'specially for us," Tony teased.

"A well-deserved step up from the student staff quarters," Simon replied.

"Crazy that the Suites are going to be demolished as well," Angela complained. "They're not even a decade old. So wasteful!"

"That's called progress," Simon stated cynically. "But I'm leaving all that behind. This is all that's important . . . Being together."

Paige couldn't hold his gaze.

"The Moodies always got it right," Angela said with a contented sigh as "Lovely to See You" came on. "And they're still writing awesome songs that are the soundtrack of our lives."

■   ■   ■

Paige remembered to pick up her photos the following morning, including the film that had been partly exposed. The ones of Brett sailing had been ruined, but the one of the mess of papers had survived. She was horrified to see a smudge that looked like a person in the corner of the room, staring at the photographer.

What the hell! Was that Bex?

Did that explain the strange goings-on in the cabin?

One more night. You just have to get through one more night in the cabin. Or would Bex follow her? Had that been her *silhouetted in the tower photo?*

Filming the busy regatta and interviewing participants helped to distract her.

She was glad to see that there was still plenty of camaraderie and enthusiasm amongst those on the lake. All skill levels were evident in the races, with novices laughing when their canoes went sideways, but they carried on valiantly with spectators urging them on.

After the dozen regular races in different age and gender categories, the final one was a fun free-for-all with a twist. The person in the front of the canoe had to face the stern and paddle backwards to create forward momentum.

A couple of the waterfront staff demonstrated, while another one commented over a megaphone.

"OK, boys and girls, ladies and gentlemen. Here's what NOT to do in this race. We have Erin in the bow and Jake in the stern. Erin must obviously not paddle forwards, but that's harder than you think. Here's what happens when she does. Remember, they're on the same team."

The two in the canoe stared at each other as they dug in their blades and paddled furiously forwards at the same time, making them virtually stand still, much to the amusement of onlookers.

Then Erin did a stroke on one side and Jake immediately followed with one on the other side, which made the canoe start spinning, evoking appreciative laughter.

"So, Erin and Jake will now demonstrate the proper technique. Something you might wish to master if you can't take your eyes off each other."

Erin blew Jake an exaggerated kiss which he caught and held to his lips.

Perfectly coordinated, they paddled an unwaveringly straight line. Paige knew how much time they must have spent to perfect their antics.

"And one final caution. This ending is NOT recommended if you're planning a romantic evening together."

Erin and Jake splashed each other with their paddles until they were dripping wet. Cheers and applause rippled out across the lake.

"Erin and Jake are part of our talented waterfront staff. You can also see them in our weekly waterski show on Wednesdays. They made the backwards paddling look easy, but now it's your turn, competitors, so take your places and good luck!"

There was chaos and uproarious laughter as canoes ended up going in random directions and colliding harmlessly with others as water was splashing everywhere.

Simon handed out the winning ribbons for all the races afterwards. But everyone who participated received a powder blue one with gold lettering saying "Westwind's 99th Regatta, 1997".

Then he addressed the crowd. "Guests, staff, neighbours, and everyone here who loves the lake as much as we do, thank you for coming out for Westwind's final regatta, and for your unfailing support over the years. Some of your families have known our resort and my family for over a century. We all have stories that are dear to our hearts and the essence of summer life on the lake. Some of you have told me that one of the treasured constants in your lives has been to enjoy our double-decker ice cream cones and butter tarts as well as our dances."

There were plenty of chuckles and hoorays.

"I hope that the new Westwind will still provide you with good food and entertainment, and remind you at least a little of its remarkable past."

There was tremendous applause, and several people were dashing away tears, Paige noticed, suppressing her own. This really brought home how much Westwind itself helped to define the lake culture, and how much the community would miss it.

She'd noticed how hard Simon had kept his own emotions in check – the twitch of a muscle in his jaw, the rigid shoulders – and seemed to feel those within her own being, as if they were tethered together.

Standing beside her, Angela remarked, "Is it my maternal hormones that are making me feel like having a good cry now?"

Tony, on her other side, pulled her close. "I think at least one more love match is being made here. Look at Erin and Jake. Remind you of anyone?"

The three of them watched as Jake put his arm around Erin's shoulder and whispered something in her ear, making her smile happily and lean into him.

"Westwind magic still at work," Angela proclaimed.

Paige felt a sharp stab as she wondered why that magic hadn't worked for her and Simon.

■ ■ ■

After a delicious prime roast beef dinner and fine wine, Marshall and his guys filmed a bit of the dance before returning to Arcadia. Paige accepted the Vanderbecks' invitation to meet at the pavilion, along with Simon. The band was playing "Sweet Child of Mine" as they arrived.

"I haven't done this since the '80s," Simon admitted. "Veronica doesn't think it's professional of us to take part, but our family always has, to some degree. Anyway, it's the last summer, so why not enjoy all of it?"

"Your participation is part of why we feel so at home here," Angela pointed out.

"Damn right! This is just like the good old days," Tony said cheerfully.

The band played popular rock from the '60s on. When they started "Old Time Rock and Roll", Angela jumped up and said, "Oh, this is one of *our* songs!"

She meant that it was one that they had performed in the talent show.

Tony joined her, urging, "C'mon you two!" to Paige and Simon.

They looked at each other tentatively. Simon held out his hand and Paige took it, her heart singing at his touch.

As they danced next to their exuberant friends, it felt to Paige as if the past ten years had fallen away. She allowed herself to be joyful, to revel in the moment.

"Rock and Roll Music" had them all laughing as they danced together.

During "Hungry Eyes" Simon gazed at her so intently that when "Nights in White Satin" followed, she surrendered herself gratefully into his arms. He drew her ever closer, and she had to resist laying her head on his shoulder. She could hardly bear the visceral closeness that made her long for so much more.

They moved away from each other reluctantly when the song ended, surprised to find Veronica at their side, a plastic smile belying the anger in her eyes.

"Sorry to interrupt, but some issues require Simon's attention in the office."

He looked skeptical, but said to Paige and the others, "It seems that work beckons. Enjoy your evening."

"She's a bundle of joy, as usual," Angela commented snidely as the three friends sat down.

"Ang," Tony cautioned.

"I'm sure there's nothing so pressing it couldn't wait a while!" Angela looked like she was about to say more but clammed up.

"Well, it's been a long day, and another busy one tomorrow, so I'll head back and make sure I have my questions ready," Paige said.

She already did, so there was nothing pressing she had to do except finish packing for her move to the inn.

But she needed a distraction from the emotions and desires that being held so intimately and sensually with Simon had aroused.

Discovering more about her grandfather might help, so she opened the bundle of letters he'd sent to Edward.

Roseneath Manor, Oxford

Boxing Day, 1922

Dear Edward,

I trust you had an uneventful journey home, and that your bride tolerated the sea voyage better this time. I doubt there is much else that defeats her.

I must say that Florence's maturity of demeanour, strength of character, and wholesome good looks are a refreshing change from giggling debutantes.

She has such enthusiasm for her life's work that you've obviously been smitten by that as well. Now that you've both given me a better sense of Westwind, I envision you as the amiable host of a country estate inviting guests to enjoy his idyllic environs.

And all thanks to that book you found in Pater's library, written by an old friend thirty years ago. I know you were enthralled by the chapter about his summer-long stay on a private island in Muskoka. How lucky that you were able to locate it according to his references to nearby Westwind, despite the island's name having been changed, and its cozy cabin now replaced by a summer mansion.

Remarkable that Florence's parents recall the affable young Englishman who came regularly to purchase supplies from their farm and kitchen to augment his diet of freshly caught fish.

That this was meant to be is reinforced by your father giving you funds to buy into Westwind instead of disowning you for not following the Davenport men into the family firm. I suppose he doesn't want you to be deemed a fortune hunter, and realizes you're not cut out to be a solicitor. Of course, you did present him with a fait accompli, and at least one son is content to follow in his footsteps. What a wonderful escape from a life you never wanted!

I, on the other hand, am but a mediocre scholar, and wouldn't be accepted into academia just because Pater is an esteemed professor at Oxford. Cedric would have been brilliant. But I have yet to discover my path. I know that my scribblings won't pay for my keep. But I will begin by assembling them. Including the poems I wrote when we spent those memorable summer weeks rambling the hills of the Lake District and the dales of Yorkshire. Discussing our dreams. Envisioning the women who would steal our hearts. You have done well in both regards, my friend! Had I come with you as originally planned, I wonder if I would have found my future in Canada as well. But, of course, Enid's wedding was not to be missed.

Christmas was still an ordeal since Cedric and Imogen are no longer with us and Grandmother is very frail, but we're thrilled that Enid is with child. God willing, I shall be an uncle when May flowers bloom. I was deeply touched when Pater encouraged me to pursue my "literary talents" – his words! - and offered to publish my poems as my Christmas present. I will send you a copy.

The more I think about the unique and adventuresome life you're embarking upon, the more I envy you. I should consider exploring the byways of our storied isle to see if there is someplace that speaks to *my* soul. If not, I might visit you next summer to discover if my destiny lies in your new world as well.

Your fellow traveller, Cliff

March 27, 1923
Dear Edward,

Having just adjusted my thinking of you becoming a father, I was terribly saddened to hear that Florence lost the child. Mater said it's devastating even so early in pregnancy, but to assure you from her own experience that next time could be perfectly fine, so not to lose hope.

We all send our love and best wishes to you both.
Cliff

Basildon Books,
St. Ives, Cornwall
July 29, 1923
Dear Edward,

You can see that something monumental has happened since I last wrote. I have found my own little corner of paradise!

After Grandmother passed away in January, I began to reminisce fondly about summer holidays we enjoyed at the various seaside houses she rented on the "Cornish Riviera". I suddenly had a desire to revisit those places where we children and our cousins had the freedom to explore coastal paths and beaches, turn subtropical gardens with palm trees and exotic towering plants into jungle adventures, and "mess about in boats" along the Helford River.

I believe I mentioned that Grandmother had been an heiress and widowed young, so she was financially independent for most of her life, and able to indulge her two sons and several grandchildren. She has left each of us the incredible sum of £5000, with the bulk of her estate split between Pater and his brother!

With that windfall, I thought I would return to Cornwall on a coastal walking tour, seeking my muse. I'd forgotten how much I love the everchanging sea, and was particularly captivated by the wild and rugged north coast, which I had never seen. Daily I documented my impressions along the way, seeking unusual places and ancient tales, and thinking of turning them into a book.

I got as far as St. Ives where, at the corner of a narrow, cobblestoned street, I discovered a treasure trove of a bookshop, all higgledy-piggledy but with rare used books as well as new. And it was for sale! As you can see, it is now mine in name and deed, along with the flat above, which is my new abode. I am but steps from the harbour and can glimpse the Celtic Sea from my windows. What bliss!

Enid's baby daughter has brought great joy to the family....

One missive was written in a notecard with an evocative watercolour painting of a golden beach leading to St. Ives harbour, the aqua water innocently calm against an incoming storm of indigo clouds.

A year into my new life, I can assure you that I'm enjoying myself immensely. The weather is mild even in winter and sunnier than the rest of the country, so we do get tourists year-round.

I have a small circle of friends – artists and writers who are also inspired by the area. One particular friend, Talia, is a war widow and painter who sells her delightful watercolours to the tourists, but also helps out in the shop to earn extra money. We're great pals but have no romantic intentions.

This is one of her creations, which I persuaded her should be turned into note and postcards. Tourists can take home copies of her art, and those who can afford it, can buy her originals, which we display in the shop. She has created a dozen different scenes of the ancient town with steep, narrow streets leading to the busy harbour, enticing beaches, dramatic cliffs, and the stalwart Godrevy Lighthouse on its tiny island lashed by the furious sea or afloat on a tranquil sunset. Since I produce and sell them, we both benefit from the popular items, and my flat has become my personal gallery of her original works. Can you tell that I'm in my element?

I'm intrigued by the new wing you've built, especially the screened sleeping porch. How tropical your summers must be to require you to sleep outdoors in the buff! Do send a photo. Just the porch will do.

Paige chuckled. And she was delighted that from then on, all Christmas correspondence was written in one of Talia's stunning art cards. There was no surname in the attribution, just her first followed by a sketch of a swan. Unless that *was* her name! She was probably long gone, but perhaps her art had survived her.

August 21, 1926

Dear Edward,

I've met the woman of my dreams! Six weeks ago, the most beautiful girl I have ever seen walked into my shop to purchase the latest Agatha Christie novel for her grandmother, who was ostensibly chaperoning her and two female cousins for a lengthy holiday at the Tregenna Castle Hotel. She confided that they were persuaded by their parents to look after their granny, who had spent many happy vacations here with her late husband.

I could see from Fenella's sea-green eyes that the attraction was mutual. She asked if I played tennis, since they needed a fourth. Of course I agreed.

With Talia helping at the shop, I was able to take time off, and soon Fenella and I were spending part of every day together – dances at the hotel, rambles along the cliffs, and outings in my motorcar to show her the attractions of both coasts. Her cousins were supposed to have been with us, since Granny wanted only to relax in the gardens at the hotel with her books, so they pretended to come along while actually going to the beaches in our absence. Fenella inspired several poems, which she was thrilled to receive.

After this romantic whirlwind, we are now tentatively engaged, pending her parents' approval. Her father is a Member of Parliament, backed by family money from the tea business.

As luck or Providence would have it, her granny lives not far from Grandmother's former estate near Henley, and recalls meeting her at some social functions, Basildon, being an uncommon surname. Surely that will stand me in good stead with them all.

Fenella has four older sisters and a younger brother. The eldest married a minor aristocrat, the second, an American businessman and now lives in Boston, the next is a Bohemian who has severed ties with the family, and the fourth is horse crazy so she wed a horse breeder. Fenella said that as long as she doesn't have to live over the shop, there shouldn't be any reason I wouldn't be accepted.

I should have enough money left from Grandmother's legacy plus my earnings to purchase a respectable house with a garden and, hopefully, a distant sea view.

I do hope you'll be able to meet Fenella if you return for your autumn interlude in the Old Country....

*Far Horizons, St. Ives
June 1, 1927
Dear Edward,
Our honeymoon in Paris was a great success, and my bride is now eager to decorate our new home. I'm delighted that she likes it as much as I do.
What a stroke of luck to find this modern house perched on the hillside with magnificent views of the sea from its many large windows! It has a generous garden with a splendid stone terrace from whence we can also observe the sea in all its moods - serene, seductive, tempestuous, terrifying.
It's less than half a mile from the shop, thus an easy walk, and I can actually see the edge of the building from our height.
Talia was happy to take over the flat, and also to take charge of the shop more often so that Fenella and I have time together. Summers are so busy that I usually have little time to myself. You know all about that!
We have a guest bedroom for you if you visit this fall....*

It was strange to read her grandfather's thoughts when he was younger than she was now. No matter how close she had been to Delia, Nan had always been an elderly lady, and Paige had no inkling of what thoughts and dreams she'd had when she was young. These letters provided a unique glimpse into Cliff's past.

And she could see the fractures in the marriage forming quite early on.

*Far Horizons, St. Ives
September 1, 1928
Fenella misses her family and their "exciting" social activities, so she frequently visits them. I go along for a few days when I can, but she stays for extended periods. Shopping trips to London with her cousins and country house weekends at her titled sister's estate leave her exhausted and fractious when she returns. She's not fond of my friends, whom she fears may be immoral Bohemians (like her*

wayward sister "living in sin") or dreaded Communists, since they seem to "revile prosperity", which is nonsense, of course. They just don't prioritize accumulating wealth, but rather, gain satisfaction from their creative endeavours. Any income beyond that necessary for comfortable living is a welcome bonus.

Now that she's with child, Fenella's feeling the constraints of her condition and bemoaning the reality that she'll have to settle down to domestic life and curb her travelling. Fortunately, she has an allowance for a couple of domestic staff through her dowery, so a nanny will join the cook-housekeeper, the latter having a home to return to at the end of the day.

The following years delivered more tidbits of a crumbling marriage, after the initial elation of their daughter's birth. And it seemed that 1932 was the last time that Edward visited England.

Far Horizons, St. Ives
October 31, 1933

I must say I miss your annual visit, but of course you can't leave Florence when she's enceinte. I will pray that this time all will be well, and you can enjoy fatherhood as I do.

Although only four (and three-quarters, she keeps reminding me), Isobel is precocious, already reading simple books with me. She particularly loves Winnie-the-Pooh and Beatrix Potter stories. She has inspired me to write little nursery rhymes for her, which she helps me create. What fun we have! She's my greatest joy.

I think that Fenella and her sisters suffer from having had a series of incompetent governesses. Their father believes girls don't need education beyond speaking French and comporting themselves in society. Their younger brother – the long-awaited heir - received the finest at Eton but was sent down from Oxford. That I achieved a First there rankles them both. The heir has been shipped out to the family tea plantation in Ceylon.

Isobel also loves to draw, and is illustrating our verses under Talia's tutelage, which both enjoy.

Talia has married the sculptor you met last year, and they have a house and studio not far from the shop. Thankfully, she still helps out. She sends her best and says she'll miss your weird and wonderful tales of life in Canada.

Again, no surnames, but Paige was hopeful that Talia-possibly-Swan and her sculptor husband would trigger some information from the Tate Gallery in St. Ives.

Paige was determined to also try to find where Cliff's bookshop had been. She already had an inkling from descriptions in the letters, especially with regard to a church between him and the harbour. But she didn't remember the ancient part of the town well enough to picture it. If it was the medieval church she was thinking of, she did recall having a strange feeling of déjà vu there. And a house named Far Horizons could still exist.

What fun mysteries to unlock for information about her grandfather's life. And she definitely wanted to know about Isobel. Her aunt! She could surely still be alive. As could Cliff's sister's children and grandchildren. But Abigail was probably right that she should never reveal her kinship to them.

Paige was interested to realize that Cliff had also married unwisely and was happy with a divorce. It made her feel less like a failure to admit defeat and move on.

But she did wonder how Nan would have felt leaving behind her treasured home and cottage, her dearest friend, Esther, and the comfortable life that she'd made for herself in the vacuum of her marriage. And if love was strong enough for no regrets, just ecstasy at being together in Cornwall or wherever they ended up.

Paige tried not to dwell on the intense connection she had once again felt in Simon's arms. And what that could mean.

We touch as two, become one
Nothing twixt my love and me,
Our souls sing in harmony
And vow to share eternity.

Chapter 13

"You're always welcome to stay here," Simon offered Paige when he delivered her things, as well as the latest box of documents she'd been going through to his boathouse suite after Sunday breakfast. Her suitcases would be transferred to the inn later. "Freshly cleaned and no dock spiders."

The boathouse was built in the early '20s to shelter the family's rowboat, canoes, and the two motorboats crafted by Fred Hawksley, as well as providing a private retreat on the upper level for guests. It was a lofty, airy space, with the bedroom and sitting room both having unimpeded views of the lake through French doors opening onto the deck, as well as through the windows on three sides. There was a bathroom with a granite shower stall, and a kitchenette with a sink, bar fridge, microwave, kettle, and coffee maker. Comfy chairs and a couch faced the distant islands, while an ample new desk and office chair were situated in front of one of the windows looking towards the wharf. The long, partly roofed deck hosted inviting Muskoka and lounge chairs.

It was very tempting, especially since Cliff had stayed here.

But she didn't want Brett here, where she and Simon had secretly, blissfully made love numerous times that last summer. Although they'd tried to evade Rebecca, she'd obviously been spying on them. The thought made Paige shiver, as if Bex were here now. Still watching.

"Thanks, I'll keep that in mind."

He looked at her as if reading her thoughts, and turned away, saying, "The offer stands if you change your mind."

"I appreciate that. OK, I'll just grab my camera and I'm ready to go."

Simon was taking the day off, and they were meeting Marshall and his crew at the Hidden Cove Lodge. Because the dock there was unusable, they drove over in Simon's Volvo.

Ignoring the *No Trespassing* signs, they bumped along the potholed gravel access road only a few miles away. The woods were encroaching so that there was barely one lane, although someone had been keeping the centre cleared for vehicles.

A deer suddenly leapt out in front of them, and Simon slammed on the brakes, barely missing it.

"Good thing we couldn't drive any faster along here!" he said with relief, as he slowed to a crawl. "We're the intruders now."

"Maybe there'll be deer to film around the resort. That would add a nice touch."

But all they saw were a few turkey vultures peering down at them from the edge of the roof smashed open by an uprooted pine, and a dozen or more perched in the trees above.

Paige found their silent scrutiny unnerving.

"This decay into oblivion is the stuff of nightmares," Simon admitted as he parked behind the derelict hotel.

"I dreamt about Westwind being engulfed by a monstrous creeping vine the other night," Paige ventured. "And dead people were looking out at me. Including Bex."

Before Simon could respond, his cell phone rang.

"Hi, Tony.... Yes, we're fine.... Oh! Well, we almost hit a deer. ... Not at all. I appreciate you looking after them.... Sure thing!"

Paige held her breath, suspecting what Simon was about to say.

"The clock chimed."

They looked at each other with trepidation.

"Tony heard it as well, but the Pembrook sisters were upset, so he offered to call me."

"Let's hope the deer was the reason." Although she didn't think it had been a life-threatening situation.

As if reading her thoughts, he replied, "Those can be serious encounters. A heavy, hooved body flying through the windshield."

But as the film crew's van pulled up behind them, he said, "Maybe you should stay in the car."

"Only if you do," she challenged.

He hesitated. "Then we'll stick together."

There had been a short downpour in the early morning and there was hardly a path through the dripping, sometimes waist-high vegetation to the veranda.

"We have to be careful where we tread," Marshall warned. "*Use at your own risk*, I was told, and no entry into the lodge. It's unsafe. Paige, you walk behind one of us, and if something cracks, back off!" he ordered sternly, and then winked at her.

The white paint had flaked off most of the building, exposing weathered and splintered wood. The resort had always been more rustic than Westwind, several extensions seemingly cobbled together at different angles and tied together with uneven veranda railings made of sticks topped with thin logs. The veranda roof was supported by crudely hewn poles, some split along their length. That had once given the building antiquated charm, but now it seemed slightly sinister.

Vigorous saplings were muscling up through broken boards, reclaiming dominion on the open end of the veranda, so they avoided that section. But even under the roof, boards were spongy and rotting, so they stayed close to the building.

Paige and Simon took photos while Pierre was filming. Terry wandered onto the rocky promontory, since he wasn't needed until their next stop.

The main level door and window openings had boards zigzagged across them, which left large gaps to see and film the inside.

The reception desk still looked solid, as did the bottom of the staircase next to it. But the landing partway up was open to the sky two stories above, and littered with broken beams and years of decomposing leaves and twigs. Pinecones paraded down the stairs.

In the lounge dominated by a massive fireplace constructed of random-sized boulders, stained wallpaper hung limply from some walls while black mould claimed others. The ceiling buckled ominously in places. Bright green moss, studded with broken glass shards, grew luxuriantly on carpets. Cobwebs were everywhere, making Paige shiver.

She and Simon went ahead while Marshall was directing Pierre for interior footage. Their photos would inform the script, and were easier and more descriptive than writing notes.

Beneath the spray-painted "Highway to Hell" graffiti on the far wall of what had probably been the dining room, Paige noticed a bevy of empty beer tins marching six abreast towards the centre of the room littered with chip bags and overflowing ashtrays inside a circle of deflated air mattresses. Judging by the number of cans, this had been a party scene for a large group or the regular haunt of a small band of rebellious teens.

The boards blocking one of the tall windows, which stopped a couple of feet short of the floor, had been pried loose and hung from just one nail on either side. The window opening had been mostly cleared of glass, and the shards inside had been roughly swept into piles, making for easy ingress. She snapped a couple of pictures.

Simon was standing by the railing taking a photo of the veranda that kept meandering along. "This is a cool perspective! A crooked line of pioneer craftsmanship. Really tells a story of how home-made some of these places were."

As she headed towards him, the hair at the nape of her neck suddenly stood on end and she had an overwhelming sense that something catastrophic was about to happen. An image flashed through her mind. She flew to Simon, screaming "Run!" and yanked him back just as there was a tremendous crack.

She dashed to the window opening and jumped through. Simon joined her just as the veranda roof collapsed and crashed through the rotting floor.

He pulled her toward the windowless back wall and embraced her protectively as everything shook and debris flew, shattering windows. It seemed as if the entire building were imploding. But Paige realized that they'd been under the short section that had second and third floor balconies, which had rested on the veranda roof.

When the dust settled, they could see nothing but a pile of sodden, splintered wood where the veranda had been, and the unconcerned blue sky beyond.

"Marshall!" she cried frantically.

"Watch where you're walking," Simon cautioned, trying to avoid broken glass as he led her through the lounge. Fortunately, she was wearing rubber soled boating shoes and not sandals.

She almost wept with relief to see that where Marshall and Pierre had been filming was now on the precipice of the severed veranda, with the broken roof drooping precariously, but that they, along with Terry, were yelling and waving from solid ground beyond.

"We'll make our way to a back exit," Simon shouted to them. "We might need help getting out."

Marshall gave two thumbs up.

It was eerie to be barricaded inside a crumbling building, which reeked of mould and rot and other putrid smells, Paige thought as they walked down a dark hallway alongside the stairs. Simon was brushing away the cobwebs in their path. She jumped when something dashed past her, but it was just a chipmunk.

They passed the closed doors of "Gentlemen" and "Ladies" washrooms, a corridor that led to the vast kitchen in one direction and probably offices in the other, to a foyer where they found an outside door.

Simon unlocked it and drew back the thick bolt. The opening was criss-crossed by solidly nailed planks, and beyond it was the leaning trunk of the hefty pine that had crashed through the roof, its shallow but extensive tangle of roots reaching skyward. Afraid that the building was now more soggy matchsticks than robust wood, Paige was nervous being beneath the tree's descending path.

Marshall, who was scanning the back of the building, came over to them. Fortunately, there was no veranda along this side.

"I've never been so ecstatic to see anyone in my entire life! But we still have to extricate you safely. So, the last room to your left has a slider window that isn't too far off the ground. It only has two boards across, which we can easily pry off. The guys have gone to fetch tools from the van. Or we can call the fire department to rescue you," he teased.

"I think we can manage the first option," Simon retorted with a chuckle.

When they located the room, Terry was already atop a step ladder removing the wood. From her previous work with the crew, Paige knew that the van was like Mary Poppins' magic carpetbag, containing seemingly odd and endless things that usually came in handy at some time.

Simon unlocked the window and lifted out the panes, albeit with some difficulty, as the building had been settling. They handed their cameras to Terry.

Paige was glad she was wearing a split skirt, but it was still awkward to throw a leg over the chest-high window.

Simon squatted and offered a knee. With his boost and her hands on the windowsill, she swung her free leg onto the ladder, which Marshall and Pierre were steadying on the uneven ground below. Simon wasn't far behind.

"Jeez, that was a helluva close call!" Marshall said, giving Paige a relieved hug.

"How did you know to warn me?" Simon asked her.

"It was only an instant before. A premonition."

"Thank your guardian angel for that!" Marshall proclaimed.

Thank you, Nan. And Granddad.

"It was bizarre, but from the bluff I saw a dozen or more vultures land on the top of the third-floor balcony roof. And suddenly everything collapsed!" Terry said.

"I heard the terror in your voice when you shouted, Paige," Pierre said. "But it all happened so fast that we didn't even run until we saw you leap into the building and everything started to come down. Luckily, we were close to the stairs."

"Thank God that you noticed that unblocked window," Simon added. "We probably wouldn't have made it far enough away along the veranda."

That sobering thought struck silence.

A vulture circled down towards them with a guttural hiss. They began to duck but it rose majestically on its immense wingspan.

"That was creepy," Pierre said.

"We had vultures around our farm when I was growing up," Terry said. "Seems like that's the only sound they make. When they feel threatened. But they're no threat to us. And only eat dead things."

"I trust they weren't trying to hasten our demise for their larder," Marshall quipped. "OK, let's get some exterior footage from a distance and then split. Demolition begins here Tuesday. We'll film that from the boat."

In the car, Simon suggested, "Maybe we shouldn't tell anyone what happened. It might upset the sisters."

"Unless they don't believe the deer story. They have an uncanny knack of knowing what we're thinking."

"True enough."

Simon glanced over at her. "How can I ever thank you for saving my life? You should have just run."

"That's not what friends do," she replied, trying to keep the mood light. "I reacted instinctively. With Delia and Cliff looking after me...." She realized her blunder.

"What does *he* have to do with anything?"

Fearing that Simon was going to break down her defences, she thought it best to divert his attention. Admitting the truth about Cliff was less dangerous than the truth about herself.

"That's tragic. And amazing. So, you're actually his granddaughter! Wow! Another secret the sisters managed to keep all these years."

"What are their other ones?"

"Not mine to tell," Simon admitted, keeping his eyes on the road.

"I can guess that Emmeline and Edward were lovers."

He shrugged.

"Well, I'm happy for them, although sorry for your grandmother, if it's true. Just as I am for what little time Nan and Cliff had together."

"Things aren't always what they seem."

                ■   ■   ■

After a busy afternoon out in *Diva*, filming at Windermere House and other places on the lake, Paige and Simon returned by boat from Arcadia. Marshall and his guys were going to have a relaxing evening there, and feast on frozen meals which Duncan had supplied to keep Marshall properly fed. Although he knew how to cook, he was apt to open a tin of stew or settle for a TV dinner.

Simon had work to catch up on, so Paige was planning a quiet evening reading Cliff's novel.

Her new room offered a much different perspective of the resort than the cabin had. Set atop a gently sloping rise, the inn already had a high perch, but from the third floor there was an even loftier view of the dock, lake, and busy waterfront activities. Majestic maples provided a sculpted, shady canopy and tall pines punctuated the scene without blocking her view.

Because it was changeover Sunday, some of the kitchen and dining room staff took their half day off by sunbathing on the dock, swimming, and canoeing. Cottagers arrived for ice cream or food and drinks at the rooftop bar, as did those too early to check into their rooms, but eager to begin their vacations.

Paige already felt much more part of the social life here, and was reassured by being next door to the Pembrook sisters.

Like their room, hers had a couple of comfy wingback chairs, coffee table, dresser, and an armoire hiding a small TV, bar fridge, and coffee maker, but no desk or other work surface. These old-fashioned rooms were still intended for carefree holidays and plenty of time spent on outdoor activities or in communal spaces.

There were two single beds, which would annoy Brett, but they could be pushed together to make a short king-sized bed.

A picture window flanked by screened casement windows dominated the end wall next to the screened door onto the spacious roofed balcony, where two Muskoka chairs sat invitingly.

The only other balconies in this building were the two below them, which sat atop the roof of the veranda that stretched along the front of the inn to the north end of the building, where she could see the fire escape. If she couldn't get to it from the far end of her hallway, she'd only have to clamber down a veranda post from her balcony to the top of the railing below and hop over. *Yeah, right.* But after what Marshall had told her about the many inns that had succumbed to fires, she knew it was a serious consideration.

At this height, Paige figured she wouldn't even need to close her curtains for privacy, except when changing into pjs at night. What a treat to watch the sunrise from her bed!

Having spent most of her previous summers in the same two-bedroom cabin, it was interesting to experience the original inn, which had so many decades of history behind it.

But when she stepped into the hallway and was confronted by the door to the tower, she tried to ignore the twinge of uneasiness.

▪   ▪   ▪

She was about to go down to dinner with the Pembrook sisters when her room phone rang.

"So you are there, babe! I couldn't reach you on your cell."

"I have a room in the inn now. Bad reception perhaps. Sounds like you're at a party." She could hear chatter and laughter in the background. Plenty of women's voices.

"Dean's wife invited a few neighbours over. We just got back from a terrific afternoon of sailing."

She could almost see the self-satisfied smile on his face, and had a sudden vision of his arm around Alexis as he dutifully called little wifey.

"How nice for you."

"Everything going well there?"

She could tell from his voice that he was focusing on someone else as they spoke. And also, that he'd already had a few drinks.

"Sure. Narrowly avoided getting killed today, so I'm fine."

He chortled. "You do have a quirky sense of humour."

"It helps me deal with unpleasant situations. You seem to be enjoying yourself."

"It's a blast spending time with my old friend. Stunning place, terrific hosts. We're going to stay in touch more. Anyway, I just wanted to check in with you."

"I'm off to dinner now."

"Sunday turkey?" he asked snidely, since that's what they'd had when he was here.

"That's right. One of my favourites."

"Dean has his own gourmet chef. Best surf and turf I've ever had. Well, enjoy yourself in your ancient inn. I'll let you know when I'm home."

Paige slammed down the receiver. *Bastard!*

But then she realized that was exactly why she needed and wanted to leave him. She would tell him when he came up for the weekend, although she didn't really want to have a confrontation here. But it seemed harsh and impersonal just to phone and say, "I want out. Don't bother coming."

She was in a better mood when she joined the sisters for dinner, and filled them in on the places they'd filmed that afternoon.

"It's sad that so many resorts have vanished. But I guess it's also rather telling that most of them have been replaced by single cottages," Paige said. "We filmed some mega-mansions today, which we'll juxtapose against historical footage."

"People complain about the rich flaunting their wealth with ostentatious lakeside estates, but they're no different from the 12-bedroom, 8-bath, 10,000 square foot cottages built by millionaires in the last century, now deemed historical treasures. And those weren't even all-season," Abigail scoffed. "Except that they were usually tucked into the landscape so that you *couldn't* see how enormous they are."

"Arcadia only has eight bedrooms and four baths," Paige said with a grin.

They laughed.

"Now tell us what *really* happened this morning, dear," Emmeline prodded gently.

"What makes you think something did?" Paige asked, not looking up from her apple pie and ice cream.

"I sensed that it wasn't the deer."

"Em didn't stop fretting until we saw you all return for lunch," Abigail added.

"I'm sorry we caused you such distress, Miss Emmeline!"

"Tosh! We can't help worrying about our cherished friends. But that's not your responsibility. Nor is danger something you should keep secret. In fact, Edward's clock warns us so that we have a chance to intervene."

"You're right." She downplayed the danger when she gave them an expurgated summary of the events.

They looked at her with raised eyebrows. Hastily she added, "I'm sure knowing about the clock chiming put me on high alert. So thank you for that!"

"Your sixth sense," Emmeline said. Her expression softened as she placed her hand on Paige's. "We have much to be thankful for right now. If you need any help or just some company, let us know. You've had a terrible shock."

Paige could almost feel Emmeline's blue eyes probing her mind.

"An early night, I think."

"We sleep lightly these days, so knock loudly on the wall anytime."

"That's very reassuring." Paige hesitated. "You haven't felt anything unusual from the tower across the hall, have you?"

"Never! In fact, it was one of our favourite places. We felt so privileged to be included in the cocktail hours that Edward presided over there. Camaraderie with like-minded souls. Fascinating conversation."

"I wish I could have experienced that! I sometimes feel that I did, in a way. I have strong images of the '20s and '30s. Or at least I think they are."

"I expect you felt those through Cordelia's dress as well as Arcadia. Artifacts from the past seem to retain impressions."

■   ■   ■

Emmeline knocked on the open office door. "May I come in, dear boy?"

"Of course," Simon replied, rising from behind his desk.

She shut the door firmly behind her. "We'll be undisturbed?"

"Yes. Veronica's at the pavilion."

She sat in the chair opposite his. "Tell me what happened today. Paige was rather vague, so I expect she was sparing us the worst."

He hesitated. "It could have ended badly."

"How badly?" She riveted him with her sharp eyes.

He tried to minimize the risk, but she realized, nonetheless. "So, you could both have been killed."

"Possibly."

She sighed deeply as she leaned tiredly into the chair. "Thank God for her instincts. And Edward's warning!"

"Yes."

"When are you going to realize that she still loves you? . . . Oh, I know I promised never to interfere in your life, but she's *hurting*. I can feel it!"

He ran his fingers through his hair. "She's married."

"Not happily, Simon."

■   ■   ■

"Hey, Kiddo, how are you doing now?" Marshall asked over the phone.

"I'm OK. Reading Cliff's novel, so that puts me into a different space."

"Good!" He hesitated. "I don't want to distress you, but thought you'd better know. Terry confided that he saw something so bizarre that he didn't say anything at first. But he realized it could be a portent."

Paige tensed.

"Before the vultures descended onto the upper balcony, he thought he saw a girl with red hair standing there. It was just for an instant, which is why he didn't believe his eyes. But it's been bothering him. He has a sensitivity to *atmosphere*, as he calls it. Asked me if Arcadia has ghosts."

"Oh my God, that sounds like Rebecca!"

"That's what I was afraid of. Do you think she's been orchestrating the strange incidents?"

"I think she's been trying to scare me away. But I can't believe that she'd harm Simon. She was obsessed with him. He just told me a couple of days ago about how difficult she'd made his life."

"Hmm."

"Oh hell! I know what you're thinking!"

"Was she vindictive?"

"She had the potential."

Paige remembered Bex bragging to her that she'd been expelled within a few weeks from Brightwell Academy in Toronto, where she – like all Hawksley girls and their Rowan cousins in decades past – had been sent. "The Davenports were going to ship me off to another boarding school in the city, but I threatened to burn it down if they did!"

"Why?" Paige had asked.

"Because I don't want to be shuffled off like I'm just a nuisance! At least Simon cares about me and he comes home some weekends! So I want to be *here*!"

Simon's prestigious private school at the top end of the lake was only a twenty-minute car or boat ride away.

"I don't care that it's a frigging long bus ride to the high school in town! And I stay with the Rowans when the Davenports need their *winter holiday*." She'd said it as if that had been a huge imposition on her life.

"Be careful. Both of you," Marshall advised.

Chapter 14

Paige wondered why the hall lights were so dim and unable to dispel the thick twilight gloom. The opening to the tower was less dense, as if long fingers of dawn were reaching down along with the music that summoned her.

"I Know You're Out There Somewhere"

"Simon?" She started up the stairs. Faint laughter and whispers drifted down, but she couldn't make out the words.

But only Bex was at the top of the stairs. Exultant. Crazed. Her wiry red curls seemed ablaze as she threw back her head and laughed maliciously. Like a glowing match, she set the tower around her on fire.

Paige fled down the stairs that kept twisting and turning as heat and smoke chased her, until she finally reached the bottom. But the door wouldn't open.

She screamed as the flames licked closer.

And awoke with a pounding heart and a panic attack about to seize control.

Careful not to disturb the sisters, she went onto the balcony, breathing deeply of the life-affirming air and finding solace in the infinite stars on a moonless night, perfectly reflected in the bottomless black lake.

Knowing that sleep would elude her, she decided to take her camera and tripod down to the waterfront. She dressed quickly and was glad that the old wooden door could be closed quietly. She didn't want to disturb anyone at 3:30 AM.

Glancing at the door to the tower, she shivered and hurried away. The wall sconces above the dark Victorian wainscoting flickered, making the empty hallway sinister. For a moment it felt as if only ghosts dwelt behind the dozen closed doors.

She was relieved to be outside and glad that the landscape lighting was adequate to find her way, yet reduced from its pre-midnight festiveness that included fairy lights around the rooftop bar and well-lit paths.

The lights at the corners of the gazebo on the wharf were subtle enough that she was able to shoot towards the south without too much ambient distraction. Fortunately, there were no blazing cottage lights spilling onto the glassy lake, merely pinpoints on distant docks that shimmered across the water amid the sparkling stars and magnificent Milky Way. It was awe inspiring.

Through her lens, a canoe emerged from the darkness along the shore. Despite the nighttime silence, there was barely a sound from the rhythmic dip of the paddle. Paige held her breath, wondering if it was another glimpse into the past or an apparition.

"It's a magical night," Simon said as he came closer. "I couldn't sleep either."

She sighed with relief. "Amazing what we miss when we snooze. This is far better."

She snapped a photo of him adrift between the sublime heavens and envious lake. "Do you do this often?"

"When I need time to myself. To escape the busyness of summer days. To seek my place in the universe. Usually, I just skinny-dip from my boathouse. That's when I really feel like I'm part of this glorious nature."

Paige wondered if she'd ever have the courage to brave the lake in the dark again, despite fond memories of skinny-dipping with the women at Arcadia.

"But tonight, it's to celebrate still being around to do so. Thanks to you."

She could feel him drawing her close, and was glad she couldn't see his face too clearly or it might be her undoing. "And thanks to our grandfathers and Nan."

He chuckled. "Good champions to have in our court."

"Simon . . . Marshall told me something disturbing." She went on to relate Terry's sighting.

"Hell!" He dropped his head as if in anguish, and then looked at her. "How do we rid ourselves of Bex's vicious meddling?"

"I don't know. I've asked her nicely to leave us alone."

"Then I will as well, next time she's near. And *not* nicely if necessary."

•   •   •

At breakfast, Paige said to the sisters, "My door was so stuck this morning I thought I'd have to call for help." She'd been surprised, since it had opened easily in the middle of the night.

"That's the arthritic old building showing its age," Abigail said. "Like us, it doesn't do well with the humidity."

"I don't like having the AC on, especially here. It was lovely to have the door and windows open to feel a gentle breeze and hear the nighttime sounds of nature."

"Our sentiments exactly!"

"Did you go out for a walk in the night?" Emmeline asked.

"Not sleepwalking, fortunately. I went to take photos. There was a spectacular sky."

"Indeed! I looked out as well. It didn't feel like a night for sleeping." Emmeline's smile seemed to indicate that she had seen more than she was letting on.

Before the sisters could wheedle information from her, she changed the subject as she nonchalantly buttered her toast. "You can tell me to mind my own business, but I'm curious to know why neither of you married. You're both smart, talented, accomplished, beautiful women. I can't believe men weren't lining up to win your hearts." Her crispy bite from the bread put paid to their previous conversation.

Abigail chortled. "Thank you for putting intelligence before beauty. And there's your answer. We seemed to intimidate men."

"Also because we told them that our careers were important to us," Emmeline added.

"It was difficult to find men like our father, who didn't look at us as ornaments or possessions. It wasn't easy to be an independent woman in those days. Bluestockings they called us derisively because we'd gone to university."

"But your parents encouraged you?"

"Oh yes! Mother had strong opinions about women's rights and abilities. She wasn't allowed to attend university – that was before the turn of the century, when women weren't admitted. Convinced that the way for women to gain equality was for them to be as educated as men, she became a teacher and encouraged girls to dream big and fulfil their potential.

"She was thirty when she met Father. Her soulmate, who believed in her and her ideals. He'd had rheumatic fever as a child, which left him with a damaged heart, so he was privately tutored at home and thus had a different perspective on life than most men. His was also a kind heart, and he was a thoughtful, sincere person. So, she agreed to marry him, which meant she had to quit her teaching career. Not something she did lightly. Married women weren't allowed to teach in those days."

"So my parents have told me!" Paige admitted.

"Father worked in the family printing business, which he'd inherited, and it provided us with a comfortable life. Mother helped him with correspondence and record keeping, but also became a volunteer in the community, teaching English to immigrants. Always encouraging the women to strive beyond the narrow boundaries defining 'wife' and 'mother.'"

"Until she fell gravely ill with the influenza in 1918. I remember how scared we were that we would lose her," Emmeline said. "I was six and Abby was eight."

"She recovered slowly, but never completely. Which is how we ended up spending every summer here. She was so proud of us getting into university, and took great pleasure in hearing about our classes. She delighted in reading the prescribed texts, which would stimulate dinner table conversations.

"Father was devasted when she died in '32. His damaged heart was now completely broken, and he passed away only three months later."

"Reminding us what he and Mother had always advised – seek fulfilment and happiness, and choose a partner wisely," Emmeline added.

"Ergo, we remained single. That doesn't mean we didn't have *romances*," Abigail said with a twinkle in her eyes. "You probably know that the Roaring Twenties were rather wild – a reaction to the enormity of death and uncertainty of life brought about by the war and the pandemic – and rapidly changed society. Somewhat like the '60s – except it was 'free love', booze, and jazz in our day, not 'sex, drugs, and rock and roll'. But I have no regrets. Ironically, the men I dated had qualities I admired, but which would have made them lousy husbands. They were ambitious, charismatic, and dazzled by their own brilliance."

Paige chuckled. "It's so much easier for us these days, when it's no longer sinful to live together before or without marriage, or have children out of wedlock."

"Or scandalous and difficult to divorce," Abigail said pointedly.

• • •

Paige and Simon had cleverly choreographed the filming of him discussing the resort, based around vintage photos, which they'd already selected, and film clips that Abigail said she could provide.

Former staff from different eras had engaging tales of their experiences and the bonds they had formed with the Davenports, this loyalty bringing them back whenever possible.

Paige could tell that Simon was deeply touched by their sentiments.

They had fun interviewing the two dozen members of the exuberant Skipton family, who travelled from various locations in Canada and the United States for their bi-annual family reunion week. The grandparents had honeymooned here post-war and had brought their five children for a few weeks most summers. The one who lived in Toronto was now considering buying into the Westwind Beach Club so that the clan would always have a foothold here.

Paige had helped to teach a few of the oldest grandchildren, now in their early 20s, to waterski, so it was a reunion for her as well.

The Pembrook sisters were eager to catch up with the elderly Skiptons, with whom they had often socialized over the past forty years. They had become part of Edward's circle, the Professor (now Emeritus) leading lively discussions on Canadian identity and culture, or lack thereof.

Over cocktails on the veranda with them, Emmeline felt that extra link to Edward, and revelled in those happy memories.

"I feel like I missed out on a great summer job when I was young," Pierre said during the crew's dinner that evening. "I worked in a stinky factory in the city. This would have been paradise."

"And I was stuck on the farm," Terry said. "But at least I was able to work outdoors."

"There'll be fewer summer jobs for students as resorts close or become four-season," Simon speculated. "And it's the end of the waterski school here."

Breaking the melancholy silence, Marshall quipped, "I hope you sold them the butter tart recipe. That's gotta be worth a million bucks."

They laughed.

But Paige felt overwhelmingly nostalgic, and sad that this was all going to change so drastically. She would never again be part of what had sustained her soul.

■   ■   ■

"Hey, babe, is this a good time to talk?" Brett asked.

"As good as any." She had just returned from dinner and had been expecting him to call. "I take it you're safely home."

"Yes. It was a terrific weekend."

There was a long pause, and she sensed what was coming.

"You were right. About several things. It's been fun, but it was a mistake."

"Is this about Alexis? Chad said I should ask you about her when he groped me at your parents' pool a few weeks ago and suggested we retire to the cabana."

"What the hell?! . . . Jeez! I'm sorry, Paige."

She said nothing into the silence.

"I'll get him for that! The bastard! . . . But he's right."

"Why didn't you tell me sooner? Why the elaborate ruse of buying a condo here?" She couldn't help the bitterness.

"I wanted you to have something that would make you happy."

"Since you couldn't anymore. So what happened to that?" She suspected his father had nixed it.

"It just makes things more complicated."

"You don't have to buy me out to ease your conscience. I've spent too much time feeling miserable and inadequate because I suspected you were having affairs."

"Not plural."

"That's some consolation, I suppose," she scoffed. "But I was going to end this as well."

He was momentarily silent, probably surprised that she didn't consider him good enough. "Because of Simon?"

"No. Because I want my freedom. To be happy again. In whatever way that works for me."

"I see." He paused. "I never wanted to hurt you, Paige. You're a sweet, kind, wonderful person. I still love you as a friend."

She felt a pang as some happy memories surfaced.

"You can take over the house," he offered. "It was never my style. I'll opt for something modern."

And grandiose enough to suit Alexis.

"I have no desire to live there now, so let's just sell it. I'll come to pack when it's convenient. I have a busy few weeks here."

"There's no great hurry. And I won't be around much."

Were you ever really? "I'll have my lawyer contact you."

"Paige..."

"Goodbye, Brett."

She had a cathartic cry despite feeling relief that it was finally over. After she rinsed away the tears, she phoned Marshall.

"Could you please ask Larry to recommend a divorce lawyer?"

"Aww, Kiddo, I'm sorry. But not surprised."

"Why?"

"Gavin overheard some talk at the restaurant that Brett's old flame was winning him back."

"Oh, hell! The talk of the town now, are we? I'd already decided that I needed to liberate myself. Being back here in my favourite, happy place has made me realize how *unhappy* I've been for a while. And how you can become lulled into complacency and inertia even when you're often miserable.

"I should have trusted my instincts and not married Brett. But he was persuasive, and I was flattered that a rich, handsome, talented Prince Charming swore he loved only me. At first, he made me feel like the most important person in his life. But then he became too busy to spend much time with me. He had more *business* dinners and trips where I wasn't included, and I began to suspect his fidelity.

"So, I'm hurt and insulted, but not heartbroken. And actually looking forward to my new life."

"Good for you!"

"Don't turn down any business from Brett on my account. It should be a relatively amicable parting of ways."

"Larry will ensure you get a fair settlement. He has divorce attorneys on staff used to dealing with wealthy people."

"Not sure I can afford them!"

"They'll more than earn their fee, Kiddo. Brett's father's a bit of a bastard, I've heard. He'll try to find ways for Brett to not pay his dues. Even if he wants to."

"I'm not surprised. I don't even want to go back to the city. I'll go home."

"You can stay at Arcadia anytime. I know my parents enjoy your company, and Dunc and Gav would spoil you when they're here."

"Thanks! I might have to do that to finish my interviews with locals and archival research here."

"Are you OK for tomorrow, or do you want some time off?"

"There is nothing I'd rather do than work."

"Need a shoulder to cry on?"

"Nope, but thanks. We can quietly toast my freedom next time we dine."

He chuckled. "Atta girl!"

"By the way, I'm not going to tell anyone else yet, except on an as-needed basis. And I don't want my parents to worry while they're abroad. But I don't mind if you tell Duncan and Gavin, since they already know something's wrong."

Not long after, Paige had another call.

"Hello, Pet. Gav and I are sorry things haven't worked out for you, but Marshall says you're actually happy to get out of that relationship. That's brilliant! We've been worried. Let us know if there's anything we can do to help."

"That's so kind! I'll look forward to a freedom celebration with you soon."

"We'll host it here or at Arcadia. Whenever you're ready."

"I'd love that! Thank you. You've made me feel valued. I haven't in Brett's world."

She heard the catch in Duncan's voice before he said, "Nothing but the best for you, Pet."

"Love you both."

Chapter 15

The hands clawing at the canoe almost reached her this time. Paige awakened in relief, but was momentarily confused as to where she was. The pre-dawn light creeping in gave some form to the room.

An icy breath touched her, shocking in the warm night. She jumped out of bed and turned on a light. There was nothing obvious in the room. Just an eerie sense that she wasn't alone.

Something shone on the carpet beside the wastebasket. It was the silver dragonfly necklace Brett had bought her. She'd left it on the dresser beside her talisman rock and on the other side from the bin, so even a strong gust blowing through the screens couldn't have carried it that far. And she wouldn't have done that herself. Would she? Had she sleepwalked and thrown it on the floor in anger? But it was a work of art that she treasured and wore daily. A farewell present from Brett, she figured. And bought in Port Carling, it symbolized the end of her life with him and her return to where her heart belonged.

"Bex, stop playing your nasty games! I wish you'd go away!"

She thought she heard a faint chuckle, but a mourning dove landed on her balcony railing and began its familiar lament. She knew that its wings made a strange cackling noise.

There was no point trying to get back to sleep, so she showered, dressed, and took her camera to her boathouse "office".

Although the house was on higher ground, the boathouse had been set south of it so as not to impede any lake views. And also, Paige suspected, because the rocky shoreline dipped down on that side. From a small bridge, a few steps led up to the suite's door, and a longer stretch of stairs angled down to a flagstone terrace, which was sheltered from the resort as well as the house and the prevailing winds. A round dining set with a sky-blue market umbrella and several white Muskoka chairs were interspersed with flowerpots spilling over with colourful annuals. A hot tub was tucked up beside the building.

The terrace adjoined the dock that flanked the south side and the entrance to the three boat slips inside, one occupied by *Miss Chief*. Through there, the dock along the other side of the building could also be accessed. Both had swim ladders at the deep ends, but there were also a couple of steps from the terrace into the lake.

Crossing the short bridge to the suite felt like entering sanctuary. Paige made coffee and got to work, glancing out occasionally to check if there was a photogenic sunrise blossoming.

She tensed when she heard footsteps on the stairs.

There was a knock on the door and Simon entered saying, "You're an early bird." He was in his bathing trunks with a beach towel draped around his neck. "I noticed the light was on, and just wanted to be sure that everything was OK."

"I thought I'd get an early start."

"You can join me for a swim, if you'd like."

"Sure!" She was glad she'd left a bikini here and changed quickly.

Swimming parallel to the shore and away from the awakening resort, she was reassured to have Simon as her safety barrier to the deep water. It was invigorating.

They swam as far as a rocky point where the undulating Ridge Dragon nosedived into the lake, and where the water became deep. It was the southern boundary of the Davenport property, so they turned and did a few more laps, and then sat on the terrace to watch the sunrise as they dried off.

"I can't think of a better way to greet the day," Paige sighed contentedly.

"I realized when I spent those years in Toronto that I'm not a city person for long," Simon admitted. "At least I was home in the summers then, but I would miss this every day if I had to live there now."

"Do you still swim from the time the ice is out in spring until late fall?"

"Yup. The hot tub helps."

"I envy you." He looked at her curiously, so she elaborated. "Now that I've reconnected with the lake, I realize how much I've missed it. Of course, I can always stay at Arcadia."

"You're welcome to stay here anytime."

She couldn't look into his eyes.

"Perhaps I could come when Angie and Tony visit." She would feel awkward staying here with just Simon and Veronica.

"Sure thing." After a weighty silence, he declared, "Well, I'd better get to work. Be careful out there today."

Simon didn't need to be with them when they filmed the demolition of the Hidden Cove Lodge. Paige certainly didn't want to be around when much of Westwind was doomed for the same fate this autumn, although Marshall wanted to capture that as well, of course.

She was thankful that she had *Miss Chief* and didn't linger. She boated into Port Carling and spent several hours in the museum and the library archives. She was to meet the crew again mid-afternoon at Westwind to film the hotel's mahogany day cruiser taking guests out for an hour-long sightseeing trip.

The 38 ft. *Westwind Lady* was a work of art and labour of love – the largest boat that Fred Hawksley built. The enclosed cabin was finished with elaborately carved oak. Carefully maintained for the past seventy years, she was little changed in appearance, although a few things, like the engine and wicker chairs, had been replaced over the years.

"Simon took our wedding party and immediate families out for a sunset cruise after our rehearsal dinner," Angela told Paige on camera as she and Tony waited to board. Their photos of that occasion would illustrate that point. "It was incredibly romantic. So, we don't miss an opportunity to sail on this magnificent old gal."

"And it was a thrill to drive her when I used to take guests out," Tony added. "She glides majestically through the water as if she rules the lake."

"She wasn't built for speed, but to carry lots of people in comfort, and was a much bigger part of the resort culture in the old days," Abigail elucidated. "As well as daily picnic, adventure, or sunset outings, there were afternoon tea cruises. In the British fashion, we were served little sandwiches and cakes from silver platters on crested china. It was all so civilized," she concluded with a smile.

"Simon said that the new owners were keen to have her, so she'll give the revamped resort a tangible connection to the past," Emmeline added. "Which will be lovely."

At dinner, Paige asked the sisters, "So, tell me more about Fred's family and the marina."

Abigail replied, "Fred was only interested in boats, which is how Florence ended up being in charge of the inn. He began working winters at the Ditchburn factory in Gravenhurst at the age of fourteen, so he had six years of boatbuilding experience before he went off to war. In the summers, he'd run the inn's boat livery. That's how the marina began and where he built his own boats after the war."

Paige remembered how furious Rebecca had been when Richard didn't allow her to drive either of the boats that Fred had built for the resort. She claimed they were hers, and he had no right to stop her. Simon had to step in and tell her that Fred's parents had commissioned and financed the boats, and that she still needed a few years of supervised experience before she could be in charge of them. If she behaved herself.

"It was tragic that after his own horrific experiences in the first war, Fred lost his son and only child, Will, in the second. His wife had died in childbirth in the '20s, so Will had been his whole life. He loved working on the boats with Fred. Hardly more than a boy, Will had just married and had his own son when he joined the RCAF. He was a bomber pilot, killed in action in '44. Fred was shattered. His daughter-in-law and grandson stayed with him, and helped to run the marina until Fred wasted away in the mid '50s. He stopped building boats in '44. Stopped living, really."

"And Will's wife - Rebecca's grandmother - never remarried?"

"Not as far as we know. She kept the marina going for a few more years, but her son wasn't interested in the business, so she sold it. That was the last we heard of them until Rebecca came to Westwind."

"She had a false sense of entitlement to this place," Emmeline stated, as if reading Paige's thoughts.

And Bex was still fighting for it.

■   ■   ■

It had been another blistering day and Paige craved a swim after dinner, but she didn't want to bother Simon. He was probably busy, since he hadn't invited her over, and they already had their shooting schedule ready for tomorrow.

There were families still in the pool, but she didn't want to be in a crowded, boisterous place.

She decided to at least cool off in the lake before tackling more research. She stepped down from the terrace into shallow water where the sand was firm underfoot, but didn't move beyond waist-deep, despite having her pool noodle in hand. The lake didn't seem menacing in the golden hour.

"You shouldn't be in there on your own," Simon chided, striding onto the dock in his swim trunks.

She breathed more easily. "I wasn't planning to go far. Just get cool."

"Let me know next time," he said before jumping in beside her. "I need this as well. And this is a perfect time of day."

The wind-whipped ripples had subsided, and long, cooling shadows reached into the lake. Distant, sun-kissed islands blushed.

A canoe appeared from around the "Dragon's Point" to the south. "That looks so inviting!" Angela said when she and Tony paddled up to them. "May we join you? I'm boiling."

They were in their swimsuits.

"Of course!" Simon said. "Just pull up to the dock. I'll return the canoe in the morning."

"You're a brick!" Angela said.

Simon went over to help her out.

"Ahhh, bliss!" she exclaimed as she immersed herself in the lake. "Little Nipper's already makes me feel hotter and heavier, so now I'm more my old buoyant self."

The water was warm enough that they stayed in, chatting, until Angela declared she was turning into a prune. They settled into the Muskoka chairs on the terrace with drinks, which Simon fetched from the boathouse fridge.

As the stars began to populate the descending night, Angela said, "We brought our new video camera. It's like yours, Simon, so will you give us some tips on filming? We want to practice before Nipper arrives."

"Sure! How about before we head out on the Segwun tomorrow?"

Tony and Angela were signed up for the luncheon cruise on the steamship, which Marshall got permission to film. Paige was going as part of the film crew, and Marshall had persuaded Simon that he shouldn't miss the final time that the legendary steamship sailed to and from the historic inn. He also wanted him to do some filming, not only to get practice, but also because there was potential for different shots on the ship and of the passing scenery.

"Perfect!" After a contented sigh, Angela added, "This is how summer days and nights should always be. It's so easy to feel young here. It's like . . . you know . . . when you hear a favourite song and you're instantly back there again, at a particular place. With a special person." She looked lovingly at Tony, who took her hand and kissed it.

"Magic happens here," he said simply.

"Maybe with the help of those butter tarts," she joked.

They all burst into laughter.

"What's the secret ingredient? Fairy dust?"

"A sprinkling at least," Simon replied with a grin.

■   ■   ■

The white ship rising from the green hull and punctuated by the red and black funnel dominated the wharf and thrust Emmeline back half a century and more. Travelling by express train to Gravenhurst and then boarding one of the steamships for the hours-long journey to Westwind had been their summer routine for over thirty years.

How thrilled she had been when the Segwun had been restored and now served as a living history tour boat. She and Abby sailed on her as often as possible. So, she was flooded with poignant memories as the engines rumbled impatiently beneath, eager to set sail.

With a throaty blast of her whistle, the steamer pulled away from the wharf.

"Welcome aboard, ladies and gentlemen. This is your captain. The crew and I hope you enjoy the two-hour cruise of Lake Rosseau, and through the past.

"The RMS Segwun is 110 years old, making her the oldest operating steamship in North America. You can purchase post cards and stamps in our onboard gift shop and drop them into our mailbox. They will be franked 'RMS Segwun', so you might wish to mail one to yourselves as a souvenir.

"Segwun is an Ojibwa name meaning 'springtime'." He went on to give a brief history of the ship and her sisters in the fleet that had helped to open up and sustain this once remote wilderness to settlers and tourists.

Emmeline and Abigail proceeded to the elegant dining room, with its panoramic views of the lake, for the first luncheon seating. That truly was a trip into the past - the warm wood panelling and the bentwood chairs with William Morris inspired upholstery evoking a genteel, bygone era.

While Pierre began with the sisters, Simon was filming Westwind as it grew smaller, finally disappearing as they passed between two islands. Standing next to him on the deck, Paige felt the poignancy of the moment for him and herself.

But they were distracted as a multitude of private boats – many of them antique, hand-crafted launches by renowned Muskoka boatbuilders like Ditchburn and Greavette – came alongside to cheer and wave at another lake legend still sailing. Passengers waved back and the ship responded with a long blast and two short toots.

The Captain also gave the "Master's salute" to cottagers on their docks, who were waving gaily to the passing ship whose now infrequent trips to this upper lake were a noteworthy event. For many of them, the Segwun and her fleet had been the only way their ancestors had been able to access those cottages until well into the 1930s, when reliable roads were being built.

While Simon kept his lens focused on the passing scenery, Paige approached several passengers, asking if they'd be willing to say a few words on camera about the cruise and their connection with or thoughts about Muskoka. Terry was ready with the microphones when Marshall and Pierre joined them.

The Pembrook sisters sat in the breezy shade on the aft deck for the latter half of the tour, absorbing the experience. Emmeline felt the past reaching out to her, reminding her of those vibrant, heady days of her youth.

As the ship neared Westwind, the sisters stood alongside Simon and Paige at the bow, all gazing emotionally at the iconic resort that stretched almost half a mile along the shoreline.

Guests and passengers who had dined at the inn occupied every chair along the waterfront, stood along the railings of the sundeck bar with holiday drinks in hand, and lined the peripheral docks ready to admire the venerable vessel once again.

When they had docked, Paige noticed Simon watching the Pembrook sisters shuffle along the wharf arm in arm, Emmeline, in particular, looking unusually stooped and frail. It tugged at her heart to see them like that, and to see Simon wincing.

The film crew had had a quick and early lunch, so they enjoyed a snack of coffee and butter tarts on the rooftop bar after filming the departing ship.

The waterfront staff was gearing up for the waterski show – a weekly tradition since the '60s. The spectators grew as cottagers watched from boats idling at a safe distance.

"It's good to see so many talented and enthusiastic young people still embracing the sport," Angela said to Paige as she filmed parts of the show for video practice and Paige photographed it.

"It's such a part of lake culture, how could they not? Summer life is different on a lake. I've missed that."

"And we've missed you," Angela said, looking at her fondly. "We do love it here. It reminds us of those happy, carefree days of youth when we had few responsibilities and plenty of fun. Now we're 'adulting' and about to produce spawn that will consume all our energies and resources." She chuckled.

When filming wrapped up for the day, Marshall said, "We're going back for a swim and an early dinner so these guys can head home to the city for a few days with their families. Pierre is a master with barbecue tongs, so he'll cook steaks."

"I'll ask the kitchen to pack you a hamper of salads and desserts," Simon offered, it being the mid-week buffet.

"Terrific! . . . Paige, let's go through your notes tomorrow. Simon, can you bring the Pembrook ladies to Arcadia in the morning? Sandy Wyndham sent me the Muskoka documentary they made in '46, so I'd like you all to have a look at it and see what bits we can use. I expect they wouldn't mind."

"I'm sure they'll be delighted."

After seeing the crew off from his boathouse, Simon looked weary when he said to Paige, "I still have office work to finish, but need a dip first. Want to join me?"

"Absolutely!" Not only because of the unrelenting heat, but also because she wanted to support him.

Seeing from the Segwun the entirety of what his family had slowly built over four generations was impressive; knowing that it was soon to disappear must be difficult, no matter how much he craved his new-found freedom. She could almost feel his guilt and sense of betrayal, especially regarding the Pembrook sisters.

"But you don't have to stick close if you want to swim out further," she said. "I'm fine in the shallows." She did feel more confident in the lake now.

"We advocate the swim buddy system, but I'm not good at heeding my own advice. This is more fun anyway."

She was happy to see him smile.

After a refreshing swim to the Dragon's Point again, Simon asked, "Is Brett arriving Friday?"

"No . . . He's busy," she replied without looking at him.

"Tony and Angie are coming to the house for dinner. Will you join us?"

"I'd love to!"

"Great! Well, I'd better grab something to eat and get to work."

Paige was glad that she kept a few of her things in the boathouse suite, including a change of clothes after swims. She would love to stay here, seeing the reflections of sunlight off the water dancing around the rooms, hearing the rhythmic waves, feeling the playful breezes squeezing through the many screens. She might yet take Simon up on that offer, especially now that she didn't have to care what Brett thought.

But what would Veronica say? That Paige was encroaching?

She poured herself a glass of Sauvignon Blanc from the open bottle in the fridge, and sat on the deck, watching the activities wind down as dinner time approached. The ski boats were returned to their berths in the long boathouse beneath the rooftop bar, sunbathers on the wharf gathered towels and headed back to their rooms, while guests in evening wear climbed the outside stairs to the sundeck for a preprandial drink.

Even the lake traffic calmed as boaters returned to cottages. With every breath, Paige felt that she was imbibing the summer lake ethos, with remnants of the past as well as the sensuous present. It was sublime.

She hadn't noticed the canoe approaching from the south, but the occupant looked strangely familiar. As he neared the boathouse, he rested his paddle across the gunwales and drifted, gazing pensively at the lake.

Paige gasped. He resembled Cliff! She jumped up and went to the railing, staring with disbelief. As if he sensed her, he looked up and smiled. It seemed like minutes that their eyes were locked and souls touched. Then he just faded away like early morning mist.

She grabbed the railing to steady herself, quivering with awe and trepidation. Wondering if her mind was playing tricks. It was as if that photo of him in the canoe had come to life.

She eased back into the Muskoka chair to review what had just happened and cement it into her memory. She had surely just been given a gift.

"Thank you, Granddad! I wish I could tell Dad about you. I think he would understand."

■   ■   ■

After dinner, Paige went back to the boxes in the boathouse suite, although she really wasn't in the mood to do any more work. So, she was excited to find a bundle of letters, still in their original envelopes, addressed to Edward from Mrs. Gilbert Ryeland in Oxford. Somehow, she knew that was Cliff's sister – her great-aunt! – who now had a married name and a street address.

September 29, 1937

Dear Edward,

It is still unfathomable that Cliff is gone - that I will never again laugh with my little brother, see his infectious grin, hug him close. My parents have aged a decade since receiving your cable, and I fear that Mater is suddenly very frail, her spirit broken by having now lost three of us children.

The photos you sent are greatly appreciated and do help. Cliff does indeed look like he was having the time of his life. I'm grateful that he was so happy in the end. And that's thanks to you, so please don't feel that you could have done anything to prevent this tragedy.

Thank you also for sending his Muskoka poems, which we all treasure. What a beautiful place you must live in to inspire such rapturous verse. I agree that "Love Eternal" is a joyful celebration of a deep love. Which of the three beauties who appear in so many of the photos do you think captured his heart? How I wish he'd had a chance to share eternity with her. Perhaps that will yet happen. And for now, he dwells in her heart as well as ours. There is something oddly comforting in that.

Of course we don't mind that you made copies of his poems. But I think it best if you keep his unfinished novel. The poems are complete unto themselves, revealing little parts of Cliff, even his creative process through his editing. But an unfinished literary work is like a wound that can never heal. That would break Pater. He had such faith and pride in Cliff's talent, as he did in Cedric's. Neither was allowed to flourish as they should.

Rest assured that I will look after Isobel even if I must fight to do so. She's stayed with us for several weeks and most weekends since Cliff left, and I will ensure that frequent visits continue. She doesn't completely grasp that her beloved Papa won't be returning. We don't dwell on that, hoping that time will dull the pain of his absence. But we also don't want her to think that he willingly abandoned her. It's heartbreaking to watch an eight-year-old deal with this crushing loss. Fortunately, she and Hazel, who is only a year older, are best of friends. Hazel is most protective of her little cousin, as if she understands and wants to ease her pain.

I have given Izzy your love from "Uncle" Edward. I expect she'll be happy to hear from you, as she speaks fondly of you, and really does think of you as an uncle. So, write to her here, and I'll make sure she receives your letters. I will definitely keep you updated.

Talia was heartbroken by the news. She will keep running the shop until we find a buyer. The money will be put into a trust fund for Izzy, which Cliff wanted you, Gilbert, and me to administer, so I hope you agree to this.

Thankfully, Cliff made a new will, leaving everything to Izzy, with us and your brother Arthur as her solicitor to oversee the estate until Izzy is twenty-one. Fenella can't hide her delight that she'll be spared the scandal and disgrace of a divorce – having now taken on the mantle of grieving widow - but is livid that she inherits nothing, having already received a share of the house sale. A generous allowance for Izzy's care will be given to her, of course, but we'll have to ensure that it's wisely spent on the child, not on couturier gowns and folderol for Fenella.

We all send our love,
Enid

Paige wondered if Enid would have been secretly happy or scandalized to learn of Cliff's lovechild. She tended to think the former. She wished she had time to indulge in this treasure trove of letters from her new-found family, but for now, she sampled a few more letters from the following three decades to discover what had happened to people.

February 9, 1944
Dear Edward,

... Fenella is ensconced in her husband's draughty Scottish castle with her infant son, as their London townhouse is closed for the duration. Having some sort of war work to do, the Laird has a suite at the Dorchester Hotel, which is supposed to be bomb-proof. I believe she often pops down to London alone to be with him.

She is relieved to have Isobel living with us. It's obvious that she cherishes the boy, destined to become Laird, of course. Izzy finally realizes that Cliff truly loved her, but her mother has always been indifferent. I do think Fenella was jealous of the bond between them.

So, we're delighted to finally be her legal guardians, as the Laird wanted no reminders of Fenella's "disastrous" first marriage. Or any claims from Izzy to his estate.

The poor child has taken it all rather stoically, although I'm sure she's aching inside, having essentially lost her mother as well. Fortunately, Talia, who has no children of her own, is more caring and invites her to St. Ives for a couple of weeks every summer. It still feels like home to her, and where Cliff's spirit is most alive. Talia continues to mentor her artistic talents, as you've noted in her yearly hand-painted Christmas cards to you.

Izzy is enthralled by your invitation to spend a summer at Westwind once the war is over. I sense that having seen the photos of Cliff's visit, she feels she can connect with him there. Hazel and I would be absolutely delighted to accompany her. We eagerly discuss the adventures that await - blueberry picking, sunset cruises, picnicking on uninhabited islands - and all the other delights of your beautiful resort, which you have so enticingly described. The girls are already planning costumes for the ball and a duet for the talent show. We pray that it won't be too many years before we're with you.

The food parcels you have sent these past four years have been so welcome and thoroughly savoured. We're astounded by the maple syrup tapped from your own trees, and your home-made blueberry jam. What sublime treats at the best of times, but especially with our rationing. Enjoying those at your tranquil, lakeside setting will be even more special.

So, thank you, dear friend, for your continued support, and for giving us something truly wondrous to look forward to in these dark times.

Enid

Paige was surprised by this impending visit and wondered why the Pembrook sisters never mentioned that they had met Isobel and Cliff's family. She skimmed through a few post-war letters until she found one dated September 1947.

Dear Edward,

Being back home in this dreary, battered country still under rationing is sad. Thankfully, we have unique and magical memories of summer at Westwind to sustain us.

Your Richard is a delightful and accomplished lad, whether at the piano (like his father) or on the water. The girls had great fun with him, especially learning how to canoe and waterski. What extraordinary experiences! The girls proudly wear their Indian moccasins as slippers.

They haven't stopped talking about marvellous Muskoka and their amazing boathouse suite. I think Izzy was particularly happy and moved to stay where Cliff had.

I must admit that the skinny-dips I did with them in the discreet darkness beneath breathtaking stars was mesmerizing and unforgettable.

So, I understand Cliff's poem "Eternal Love" now. And I can see how he would have fallen in love with the scenery, lifestyle, and one of the lovely and remarkable Pembrook sisters, if not someone else. Your place is romance personified, so it's not surprising you fell under its and Florence's spell. How many other relationships have begun and blossomed there?

But how tragic that Cliff and his lady love had no chance at a life together.

My friends are agog at my descriptions of the beauties, amenities, and gourmet cuisine at Westwind, so don't be surprised if you receive reservations from them some day. That includes your brother Arthur. I can't understand why none of your family has hitherto come to visit you.

We also appreciated seeing Cliff's grave. What a serene spot. It was strange, but I actually felt close to him there, as if touching his headstone gave me some spiritual connection to him.

I do think Izzy felt some closure, seeing where her Papa spent his final, joyful days and now rests. Meeting the Pembrook sisters, who spoke so highly of him and with light-hearted anecdotes, also helped. How kind of Abigail to film the girls at various activities and offer to send that to us. What a souvenir!

Izzy is even more resolved to follow in Cliff's footsteps, beginning by excelling in her English studies at Oxford. She plans to return to St. Ives afterwards and buy back the bookstore with her inheritance. It's ambitious and perhaps untenable, but she's a determined and independent young lady. Cliff would be so proud.

Thank you again for a splendid, incomparable holiday, dear friend! How delightful to now be able to picture you in your enviable environment.

Enid

Paige eagerly skimmed ahead to see if Isobel had accomplished her dreams.

Boxing Day, 1950

Dear Edward,

Your Christmas gift boxes were once again the highlight of our celebrations. Your sweets in all their delectable guises are particularly welcome. Even when sugar is no longer rationed here, I will still appreciate receiving maple syrup, of which I've become very fond. I use it in baking and call it my secret ingredient when my friends rave about my cakes. As it is in your marvellous butter tarts. The girls – young ladies now, of course – adore their silk stockings and the yards of exquisite fabrics, fancy buttons and ribbons for new dresses.

Which is particularly appropriate since we're preparing a wedding trousseau for Isobel. She first met Matthew in his family's bookstore on the High Street, although he was also reading English at the university. So, she'll still eventually own a bookshop, but not in St. Ives. Having attended Cliff's alma mater and having lived in Oxford all these years now, she feels close to him here.

She's been working with Matthew at "Wetherby's" since they both graduated in the spring – both achieving "Firsts"! - and have plenty of ideas of how to "modernize" and enhance the bookstore experience. They believe that adding a café where literary readings and discussions can take place would be a draw as well as a boost to authors and a contribution to the larger community.

We are delighted to see her so engaged and happy in her career and with Matthew. They are an ideal couple. He doesn't yet know that she's about to inherit a tidy sum when she turns twenty-one in two months. I expect she'll want to invest some in expanding the shop.

Fenella offered to pay for the wedding, to be held in London with her organizing everything - to impress her peers and show what a good mother she is, of course, although she's rarely seen Izzy these past few years. So, Izzy hardly knows her half-brothers. I think Fenella is intimidated by having an intelligent, talented daughter.

Izzy flatly refused the offer and told Fenella that she and her family would be invited to the wedding in Oxford should they choose to attend. I'm so proud of her for standing up for herself. I'm sure it wasn't easy.

I was glad to hear from your brother how much he and his family enjoyed their visit to Westwind this summer, and that your mother was finally able to see you in your element. Unfortunate that your father was too busy to join them, but I'm sure he's heard nothing but praise from the others. They were certainly impressed with how luxurious your "wilderness" retreat is. . . .

January 27, 1951
Dear Uncle Edward,
We are flabbergasted by your extremely generous offer of a honeymoon at Westwind and extravagant round-trip tickets on the RMS Queen Mary! I appreciate that you want me to experience the voyage that Papa had, and I've heard that second class is as luxurious as first class on other liners. Staying for a month in your boathouse suite again will be heavenly! I can't tell you how excited I am! As is Matthew, especially having seen the film of our last trip.

We can hardly wait to start our new life together, and this journey to your summer paradise will be an unforgettable beginning.

Thank you with all my heart!
Love, Isobel

Chapter 16

Paige was startled from a pleasant dream of swimming in the sandy shallows of the calm lake, blessed by the benevolent sun. She was facing the early dawn heralded by the soul-stirring cry of a loon. But that blissful moment was shattered when she sensed something behind her.

She rolled over instantly. There was nothing there. But her door handle rattled slightly. Faint footsteps seemed to start from just outside her door. Going across the hall to the tower. The creak of a door opening. Silence.

What the hell? If it was a spirit, it wouldn't have to open a door. Was Veronica or someone else trying to scare her?

Her imagination? Her PTSD kicked into high gear again by the eerie and recent life-threatening incidents?

She held her head fiercely as if to contain the demons.

▪   ▪   ▪

"I've discovered some fascinating letters to Edward from Cliff's sister and his daughter, Isobel," Paige told the Pembrook sisters at breakfast. "You didn't mention that you'd met them." She tried not to look accusing.

Emmeline sighed. "It was so long ago."

"We were lucky if we had a couple weeks here in those days, since we were both immersed in our careers," Abigail added. "So even when we saw them, we had little time to interact. But they seemed like the kind of people we would have chosen as friends."

Paige smiled. "No better accolade."

"You probably know more than we do, if you've read their letters."

"I know that you both impressed them, and Enid was happy to think that one of you might have been Cliff's true love."

Abigail guffawed. "Gracious me!"

"She also called you 'lovely and remarkable' ladies."

They smiled.

"We saw Cliff's daughter twice more," Emmeline offered. "On her month-long honeymoon and again in the late '60s with her two teenage children. Edward still visited Britain occasionally, but I'm sure she wanted to see him as much as to show the children Westwind. Edward died a couple of years later, so they never did meet again."

"But presumably wrote. More treasures to unearth. Thank you for that," Paige said happily.

"She also brought books for Simon, who was a toddler at the time. Cliff had written some nursery rhymes for Isobel when she was little...."

"I came across that in a letter!"

"Isobel was quite an accomplished artist, so she illustrated them, and found a publisher. She wrote and illustrated a few more books of rhymes and little tales for her own children, which were also published. I believe she enjoyed some modest success in Britain."

"That's exciting! I'll have to check Simon's bookshelves. At least I know her married name! But now I'm heading over to Arcadia, so I'll see you there soon."

■   ■   ■

"This is splendid! Tastefully modernized, but retains its historical essence," Abigail said when they arrived at Arcadia.

Marshall had moved the ornate pool table into the expansive living room, where it was an attractive antique and got more use. He'd turned the former billiards room into a theatre room, with a huge screen at one end and deep leather chairs for viewing.

Clipboards in hand, Paige and Simon were going to note footage that they thought could be used, with the others making recommendations as well.

The 30-minute documentary, "Not Just a Pretty Place", began with a stunning shot of sunrise sparking diamonds off a pristine lake, with the siren calls of loons and gentle lapping of waves as the only soundtrack. The rugged, uninhabited landscape of granite and pine would have looked the same before any human had ever set foot there. But a mahogany launch suddenly raced across the scene, slowing as the camera followed it, passing impressive cottages and boathouses, and coming up to the grand Royal Muskoka Hotel.

The film interspersed black and white footage and photos with the 1946 colour film to illustrate the history of Muskoka from the land of indigenous peoples to the pioneer farms, lumbering, and steamships that opened up the area, and the tourism that arose to sustain it, including Westwind.

"I didn't know we were featured in this!" Simon exclaimed.

Abigail chuckled. "I also consulted on the script."

There were humorous contrasts between swimmers engulfed from head to toe by woolen bathing costumes at the turn of the century and the sassy two-piece suits worn by the ladies of the '40s. And sombre, surprising reminders of war, showing the Royal Norwegian Air Force training their boys at the Muskoka Airport, and a lakeside German Prisoner of War Camp nearby with a cordoned-off swimming area.

"Beautifully edited, Miss Abigail," Marshall praised when the film ended.

They all agreed.

When Simon and the sisters had gone, Marshall said, "So, part of next week's plan is to film the location of the former POW camp in Gravenhurst, which is just a waterfront park now with a few stone remnants."

"It was amazing to see the old photos in the film! Dad told me about passing it on the steamships when he was a kid, and seeing 'the enemy' swimming behind a barbed wire boom. That seems incredible!"

"Sure is, and few people know about that now. There was a hotel on that site at the turn of the century, and then a private TB sanatorium that closed during the Depression and was turned into the POW camp in 1940. Ironically, after the war it became the largest Jewish summer resort in Canada for over a decade. See what you can find at the Gravenhurst archives next week."

"Sounds fascinating!"

"Now, a swim before lunch, methinks. And we'll plan to wrap up early. Monique is arriving this afternoon and returning to the city on Monday morning to beat the weekend traffic. Time to have some fun and regenerate. Which means you take a long weekend off, OK?" He skewered her with narrowed eyes.

"Yes, boss!" Paige giggled.

As they dined on Duncan's gourmet burgers and leftovers from the Westwind salads, Paige told him about this new world she had fallen into as she was connecting with her grandfather's family through the letters.

"That's cool! I wonder if your dad would like to know that as well."

"Exactly what I was thinking! I'm so torn! Trying to figure out how to approach the subject without giving everything away. He can't *unknow* it later."

"Uncle Raymond wasn't the best father. Tom doesn't resemble him in looks or demeanour, so he might have wondered if they were actually related. Perhaps he even fantasized about having a different father. He's not naïve, Kiddo. He was devoted to Delia, but gave his father a wide berth, like the rest of us did."

Marshall creased his forehead in contemplation. "It just occurred to me that Tom might know about his real father. Perhaps that's why he was so insistent that Dad didn't have to pay him the appraised value for Arcadia. I heard him say that he couldn't afford the fifty or more thousand it would take to keep the cottage from deteriorating, but he could accept at least that much less for the sale. He said the most important thing was to keep it in the family."

"A family descended from your great-grandfather. Not mine... Oh, I wish I could ask Gran what to do!"

"Try it."

"I will!" She hesitated, but then told him about seeing Cliff in the canoe.

"Holy shit!"

"Don't look at me as if I'm crazy."

"Not crazy. Gifted? . . . Plagued?"

"Not that. It was a wonderful, soothing yet exhilarating experience. It was as if he was reaching out to tell me that he was happy to be my grandfather. Approved of what I was doing. Even giving his consent to my finishing his novel." She looked up at Marshall as if emerging from a trance. "But now I question whether I should, knowing that he has a talented daughter who is also a writer."

"Ah yes. Well, first check to see if she's still around. Then you should contact her. You don't have to mention your connection at first. Tell her you're a friend of Edward's grandson, and discovered Cliff's manuscript at Westwind. Take it from there and see what transpires."

"Wise as always," Paige replied with a grin.

"That's the definition of an older cousin," he joshed. "Let's finish our wine on your rock. Best place for our celebratory drink."

Once they were seated on the warm granite with gentle waves massaging their legs, Marshall toasted, "Here's to your newfound freedom."

"I still find it hard to remember that, probably because my life hasn't noticeably changed yet, and I haven't told anyone."

"Maybe you should." Marshall looked over at her. "So . . . were you and Simon lovers?"

Paige almost choked on her wine.

"I've noticed how you two gaze at each other. Like there's a deep connection. And longing."

She looked away and finally said, "Only that last summer. But I couldn't come back.... So we lost touch."

"I didn't know at the time, or I would have responded differently. Simon saw me at the sundeck bar buying my usual summer treats. Must have been '89, because when he asked about you and your parents, I said that you hadn't been able to face coming back to the lake after the accident a couple of years before. I mentioned that you'd wrangled a summer job with the local newspaper to write articles relating to the town's history."

Paige had loved that job, which had occupied her summers throughout her university years, even though it hadn't paid particularly well.

"I didn't realize he might have been fishing for more personal info," Marshall concluded.

"No one knew about us, although the sisters and Tony and Angie suspected. Only Rebecca had found out. Anyway, it's too late now."

"It's never too late. Talk to him. You know what the Moodies said about love eternal not being denied."

■   ■   ■

But Paige couldn't find the words that evening when they were swimming, or afterwards as they sat drying off on the boathouse deck in the still sweltering heat.

She told him about the letters, and what Emmeline had said about Isobel's children's books.

"Isobel Wetherby! I used to read those when I was a kid. Loved them."

"May I see them?"

"Of course."

Paige threw on a gauzy beach cover because it felt awkward wandering into a house half naked in a bikini. And in case Veronica came upon them and got the wrong impression.

On the lowest shelf in the library was a collection of classic children's picture books.

"I used to sit here and just pull them out to read. Mom taught me early on to replace them in the right spot," Simon said with a poignant smile.

It suddenly struck Paige how young he was to have lost both parents. For a moment he looked so vulnerable, like a lost little boy, that she had to restrain herself from wrapping him in a comforting hug. But she put her hand on his arm and said gently, "I'm so very sorry not to have seen your parents again. It must be hard for you."

He shrugged as if to cover a momentary inability to speak. "They're everywhere in this house. Which is why I'll never sell it. It'll be a cottage if need be."

"You can do a lot of work from here. Have a *pied-à-terre* in the city when you're in the studio editing."

"Or set up an editing suite here."

"That's true!" Paige was getting excited. "If Marshall wants us to be the documentary team, perhaps he actually needs another studio."

"I can easily finance it if that's going to be my new career." He grinned, and the sadness evaporated. "OK, let me pull out the books."

Her suit still damp beneath the airy dress, Paige plunked herself down on the floor, crossed-legged, and Simon joined her.

"These illustrations are adorable!" She chuckled when she skimmed the clever rhymes. "How delightful!"

"I'd forgotten that one book was co-authored by her father," Simon admitted as he handed her that volume.

She stroked the book reverently before opening it. "It's amazing how odd and thrilling it is to discover the things I was reading about in letters."

"Take them all to the boathouse with you."

"Gosh! Thanks!"

"Do you want to reconsider moving in there?"

"Actually . . . Yes. I've been spooked in the inn."

"Is that why you've been up in the middle of the night and working in the boathouse way too early in the mornings?"

"Yes."

"You should have told me! OK, then let's fix that right now. You go pack and I'll come round with the cart in half an hour, if that works. And bring your car around to the parking area by the carriage house."

"Perfect!"

Paige went gaily off to her room and felt liberated as she threw things into her suitcases. It was almost as if this was a real step away from Brett and into her new life. She had envisioned him here with her, complaining about the room and infusing it with biting sarcasm. But he didn't inhabit the boathouse suite in her mind.

Her bags ready to go, she knocked on the Pembrook sisters' door.

Emmeline opened it, having been expecting something. "You look chipper. I thought I heard you singing."

"I feel lighthearted! May I pop in for a moment?"

"Of course!"

"I'm moving into the boathouse suite. I've been having bad dreams here, and seeing things again. . . . And - strictly between us! - I want you to know that Brett and I are getting divorced. I have to tell someone to make it feel more real."

"That obviously suits you," Abigail said with a broad smile. "Well done!"

At last! Emmeline thought.

∎   ∎   ∎

Paige had the best sleep since she'd arrived at Westwind. Because the deck was only accessible from the sitting room, she had left all the screened windows and doors, including her bedroom door, open, so the suite was freshly swept by all the cross-breezes, and she hadn't needed the ceiling fans.

Before leaving her to settle in, Simon had checked for spiders everywhere, even in the rafters below, and had declared it pristine. She'd stacked her empty suitcases in front of the entrance in case she sleep-walked, so she'd felt safe and comfy despite the lack of air conditioning in the persistent heat. It was marvellous to watch the sunrise from her bed.

Simon had told her to turn on the outside porch light at the entrance when she was up and ready for a swim. But she already heard gentle splashing and went to look over the railing. She watched his strong strokes as he swam straight out into the lake. Her body remembering his made her crave his touch.

When he turned, she waved and yelled, "I'll be right down!"

"This is deliciously refreshing," Paige said as she slipped into the water. "Is this heat wave supposed to break anytime soon?"

"Let's hope so. It's been so dry most of the summer that the fire risk is now in the red, so we can't have our campfires in the evening."

"Even though they're on the beach?"

"The woods are tinder-dry, so any stray sparks might ignite them."

Sing-alongs around the campfire had been a tradition for decades, especially for the kids.

"What's on your agenda for today?" he asked as they dripped off on the terrace chairs.

"I should do some research at the local libraries, but Marshall insisted I take the weekend off. So, I'll indulge myself in the books and letters on my wonderful deck. Interspersed with kayaking and swimming at the beach with my noodle."

"Actually have a holiday. Which you've hardly had these past three weeks."

"Strange to think that if we hadn't started the book and the documentary projects, I'd be going home on Sunday."

Back to the increasingly miserable half-life she'd been living with Brett. The very thought was now unbearable. She almost told

Simon but wasn't ready for what that might unleash. Better to revel in this ecstatic new life. "This is so much more fun!"

"Good! But don't go far and stay close to shore. The weather will break eventually." He looked at her earnestly. And didn't have to spell out the consequences.

■   ■   ■

Paige went to the gift shop after breakfast to pick up some Westwind golf shirts and towels for her parents, afraid that the selection might have dwindled by the time they arrived for their September week, and had fun choosing baby clothes and a cuddly teddy bear sporting a Westwind T-shirt for Tony and Angela's little Nipper.

Then she went kayaking while the lake was still calm. The sun-churned wind usually picked up by 11:00, but it was another hot day, the sky bleached and thick with humidity. A breath of wind would have been welcome. But she didn't stray far from the shore or the resort.

She had a cooling dip at the beach when she returned, and was happy to get back to her new domain. It was a beautiful, peaceful haven that made joy well within her whenever she entered it.

She immersed herself in Edward's correspondence and discovered packets of photos that must have accompanied the letters over the years. One marked "Isobel" illustrated a precocious girl growing up into a beautiful and accomplished woman. She particularly liked the ones of Izzy reading and shelving books in Cliff's little bookshop. Not surprising then to see her in charge at the impressively large Wetherby's, which was surely a bibliophile's delight.

Paige intended to visit there as soon as possible.

■   ■   ■

With side dishes and desserts from the inn and Simon's perfectly cooked steaks, the dinner with Angie and Tony on the screened veranda at Simon's house was enjoyable and relaxing. They were delighted with Paige's baby gifts, Angela saying, "We should stock up on different sizes for Nipper if these are going to become obsolete now. And some for us, too!"

"The place will have a new name and logo," Simon agreed. "I guess I'd better make sure I have a good supply as well. To last into my dotage."

They chuckled.

"I'm so glad we booked in for two weeks this year," Angela said as she scooped up the last of the chocolate mousse from her plate.

"Damn right!" Tony agreed. Looking at Simon compassionately, he added, "We know how difficult this must be for you, so let us know how we can help. For starters, will you come to visit us? We have a modest home on the lake, but we do have a guest room. You too, Paige."

"We have an office with a sofa bed as well," Angela added, "In case you both want to come at the same time. Your husband as well, of course, Paige."

She thought it was stupid now to pretend that she was still in a happy marriage. After a long pause she said, "That chapter is closed. If you don't mind, I'd rather not elaborate just now. Suffice it to say that it was a mutually agreeable decision."

She avoided Simon's startled look.

Angela put her hand supportively on Paige's. Then she said, "So, do you two want to have a gander at our novice efforts with a video camera?"

They did and enjoyed the footage. Simon offered some tips, and asked if he could have a copy of the two boat trips.

After they all helped with the dishes, they went back to the veranda. The band was playing in the pavilion, and the music wafting across the water was enticing.

They laughed as they danced ensemble to "Fun, Fun, Fun", "Summer of '69", and "Do you Believe in Magic".

When "I Want to Know What Love Is" came on, Paige went hesitantly into Simon's arms. But he drew her close and she couldn't resist his tender embrace. She laid her head against his shoulder and melted against him.

He'd already shown her what love is, and she'd been pining for it ever since that fateful summer. Not just the sex, but the conviction that he cared for her deeply, heart and soul. That they were two halves of a whole that was greater and more sublime than its parts. Surely she could feel his heart quickening in rhythm with hers.

But what had happened to that perfect love? Confused, she wanted to pull away from him, but the desire to seize and savour every moment in his arms was a stronger force. Could she really ache any more than she already did without him?

When the song ended, Angela said, "Gosh, I'm suddenly tired. An early night for Nipper and me, I think."

Paige saw the look that passed between her and an initially puzzled Tony, and realized what Angie was doing.

But she didn't want to be left alone with Simon at the moment, so she said, "I should go as well."

"Could you stay a bit longer? There's something we need to discuss."

She hoped he meant with the film. "Of course."

When the Vanderbecks had gone, he stood squarely in front of her and said, "We can't keep going like this, Paige."

"What do you mean?" Her heart raced in alarm, afraid that being virtually a free woman now, she was a threat to his marriage.

"Not talking about the past. Denying our feelings. . . . How did we lose each other?" he asked, looking searchingly into her eyes.

"I was still fragile, so when you didn't write back, I thought . . ."

"Wait! You *wrote* to me?"

She explained about the delay in replying to him. "So I sent the letter in May to coincide with your coming home."

"I didn't receive it. I tried to call you several times that summer, but no one answered."

"We were in Britain, which I mentioned in my letter. And I sent you a postcard from St. Ives, telling you when I'd be home."

"I didn't get that either. But I wrote you another letter that summer."

She shook her head. "It never arrived."

"How can all our letters have gone astray?"

Paige could almost imagine Rebecca having a ghostly hand in that.

"If you didn't know that we were in Britain that summer, how did Veronica? She mentioned it to me in a conversation. I thought you'd told her."

His face darkened. "The bitch! I should have realized even then that she was manipulating me! She was so helpful to my parents when Dad was in hospital, just as the season was beginning. She worked extra-long days, helping Louise in the office. And taking charge of the mail. I remember her insisting that nothing was too much for her to take on. Mom and I should be with Dad as much as possible. Said that since she was studying hotel management and had already spent one summer with us, she knew what to do. And she *was* competent."

Simon gripped his head in frustration and anger. "But she must have read our letters and destroyed them. What a bloody fool I've been! She insinuated herself into my life that summer. Trying to make me forget you. She asked if I'd heard from you and how you were after the tragedy. When I admitted I hadn't, she said that you probably wanted to leave the past behind and move on with your life. She subtly suggested that you had larger ambitions than running an inn, so there was no point in continuing our relationship.

"I applied to Ryerson and was accepted when I was still in Australia, but I was living in the same student co-op residence in The Annex, so I was hoping you would contact me there when you went to U of T. When you didn't, I called your home. Your dad said that you were doing well and attending Carlton, so I thought that Veronica was right, and it was over between us."

"He never mentioned that to me. Of course, he didn't know about us, so it probably just slipped his mind."

"When I was at Ryerson that fall, Veronica was in her last year there, so it was only natural that we spent time together. She and her mother lived in an apartment just a few blocks from my place. They often invited me for meals. I was hurt and bewildered, so I allowed myself to be seduced by her."

He looked at her in anguish. "But I've never stopped loving you."

She went tearfully into his arms. "Me neither!"

It was a divine moment, their souls bared and reuniting.

"Well, what do we have here? Infidelity?" Veronica sneered, interrupting their passionate kiss.

"Just picking up where we left off," Simon retorted. "Sidelined by your scheming!"

"What do you mean?"

"The letters that didn't arrive and weren't sent."

"I don't know what you're talking about."

"Bullshit! You took over the mail that summer."

"It was a crazy time. Not my fault if some things fell through the cracks. I worked my ass off helping out after your dad's accident!"

"How did you know I was in Britain?" Paige asked. "No one else did."

"What the fuck does it matter now? If you two were so lovey-dovey, why didn't you pick up the phone and talk to each other? Why base your future on letters?"

"Because your despicable actions made us feel rejected and vulnerable to further pain. As you damn well expected," Simon accused.

"Bastard! You're not even giving me my fair share of all this! After all I've done to keep this place going and the clients happy."

"They're *guests*, not clients. But to you it's just business. And you thought that by marrying me you'd automatically have a claim to this legacy that my family built up over generations. But I don't owe you a dime more than half of the value of this house."

"Then *you* look after this mausoleum on your own for the rest of the season! If you're not too busy playing filmmaker. I'm blowing this popsicle stand!"

"Gladly."

She snorted. "Everything's already packed except my clothes. I'll send for my boxes. And I still want my paychecks for this season."

"Don't worry. I'll even give you a bonus if you're out of here by tomorrow. I'm tired of this charade."

"Fuck you!"

"You already did," he shot back.

She marched out of the room, and they could hear her stomping upstairs.

Paige looked at Simon questioningly, astonished at the turn of events.

"She filed for divorce after I signed the papers with the developer last summer, thinking she'd be entitled to half the proceeds of the sale. Part of the agreement was that we stayed on for another year to keep the place viable and profitable, so we agreed to keep the divorce quiet until we closed this October. She was adamant that we keep up the appearance of a happy couple in public. She said she didn't want to be pitied, but I think she was more concerned about being blamed. I insisted that at least Louise, Barry, and the Pembrook sisters be told. Veronica moved into my parents' old suite, and we've managed to lead separate lives.

"She went to her sister's in Seattle for the winter and apparently found someone 'brilliant with terrific prospects', although I suspect she'd met him the previous winter."

"Oh, Simon," Paige stroked his cheek. "I know how it feels to be betrayed. Brett is leaving me for his former fiancé. But I wanted out anyway. It was a mistake to marry him. I should have acted on my instincts, but I thought you were lost to me."

"All this wasted time!"

"We have decades ahead of us. And maybe it was good for us to find our true selves. Now we can rediscover each other."

"God, how I love you, Paige!" he murmured as he held her close. "Stay with me tonight?"

"And always," he promised, taking her hand.

Chapter 17

When Paige awoke, she saw Simon lying on his side gazing at her with love and wonder. Which had been another one of her girlish fantasies.

"What are you thinking?" she asked sleepily.

"That one of my dearest wishes has come true. Waking up next to you. *Nothing twixt my love and me.*"

They were naked beneath the sheet.

"Mmmm. Mine too! What other wishes do you have?"

"That we'll do this forever."

"Our souls sing in harmony, And vow to share eternity. . . . I hope so."

They had made love hungrily last night, and then spent hours catching up, not holding back about the disappointments and heartaches in their marriages. Then they'd made love more slowly, exquisitely, before falling into a contented sleep.

"Sometimes I'm afraid to feel so happy and lucky," she admitted as she laid her head on his chest and his arms closed protectively around her. "It's like hubris, and some vengeful god will punish me."

"You don't think you deserve happiness?"

She shrugged.

"Because of Bex?"

"Grampa calls it 'survivor guilt'. It was common during the war."

"I should have been there to help you through all that," he lamented as he nuzzled her hair.

"Don't you start feeling guilty as well. We're together now."

"I wish I could just stay here with you all day, but it's going to be a busy one. Fortunately, we have good staff, well-trained, so I have to give Veronica some credit for that and for the efficient processes she put in place. It means that competent people can be given more responsibility."

"Anything I can do to help?"
"Have dinner with me."
"I think I can manage that," she chuckled.
"I'll inform people that our divorce will be granted soon, and that Veronica has left to start her new life. You can tell Marshall and the Vanderbecks the truth, if you like. Now I have time for a quick swim. Or . . . ," he began, caressing her face.
"*We touch as two, become one?*"
"Much more fun!"

■   ■   ■

Paige was a trifle shy when she joined the sisters for breakfast. Simon wished they could have had a leisurely one together, but he just munched on egg salad sandwiches in his office while he worked.

The ladies were beaming.

"Simon spoke to you?"

"Oh yes. And couldn't have made us happier," Emmeline said. "I only wish that Simon's parents had known. They were so fond of you."

Abigail snorted. "I expect they do, considering the spectral goings-on around here."

"I thought you didn't believe in . . . spirits," Paige said quietly so that others around them couldn't hear.

"I never said that. Only that I couldn't see them myself. I feel like I'm missing out on an interesting life experience."

"Afterlife experience," Emmeline teased.

"Don't be smug, Em!"

They laughed.

"What are your plans for today?" Emmeline asked Paige.

"Some swims and maybe kayaking this morning. And reading more old letters."

"Can you find time this afternoon for a chat?"

"Of course!"

"Simon suggested we use his place."

"Right after lunch then? Best time to be out of the sun."

"Perfect."

Paige was intrigued, but in the meantime, she waylaid Angie and Tony and explained what had transpired.

"I knew she was a scheming phoney!" Angela fumed. "So smarmy on the outside, but with steely eyes and icy core. Thank God you came back, so that you and Simon found each other again. At least the inn's closing has brought something wonderfully positive."

She gave Paige a big hug. "I always thought you two were meant for each other! You definitely have to come for a visit when the inn closes. We're only an hour and half away, and it'll be a distraction for Simon. He shouldn't watch the place being demolished."

"I agree," Tony said. "But I'm assuming he'll have you by his side as he adjusts to this dramatic change?"

"To quote you – 'damn right'!"

When she informed Marshall, he said, "Excellent! I told you the Moodies are always right." She could hear the smile in his voice.

"I'm not surprised about Veronica. She gave me bad vibes. Are you moving in with him now?"

"I'm staying in the boathouse. Maybe we should take things slowly. Just to be sure."

"I'll be damned if you're not already sure. After ten years of pining for each other? Seize every moment with zest and passion. In all senses."

She chuckled. "More sage, big-cousin advice."

"You can't get married until your divorce comes through. So just enjoy living together in the meantime. By then you'll know for sure that this time it's right. And you'll have already woven a strong relationship."

"That's certainly our inclination."

"Then go for it! You're not getting any younger, Kiddo. The big 3-0 next year."

"Stop!" she giggled.

"I'm really thrilled for you both. Enjoy your weekend. But keep an eye on the weather. There could be a severe storm heading our way."

■   ■   ■

Emmeline suggested they sit on the veranda. When they had settled into wicker chairs angled towards each other, she began. "Remember what I said when we saw the Segwun approaching that morning? That I recalled that day exactly?"

"Yes."

"It turned out to be a life-changing summer. Abby and Simon know, but otherwise, this is strictly between us." Emmeline riveted Paige with her ancient eyes.

"I understand. Thank you for trusting me. But why?"

"Because you and Simon finally have a future together."

Paige sensed that secrets were about to unfold.

"It was strange and sad for Abby and me to be here without our parents that summer. But it wouldn't have made a difference. We were adults and *accomplished women*, as Edward called us. A vase of red and white roses awaited us in our usual room, since the Davenports knew that I'd graduated from university that spring.

"We arrived on Sunday along with plenty of others staying for a few weeks or the summer. In those days, dancing and most entertainments, even some sports were forbidden by law on the Sabbath. But Edward always informally played piano at the pavilion on those nights.

"He'd start with a few classics from Beethoven, Mozart, Chopin, and such. Then he'd move on to popular singsongs for the audience to join in – "By the Light of the Silvery Moon", "Moonlight Bay", and the like – putting everyone into a holiday mood. The evening was always a happy introduction or return to Westwind.

"You should realize that Edward was only a year older than Simon is now. I had just turned twenty-one."

Emmeline had a beatific look on her face as she recalled those youthful days. Paige was already captivated.

* * * * * * * * * *

Summer 1933

Emmeline was glowing, basking in the music from Edward's skilled fingers. She was convinced that he always played Debussy's "Clair de Lune" with such feeling for her, since it was her favourite.

While everyone was dispersing after the concert, Edward waylaid them, saying, "Ladies, would you do me the honour of coming to my music room for a nightcap? I have something I'd like to discuss with you."

Abby knew that she was infatuated with Edward, and as the elder, responded, "We'd be delighted!"

The music room was a surprise, with a wall of windows facing south, and sets of French doors opening onto the deep, screened veranda overlooking the lake to the east. Bevelled glass doors led into the adjoining parlour of the house. A baby grand piano took up a back corner, next to a gramophone and a two-sided fireplace shared with the library behind. White wicker furniture with sumptuous floral cushions accentuated the cheerful turquoise walls. Palm trees scattered throughout exuded a tropical feeling.

"How delightful!" Emmeline said. "In all seasons, I expect."

"Plenty of sun streams in in winter," Edward agreed as he discarded his navy blazer and silk ascot, making him look younger and more carefree. "And we have spectacular views of blizzards. So the fireplace is well used." He grinned.

Once they were seated with Martinis in hand, he said, "We were shocked and saddened to hear about your parents. Is there anything we can do to help?"

"Very kind of you, but we're coping," Abigail reassured him. "Father trained me well these past two years, so I can manage the business until it's a better time to sell. We already appreciate that you've given us the printing of your brochures and encouraged other resorts to do so as well."

"We value our long-time guests. Friends, really." He smiled warmly. "And we're so delighted with the painting you gave us for the inn's 50th anniversary last year, Miss Emmeline, that I'd like to commission you to do some paintings for us. Before you become too famous," he added with a twinkle in his eyes.

"Zowie! I'm flattered," Emmeline said in astonishment.

"You can see it has pride of place in here. Florence wanted to hang it in the main lounge, but it speaks to my soul. It's not only eye-catching, but also subtly incorporates so many of the elements that define this place."

She could hardly contain her excitement. "Thank you, Mr. Davenport. This is overwhelming. Wonderful!"

"Edward, please. At least in private."

"Then you must drop the Miss."

"Done! My other thought is that with the Muskoka Chautauqua sadly gone, we could adopt their admirable aims to provide enrichment for mind, body, and soul. The latter two are well served by our sublime setting and plentiful sports. But guests have mentioned how much they enjoyed our forays to the Epworth Inn to listen to lectures, poetry readings, and such."

Her family had always participated, with Mummy particularly interested and supportive of the Chautauqua movement.

"So, to begin with, we have a botany professor staying for a month, who has agreed to take people on a weekly walk through the woods to examine the local flora, an astronomer will show us the constellations on a clear night, and a geologist will enlighten us about the Precambrian Shield that partly defines Muskoka.

"I also want to promote Canadian culture and the arts, so I was wondering if you would be amenable to giving a weekly lesson in watercolour painting *en plein air*, Emmeline, and if you, Abigail, would read and lead a discussion of literary works by Canadians.

I thought we could start with Pauline Johnson, the part Mohawk author..."

"Whose poetry includes ones set in Muskoka!" Abigail finished with glee. "Yes, of course! Mother was a great admirer of hers. She'd be thrilled as well."

"I'll reduce your charges by a week each, if that seems fair."

"There's no need," Emmeline interceded before Abby could reply. "These are difficult times for everyone."

"I insist. We've been lucky here. So, let's toast your degree, Emmeline, and our mission to showcase Canadian talent."

They raised their glasses.

"So, Abigail, have you had a chance to write more of your popular skits for our talent shows?"

"I have indeed, but I know I can't make a career of them. So, I've approached a couple of radio stations to see if they might be interested in some new programming, which I've tentatively titled 'Out and About'. CFRB in Toronto is, so I'm to write a few scripts, and if they like them, they'll give me a weekly spot on the radio!" She preened. "I have several ideas that I will explore this summer, including the ridiculous Sabbath Day laws. Did you know that it's illegal for people to toboggan in Toronto on a Sunday? That kiddies' swings and slides in the parks are locked? That a judge ruled golf on a Sunday was little different from a walk in a park, but all other sports and amusements – the ones that the working people enjoy and can afford - are still banned? On their only day off work?"

"Absurd! I expect you'll do a brilliant presentation with passion and humour, and might even bring about some changes. You must let me know when it goes on the air."

"Thank you! That's so kind."

"I envy your talents, ladies."

"Don't sell yourself short, Edward. Your command of the piano is astounding," Abby declared. "I never managed to be anything but a mediocre music student. Emmeline has more discipline and talent than I, musically."

"You were gushing, Abby," Emmeline accused later as they lay in their beds. "I hope you're not becoming infatuated with Edward."

"I might if *you* weren't already. He's a fine figure of a man with all the qualities I admire in a potential mate. Except that he's married."

When Emmeline didn't respond, Abby added, "I don't want you to get hurt, Em. I expect Edward doesn't even realize the effect he has on you."

"I can't help how I feel. Nor can he be held responsible." Even his British accent enthralled her.

"Well, don't be foolish. If you're prepared to have an affair, that's your business. Just don't expect it to end well."

They turned their backs to each other, Emmeline wondering if Abby was as indifferent as she alleged. It hadn't occurred to Emmeline to have an affair with Edward, but it must have to Abby, who'd already had one at university "to see what all the fuss was about". She'd enjoyed it immensely, but not so much the fellow she'd had it with, who was seeking a chatelaine for a wife, not an equal. So, it wouldn't be much of a leap for her to seek another. "No longer being a virgin is liberating," she'd said. "Now I don't have to 'save myself' for marriage with some fellow who might turn out to be an inept lover."

Their room was on the ground floor at the farthest end of the Lodge, with just the beach and woods beyond. Daddy had wanted them as close to an exit as possible, in case of fire, so they were right next to the Lodge's back door.

Their bay window overlooked the lake down a short slope thick with ferns and a constant parade of colourful perennials. Edward had brought his love of English country gardens with him, which made Westwind more elegant and beautiful than the other resorts. Cottagers often boated past to see the everchanging gardens, overseen by a dedicated team, even in these lean times.

There was no reason to close their curtains, so a crescent moon and ambient lights from the distant wharf shimmered across the water and provided enough illumination for Emmeline to see the connecting door to the room that had been her parents'. Now, forever locked.

Daddy had only been with them for a week at the beginning and end of the summer, plus two middle weeks when he could manage them. So, when Mummy had been alone, the door had always been left open, and they had talked to her in the darkness before sleep claimed them.

Emmeline tried to stifle her sobs.

"I miss them, too," Abby lamented. "But we'll always have each other. No matter what."

■   ■   ■

Emmeline dressed quickly in her flared sailor slacks, red and white striped jersey, and navy cardigan to stave off the morning chill. She let herself out quietly, painting supplies in her bag, and hurried over to the far end of the flagstone terrace along the shore. She wanted to catch the elusive dawn, accompanied by the call of a loon, both of which always touched her soul.

She knelt to scoop water into her jars from the lake, and then perched on the garden wall which, along with a riot of flowers, seemed to be holding back the hillside sliding towards the lake. With the jars at her side, pan palette in hand, and paper block on her lap, she quickly placed colours so that the bristling, distant islands and the rectangular gazebo at the end of the dock began to take shape. Clouds bloomed from the twilight and promised a magnificent celestial display. She'd have to work quickly to capture the rich, brimming hues of sunrise.

"You're out early," Edward said, coming up beside her.

"I hate to miss one of the best times of the day. Do you ever sleep?" she asked without looking at him. She knew that he didn't retire until all the guests had.

He chuckled. "Not more than necessary in summer. Every moment is special, and I've already enjoyed my morning dip. Do you mind if I watch you paint?"

"Not if you don't mind my ignoring you."

He laughed fulsomely. "I will refrain from interfering with the creative process and just marvel at it."

She tried not to let his presence distract her. His silence helped, and she was completely absorbed in her painting once again.

She finished as the fire-edged clouds in the smoky purple sky, reflected in the still water, began to fade into placid white against a gentle blue morning. And was surprised that he was still there.

"That was magical," he said simply, yet with such reverence and respect that her heart sang. "And that is definitely a painting for our house."

"I could add more detail and definition now that I have the shapes and colours."

"It's perfect the way it is. It seems more alive than a studio creation. Evokes emotion as well as capturing a unique moment in time."

She beamed. "My thoughts exactly! I'm lucky to have work creating graphics for some of our clients at the shop, but I love the freedom to paint what inspires me, so thank you for this opportunity."

"We benefit as much as you," he assured her. "Now come and make yourself comfortable in a chair while I fetch us some coffee," he said, holding out his hand.

His touch felt as if they were connecting on some visceral, yet profoundly spiritual level. He looked at her quizzically, as if surprised, and released her hand reluctantly.

She needed a moment to calm her own shock, and stammered, "Oh, you have new chairs."

"There's a story behind those. Let me know what you think when I return with our coffee."

"The most comfortable chair I've ever sat in!" she declared when he handed her a cup.

He grinned. "Delighted to hear that. They are a new venture of mine and Fred's – the Westwind Chair Company. Last year, an American guest suggested that we should have Adirondack chairs here. I ordered one from New York to see what it was like, but decided that it could be even more comfortable with a few contours to better suit the body. Fred was keen to try the design changes, so he built these first four when he'd finished his latest boat. We'll see how our guests like them this summer. Then we'll hire craftsmen to build more, and start selling them at the marina if they become popular enough."

"You are enterprising, Edward!"

He shrugged. "Making people comfortable and happy here is our main objective. We also provide as much work for the locals as possible. So, bringing in extra money is a bonus."

Emmeline suddenly wondered if his offering her and Abby projects was a way of distracting them from their grief. "It means so much to us that this is our second home. Especially now."

"No supportive relatives?"

"Older cousins who are scandalized that we're university educated," she scoffed. "Little wonder our parents kept their distance from them."

"I was the black sheep. I think my father was relieved that 'the colonies' took me in. My family has never even come to visit. Of course, I've been going home for several weeks every autumn, but they show only cursory interest in my life here, and don't acknowledge what I've accomplished."

He looked out pensively but contentedly at the scene before them. "But I felt that I belonged here almost the moment I arrived. My destiny." As if coming out of a trance, he added in embarrassment, "Do forgive me for being such a bore."

"Not at all! It was spoken from the heart. But you have every reason to take pride in this place. You provide fun and relaxation in a beautiful, invigorating, healing environment for hundreds or even thousands of people each year. And support your community. What could be a better contribution to society?"

He smiled at her. "Thank you for that accolade. You're wise for your age."

"Abby says I'm an old soul," she replied with a grin.

"A sensitive, compassionate one," he murmured, looking deeply into her eyes.

Flustered, heart pounding, she was the first to look away.

■   ■   ■

She fell even more in love with him over the next days as he found opportunities to be alone with her, watching her paint, and invited her and Abby to his cocktail hours in the tower room or on the private terrace by his boathouse on hot days.

One day, he took her along the path to the top of the Ridge Dragon - so named by Florence and her siblings as kids. "This is off-limits to the guests, so don't tell anyone."

"What a view! I will bring my paints next time."

They sat on a boulder as they stared over the lake reflecting a pure blue sky occasionally wrinkled with gossamer clouds. White sailboats listed as they skimmed across the water. The resort buildings to their left, the golf course spreading out behind and beyond it, and the Hawksley Marina in the bay further along showed how extensive the property was.

"The first time I sat here, I realized that I wanted always to have this as my domain. Silly to think that anyone can lay claim to billion-year-old rocks," he admitted. "But for a person's lifetime, he or she can believe that. It's rather reassuring that we can feel like a part of this ancient landscape as well as the even older nighttime heavens. Makes it easier to believe that our souls carry on without our earthly shells, and contemplate what adventures await."

She accepted the cigarette he offered, although she rarely smoked. It was a rite of passage for modern young women to illustrate their independence and nonchalance by gracefully putting a gasper to their lips. But it did help to put her at ease at times.

"Do you believe in soulmates?" he asked.

"Yes. I've felt the possibilities." Especially when he touched her. "But I think it doesn't necessarily have to be with a lover. Best friends can be, and even places, in a way. My soul feels nurtured here. I hug trees sometimes," she said with a self-deprecating chuckle. "To show them how much I admire and appreciate them. I believe every living thing has a vital *essence* or soul, if you will, and even rock and water and sand can resonate with us. Sustain and comfort us."

Mummy had advised never to pretend to be what you're not. If the man you love doesn't respect and appreciate you for who you truly are and what you believe, then run for the hills!

She breathed a sigh of relief when he said, "That's profound. But now I shall hesitate to step on the grass."

She laughed. "But that's how the earth can connect with you. Even better in bare feet, though," she said as she slipped out of her canvas Mary Jane sandals and felt the warm granite beneath.

"Agreed," he said, removing his shoes and socks. "Where this ridge slides into the lake, there's a spot I like to stop and sit when I'm swimming, known in the family as the Dragon's Point. It makes me feel even more connected to this place. The rocks resonate with me, too."

She grinned joyfully.

Looking at her feet, he said, "Do you know why women were required to wear bathing stockings and shoes when swimming, before the war?"

"To match those hideous wool bathing costumes that Mother said were wont to drown you?"

"That too! But primarily because their bare feet and shapely ankles were considered too arousing."

They gazed into each other's eyes, and he kissed her gently and then more deeply as she moaned. He cupped her breast, which sent waves of desire flooding through her.

All her resolve to distance her emotions from him disappeared.

"I'm sorry!" he groaned as he drew away from her. "That was inappropriate."

"No, don't stop. I want this as much as you do," she panted, unbuttoning her blouse.

He freed her breasts and kissed them while he stripped off her clothes and brought her to a point where she thought she would explode with ecstasy. The momentary pain of their coupling was like an exquisite piercing of her soul, allowing his to flow into and mingle with hers.

When they'd finished, he held her tenderly in his arms and said, "You are a remarkable woman, Emmeline. But you shouldn't have let me take your virginity."

"I'm glad to be rid of it," she said with grin. "It was an encumbrance redolent of outdated morality."

"You believe in free love, then?" he asked, offering her a cigarette when they were dressed and seated beside each other again.

"I believe that neither church nor state should tell men and women who and how and when they can love. But I am sorry if this affects your marriage."

"Don't be. That's primarily a business partnership. We're best of friends, but Florence has never been much interested in marital intimacy, except to have a child. After her fourth miscarriage last year, she declared that she didn't want to risk trying again.

"She told me I should find myself a mistress, if I needed one. As long as I'm discreet. But I had to promise to never end our marriage. It gives us both respectability, which we need to keep this place running successfully. Since I've invested all my money in Westwind, I can't leave anyway."

"I would happily be your mistress, Edward. I'm in love with you. But I don't expect marriage. Just *your* love and devotion in return."

"Dear God, Emmeline! Are you certain? That's a huge sacrifice."

"Not if it's the only way we can be together. Why should we require a document to bind us if our hearts do?"

He kissed her passionately. "You've just made me the happiest man alive!"

She laughed with delight. "Now we have to figure out how to make this work."

"Come to my boathouse at midnight. Everyone else will be asleep. Florence and I have separate bedrooms in any case."

She met him nightly in the boathouse suite. Sometimes they skinny-dipped in the private cove after making love and aroused themselves again.

Abby just shrugged and said, "I hope you're taking precautions."

"Edward is." Although not when they were in the lake. It was too difficult to stop for something that also diminished their pleasure.

"I have to admit I'm envious. And a bit surprised that you're so daring."

"I'm not. Just madly in love."

"And lust. I remember how that felt. I really must find myself a fellow here, or I'll have a very dull summer in comparison."

Emmeline giggled.

When Abby had to go to the city for several days because some business required her attention, Edward easily slipped into their room next to the back door of the Lodge and stayed with Emmeline until almost dawn.

Her most fervent wishes had come true. That was the magic of Westwind.

* * * * * * * * * * *

Having given Paige the gist of this, Emmeline said, "But, of course, things are never that easy or uncomplicated."

Paige wasn't shocked, only a bit surprised at Emmeline's casual approach to sex over sixty years ago. She hadn't realized how prevalent the free love movement had been at that time.

"Before the summer was over, I was pregnant."

Paige had been expecting that. And realized that Emmeline was Simon's grandmother.

"I did believe that marriage is important when children are involved, giving them rights and status that they wouldn't otherwise have in those days. No child should ever be considered *illegitimate*. That's like denying them humanity!

"Edward said that he and Florence would adopt our baby, if I was willing. I could see the child every summer at least." Emmeline looked pensive and sad as she peered back sixty-four years. "I knew that was the right thing to do, wrenching as it was.

"Florence had a slightly different idea. She could pretend that she was pregnant. Pad herself out until she could go to Florida after Christmas. The regular guests wouldn't see her again for nine or more months anyway. It was just a matter of fooling her parents, because she didn't want them to know the truth about her relationships or fail to produce the heir they had been hoping for. They were in their sixties and would both be gone before they had to witness another war.

"I agreed to the subterfuge. I hid my pregnancy as long as I could, and then took to my bed with influenza, as far as friends and neighbours were concerned. So, a healing sojourn with distant family in sunny Florida was quite understandable.

"Edward rented a seaside villa in Palm Beach for all of us, including Lucinda. Abby was able to join us for a month, but then had to go back to look after the business and start her weekly radio broadcasts. It wasn't until Florence and Lucinda shared a room that I fully understood the nature of their relationship. So, Edward and I were blissfully together for those three months.

"It was a truly wonderful time! We became a big, happy family, each of us content within our own skins, our romantic relationships, and with each other. And that mutual love and respect stayed with us throughout our lives. We even spent two months there during the next four winters, before the war and while Richard was a toddler.

"Anyway, we came back to Toronto in late March, where Edward had rented the three of us a flat. Lucinda was off to spend time with her family, who liked to winter in California. Edward hired a midwife, which wasn't easy, since they weren't completely legal, but we were close to Women's College Hospital if anything went wrong. I was Florence, and she was my cousin Emmeline, come to help.

"The birth certificate named Florence as the mother, of course. That was hard to bear at first. But I realized it was in Richard's best interests as well. I did get to name him. After Father." She smiled.

"He was bottle fed after the first week, and Florence could claim she had trouble breast feeding. And that it would free her to work more easily.

"They took him home to delighted grandparents, and Abby and I went to Westwind for the entire summer again. So, I did get to see my precious boy quite often. Edward was so proud of him. And he was even more in love with me. We took extra precautions that summer. And for the next thirty plus years."

"Wow! What a love story."

Emmeline smiled. "Oh, yes. He also came to stay with me for weeks at a time in Ottawa, after Abby got the CBC Radio job in '38. Not many 'real' marriages were as happy. As you know.

"I've never regretted anything. Except perhaps that '38 was the last full summer we could spend at Westwind until we retired. But establishing careers was also important. I moved to Ottawa with Abby, of course. That's when I managed to get a job at the National Gallery.

"Ironically, the war was good to us. Edward was determined to do his bit, having been too young last time, and volunteered with the RCAF once he heard about the British Commonwealth Air Training Plan, and the hundred plus new airfields being built to train aircrew in Canada. He figured his experience feeding hundreds of people three times a day would be useful for their messing arrangements.

"It helped that he'd been in the Officers' Training Corps when he and Cliff were at Oxford. So, the RCAF made him an officer and put him in uniform, of which he was so proud. Headquarters were in Ottawa, so he was stationed there, although he also travelled across the country to the various training schools to help implement, inspect, and so forth.

"He visited me often. To our neighbours and friends, he was a British cousin who had emigrated to Canada in the '20s. To me, it was almost five years of bliss."

"Gosh!"

"But it was difficult to get time off in those days. Abby usually worked sixty-hour weeks at the NFB. She loved writing and editing those short documentaries that were shown in cinemas before the main films, eventually producing and directing them. But it meant that we were lucky to get a week at Westwind together. Things eased up after the war, of course. Richard was eleven by then."

"So, when did he and Simon find out the truth?"

"Edward and Florence decided that it was only fair to me for Richard to know. They thought it might be easier after one of them had passed away, for the other to tell him.

"He took it hard at first, but Florence assured him that he was always her beloved son, even if not biologically. That my generous gift to them was also for love of him, for what was in his best interests. And that my relationship with Edward had preserved their marriage, not ruined it. She said that they owed me a huge debt of gratitude, and that she hoped he would love and appreciate me as much as they had.

"By that time, there had already been the '60s sexual revolution, which took free love to another level, and has only continued to evolve, as you know. So, he didn't condemn us for that, once he had a chance to contemplate our relationships.

"I spent a lot of time with Florence during her last summer. And Richard saw the genuine affection between us. I think that's when he realized he'd always had two loving mothers in his life and forgave us all for the secrets and lies."

Emmeline hastily brushed away a tear.

"Richard told Simon before he went to university, and asked me to flesh out the tale, which I've just told you. Simon already thought of Abby and me as aunts, but after his initial shock, was delighted to still have a grandmother and a real great-aunt. So, he became even more attentive and caring. And now we virtually stay for free.

"It would have aroused suspicion among staff had Edward done that, but we had the means to pay, and he always brought us lavish gifts. But Simon insisted, and assured us that being the most loyal customers earned us a huge discount in anyone's reckoning," she concluded with a smile.

"You've never told anyone else this? Not even Veronica?"

"She didn't resonate with me," Emmeline replied with a wink.

Paige chuckled and went to hug Emmeline. "Thank you! May I call you Granny?"

"Simon calls me Gran when no one's around. He's another great joy of my life, and now you're augmenting that. I've been so lucky."

"So are we, to have you. Were you already grooming our friendship when we were kids?"

"Just giving you opportunities to share your talents and interests. I thought it a lovely idea that Edward's grandson and Cliff's granddaughter might fall in love. They would have approved wholeheartedly."

"And I bet you wished that," Paige said with a grin. "Invoking Westwind magic."

"Westwind is magical without my intervention. But I did think it might help," Emmeline responded with a twinkle in her eyes.

■   ■   ■

Paige went to meet Simon at his house for their prime roast beef dinner, delivered from the kitchen. Even Brett had praised that traditional Saturday night meal, which included perfectly baked Yorkshire pudding from Edward's mother's recipe, and sherry trifle for dessert. All very British, Paige knew, from her travels there.

She dressed in her favourite summer outfit – the floral one that Brett had thought so sexy that last weekend he was here - but without the turquoise jewelry that had celebrated their second anniversary. She felt like an excited schoolgirl going on a special date.

She brought her key in case he wasn't home yet. But the front door was open. She heard the piano and went towards the music room, expecting Simon to be there. She realized the tune was "I'm Still Standing" - the Elton John song that had become Rebecca's anthem.

Paige's sudden vision of Bex "still standing" among the lake bottom weeds sent a frisson of fear through her.

She entered cautiously. The music stopped. There was no one there. The room was uncannily quiet, as if it were holding its breath. Paige tensed, expecting Bex to suddenly materialize.

She shrieked when a hand touched her shoulder.

"Paige!" Simon said, taking her into his arms. "What's going on? I heard music and thought you were playing."

"She's still here! Tormenting us!"

He turned to the empty room and said firmly, but not unkindly, "Bex, you don't belong here anymore. Go to your parents. Realize that they didn't choose to leave you, and stop being so angry. Rest in peace. And leave us alone, for God's sake!"

As if the room had suddenly been unmuffled, the sounds of boats and lake activities were now faintly noticeable, and Paige realized she hadn't heard Simon approach at all. It was as if Bex had sucked all the life and sound out of the room. It gave her the chills.

But now everything seemed normal again, the house feeling relaxed and comforting, not threatening.

His arm around her shoulders, Simon escorted her onto the screened veranda, where domed platters awaited them on the dining table. He poured them each a glass of exceptional wine and toasted, "To the love of my life. And to our future together."

He pulled a small box out of his pocket and handed it to her. "I brought this back from Australia for you. Will you wear it as a token of my love?"

It was a sparkling blue sapphire in a square nest of tiny diamonds set in a white-gold band. "It's gorgeous!"

She had removed her ostentatious diamond engagement ring and wedding band yesterday, so she slipped it onto her finger. "Almost a perfect fit. Thank you for this and the love that it holds." She kissed him.

"I kept it as a reminder of you. But I've dreamt of this moment. In my *Wildest Dreams*." He grinned.

"Marshall said that the Moodies always got it right."

Chapter 18

A sinewed hand reached out of the punishing waves and yanked her away from the overturned canoe....

Paige awoke with a gasp. She began quivering as panic raced through her like an electrical current. In the grey twilight, it took her a moment to realize where she was.

Simon stirred as she began to weep. "Hey, what's wrong?" He gathered her into his arms and stroked her head soothingly.

"I remember what really happened. Oh God! . . . I might have killed Bex." She looked at him in anguish.

"What?"

"She tried to drown me! I suddenly remember everything. I've suppressed that all these years.

"When the canoe capsized, we both came up on the same side – away from the cottagers who came to my rescue. She manoeuvred close to me as we clung to the gunwales. Then she cried, 'He's mine, bitch!' and grabbed my ponytail, forcing my head under the water."

"Christ!"

"I tried to fight her, but she was behind me and put her knees on my back, pushing, keeping me under. Insanely strong. I remembered what to do when a drowning person grabs you. So I swam down and away. She didn't let go of my hair at first, so I kicked as hard as I could to propel myself. And I hit something. Maybe I knocked the wind out of her. I barely had enough breath left to surface, but when I did, I was on the other side of the boat. Oh, Simon! For a decade I blamed myself for not saving her. But I'm probably *responsible* for her death!"

"No, Paige! You can't think like that. It was self-defence. Even if you did kick her in your attempt to escape, it's not your fault."

He held her tightly. "Start at the beginning. Tell me everything that happened that day."

She didn't hold anything back. It was a relief and a purge to finally tell him everything. And she realized that she wasn't responsible for anything that led to Rebecca's death, but it was healing to hear him say it.

They had their morning swim under a marbled slate sky that seemed to trap the heat and humidity, making it hard to breathe. The water looked like molten pewter as a smudge of sun reflected off it. Beautiful in its moodiness but threatening.

Paige felt unsettled, but not just by the intense heat.

By the pricking of my thumbs, Something wicked this way comes.

"There's potential for severe thunderstorms with gale force winds today," Simon informed her as they sat on the edge of the terrace dangling their feet in the water. "Let's hope something clears the air before the next contingent of guests arrives. So don't go out in a boat. OK?"

"Don't worry. I'm sticking close. In fact, give me something to do, where I can be by your side." She grinned as she wrapped her arm around his and leaned against him.

She had a nagging feeling that she shouldn't stay here alone today. If there was violent weather, she would be separated from everyone else, and it was a few hundred yards to the inn. With lots of trees enroute.

"Start by having breakfast with me. Speaking of which, I'd better get going. Another full house this week."

As they ate egg sandwiches in his office, Simon was going through the guest list taking note of those who weren't leaving today. "Since there aren't many of you, we need to know who *is* here and where, in case there's an emergency. Especially with bad weather expected."

"Is that so you can do a head count in case of a tornado or some catastrophe?"

"Exactly! On rainy days, people aren't inclined to arrive early to spend time on the beach, and those already here will likely head into town for some shopping and lunch. The cottagers don't flock to the sundeck bar, so it will be pretty quiet for a while."

Consulting his computer, he said, "It looks like we don't have anyone else on the sisters' floor. One couple on the second. Two families in the Lodge, just Tony and Angie in the Suites, and four cabins occupied."

"So, you have lots of people checking in this afternoon."

"The usual Sunday. All hands on deck."

"Do you have a couple of minutes this morning to pose for a photo with me? I want to capture this moment. For my parents as well." She held out her hand with the sapphire. "I expect Angie or Tony would be happy to oblige."

He must have sensed her urgency. "Of course! Bring them over after breakfast and we'll pop onto the veranda."

She smiled but was spooked by her escalating anxiety. *Stop being afraid to be happy! Otherwise, you'll be the cause of your unhappiness.*

"After that, you should tell the sisters what really happened with Bex. I think the more people you trust with the truth, the more you'll truly believe it and relinquish the guilt." He caressed her cheek gently. "I love you, Paige. Nothing will ever change that or come between us again."

She tensed. *Don't tempt the gods, Simon!*

But she smiled joyfully as Tony took a photo of Simon hugging her close to his side and holding her hand to show the ring, which Angela declared, "Beautiful, and so *you*, Paige".

Before getting back to work, Simon said to them, "There's a small craft warning out now, so stay safe. The staff are putting the boats under cover and not letting people take out any vessels."

The wind was already licking up waves.

"Hopefully the storm will be a relief, and not just create more humidity," Angela said. "Meanwhile, Nipper and I are staying on the deck or in the air conditioning, reading a novel. After our swim."

"And I have some scientific journals to catch up on, so a lazy day for us," Tony concluded.

The Pembrook sisters had watched the proceedings from a nearby bandshell bump-out of the veranda and were eager to see Paige's ring when she joined them.

"Simon has good taste. Like someone else I know," Emmeline said, holding out her right hand to reveal the Art Deco sapphire and diamond ring she had worn for over sixty years.

Paige looked at her questioningly, and she nodded.

"I've always admired that ring! Now I understand it. Simon decided it was premature to call mine an engagement ring, since my divorce proceedings haven't even begun. He called it a *soulmate ring*."

"What a lovely idea! Since that's relevant to only you."

Suddenly serious, Paige said, "He suggested I tell you about Rebecca. What really happened that day."

They were shocked. "But not completely surprised," Abigail added. "When she first arrived, she admired and emulated you. But by that last summer, she wanted to *be* you. I could see the jealousy in her eyes, which worried me, because I didn't trust her. But what she did was . . . just evil!"

Emmeline said, "Perhaps now that some of us know the truth about what happened, she'll finally leave you alone."

"I wish she would! She was at the house again last night," Paige admitted.

The sisters looked at each other.

"Can we impose upon you to stay close to us today?" Emmeline asked. "There's a nasty storm coming. I'm sure you feel it as well. We'll present a united front should there be any . . . interference."

They held out their hands to her and she took them. A circle of three.

· · ·

Paige decided this might be a good time to be distracted by Cliff's novel. It was so easy to disappear into the story.

But on her way to fetch her copy from the boathouse, she had the sudden urge to tell Angela and Tony about Bex as well.

The six Water's Edge Suites were attached units with their entrances at the back and large decks perched above the shoreline. The Vanderbecks' was at the north end of the row, which gave them the bonus of a large side window overlooking the wharf and with a view up to the inn.

"This is nice! Very modern and posh," Paige declared as she was invited inside. As well as a king-size bed, there was a sofa bed, an armchair, and a desk with an office chair. The décor was more urban chic than cottage cozy, and Paige suspected Veronica's hand in that. "And great views."

"We like having the extra window, so this has been our regular unit since these were built," Angela said. "Thankfully, we get the former-employee discount."

"I feel a bit awkward," Paige began when she was seated. "But I think Simon is right that I need to talk to people I trust."

"I'm delighted to be included then," Angela assured her.

"And me," Tony agreed.

Trying not to sound pathetic or seek pity, she gave them a summary of her PTSD before telling them about finally discovering the truth.

"Oh my God, Paige!" Angela went over to hug her, barely able to speak.

"Bloody hell!" Tony said. "I knew that kid was troubled, but we all tried to help her. And Simon went to heroic lengths to be nice to her and keep his temper in check, especially when she flew off the handle."

"But that's not all, is it?" Angela asked astutely.

Paige hesitated. "You're going to think I'm crazy, but... she's still here." She told them a few things that Simon and Emmeline could corroborate, ending with the piano playing last night. "So, I thought if you knew, she might finally give up and go away."

"Oh hell!" Angela paled as she said, "I thought I saw a shadow lurking behind you when you two were dancing the other night at the house. Indistinct, so I thought it was a trick of the encroaching darkness, since we only had candles burning and casting flickering light. And when I looked directly at it, it vanished. Oh my God!"

Tony came over and embraced them both. "Tell us what we can do to help, Paige."

"Just having your support is important. But be vigilant and take care."

Back at the boathouse, Paige called Marshall.

"Jesus Christ, Paige! No wonder you've been so traumatized. Do you want me to come over?"

"Thanks, but I'm being well looked after. I promised the sisters I'd hang out with them while Simon works."

He guffawed. "You're in good hands then."

"Anyway, it's getting bad out there. I just thought you should know."

"Damn right! I hope you can finally put all this horror behind you and heal. Start a new life."

"I realize now that Brett was part of the broken me, pretending everything was OK, but grasping for validation. Now I'm off to a good start. Being with the people I truly love. So, make sure you look after yourself as well."

"No worries there. But I'm going to have a hell of a time keeping Dunc and Gav from rushing up here to hug you."

She chuckled.

Noticing how agitated the lake was becoming under the gloomy sky, she closed the windows and grabbed Cliff's manuscript and her camera.

The breeze was like hot, sour breath as she made her way back. The tall trees were trembling.

The resort seemed frantic as people moved out, eager to get underway with the forecasted storm spoiling extra beach time, and hoping to avoid a messy drive home.

She joined the sisters in the bandshell. Abigail had her Super 8 camera handy.

"Feels like a doozy of a storm coming in," she said. "I'm going to film this suffocating calm before all hell breaks loose. That'll be part two."

"I'll come," Paige offered. "The sky is strange and wondrous and rather terrifying."

"So, good photos then. Especially with the wharf empty of people and boats."

"This does feel eerie," Paige said as they walked to the garden above the terrace. "Places that usually cater to crowds seem forlorn and spooky when they're deserted. Simon must find it strange here for half the year."

"Edward said that once the guests left, he felt the enormity of his domain. I think it's partly why he built the wall and tree barrier to separate the house from the resort – for privacy in summer and to make his home feel more intimate the rest of the year. But it and other things were built during the Depression to give work to local people."

Paige was trying to imagine living here with Simon year-round. Perhaps it would be a good thing to have a four-season resort next door, but not too close and not too large. She had to admit that having a restaurant just steps away was a bonus, and wondered if she and Simon could get privileges or a membership to use the indoor and outdoor tennis courts and pools.

What a thrill it was to think of a future she hadn't even imagined before!

But that thought also made taking these photos more poignant.

She shot the lake through the flowers and over the contented row of Muskoka chairs perpetually waiting to show guests the splendid view. On the stone terrace, she photographed across the chairs to the lonely dock. She wished that both could be preserved in some way. They were a defining part of the iconic view of the resort from the water.

Paige and Abigail returned to the veranda when whitecaps began crawling in.

"Everyone has finally checked out," Simon said when he joined them. "How be we have burgers and fries in the family dining nook?"

They readily agreed.

The nook was a discreet alcove by the entrance to the dining room from the lounge. It gave the family oversight of the meals, while offering some privacy. Paige had usually seen Simon and his parents there in the old days, but hadn't noticed him or Veronica there at all. She suspected that Veronica felt it unprofessional to dine with her guests, and Simon probably ate at his desk or back at the house once he was off duty.

As if he'd been reading her thoughts he said, "This is nice! I haven't dined here since Mom got sick."

"Looking like a matinee idol in his navy blazer and silk ascot, Edward used to greet each guest at dinner, asking how their day had gone and making us feel as if we really were guests in his house. After everyone was seated, he would finally have his meal," Emmeline elucidated.

"And we had fun changing from our summer frocks or shorts into evening wear," Abigail added. "Most ladies wore jewels as well. So, every evening felt like a special occasion."

"I'm glad that you have film footage of that," Simon commented.

"That's one of the customs that younger people will marvel at," Paige agreed.

"And we became a summer community," Emmeline said. "Now, most people just want to keep to themselves for their week or few days here."

"Which is why '87 was the last time we had a masquerade dance," Simon reminded them.

Noticing the trees being increasingly tortured by the wind as the noise intensified, Paige began to feel that paralyzing panic gripping her.

Simon took her rigid hand in his and gave her a reassuring squeeze. "I need to get back to work. But you know where to find me. You can always sit in my office and read."

She tried not to look desperate as she smiled and replied, "Don't worry about me. We three will look after each other."

Simon kissed her tenderly on the lips when he rose. "We have promises to keep." He winked at her.

And miles to go before we sleep, she paraphrased Robert Frost's poem. *Many many miles! . . . If only I could believe it!*

The ponderous sky was turning indigo as angry clouds coalesced and pressed down to smother the lake. The wind roared as it thrashed the trees, whipping the smaller ones nearly to the ground. Severed leaves and small branches were flying horizontally.

"I won't go off the veranda, but here comes part two," Abigail announced.

Paige grabbed her camera and went along. Facing her storm phobia was something else that she needed for healing.

Abigail captured a couple of the heavy Muskoka chairs on the waterfront terrace being picked up and flung into the lake as if they were made of popsicle sticks. With her telephoto lens, Paige snapped them bobbing crazily in the waves smashing against the rocky ledge, sending spray high over the terrace. Thunder growled in the distance.

Emmeline was agitated, feeling something dire was about to happen. Stepping onto the veranda, she urged, "Do come back inside!"

As they did, Edward's clocked chimed.

They looked at each other, aghast.

Simon rushed into the lounge. "What the hell?" He pulled Paige close with one arm and extended the other to embrace the sisters. For a moment, they huddled together as Paige and Abigail closed the circle.

Louise came in, saying, "Simon, we've had a call from the guests in cabin 12. They were trying to come back from Port Carling, but there's a big tree uprooted and blocking our road. I told them to go back to the village and find somewhere safe until the storm's over."

"Thanks, Louise! Ask Barry to get a crew together so we can deal with it as soon as the worst of this has passed."

When Louise had left, Simon cautioned, "Stay inside. The veranda might not be safe if any trees come down."

"Please don't go out there, Simon!" Paige begged.

"I won't. Not yet. But we'll have to clear access before several hundred people arrive."

She clung to him as he gave her a hug before leaving.

The women were left wondering for whom the bell tolled this time.

In the lounge, Emmeline paced and then declared, "I need something from the room."

Abigail had gone to the ladies' washroom.

"I'll help," Paige offered, following her. "But let's hurry."

She didn't want to be on the top floor when the worst of the storm hit. While she had once loved watching raging thunderstorms, she now wanted to stay cocooned in the middle of a building, away from windows.

The housekeeping staff seemed to have finished with the rooms up here, as there was no cleaning cart present. Knowing that there was no one else on this floor at the moment suddenly made the hallway feel menacing. Paige refused to look at the door to the tower, although she felt like something sinister might suddenly emerge from it.

But she didn't close the door behind them because she feared it might stick in this humidity.

Thunder was creeping ever closer.

Emmeline grabbed a well-worn leather satchel and stuffed several envelopes into it from the coffee table.

"May I ask what those are?"

"Edward's letters to me. And photos. I don't bring all thirty-eight years' worth. Just my favourites."

"Oh wow! I haven't found any letters from you to him."

"Florence gave those back to me after he died."

"How thoughtful!"

Emmeline felt compelled to add the rest of her jewellery from Edward, carefully wrapped in a travel bag, into her satchel. She grabbed Abby's as well, since she had unique keepsakes from old suitors.

An ear-splitting blast shook the room.

"Have we been hit?" Paige cried. She turned to look into the hallway, but the door was closed.

Her blood ran cold. She rushed over and pulled frantically at the door handle. It was stuck fast.

She picked up the phone to call down to the front desk for help. There was no dial tone. And her cell phone was in the boathouse.

But there was ominous crackling outside the room. And the whiff of smoke.

The fire alarm began braying in the hallway.

"Oh, dear God," Emmeline said. *What have I done? Edward, you must help us now.*

Terrified, enraged, Paige yelled, "Stop this right now, Bex! I wish I *hadn't* wished to speak with you. But I realize now why you've been tormenting me. You were trying to scare me away before Simon and I reconnected. And before I remembered that you tried to kill me. Well, it's too late because I did, and I've already told lots of people! If you're looking for forgiveness, you won't get it by hurting Simon and everyone he loves. But you can still redeem yourself if you leave us alone. Begone from this world, where you no longer belong! Then I can begin to forgive you."

There was a guttural hiss, like the turkey vulture had made, which faded away on an icy breath that whipped around the room.

Paige felt an enormous sense of relief, as if she'd finally divested herself of Rebecca's curse. But it was only momentary. Smoke was seeping in under the door. She knew better than to open it. She hurried into the bathroom and soaked a large bath towel in water and stuffed it against the gap.

She picked up the phone and this time there was a dial tone. But no one answered.

■   ■   ■

The lightning strike to the tower had shaken the entire building.

And Edward's clock chimed again.

Abigail was frantic when Simon joined her. "I don't know where they went! But Paige left her camera and Cliff's manuscript. They're not outside, so they must have gone to our room."

The fire alarms screamed.

He raced up the stairs and made sure that the guests in 205 were not in their room. He'd already passed the chambermaids, whom he ordered to evacuate the building.

But smoke was billowing dangerously down the stairwell from the third floor.

He cursed as he turned back. He tried to call the room, but the line was dead. Louise had already summoned the fire department and warned them there was a tree down.

"Ask Barry to meet me out front with as many guys as he can round up, Louise. We're going to have to fight this ourselves until help arrives. And then get yourself and everyone else out of here ASAP."

The clock chimed eleven times.

"Grab Paige's and your things and go to the pavilion as fast as you can, Aunt Abby, and stay safely inside," Simon urged, back in the lounge. "I'll bring them to you. They'll be on the balcony if they're up there."

In the Water's Edge Suites, Angela looked out the side window after hearing the explosion. "Oh my God! The tower's on fire!"

It was alight at the top like a candle.

Tony joined her. "Bloody hell! Everything's so dry; that's going to spread like wildfire. I'd better go help! There are too many trees around here, so you should go to the pavilion. Remember the protocol for staff to gather there?"

"Yes, and maybe I can be of some help."

"But promise not to go out until the storm has passed. And if the fire spreads towards the dock, get to the marina. I'll find you!"

"Tony, please be careful. Nipper and I need you."

"You bet! Likewise!" He gave her a quick hug and kiss.

Angela grabbed the video camera and began filming the fire engulfing the tower as they walked together to the beginning of the wharf.

"Oh my God! There are people on the third-floor balcony! It looks like Paige and Emmeline!"

Paige saw them and started waving frantically. *Thank God someone knew where they were.* But she couldn't see that fire had burst through the roof from the vast, parched attic above the third floor.

A blinding flash of lightning was almost immediately followed by deafening thunder. As if ripped open, the inky clouds released torrential rain driven by the furious wind. Abigail seemed to be propelled by it as she hurried towards the wharf.

"Inside quickly!" Tony said to them both before he bounded up the stone stairs that led to the inn. Simon, carrying a ladder, gestured to him that they would be going up the fire escape staircase on the north side of the building.

Paige saw where Simon was headed and helped Emmeline roll over the waist high wall to what had been Paige's balcony. Like Paige, Emmeline wore a culotte-skirt, but one that reached her knees. Paige took Emmeline's satchel and slung it across her shoulders.

The second-floor landing of the fire escape was at the level of the roof over the front section of the dining room, with just a low railing to hop over. That roof was wide, with a gentle slope, but a short, steeper slope fanned out from the base of the second-floor balcony where it jutted out from the rest of the building. That was where Simon and Tony had to set up the ladder. The drenching rain was dampening the fire above their heads, but also making the shingles slippery. They knew they had little time to waste.

They steadied the ladder against the vicious wind. Paige grabbed it at the top and urged Emmeline to climb onto it.

"You should go first, dear. I'm not good with heights."

"Don't look down. Just straight ahead. And find each rung with your foot before putting any weight on it. Slide your hands down along the sides, but don't let go. You can do it, Gran. Please!"

She looked at Paige in regret, but suddenly saw Edward behind her. He smiled and nodded at her, and then disappeared. Gathering her courage, she flung a leg over and found purchase. Then the other. Slowly, painfully slowly for those watching, she managed to get down.

One of the staff had come to help, so he had her back by the time she was within reach and helped her down. Paige dropped the satchel to them, and he led Emmeline away quickly.

Paige hesitated as a ferocious gust of wind nearly ripped the ladder out of her hands. She had held it tightly against the railing when Emmeline descended, and wondered what would happen when no one was holding the top for her.

Startled by a brilliant flash of lightning and the sonic boom of thunder overhead, she let go of it.

As if blasted by the shock waves, the flaming tower collapsed through the seething roof, sending fiery sparks skyward and debris cascading onto and over the lower roof where Simon and Tony were standing. Leaping to safety on the second-floor balcony in front of them, they dropped the ladder, which the wind flung into the garden below.

Paige tried not to panic as the merciless fury and heat of approaching fire became more intense. She leaned over the rail and was relieved to see Simon unscathed, looking up at her.

"I'll be right there!" he shouted.

Barry and his gang arrived below the building with hoses, shooting water onto the lower roof to keep a safe path open, and trying to reach the roof above Paige.

"Get to the pavilion, Tony. I can manage this," Simon assured him.

Holding onto the square corner post, he hauled himself onto the railing right below Paige.

She looked at him fearfully.

"We can do this, sweetheart. Climb over. There are a couple of inches of floor there. Hang onto the balusters, step onto my shoulders, and then climb down me, just like when we were waterskiing."

She kicked off her sandals and flung them onto the wide roof below. Simon hooked his left arm around the post and had the other ready to assist her.

They did the maneuver flawlessly. Once she stood beside him, they scrambled off the railing and ran between smouldering debris to the stairs, gathering her shoes en route.

There was a huge cheer from the onlookers and those manning the hoses.

Once they were safely on the ground, Simon took her into a fierce embrace. "I was so afraid I was going to lose you again, my love," he whispered before ushering her down to the pavilion, where some of the staff and a few guests had gathered.

There was another cheer as they arrived on the dock.

"I caught all that on film," Abigail informed them.

"As did I on video," Angela said. "Elegantly done, you two!"

"You were supposed to stay safely inside!" Simon protested.

"That's what I said!" Tony agreed, his arm around Angela.

Abigail harrumphed. "When have I ever taken orders from a man? Besides, you can't be a great filmmaker if you don't take risks."

"I'll remember that next time you tell *us* to be careful," he shot back with a grin.

He went over to Emmeline, who looked shocked and dejected. "You did well getting down, Gran," he whispered to her.

"I felt that Edward was with me every step of the way.... But I should never have gone up there in the first place. That put us all in grave danger."

"I expect he was looking out for us. Anyway, you weren't to know what would happen, so please don't worry about it. I love you, Gran. C'mon, let's get inside."

She smiled gratefully. But she *had* felt impending disaster. Although not from the tower. It's where she'd often met Edward, once she and Abby had moved into the room across the hall, especially when the boathouse was occupied. She'd had a key. By that time, it was as much for companionable time together, like any married couple, as for sex.

One of the staff was passing out towels from the waterfront booth, so Simon draped one around Emmeline as he led her to a chair inside the pavilion. Towelling off, the others joined them.

"Now that everyone is safe, I don't think I can bear to watch anymore," Angela said, wrapping up her sopping long hair.

"Complimentary food and drinks, so order whatever you like," Simon said to the group of mostly staff. "It looks like this will be the sundeck's last day."

There were muted expressions of sadness amid the stunned silence as the enormity of the situation sank in. Without the old building, there was no resort. Even if all the other accommodations survived, there was no kitchen or dining room to handle all the guests. If they would even be permitted to be on site.

Simon took Paige aside and said, "I have to go and do God-knows-what to deal with this disaster. Let's invite the sisters, and Tony and Angie to stay at the house. Ask Emmeline if she and Abigail want the boathouse suite. I think it's special to her. And move in with me tonight."

"Gladly! . . . Oh, Simon, it shouldn't have ended this way. I'm so sorry. And thank you for your brilliant rescue. Thinking about our waterski routine overshadowed my fears – of the storm, the fire, Bex. I love you so much!"

They kissed passionately. "More of that later," he said with a grin. "Now you try to relax. Thankfully, the wind is blowing the smoke towards the beach, not the dock, so this is the safest place for people to be."

"Can I help with anything?"

"Look after the sisters. We've been storing the overflow inventory of Westwind clothes in one of the bedrooms in the house. Perhaps they should get out of their wet clothes, so take them there to get outfitted for the time being."

"I'll get the rooms ready as well."

"Great! We'll put Tony and Angie in my parents' old suite on the north side, where Veronica's been staying. Unless the sisters want that one. You'll find clean sheets and towels in the ensuite closet. The boathouse has its own linen closet, and there's one in my room."

Simon had moved into his grandparent's suite once Florence had passed away, but Paige had never seen it. Although that wing had its own back staircase and even an outside entrance, it had been too risky for them to meet there, especially with Bex around.

"OK. And I'll check the larder."

"You won't find much, since we always eat at the inn in the summer. I'll see what supplies are left from the sundeck bar. We might be eating burgers and fries for a while."

"But probably not butter tarts."

He smiled. "That's OK. Mum taught me how to make them. Every generation trained a family member to take over the kitchen if necessary."

"And you had no competition."

"Exactly!"

"A man of many hidden talents, then."

"I guess you'll find out."

"I can hardly wait!"

There was such love in his eyes that she *could* hardly wait to be in his arms again.

The rain eased up, and the wind finally abated as the thunderstorm moved south.

As Simon had feared, the fire had ample fuel inside with nothing to stop it, and rampaged through the old building.

No one wanted to leave the pavilion yet. It was as if they needed to stay together - to watch, to mourn, to feel the comfort of others in the final few hours of the resort's existence. It was still hot, although not so humid, so they were drying off nicely.

Louise and her team set up a temporary office inside the sundeck bar while the phone line was still active. They were already fielding calls from resorts, hotels, and motels within a thirty-mile radius, offering what few rooms they had available to incoming guests.

The rain and the firefighters from four stations, who had finally managed to get through, prevented any spread to the other buildings and trees. Being upwind, the nearby staff quarters were spared. Fortunately, no one had been injured.

But the inn kept burning. No amount of water could stop the inferno.

Once the lake had calmed sufficiently, boaters came by, word having spread that the legendary resort was ablaze. They offered help – food, clothes, accommodations for guests and staff who couldn't get home today. It was an incredible outpouring of sorrow and support from the local and summer communities.

Marshall arrived with Monique. "We could see the smoke but didn't realize it was from here. A friend at the Country Club called me with the news. This is heartbreaking. But I'm mightily relieved to see all of you hale and hearty."

"Have a look at my video," Angela offered.

"Jeez! You must have a guardian angel, Paige," Marshall said afterwards as he held her close.

Paige was shocked at how tense the rescue had been. And hadn't realized that only a few minutes after they were safely on the ground, the rooms were alight and shooting out tongues of flames to consume the balconies.

"I caught that on film," Abigail said to Marshall. "Which will be yours to use exclusively for the doc."

"Awesome. Thank you!"

"Em was quick enough to grab the films I'd already shot and add them to her bag. She knows what's important to me. Along with our wallets and car keys. Everything else is lost but can be replaced. An excuse to buy a new wardrobe," she chortled.

"What's your dress size, Miss Abigail? And Miss Emmeline's?" Monique asked. "I'm going to make a few calls. There are some lovely boutiques in the town and the village."

"That's kind of you, dear! We're both 10s."

"I'll say you are," Marshall quipped.

"You are a tease!" Abigail laughed.

He winked and then said, "I'm going to capture more of this activity. Including the generosity of the community and their obvious fondness for this place. Want to help with the interviews, Miss Abigail?"

"You bet!" She was suddenly energized.

Paige went and put an arm around Emmeline. "Simon was wondering if you preferred the boathouse suite to a room in the house as your new accommodations."

She brightened. "Oh yes! How thoughtful. But are we kicking you out?"

"Not at all! I'm moving in with him. Another step into our new life."

Emmeline drew her close, too emotional to speak. *How badly wrong that could have gone today.*

"I think we could both use a drink. Martini? Wine?"

"Martini. Stirred not shaken. Edward said 007 got it wrong."

Paige laughed.

They sat overlooking the lake through the bank of windows in the pavilion as they sipped their drinks. Neither could bear to watch the inn dying.

Paige glanced around the long building that had been a gathering point for tens of thousands of people during its seventy-three years, and where she had made many fun memories for ten of those.

She photographed the lake views, the empty stage, the people congregating, and Emmeline holding her precious satchel on her lap as she gazed out with wounded eyes that had witnessed so much here. Paige could only imagine how entwined Emmeline's life and sentiments were with this place.

She went over and gave "Gran" a hug and kiss on the cheek.

"Goodness!" Emmeline said, startled out of her reverie.

"I'm so glad you were able to retrieve what you hold dear. And that I was able to help. Don't ever regret that."

Angela and Tony were delighted to accept the invitation to stay in the house.

"But we don't want to be a bother," Angela insisted. "Let us know what we can do to help."

"Just having friends around right now is a big help."

When Marshall returned, he told Paige, "You and Simon are off film duty while you deal with this disaster. Tony, would you do me a favour and drop Monique off at Arcadia? She has some shopping to pick up." Marshall handed Tony the keys to *Diva*, but before releasing them, cautioned, with a piercing look, "You know that I value both of these ladies very highly."

"Yes, indeed," Tony chuckled. "I will guard them with my life. And appreciate the honour of driving this magnificent launch. I'll take Ang along, if I may."

"Go for it!"

It had stopped raining, so people migrated from the pavilion to the rooftop bar, where they dried off chairs with their towels, and themselves, in the blossoming sunshine. Marshall caught that on film as well, while Abigail fetched herself a Martini and joined her sister and Paige.

"I've had a chance to reflect on what happened on the balcony after you got down, Gran," Paige said. "And I've realized that if the wind gust hadn't almost torn the ladder from my hand, making me pause, and then the lightning and thunder scaring me into letting go of the ladder, I would have been on it when the tower collapsed, and we three would have been in the path of the burning debris." It sent a shiver through her. "I think there was a 'spirited' hand holding me back."

"I asked Edward to help us," Emmeline announced, profoundly thankful that he had apparently responded.

When Tony and Angela returned and joined them, she said, "Arcadia is amazing! But it was heart-rending to see the huge plumes of smoke as we drove back. This is so unreal. I feel as though I'm in a bizarre nightmare."

Most of the local media had left by the time a crew from the closest CTV station arrived and began interviewing people. They sought out Angela because someone had told them she'd filmed the epic rescue. Paige was glad that Marshall was there to advise.

"I think you should give them approval to use it, but don't sign away the rights. It *was* heroic. Because it had a happy ending, viewers will rejoice. It's very cinematic, and I don't think Hollywood could have done it better."

Paige chuckled. "But I didn't sign up for the gig."

"Which is why it's even more dramatic."

After the TV reporter had briefly interviewed her and Emmeline, Paige realized that the sisters were drained.

"Come to the house with me, and I'll get you settled in with your new Westwind wardrobe," Paige said to them.

"Won't we be fashionable then," Abigail jested.

Paige told Angela, "Why don't you go and pack, and we'll find some staff to bring your luggage to the house. I'll get the rooms ready."

"Let me help when I get there. You've had a tough day, to say the least."

"It's good to keep busy. But sure, thanks!"

Paige offered each sister an arm, but Marshall came over and offered his to Abigail.

"If I were forty years younger, I'd think you were flirting with me, Marshall."

"If you were, I *would* be," he asserted with a cheeky grin. "But I feel privileged to know you, Miss Abigail. You are a legend in the industry."

"Do stop, or I might get an inflated opinion of myself," she cackled. "But I have always appreciated the attentions of a talented and handsome man."

"Now who's flirting?" he riposted. They burst into laughter.

He left them at the entrance, saying, "Well, back to recording this historic event. The films and photos we've all shot recently and over the years are even more important now."

At the house, Paige found the boxes of monogramed clothes, pulling out sweaters, golf shirts, capris, track suits, pajamas, bathing suits, and bathrobes for the sisters. They were sitting on the balcony of the boathouse in quiet reflection as Paige quickly packed her suitcases and changed the linens on the double bed she'd used. The other bed hadn't been touched.

"Is there anything I can do or get for you before I head up to the house?" Paige asked. "A cup of tea or coffee? There's wine and Perrier in the fridge."

"No thank you, dear," Emmeline said. "This is perfect for the moment."

"Don't worry about us," Abigail added. "I'm sure you have plenty to do, so you let *us* know when you need help."

Paige felt awkward at first, going into Veronica's room, which had been left in a mess, probably in protest. Drawers hung open, garbage bins overflowed, towels dumped on the bathroom floor reeked strongly of Veronica's cloying perfume as if she had doused them with an entire bottle. "Fuck you!" was scrawled in red lipstick on the bathroom mirror.

"Likewise!" Paige stated aloud as she briskly began the clean-up, determined to wipe away every vestige of Veronica from the house.

Angela joined her, saying, "What a lovely room. With a screened porch. Cool! Tony's borrowing Simon's cart and trundling our luggage over. We can't bring the car until the firetrucks move. OK, so let me take over here and you do whatever else you have to."

"Just the bathroom left to do here."

"Nice message," Angela said sarcastically as she stepped inside. "And what a stink!"

Paige had already opened all the windows and the French doors onto the porch, turned on the ceiling and bathroom fans, and deposited the towels outside the back entrance, but the odour lingered.

"Can you manage, Ang? Don't want to nauseate you and little Nipper. There are four other bedrooms to choose from."

"If you can find me some baking soda, vinegar, and a shallow bowl, I can remove the stench."

"Of course!"

When Paige delivered the items, Angela poured some baking soda into the bowl and set it on the bathroom vanity. Then she sprinkled soda on the tiles where the towels had been and poured some vinegar over it. As it foamed, she said, "I'll leave this for a while and then clean it up, good as new! But I was thinking you might want to do a *cleanse* of this room and the house."

Paige looked at her curiously.

"I've long had a fascination with the potential healing properties of plants. Sage has been used by many cultures, including some of our indigenous peoples, for cleansing and removing *negative energy*. I think Rebecca and Veronica qualify for that label! But you probably don't want to burn anything at the moment, so just having sage leaves out like potpourri can help. And the turkey-stuffing variety works, although it's not the most potent of the sages."

"That *is* fascinating! I'm game!"

"We'll put a bowl in every room. There was always some growing in the chef's herb garden, so I'll check that out later if it survived. And I noticed that there's plenty of soothing lavender in Simon's garden, so I don't expect he'll mind if I harvest some."

"Will our guys think we're loopy?" Paige asked with a grin.

"Nah. . . . Witches, maybe."

They giggled.

Paige stepped into Simon's suite of rooms with excitement and awe as she realized that this was her new home. Something she had wished for, but never fully envisioned, even in her *Wildest Dreams*.

The short hallway that ran perpendicular to the main one and along the wall that had originally been the outside of the house was a gallery of paintings, including ones by Emmeline. There were a few of St. Ives by Talia, and several collages of watercolour Christmas cards from Isobel, each showing increasing artistic skill. No wonder Paige hadn't been able to find them among Edward's correspondence.

Taking up the entire front of this wing, Simon's expansive bedroom with adjoining dressing room overlooked the lake, partly through the sleeping porch as well as a large bay window facing south. Two easy chairs flanking a round table had a view of the boathouse, Dragon's Point, and distant islands beyond. It looked like a lovely spot to enjoy a quiet read or morning coffee.

The porch, facing east, had an exterior wall of modern, screened casement windows, but only a single bed tucked under one of the open windows to the dressing room. There was plenty of space for another, even with a couple of wicker chairs providing a tranquil spot on a hot night.

The bedroom had a few of Simon's paintings and photographs on the walls. But Paige was surprised to find a photomontage of the two of them together over the years – painting on top of the Cliff Dragon with Emmeline, canoeing, waterskiing together and alongside Angie and Tony, in costume, on stage with the others for the talent show, sitting side-by-side on the end of the wharf. She could see Abigail's hand in the photos, and Emmeline's in the display. But Simon surely didn't have these here when Veronica had shared the room with him. She was touched to see that she had already become part of his life and dreams again after he and Veronica had officially separated.

Unpacking her suitcases solidified this commitment.

The dressing room was astonishing in its size and the beautifully crafted, built-in drawers and cupboards. One side was filled with Simon's things and the other was empty. Thankfully, there was no lingering scent of Veronica there.

Paige knew that Simon's parents had done a major renovation to the house in the early '80s, adding walk-in shower stalls and practical vanities in the three bathrooms and a powder room downstairs. They removed a couple of walls to free the kitchen from isolation at the back of the house. Tastefully modernized, it flowed past an island into the dining room, which opened onto the veranda dining space. That area was bathed in light from windows on three sides of the building.

It was a truly beautiful house in a magnificent setting.

Tony appeared with their luggage, and Paige left the Vanderbecks to settle in while she had a refreshing shower in the spacious, granite-walled stall, and climbed gratefully into clean clothes. Then she went to see if she could help Simon.

She was shocked to see that the inn was now a just a smoking heap of rubble with only the two granite fireplaces standing defiantly. Firefighters were still pumping water onto the remains to quench every last spark.

She found Simon partway up the road with several staff, dealing with a line of cars of incoming guests. They had clipboards to record people's particulars in case information was lost in the fire, although quick-thinking staff had rescued the computer and important files from the office. Refunds would eventually be given, but people were also informed about what other places were able to take a few guests, so that their holidays weren't completely ruined.

Simon looked exhausted. Paige just wanted to take him into her arms and comfort him.

Marshall joined her, saying, "I'm going to pick up Monique. She has some outfits and toiletries for the sisters. I've heard that the SRA has organized pizza delivery for the staff from all the pizzerias in the area."

"Wow!"

"Some of the kids with cars have already left for home, offering rides to anyone near their destinations, and others, especially the waterfront staff, have families with cottages on the lakes, so most of them weren't even here today."

Paige knew that, except for a few required to help with boat rentals and handing out equipment for canoeing, they had Sundays off, as did those running the children's programs. Like her and Marshall's experience, talented waterskiers who grew up on lakes considered it a great summer job. It was what had drawn Tony and Angela as well – his home being on a lake in Haliburton, and hers, in Orillia.

"Now that the phone system has died, the rest can't even contact their parents, so those of us with cell phones have been letting the kids use them, and quite a few are lined up at Barry and Louise's place to use their line."

"They could come to Simon's house and phone from there as well."

"Not an easy time for you guys right now," Marshall said, putting his arm around her shoulders. "I'll help you round up some students before I head out."

Tony was happy to take charge of them when they trooped into the house. Angela went to the chef's herb garden.

It wasn't a party in the sundeck bar later, but the staff appreciated the pizzas and a chance to say goodbye to their new friends. Anxious parents arrived to fetch their kids and were invited to dine before heading back.

The Vanderbecks were there, but the sisters had been content to stay at the house with Monique and a gourmet meal supplied by Marshall from his frozen Maison d'Étoiles stock.

Meanwhile, he filmed the proceedings at the bar discreetly, although he might never use the footage.

Simon made a touching speech, thanking everyone for their contribution and dedication to Westwind, assuring them they would be paid for the summer. And he urged them to look out for Marshall's documentary, *Once Upon a Summer*, as they might find themselves in it, and Paige's history of the resort, with plenty of photos. Those who needed to get to a bus station would be dropped off in the morning.

With power being distributed from the central maintenance building behind the staff quarters, all the other buildings still had electricity and water, which was pumped up from separate wells. Those who couldn't get home tonight would be allowed to stay in the Lodge, Suites, and cabins, although they might have to change the bedding themselves, since the housekeeping staff hadn't finished before the fire. The staff quarters were too close to the smoky ruins but could now be accessed to gather belongings. Breakfast, orchestrated by Chef and his pastry-chef wife, would be served at the sundeck restaurant.

Barry and a few of the locals who worked seasonally at the resort were going to stand guard overnight to make sure the fire was truly out.

"I desperately need a shower, and then how about a nightcap on the veranda?" Simon suggested, as they and the Vanderbecks walked back to the house in the twilight. Marshall and Monique had already left. "Paige and I will just check on the sisters first."

"Sounds good. We'll have a swim in the meantime," Tony said.

"I'm not exactly presentable," Simon said to the sisters when he and Paige were invited in. "But I wanted to make sure you're comfortable and have everything you need."

"Absolutely!" Abigail replied. "This a beautiful, serene space. And Monique has more than met our needs for essentials. She has excellent taste, so we'll be fashionable old gals in our new togs."

"You've always been the best-dressed ladies," Simon said with a grin. "Now I need to go and wash off the soot and scrub the acrid smoke out of my pores."

"What a difficult day for you, dear boy," Emmeline said compassionately.

"I have what's most important to me, Gran. The three of you, safe and here with me."

He kissed his grandmother and great-aunt goodnight.

At the house, they found small bundles of fresh sage leaves and teacups filled with lavender on counters and tables in every room.

"Smells lovely in here!" Paige said, grinning at Angela, who winked in response.

After the bizarre and distressing day, Paige found it relaxing just to sit in the darkness of the deep, screened veranda with a few tealights flickering, sipping cool wine and talking to the others.

Someone's boom box was blasting The Tragically Hip's "Ahead by a Century" amid energetic sounds of water splashing and laughter from the dock.

"The staff seem to be enjoying this unusual evening," Angela said. "Not that I blame them."

"Are they really going to be paid for the last three weeks?" Tony asked.

"Before I signed on for this extra year, I made sure that all our usual insurances were in place, including payroll coverage for the students and our local seasonal help, who are here until Thanksgiving," Simon replied. "And if there's any shortfall, I'll cover it myself. I know that many of the students need the money to get them through school. In fact, I've been thinking of setting up a scholarship for Muskoka kids who couldn't otherwise attend college or university. There's a huge discrepancy between the summer people and so many of the locals who have to survive here year-round, working minimum wage jobs in the service industries."

"You're so good, Simon," Angela said.

"With this windfall from what my ancestors built and left me, I want to make a difference where I can. I've helped Louise and Barry with their new venture and am investing in Adam's 'design and restoration' company. They've been indispensable to Westwind and are more like family.

"Chef and his wife have been with us for nine years and worked winters at ski resorts. They're finally opening their dream restaurant in town this fall, which I've invested in. He's another local guy who's worked hard to achieve his goals.

"Sometimes it doesn't take much to give people a bit of a leg up. So let me know if you have any cool schemes."

"Your family has already given us the most valuable things – bringing us all together while we had the best ever summer jobs, and becoming dearest friends," Angela assured him.

Simon smiled. "OK, then think of something that we could start as a team. Some sort of research project or significant habitat preservation that will ensure that the lake life we cherish will endure and thrive for future generations. We need our fish and loons and pristine waters. You'll think of something brilliant, Tony, with your expertise in aquatic ecology."

Momentarily stunned, Tony grinned and said, "Damn right, I can! That's fabulous, Simon! What an opportunity!"

"Funded by the Davenport Foundation, which I just invented, with us as Directors. And probably a few others."

"Like Marshall," Paige suggested.

"Definitely!" Simon agreed. "And the sisters, while they're able."

They eagerly discussed the possibilities, which was a welcome distraction from the events of the day.

Later in bed, Paige snuggled into Simon's arms saying, "Right now I couldn't be happier. But I also feel terribly sad because of what you and the rest of us lost today."

"Don't be. The new owner called me as soon as he heard about the fire and said that it's easier to rebuild from scratch than to renovate the old building. He assured me that the new one would resemble the old as much as feasible on the outside, but be functionally modern with greater possibilities on the inside. Windermere arose from the ashes, the same but better. Westwind will in a different and exciting way. After all, it was constantly changing and evolving over the past century. We're all going to begin anew."

"And this is by far the best way," Paige said, holding him close.

■   ■   ■

It was a placid morning, fresh and new, full of promise if you looked at the lake. But Paige found it heart-wrenching to pass the charcoaled, sodden, reeking ruins of the inn. There was such an apocalyptic void in the landscape. She squeezed Simon's hand.

Despite their tiredness, they were up early and at the sundeck restaurant to help with breakfast. Chef had arranged for an early delivery of eggs, bacon, breads, cereals, fruits, and such, and cooked to order in small batches.

"Not our finest moment," he said to them, "But no one will go hungry."

"And we're all grateful, believe me," Simon responded.

He and Paige had a quick meal and then served the staff as they trickled in. The Vanderbecks were not far behind, and happy to help.

Paige's cell phone rang. "I'm calling to make sure you're OK," Brett said. "I saw the video of the fire on the 11:00 o'clock news. Jeez, that was terrifying!"

"I'm fine, Brett. Thanks for checking though."

"It was an amazing rescue. . . . You and Simon make a good team."

"All those years of waterskiing. But yes. We're back together. His divorce is almost final."

"Ah. I'm happy for you, Paige. But also glad I had a chance to know you. Take care."

"You, too. Thanks, Brett."

Veronica could not have failed to hear the news, but she never called. Instead, a small moving truck arrived to collect her boxes, which were stored in two of the other bedrooms. Simon made sure they took nothing else.

Quite a few of the students had been picked up the night before, and families from farther afield arrived, so those who needed to catch a bus were loaded into the resort van and taken into town. They were all gone by the time the new owner and insurance people arrived on site.

Paige steeled herself to photograph the devastated, deserted resort while Simon talked to them.

With Angela and Tony seeing the tower burst into flames moments after being struck by lightning, and then filming the rapidly spreading, unstoppable fire, there was no question of what had happened.

And there was no reason to delay the cleanup or the demolition of the rest of the resort, Simon explained to Paige, the sisters, the Vanderbecks, and the senior staff over dinner on the sundeck bar. Chef and his wife had prepared a delicious steak feast as a farewell meal.

"The developer plans to start building by Thanksgiving."

There was a heavy silence.

Chef said, "Let's celebrate the Westwind that was, and will never be forgotten. Shall we pop the champagne?"

"Definitely!"

Chapter 19

The Vanderbecks were happy to stay for the week to provide moral support and help however they could. Paige and Angie enjoyed cooking together and developed a deeper bond.

The Pembrook sisters enthusiastically returned home to Ottawa to collect old films and photos to be used in the documentary, and replenish their wardrobes. They agreed to stay until after Thanksgiving when they returned.

"Think of yourselves as cottagers now, not resort guests," Simon suggested. "Anyway, you both still have work to do for the documentary, so it's good to be closer to Marshall.

"I also want you to think of this as your second home," he assured them. "And primary home if you ever want to sell your bungalow in Ottawa and come to live with us."

"Absolutely!" Paige chimed in. "It's a big place for just the two of us."

"There are other ways to fill the bedrooms," Emmeline quipped.

She sensed that it softened the blow for Simon to cling to whatever vestiges of the past he could. She and Abby were not only family, whom he truly seemed to cherish, but also custodians of the past. She hoped to be around to welcome her great-grandchildren, but her heart was full in any case. At least another of her dearest wishes had come true, and she felt - deep within her soul - that Simon and Paige would be happy.

He set up a temporary office in the living room for Louise and her staff to deal with cancelling and refunding the reservations, and other administrative work to shut down the resort. And he convinced the new owner to hire her son, Adam, to help with the re-invention of the inn, since he had a life-long knowledge of Westwind and skill in historic restoration, especially in Muskoka-style architecture. Louise and Barry were thrilled and proud.

Paige and Simon helped with the final interviews of former resort owners or their descendants, so Marshall wrapped up filming for now, and returned to the city to deal with ad work.

"You can stay with me when you come to do research at the archives," he told Paige. "I know you have to pack up your stuff from the house, but probably don't want to stay there."

"You're right," Paige agreed.

"Anyway, Duncan and Gavin are dying to meet Simon and host a celebratory dinner. They saw the rescue on the news and already approve of him."

She beamed.

■   ■   ■

Paige and Simon arrived in Launston Mills the day before her parents were due back from Britain. She was eager to see them, but there was also much that needed to be disclosed in person.

She was excited to show Simon her hometown, which he found charming, especially the tree-canopied streets of complacent Victorian homes. He was particularly impressed with theirs.

They loaded the fridge with food for her parents, and then went to dine at the lakeside inn not far from town.

"A different kind of cottage country," Simon observed as they drove past farms that dominated and sculpted the gentle landscape, and cottages, homes, and fenced estates strung along sections of the waterfront.

"Lots of people who work in town live on the lake, since it's so close. My parents considered it for a while after I went away to Carlton, but Dad would never sell the home that Nan's father built. I'm glad about that."

A place that truly was his birthright, unlike Arcadia, Paige realized.

When they had parked at the relatively modern resort, she said, "I loved growing up among all the lakes around here. The villages at either end of this one straddle waterfalls and locks and have the best ice cream stands."

"Better than Westwind's?" Simon teased.

"Different flavours, like decadently delicious Raspberry Thunder and Blueberry Blast," she said rapturously. "From a local dairy. You're in cow country now."

He chuckled. "So I noticed."

"Despite the perks here, I always treasured our summer weeks in rugged Muskoka," she said with a twinkle in her eyes.

"Ah, but you have yet to experience winter there. Snow-muffled silence. No neighbours. Yet."

"I'm looking forward to being snowed in with you."

He laughed as he pulled her close.

"Before we go into the restaurant, I want to show you the impressive log house that's now 160 years old."

It sprawled on the manicured lawn closer to the lake than the main inn, surrounded by a lichen-encrusted split-rail fence and landscaped grounds shaded by mature maples and lofty evergreens. A sign proclaimed "Langford Manor".

"It's enormous for such an old log building!" Simon commented.

"I wrote an article about its history when I worked for the local newspaper, so I'll bore you with the details at dinner."

"Impossible! I'm all ears!"

Over a delectable meal in the elegant restaurant, she recounted how the pioneering Langford family had cleared the land for a farm, but discovered that cutting down the seemingly endless primaeval forests was more profitable. The Langford lumber baron constructed the substantial, square-timbered house before eventually building a stone mansion in the nearby village. One son took over and expanded the farm.

"So, this remained a working farm until the 1960s, when it became a golf club, and the historic house was turned into a restaurant. But it was so popular with locals and boaters that the owners built this chic country inn and turned the log house into luxury suites and small reception rooms."

"I sense there's more to this fascinating tale," Simon ventured, eyeing her with amusement.

"You've read my thoughts!"

"I'm afraid you can't hide them. They escape through the glow in your eyes and the enthusiasm in your voice."

She beamed. "Well, the crux of this tale is that one of the Langford daughters - Eliza - married my great-great grandfather, which is how *he* then got into lumbering. So, the old log house is part of my history."

"That's awesome! Odd how you now know more about my family history than I do, and I know very little about yours."

"Eliza kept a meticulous record of everyday life – the weather, wildlife, chores, crops, people, plagues, events, entertainments, and so on - with amusing anecdotes and thoughtful insights. She also illustrated her journals with detailed sketches, and was well-read and smart. So, they're a fascinating record of backwoods life that's a treasure trove for historians. Dad has spent years editing and fleshing them out with historical context, and plans to print them."

"What a legacy! I'm looking forward to reading them. Obviously, her creative talents were passed on to you, but I'll let you know what else I discover."

She chuckled. "No more skeletons in the closet, I hope!"

Paige had never told Brett any of this. When they had lunched here, he hadn't been interested in its history.

"I wanted to get married here," she confessed as they lingered over dessert and coffee. "And we were actually able to arrange a wedding for October. There's a lovely ballroom with a wall of windows overlooking the lake. But Brett's parents decided there wasn't enough *suitable accommodation* here or in the area for their friends. So, they booked a grand ballroom at the Royal York Hotel in Toronto for late November and paid all the expenses. It was very posh, of course. But it felt impersonal to me, having little say in the arrangements, and a place that wasn't part of my world. I already realized that I was probably in over my head with those people."

Simon took her hand and kissed it. "This place is perfect," he assured her with such adoration in his mesmerizing blue eyes that she wanted to melt into his arms. "Mrs. Davenport?"

"I can hardly wait!" 'Paige Davenport' sounded so right.

Before they left, they sauntered down to the lake as the moon began to crest the horizon. "I think the stars are saying 'I love you'. And this *is* heaven!" she quipped, referring to the Moody Blues song "Is This Heaven?"

He put his arm around her as he responded likewise. "And the universe is ours again. Did you ever think that would happen in *Your Wildest Dreams*?"

"A never-ending dream. Because you always felt like a part of me." She chuckled and added, "We could have an entire conversation with snippets from the Moodies' songs."

"So, you know you'll always be in my heart."

"I wished for that. And no one can love you like I do."

"Thankfully we're not living in *The Land of Make-Believe* anymore."

They burst into laughter and hugged each other joyously. And Paige realized she was no longer afraid to be happy.

Back at the house, there was one more thing she wanted to do before bed.

It had puzzled her that Delia had left her copy of Cliff's poetry book at the cottage, where she'd spent only three or four months a year. Paige wondered if there was another one at their Launston Mills home. And if so, had her father discovered it?

She and Simon searched the bookshelves in the library but found nothing.

"You still have the painting I did for your eighteenth birthday," he noted, pleasantly surprised, as she led him into her bedroom. It was a watercolour of her sitting on the Dragon's Point, feet in the water and hands splayed on the granite, her fair hair spread like a cape around her shoulders as she gazed pensively at the distant islands. It hung where she could easily see it when lying in bed.

"Of course! It captured my soul. It's so special to me that I've always kept it here. I know this sounds crazy, but I didn't want Brett or anyone else to share it. He only slept in this room for a couple of brief Christmas visits. And I put the painting away."

Brett had always found excuses for not coming to visit her parents, and had urged her to go on her own on weekdays so as not to interfere with weekends, which often meant hosting or attending dinner parties and events with his friends.

"So, you've always been with me in spirit and in my thoughts," she said.

"Could you tell I was already in love with you when I painted that?"

"I wanted to believe it, but after the accident, I doubted that. And everything."

"Don't ever doubt again. You are my world, Paige," he said, taking her into his arms.

She was overjoyed to awaken in the morning with Simon sleeping next to her. The reality was even more exquisite than her teenage daydreams had been.

She rose quietly from bed so as not to disturb him, and wrapped her nakedness in a silk dressing gown. She tiptoed out barefoot, and then hurried down the broad staircase to the sunroom, which was just beginning to lighten with the dawn.

She went over to Delia's chair and had a powerful sense of her presence, as if she were sitting there awaiting the first rays of daylight to illuminate her.

"I'm so glad you're here, Nan. I want to tell you how much I love you and wish that I had known my real grandfather. I hope you told Dad, because I believe he would be happy to know about Cliff as well. And I have lots to tell him. If I may."

Paige had a momentary flash of inspiration. "Of course! Thanks, Nan!"

She went into the library, which was also her father's office, and sat down at the heavy oak desk built for her great-grandfather. In the second drawer on the left, she found a leather-bound notebook. She gasped with delight when she recognized Cliff's flowing handwriting in the clean copies of his poems.

"Songs of Muskoka" - for my beloved muse

He probably didn't mention Delia's name in case Raymond found the book.

"Eternal Love" was the last entry of the collection. Tucked into the next pages was a photo of a heartbreakingly handsome Cliff in a canoe. And in the following ones was the newspaper article about his death.

The one her father had mentioned. So, he *had* discovered the truth! At least of the romance. But he surely couldn't have missed the resemblance between himself and Cliff.

How long had he known and why had he never told her?

She noticed a file folder labelled "Basildon" in the drawer. Inside were letters with return addresses from Oxford University and Wetherby's Bookshop. She didn't open them, of course, nor read the copies of the letters that her father had sent, which lay loose below.

But she surmised that he had tracked down his half-sister, and probably visited her this time.

Casting her mind back to their trip to Britain nine years ago, she realized that he'd been looking for some evidence of Cliff's bookstore in St. Ives, since he visited each one as well as artists' shops, and enquired about their history. She'd thought it was just his keen interest in the past.

"There you are! I got lost looking for you," Simon jested as he entered the room.

"My friends and I had fun playing hide and seek here," she admitted.

"I bet!"

She told him what she'd discovered, and concluded with, "Dad has some explaining to do."

"As do we," he reminded her, opening her wrap and pulling her close.

He wore only his boxer briefs. His warm skin against her nakedness quickened her pulse. He kissed her deeply and long as he backed her against the desk.

"Not here," she panted. "Some ancestor is probably watching."

He chuckled and took her hand. They scampered up to her bedroom.

Lying in his arms afterwards, she sighed contentedly, "I've never been so happy, so intoxicatingly in love."

"Not worried about vengeful gods?"

"Not anymore. Not with you."

He held her close. "Mom always told me to send positive vibes out to the universe."

"That's easy now. It's like a whole new life has suddenly opened up for me."

"For both of us. Exciting, isn't it?"

"I hardly know where to begin."

"How about with breakfast? I'm pretty handy at flipping pancakes."

"I can slice fruit and brew coffee."

"We're a good team then."

As they ate on the extensive flagstone terrace flanked by the kitchen and sunroom, Paige felt at peace with herself and the past. It was as if reconnecting with Simon had made her whole again.

She was more aware of the beauty around her – the colourful perennial gardens that drifted through the long, sun-dappled yard; the majestic old trees that had watched over her family for four generations; the exuberant chattering and singing of birds.

"Strange that this feels a bit like home to me," Simon said, slipping out of his loafers and connecting with the stone.

"That's because this is *Muskoka* granite."

"Of course it is! I can tell," he jested, as he touched his toes to her naked ones. They played footsies for a giddy moment.

"I have something else to show you," Paige said, offering her hand. His grip was sensuous and comforting.

The stone path through the grounds was already warm beneath their feet in the morning sun.

"Nan and my garden," she said when they reached a back corner of the property. It was tucked behind a ten-foot-tall hedge of lilacs and bounded by the ruins of a drystone wall encased in wild vines. The nook had a meandering river of stones flowing from a carved wooden bench through creeping thyme studded with islands of seasonal flowers. The statue of a winged fairy perched on a tree stump, reading a book, anchored the other end.

"Apparently, I started collecting stones when I was a toddler, and I was very discerning. Picking only the most colourful, or unique, or sparkly. And I wouldn't come home from the cottage without them, so Nan said we'd make our own secret rock garden."

"It's enchanting!"

"Sometimes Nan and I would sit here together and read." She paused to recall those tranquil, treasured moments.

"I only brought one more stone home after she died. From our first summer at Westwind." She pointed out a baseball-sized chunk of pink and grey granite at the foot of the statue. "I stumbled over it in the shallows and had to rescue it. Now that I know about Nan's connection to Westwind, it seems so right." And because it was like her smaller talisman.

"After what I've experienced lately, it wouldn't surprise me if your grandmother had orchestrated that."

She giggled.

"Tell me more about her. It's so neat that she was friends with the sisters. Even if only for a summer."

She did as they spent hours going through old photo albums, seated side-by-side on a sofa in the sunroom. She was touched by his genuine eagerness to know about her family and her life.

Expecting her parents to arrive by airport limo in the late afternoon, she and Simon prepared a small gourmet dinner.

"They'll be grateful for a tender steak with a divine mushroom port sauce – thanks to Duncan's recipe - and a mixed salad," Paige predicted. Thanks to Gavin, she also had the perfect wine match.

"And freshly picked corn," Simon added.

"Of course. You're in corn country, too," she jested, referring to the signs reminding tourists, and the many roadside farm kiosks selling it.

She went over and gave him a seductive kiss, and then popped a cherry tomato into his mouth.

"Temptress!" Simon accused.

She flashed him a sexy grin. "No, we don't have time," she declared, reading his thoughts.

She was nervous about suddenly having to explain Simon to her parents. But it was time to admit to their past romance and the present realities.

Simon suggested he wait in the secret garden while she broke the news. He seemed to be just as anxious.

"They'll love you, even if they don't already," she predicted. "But nothing will change how I feel."

She didn't waste any time once her parents arrived, condensing into a few brief sentences Brett's cheating, her discontent with the marriage, Veronica's sabotage, and her ecstasy at finally being with Simon again.

"We go away for six weeks, and the world has drastically changed," her father, Tom, teased.

"That's a relief," her mother, Jane, added. "We've been worried about you, sweetie. Don't think that we didn't sense your unhappiness. I do hope you brought Simon with you. I've always liked the boy."

"I have, and he's going to grill the best tenderloin steak ever!"

It was a cheerful reunion, although her parents were deeply saddened to hear about Simon's parents, and now the inn burning down. Over the perfectly cooked dinner, Paige and Simon filled in the details.

"We'll show you the video that was on the news when you come to stay with us," Simon promised. "Definitely for the first week of September, as you'd planned. The best way to start the school year now that you're retired."

"A few days would be welcome, but we don't want to impose," Jane said.

"Mum, we've already started our life together and Simon is family now. I expect we'll be back and forth a lot. You won't mind if we use this place as our *pied-à-terre* when we need to work in Toronto? It's only an hour away, and it's sometimes better to commute than to stay in the city."

"This is still your home, so you never need to ask." With a grin, Jane added, "It's wonderful to have a soon-to-be son-in-law who actually wants to be part of our family."

"I can't tell you how much this means to me," Simon confessed, stifling his emotions.

Putting her hand reassuringly on his, Jane replied, "It means the world to us, Simon."

Telling her parents about what really happened the day of the accident was harder and more emotional for all. She didn't mention the ghostly encounters with Bex, so when her mother said, "Hopefully you'll stop being haunted by the past now", she and Simon exchanged glances.

"Yes, I do think so," Paige replied.

Jet-lagged, her parents retired early. Paige left two letters open on her father's desk – the one that Cliff wrote before he came to visit Westwind the summer of '37, and the one from Enid to Edward following her brother's death.

After breakfast the next morning, Tom asked to speak with Paige in the library. Her heart was pounding as he pointed to the letters and asked, "What's this about?"

"During my research, I discovered fascinating letters from Cliff Basildon and his family to Simon's grandfather. And I know that Cliff was Nan's friend who drowned." She searched her father's face. He looked away.

"The Pembrook sisters filled in details as well, when pressed. I didn't read anything, but I noticed you had a 'Basildon' file in your drawer. Do you want to tell me what *you've* discovered?"

He sat down in resignation. From the file, he pulled out a letter and handed it to her. "Perhaps you'll understand why I didn't give you this sooner."

She took a chair opposite him and opened the missive eagerly.

My darling Tom,

You and your beloved family have been the greatest joy of my life. I didn't have the courage to tell you when I was still with you, but it's time you knew the truth. I hope it won't destroy your affection for me. I love you more than you can know, especially because of what I'm about to reveal.

I should start with "Once upon a time", for it seemed like a fairy tale come true, that magical summer of 1937. Perhaps more correctly, "Once upon a summer."

With Esther and her family in England and Raymond busy in in the city, selling the factory, I went with cottage acquaintances to the Dominion Day ball at the popular Westwind pavilion. I had no lack of partners but allowed them only one dance to discourage them from thinking I was interested in anything more.

Until Cliff Basildon approached me. Suffice it to say that we both felt as if we had been waiting for that moment for all our lives.

I hadn't realized what I was missing until I met him.

He had just arrived from England to spend the summer with his old friend, Edward Davenport.

We spent part of every day together, except the odd time when Raymond drove up from the city. I felt no guilt loving Cliff, since Raymond was neither tender-hearted nor companionable, needing me only to run his household and satisfy his self-centred needs.

During that blissful summer, Cliff convinced me to leave my callous husband and begin a new life with him in Cornwall, where he owned a bookshop. We would marry as soon as our divorces were granted, and I felt no shame to live with him "in sin" in the meantime. I was to accompany him on his return journey at the end of August, and began my secret preparations.

I relished the freedom of being on my own at the cottage, with no prying eyes to witness Cliff's evening visits or my packing.

Tragically, he drowned making a hasty retreat from Arcadia when Raymond paid me a surprise visit. Cliff was to have stayed with me in the boathouse, slipping away in the early dawn, as he usually did. But I could hear the distinctive sound of Raymond's Cadillac as he came down the last stretch of road.

It was easy enough to distract him with a tumblerful of scotch in the cottage while Cliff made his escape. But I was terrified for Cliff when a violent storm suddenly blew through. I knew he hadn't had enough time to reach Westwind.

I cursed Raymond for not having informed me he was coming, although I knew it wasn't fair to blame him for Cliff's death. Crazed with grief I couldn't express, I contemplated joining him in a watery grave.

But already feeling that I might be with child - <u>his</u> child - I had to endure. And ensure that Raymond believed you to be his.

I don't think he ever suspected, but I know he wasn't much of a father. Because of the war, he couldn't tolerate noise, and found children irritating in any case. He needed only an heir and proof of his manliness. When you chose to study history instead of engineering, as he wanted, he became even more distant, as I'm sure you realized.

In my darkest hours I wondered if Cliff's death was some sort of divine punishment for finding passionate love outside the bonds of marriage. But how empty and lonely my life would have been had I not seized and savoured those exquisite moments with him.

You kept me sane and gave me a different but powerful love to cling to. That I could see Cliff in some of your expressions, demeanor, and talents was added joy. And sometimes I felt he was with me at Arcadia, watching over us. He would have been so proud of you, and Paige.

Unfortunately, I have little to tell you about his family. Your family.

Delia mentioned Cliff's books, his professor father, sister Enid, and adored daughter Isobel.

Paige must eventually know, of course, but please don't tell her until she's much older and has experienced romantic love and passion.

I hope that you can both feel proud to be Cliff's descendants. It is comforting to know that you carry part of him in your very being.

Be assured I will always watch over you all. I hope you feel my love surrounding and protecting you.

Fulfill your hopes, follow your heart, grasp happiness in all its guises, and never stop dreaming, dearest ones.
Your devoted, grateful, loving mother

Paige looked at her father teary-eyed and said, "It's even more tragic than I thought!"

"I was going to give you this before you were married, but it didn't feel right. You were still fragile from the accident. Even more understandable now! And Nan seemed to help you through that terrible time, as she'd promised, although I found it hard to fathom. So, I didn't want to destroy any illusions you had about her."

"I understand, Dad. I'm glad that Nan experienced true love even if it was only for one short summer. And I'm thrilled to have gotten to know my grandfather through his writing. I've brought you all the family letters along with plenty of photos, which Simon says are yours to keep."

He told her about the long journey searching for and finally meeting Isobel and her family, and Enid's descendants.

"I was afraid that Isobel might be appalled to find out she had a half-brother, but she was delighted. She had read *Eternal Love* and wondered if Cliff's muse had been one of the Pembrook sisters, whom she admired. But she had photos of his visit, which also included Nan."

"Yes! Driving them around in *Miss Chief*, among others," Paige said with a grin. "I'll run up to fetch them. Let's show Mum. Simon's seen them and . . . already knows. I accidently let it slip." She looked at him sheepishly.

Tom chuckled. "Then there's no need for awkwardness."

Armed with the photos, they went into the kitchen where Simon and her mother were finishing the dishes.

"Simon gave me the secret butter tart recipe, and he's going to help me make my first batch," Jane announced with glee. "My book club ladies will be impressed."

"I'll say!" Tom agreed.

The first photo Paige showed them was the most intimate one of Delia and Cliff, which she'd found in his poetry book at Arcadia.

"Wow! And to think it's been there for sixty years and none of us ever discovered it," Tom said.

"I expect Nan was guarding it. Waiting for the right time."

After the photos and the letters had been turned over, Simon handed Tom a leather-bound notebook. "You should have this as well. It's Cliff's unfinished novel. Paige has a copy and was going to try her hand at completing it."

Tom held it reverently as he opened it.

"It's a terrific story so far, Dad. But Isobel should have first crack at it."

"We'll ask her, shall we? I promised we'd call, and I'd introduce you to her."

"Gosh! What do I say? Do I call her Aunt?"

"I'm sure she would enjoy that. You already know more about her past than I do, so I doubt you'll have much of a problem talking to her. She's very generous and engaging, with a quick wit and a droll sense of humour."

"I got that impression from her children's books," Simon admitted.

"Definitely," Jane agreed. "She gave us a set of them for our future grandchildren. I expect she'll be delighted that you two are together now. Your grandfather was a treasured part of her life, Simon."

"Maybe we can entice her to visit us. She loved our boathouse suite," Simon replied.

"We invited her as well, and she thought that next summer might work. Her son and daughter mostly manage the shop now, overseen by their father, but she still likes to run the literary events," Tom said. "She and Mum really hit it off, with their passion for books."

"Cool! This is so exciting!" Paige enthused.

"It sure is. And it's wonderful to see *you* so happy again," her father commented.

Paige wrapped her arm around Simon's and leaned against him with a luminous smile. He looked lovingly down at her.

Uncannily like the photo of Delia and Cliff.

Author's Notes

As a teenager, I was fortunate to spend unforgettable summer weeks at my friend Fay Patterson's island cottage on Lake Rosseau in Muskoka. We often went to nearby Cleveland's House resort to pick up mail and savour ice cream cones. Over the last few decades, my family and I have occasionally stayed at Cleve's – as it's affectionately known – as well as many other resorts throughout Muskoka.

Cleve's became the epitome of gracious, Victorian summer resorts to me and inspired my Westwind Inn. This, however, is a work of fiction, so Westwind and all the characters in the novel spring from my imagination.

Here are a few facts about real things in the novel:
- Windermere House did burn down as mentioned and was rebuilt within a year. In 2023 it was turned into a 4-season hotel.
- The Royal Muskoka, Wawa, and Beaumaris Hotels burned down as described. The Epworth Inn – later Wigwassan – home of the Muskoka Chautauqua, was renowned in the 1920s. The other resorts are fictional but resemble real ones, which are also gone.
- Greavette and Ditchburn were famous boat builders in Muskoka, whose hand-crafted launches still grace the lakes.
- The RMS Segwun is still going strong at the age of 137 (in 2024). A cruise aboard the iconic ship is the perfect way to experience the beauty and history of legendary Muskoka.
- "Launston Mills" is what I called my hometown of Lindsay, Ontario in my first novel, *A Place to Call Home*.

Visit Once-Upon-a-Summer.com for photos of Muskoka, Discussion Questions, special pricing for book clubs, and more! Use the QR Code on the Author page for a quick link.

If you'd like to spend more virtual time in Muskoka, have a look at my 4 "Muskoka Novels"– an epic family saga set between 1914 and 1951.
Visit TheMuskokaNovels.com

Acknowledgements

Many thanks to the following people for help with research, providing feedback, and sharing stories from their experiences as cottagers and/or working at summer resorts in Muskoka.

Alphabetically: Sandra Bradley; Shelagh Haynes; Kim Haynes; Linda Kelso; Marilas McInnis; Lawton Osler; Fay Patterson; Captain Randy Potts; Jack Rawlinson; Blair and Donna Stewart; Mary Storey and the Muskoka Discovery Centre archives; Vic and Laurie Tavaszi; Susan Wills.

Special thanks to my friend Amitav Dash of "dubs & dash" for generously creating the evocative cover design, his insightful editorial review, and ongoing marketing ideas.

I am forever indebted to my beloved family for believing in me, for their encouragement and support, and for sharing the creative journey with me. Our research ventures also provide cherished time for us to immerse ourselves in Muskoka's magic. My daughter, Melanie, keeps me on track with her creative suggestions and thoughtful editorial comments. I'm delighted that her stunning photo once again graces the cover. My husband, John, as well as giving editorial feedback, is responsible for e-books, e-commerce, and helps with e-marketing. I'm so grateful for my team!

Soundtrack

We all have soundtracks for our lives – music that transports us in a heartbeat to a particular time and place whenever we hear it. Our favourite bands had a way of anticipating and voicing our thoughts, joys, angst, dreams, and desires in a lyrical and timeless way. That applies equally to my fictional characters.

The Moody Blues became a hit with a whole new – younger – generation of fans with their "Your Wildest Dreams" hit on the album *The Other Side of Life* in 1986. Here's a list of their music referred or alluded to in the novel or relevant to the story. The songs speak of love and loss and second chances.

Moody Blues:

"Your Wildest Dreams" – *The Other Side of Life* (1986) & boxed set *Time Traveller* (1994)
"I Know You're Out There Somewhere" – *Sur la Mer* (1988) & *Time Traveller*
"Nights in White Satin" – *Days of Future Passed* (1967) & *Time Traveller*
"The Actor" – *In Search of the Lost Chord* (1968) & *Time Traveller*
"So Deep Within You" – *On the Threshold of a Dream* (1969)
"Lovely to See You" – *On the Threshold of a Dream* (1969) & *Time Traveller*
"Question" – *A Question of Balance* (1970) & *Time Traveller*
"Isn't Life Strange" – *Seventh Sojourn* (1972) & *Time Traveller*
"The Land of Make-Believe" – *Seventh Sojourn* (1972)
"Remember Me, My Friend" – *Blue Jays* (1975) & *Time Traveller*
"No More Lies" – *Sur la Mer* (1988) & *Time Traveller*
"Want to Be With You" – *Sur la Mer* (1988)
"Lean on Me (Tonight)" – *Keys of the Kingdom* (1991) & *Time Traveller*
"Bless the Wings (That Bring You Back)" – *Keys of the Kingdom* (1991) & *Time Traveller*
"Is This Heaven?" – *Keys of the Kingdom* (1991)
"Highway" – *Time Traveller* (1994)

Other songs referred to in the novel:

"Rock and Roll Music" – The Beatles (1964)
"Fun, Fun, Fun" – The Beach Boys (1964)
"Do you Believe in Magic?" – The Lovin' Spoonful (1965)
"It's a Beautiful Morning" – The Rascals (1968)
"Old Time Rock and Roll" – Bob Seeger (1978)
"I'm Still Standing" – Elton John (1983)
"Heaven" – Bryan Adams (1983)
"I Want to Know What Love Is" – Foreigner (1984)
"Dancing in the Street" – David Bowie and Mick Jagger (1985)
"Summer of '69" – Bryan Adams (1985)
"Sweet Child of Mine" – Guns N' Roses (1987)
"(I've Had) The Time of My Life" – from Dirty Dancing (1987)
"Hungry Eyes" – from Dirty Dancing (1987)
"Ahead by a Century" – The Tragically Hip (1996)

Find links to these tunes on Once-Upon-a-Summer.com

Other Novels by Gabriele Wills

The Summer Before the Storm
Book 1 of the Muskoka Novels

Muskoka, 1914. It's the Age of Elegance in the summer playground of the affluent and powerful. Amid the pristine island-dotted lakes of the Canadian wilderness, the young and carefree amuse themselves with glittering balls and courtly romances. When Jack Wyndham, the destitute son of a disowned heir, joins his privileged family at their cottage, sparks fly and life will never be the same. He schemes to better himself through alliances with the Wyndhams' elite social circle, as well as with his beautiful and audacious cousin, Victoria.

But their charmed lives begin to unravel with the onset of the Great War, in which many are destined to become part of the "lost generation".

This richly textured tale takes the reader on an unforgettable journey from romantic moonlight cruises to the horrific sinking of the Lusitania, from regattas on the water to combat in the skies over France, from extravagant mansions to deadly trenches - from innocence to nationhood.

The Summer Before The Storm, the first of the epic Muskoka Novels, evokes a gracious, bygone era that still resonates in this legendary land of lakes.

Elusive Dawn
Book 2 of The Muskoka Novels

Elusive Dawn continues to follow the lives, loves, and fortunes of the privileged Wyndham family and their friends. While some revel in the last resplendent days of the season at their Muskoka cottages, others continue to be drawn inexorably into the Great War, going from a world of misty sunrises across a tranquil lake to deadly moonlight bombing raids, festering trenches, and visceral terror.

For Victoria Wyndham, too many things have happened to hope that life would ever return to normal, that innocence could be regained. Caught in a vortex of turbulent events and emotions, she abandons the safety of the sidelines in Britain for the nightmare of France. Her fate as an ambulance driver remains entwined with those of her summer friends, all bound by a sense of duty.

Living in the shadows of fear and danger awakens the urgency to grasp life, to live more immediately, more passionately amid the enormity of unprecedented death. Those who survive this cataclysmic time are forever changed, like Canada itself.

Impeccably researched, beautifully written, **Elusive Dawn** will resonate with the reader long after the final page has been turned.

Under the Moon
Book 3 of The Muskoka Novels

The catastrophic Great War is over, but the survivors now face the final battle - to rebuild their shattered lives and protect their secrets. Some find solace amid the rugged beauty and serenity of the Muskoka lakes. Others seek to reinvent themselves among the avant-garde of decadent Paris and the opulence of the blossoming Riviera.

Meanwhile, the inevitable momentum of civilization ushers in a daring new era of scandalous excess and social upheaval that threatens the strictures of Edwardian society. On the forefront of this revolution are two diametrically opposed Wyndham cousins, Lizzie and Esme, who struggle to defy convention in the name of love and ambition. Only time will tell whether their worlds are ready to embrace change.

In this gripping third volume of the acclaimed Muskoka Novels series, Gabriele Wills vividly evokes the triumph and tragedy of the glittering Jazz Age as it seduces a privileged summer community, and we stand witness to its sultry dance on the dock, **Under the Moon**.

Lighting the Stars
Book 4 of The Muskoka Novels (Can be read as a stand-alone)

Merilee Sutcliffe's idyllic town is worlds away from the conflict in Europe. But as her patriotic friends and relatives leave for battle, German POWs march into her shocked community to become Merilee's closest neighbours, and biggest threat. Caught up in the chaos is Luftwaffe pilot Erich Leitner. Shot down during the Battle of Britain and transplanted to a lakeside prison, he discovers he has more to fear from his comrades than his captors.

While her cousin, Elyse Thornton, navigates the treacherous skies of Britain as a Spitfire Girl, Merilee becomes entangled in dangerous liaisons on the home front. Caught between worlds, with conflicted loyalties and a sense of duty, she joins the Royal Canadian Air Force

Women's Division, and finds herself in ground-zero London, focussing her photographer's lens on a city under bombardment.

Far from carefree summers on the lake, struggling to survive the relentless demands and sacrifices of war, Merilee and Elyse wonder if they dare risk their hearts as well in this epic tale of a generation torn apart by war.

A Place to Call Home

Set in the turbulent, formative years of Ontario, this compelling saga spans five decades and two generations. Barely surviving a disastrous journey on a cholera-ridden immigrant ship, Rowena O'Shaughnessy and her family settle in the primitive backwoods of Upper Canada in 1832. Her complex relationship with the wealthy and powerful Launston family leads to tragedy, and eventually to redemption.

Their lives are played out against a rich tapestry of events - devastating plagues, doomed rebellions, mob uprisings, religious conflict, and political unrest.

A Place to Call Home is a novel about Canada, and its less civilized pioneer past.

Moon Hall

Two women who live a century apart. Two stories that interweave to form a rich tapestry of intriguing characters, evocative places, and compelling events.

Escaping from a disintegrating relationship in the city, writer Kit Spencer stumbles upon a quintessential Norman Rockwell village in the Ottawa Valley, where she buys an old stone mansion, "Moon Hall". But her illusions about idyllic country life are soon challenged by reality. Juxtaposed is the tragedy of Violet McAllister, the ghost that reputedly haunts Moon Hall, who comes vividly to life through her long-forgotten diary.

Moon Hall is a gripping tale of relationships in crisis, and touches on the full spectrum of human emotions – from raw violence and dark passions to compassion and love.

About the Author

Born in Germany, Gabriele emigrated to Canada as a young child. With degrees in the social sciences and education, she's had a varied career as an educator, literacy coordinator, and website designer. She's been an active community volunteer, particularly in heritage preservation and the arts. She also produced an award-nominated feature on CBC Radio.

Her real passion, however, is to weave compelling fictional stories around meticulously researched and often quirky or arcane facts to bring an era vividly to life.

Gabriele grew up in the Kawartha Lakes, which fostered her love of "cottage country". The sublimely beautiful Muskoka lakes also provide soul food and inspiration for her writing.

Discover more on her website: TheMuskokaNovels.com

You'll find links to her Facebook Page, Goodreads profile, Blogs, Book trailers on YouTube, and more.

Gabriele is always delighted to hear from readers!
Contact her at info@mindshadows.com

If you enjoyed this novel, please share your thoughts, send comments, and help spread the word! Many thanks!

For more info, visit GabrieleWills.com

Manufactured by Amazon.ca
Bolton, ON